Carrie Border

the prequel

Nancy Jackson

WILD
IDEAS
PRESS

Book Cover Design by - Angela Westerman of
AK Organic Abstracts - AKOrganicAbstracts.com

Edited by - Andrea Hurst

Audiobook narration by - Catherine Gaffney

I am dedicating this book to Rick.

He has been my champion, and has continued to encourage me to write when no one else did. He sees the gift that God has given me to write, and won't let me lay that torch down when it gets tough and discouraging.

Thank you Rick. I love you dearly!

Chapter One

Through the haze in his mind, he could sense slithering across his midsection. Or was he caught in a horrific dream? He couldn't tell. Whatever the case may be, he could do nothing about it.

His body had been rendered useless, and his mind nearly so. It was impossible to know if this nightmare was real.

Time could not be captured. Had he been like this for minutes or for days?

The slithering again, not just across his midsection, but across his legs and arms too. His eyes were cemented shut from the brain fog, so he couldn't see where he was or what was happening.

There were no memories either. No memories of what had led to this moment. The fog would not clear so he could think, so he could remember.

He wanted to move. He wanted to crawl out from

beneath the slithering, but his mind could not give his body the command it needed in order to do so.

So he lay there as the slithering sensations increased. There were more now, and his anxiety grew. Where was he and why was he here?

Just as a small amount of brain cognizance surfaced so that he could begin to understand what the slithering was, a severe pain punctured the fog. It rocketed up his lower leg, through his pelvis, and then to his heart.

And just as his eyes flew open for the first time in hours, his heart stopped beating.

Chapter Two

Excitement tingled through Carrie's body as she stood waiting for her turn to receive the pin from the chief welcoming her into the Oklahoma City Police Department. Her palms were sweaty, and she was trying to avoid rubbing them together, so she pressed them tightly to her side.

Beads of sweat furrowed small rivulets through the chignon she had forced her honey blonde hair into. Her wavy curls were contrary, and it had taken extra time that morning to comb and spray them into place.

She had waited for this day for a long time and it was finally here. It was one step closer to her goal of becoming an Oklahoma State Bureau of Investigation Agent. Once it had seemed like a far-reaching goal, but today it felt more attainable than ever.

"Carrie Elaine Border." The voice boomed through the room.

Don't trip Carrie. Stand tall Carrie. Smile Carrie. She moved nervously forward to receive her pin and shake the chief's hand.

Cameras whirred and flashed, and she smiled big for them. And just like their quick flashes, it was over. A huge whoosh of air escaped her lungs as she stepped off of the platform and walked back to her place in the audience along with all the other cadets. Today, they all became rookies in the OKCPD.

That memory was three years ago, but it still seemed like only yesterday. Carrie was lost in it as she stood waiting for her partner, Tommy. It was bitterly cold outside, and her fingers felt like frozen sticks in her gloves. Even with constant rubbing and tucking them under her armpits, it didn't seem to help.

"Okay, let's load up," said Tommy, as he rushed by with the keys to their replacement squad car. Theirs had been hit the day before when a motorist couldn't stop on the ice. So today, they were checking another one out of the car pool. While Tommy had gone to retrieve the keys, Carrie waited outside watching the white billows of air she breathed. She should have gone in, then she wouldn't be frozen solid.

As soon as Tommy turned over the cold engine, Carrie reached to crank up the heater.

"You know that will only blow out cold air until the engine warms, right?" The half-smile on Tommy's face told her he was used to her cranking the heater and the AC each time they got in their ride.

A broad smile filled her face, "I know, but old habits are hard to break and all."

"Wow, the snow is really coming down. Going to be a fun day," said Tommy, looking up at the falling snow through the front window. It fell in huge lofty flakes that took their time floating down.

"Well, thankfully, here in Oklahoma, it won't last long. Or it usually doesn't," replied Carrie. It was true. The weather here changed like the wild mood swings of an adolescent. The morning could hold a frigid ice storm and then rocket to the eighties by two in the afternoon. Predictability was not Oklahoma weather's strong suit.

"I don't know. I watched the weather this morning, and it looked like we may be in for a few days of snow and ice." Tommy glanced over at Carrie to see her reaction. He knew how she hated the cold.

He waited for a pithy response that didn't come. When her face showed no sign of change, he said, "You seem distracted today." It was a question, posed as a statement.

"Yeah," said Carrie absentmindedly.

"What's up?" Tommy frowned. He had grown close to Carrie over the past few years and she felt like one of his daughters. If something was bothering her, he wanted to try and help.

Carrie looked at Tommy, then back out to the large puffs of white drifting onto their windshield. "I applied to the OSBI." Her stomach immediately clenched. She had said nothing of it to Tommy up to that point and didn't know how he would respond.

For what seemed like an eternity, there was only silence in the now-warm patrol car. Then Tommy turned and gave Carrie a genuine smile. He had known from the day he had met her that she was going places in her career. She had graduated with honors from the University of Central Oklahoma with a degree in criminology, and while working with the OKCPD, she continued on a part-time basis to achieve her master's degree. He knew there would be no way she would occupy a patrol car for the rest of her career.

"You'll get it." Tommy's confidence resonated in his voice.

"I was afraid to tell you. I thought you might be upset with me."

"Why would you think that?" he asked.

"Well, we've ridden together for three years now and I didn't want you to think that I wanted to leave because of anything you'd done, or feel like I was abandoning you. You've been a great partner and taught me so much. I owe a lot to you, Tommy," Carrie was sincere. What can only be learned out on the street, Tommy had taught her.

"I'm proud of you." The look in Tommy's eyes held genuine pride at his once rookie-cop.

"Thank you, Tommy." Carrie was truly grateful. She had dreaded telling him since before she had filled out the application. She knew she couldn't have gotten a better first partner and hated to hurt his feelings. Now that she had told Tommy, it felt like the weight of the world was off of her shoulders.

They were slowly moving down a street deep in urban

Oklahoma City trying to stay safe and warm. "Tommy, look over there," Carrie pointed out her window to the right. "See that guy? What's he doing?" Through the bits of snow and ice on her window, she could see a disheveled old man in a long tweed coat that had seen better days. He was looking down, fiddling with something in his hands.

Tommy signaled and turned the corner as he watched the guy Carrie had referred to. "I can't tell. Let's check him out." Tommy pulled the car over to the curb across the street and they got out. The street was slick, and it was a challenge for both him and Carrie to navigate. Even the rugged soles of their boots wouldn't grip the ice.

"Hey there, can I see your hands?" Tommy asked the guy as they approached. As they had walked up, they could tell he had shoved whatever had been in his hands into his old and worn coat pocket, and his hands remained there. Tommy was concerned he was an addict who was pocketing his drugs.

"I ain't got nothing," said the man. His voice was gruff, as was his language. It appeared to Carrie that this was probably a homeless man, but she had not seen him around the area before and it didn't appear that he had any clothing or bags with him.

"Do you live around here?" Tommy asked.

"Naw."

"What have you got in your pockets?" Tommy asked again.

The man met his question with a firm shake of his head as his eyes skittered wildly back and forth. He was growing more and more agitated.

Neither Tommy nor Carrie wanted this to escalate from nothing at all to a drastic incident.

"Where do you live?" Tommy asked.

"I got me a place back over there," the man said, and then bobbed his head in a northeast direction.

"How far over there?" asked Tommy.

The man became even more frenzied the longer they stood there.

"What are you doing out here on such a cold day? Can we help you get somewhere warm?" asked Tommy.

The man didn't answer; he only jerked his shoulders into a shrug and looked away quickly.

"I ain't doing nothin' wrong," the man said as he continued to shake his head.

Carrie was certain now that he had to be homeless, even though he said he had a place. He smelled. His clothes were in dirty tatters, and his weathered face hadn't seen a razor in a very long time.

Carrie gave her head a slight tilt that caught Tommy's eye.

"Do you want us to get you back home?" Carrie asked. The man's head shook even harder.

"Nope, nope, nope,"

"Okay, calm down. You be safe out here. Okay?" Carrie said as she tipped her head toward their car. She wanted to talk to Tommy about the situation. She felt compassion for him and didn't want to elevate his stress if indeed he was doing nothing wrong.

"Yep," said the man.

Just as Tommy and Carrie turned to go, movement caught

Carrie's eye in the direction of the man's pocket. She whirled around, which startled the man, who jerked his hands out of his pockets. Then, out jumped a mouse. It hit the snow and took off running and squealing.

The man began whining and shaking his head. He attempted to run after the mouse on the snowy sidewalk while Tommy and Carrie just watched in shock. Finally, the old man turned the corner, still hurrying after his friend.

"Poor guy," said Tommy.

"I know," replied Carrie. "That is what he was playing with when we drove up. I hate it that people are reduced to having only a rodent for a friend. And now I feel awful. If we hadn't come along, he would still have him," said Carrie. "I wonder where his stuff is? Or where he sleeps."

"He's been around for a long time. I've seen him from time to time, but that was when I rode that beat over off of Southwest 29th. He is a long way from home."

Carrie shivered as she climbed back into the patrol car. "Don't you even touch that heater," warned Tommy as he laughed.

Carrie only smiled and shoved her hands under her arms.

Carrie stood looking out of her front window, waiting for Billy to come pick her up. She was once again amazed at the beautiful day that lay before her. Had it only been a week earlier that she and Tommy were slogging through the snowy streets? Today it was sixty-nine degrees. She breathed deep and smelled the apple pie scented candle that she had just blown out in anticipation of leaving.

She turned from the window, trying to push her nervous anxiety down. Billy was late, but it didn't worry her. She was just ready to get going. He was always reliable and must have been held up at work. He had the day off, but had been called in at the last minute to straighten out an accounting error a clerk had made. His job as accounting supervisor at the small manufacturing company he worked for kept him busy and buried in a ton of responsibility.

Today was the day they had planned to go shopping for their wedding, and Carrie was excited. These types of frilly girl things weren't usually her cup of tea, but she was elated to be marrying Billy. She had loved him as long as she could remember.

Gazing down at the beautiful diamond ring on her left ring finger, she smiled as she remembered the day they had first met. It was on the UCO campus in Edmond and she was in a hurry, as usual. She had run right into him, but rather than be irritated, Billy had only laughed and helped her to pick up the pile of books she had dropped.

Carrie jerked from her thoughts as she heard Billy's car horn honk outside. Grabbing her purse and jacket just in case, she bolted out the door.

"I'm sorry I'm late. Had a last-minute phone call as I was leaving the office," said Billy.

"Oh, it's okay," said Carrie, settling into the passenger seat. He was here now, and that was all that mattered. She slid her hand in his as they pulled onto the street. It was strong, and she felt secure in his grip.

"Where to first?" asked Billy.

They had spent the night before writing down options and ideas. Carrie had never realized just how much there was to planning a wedding, and Billy really didn't care what they decided on as long as it was what Carrie wanted.

"We need to get the venue out of the way. They are booked months in advance. I can't believe how expensive they are."

"We could elope," said Billy, looking down at Carrie with a huge smile on his face. His eyebrows were bobbing up and down.

Carrie burst out laughing. She would love nothing more than to do that very thing. "Okay, let's go!" Calling his bluff would fix that.

"Our parents would kill us. Well, our moms would. Our dads would probably cheer," said Billy.

"We'd have more money for the honeymoon. We could go to Paris for a month on what this thing is costing. I was looking at dresses online. Outrageous!"

"Did you find one?" asked Billy.

"Maybe, but you'll have to wait until the wedding to see it. I have to actually go to the store and try it on, but I really liked the way it looked online." Carrie beamed when she thought about the beautiful dress. Even though she had always been a bit of a tomboy, she had always dreamed of her wedding dress and how it would be, and the one she had found online was simply perfect.

"Let's see how much we can check off of our to-do list today. Do you know what you want to see first?" asked Billy.

Carrie gave him the address of the first venue she wanted

to check out, and he headed that way. It was a beautiful sunny day with the man she loved whole-heartedly. She didn't think she could ever be happier.

By the end of the day, Carrie felt they had made quite a dent in their list. They had put a deposit on a venue, and the date had been scheduled for six months out. They were only able to pull that off because there had just been a cancellation before they had arrived.

Flowers were also ordered. Carrie had had no idea what she really wanted. She loved all types of flowers, and Billy was no help. He had no opinion about what to order. The fact that they would hold the wedding in July, right before her twenty-fourth birthday, finally led them to pick a variety of summer flowers in yellows, pinks and lavenders.

The venue they had chosen had catering options, which thrilled Carrie. That was one less thing they would have to do, but it came at a premium. They still had to choose a cake and, of course, bridesmaid dresses, as well as the men's tuxedos. There were a variety of small things like the guest book, guest favors, table decorations, and so much more, but the major items were under control and Carrie felt relieved.

"I could have worked a double shift wrestling armed robbers and still not have been as tired as I am right now." Carrie flopped onto her sofa with aplomb.

Laughter filled the air as Billy came and pinned her down, looking into her beautiful hazel eyes. "Let me up!" exclaimed Carrie, tempted to good-naturedly shake him off onto the floor. He held firm, and she loosened her resolve as he kissed her with purpose. Fatigue faded as their passion kindled.

Two hours later, Carrie woke in Billy's arms on the sofa. This was her safe place. She traced her finger along the sculpted lines of his shoulder muscles. A tickling sensation ran through Billy's body and his eyes opened to find a smile on Carrie's face.

"I'm starving," he said, as his eyes twinkled.

Dressed in whatever clothes they could randomly throw on, they scavenged through the kitchen refrigerator and cabinets. Neither one cooked, but they were able to find leftover Chinese food, chips and dip, and a not-quite stale box of Oreos. Armed with their bounty, they headed back to the sofa.

Just as they were sitting down to feast, Carrie noticed a letter peeking out from a pile of advertisements she had pulled from her mailbox. It must have been tucked inside one of them when she had initially thumbed through her mail.

As she slid the envelope out, she realized it sported the logo of the OSBI in the upper left-hand corner. She dropped her chopsticks back onto her paper plate and wiped her hands on her shirt. She felt such awe and reverence for that envelope that to tarnish it with a smear of food grime was unconscionable.

A cold draft suddenly whipped through the room, and her bare legs dimpled from the chill. She gently lifted the letter up to relish the moment. Billy had flipped on the TV and was lost in a sitcom rerun as he shoveled chips loaded with dip into his mouth. For Carrie, the raucous laughter seemed incongruous with that sacred moment.

Carrie felt surreal, as though time was standing still, and everything around her faded. This letter would change her life forever. It could be an acceptance letter, or a letter laced with regrets. Finally, not able to wait a second longer, she turned the envelope over and slid a finger under the flap. She almost felt dizzy as the letter slid from its trappings.

Just then, Billy looked over and saw the intensity of Carrie's gaze on the letter. He knew what it could be, so he just sat quietly, letting her have her moment. He was ready with congratulatory remarks or words of compassion, whichever was needed.

The stiff paper crinkled as Carrie's fingers gently worked to splay open the folds. Her heart stopped as she read their words, congratulating her on becoming a member of the OSBI. There was a part of her that had feared the worst, but this perfect day filled with love and joy was now topped off with a dream come true.

She turned quietly to look at Billy, still in shock. "They accepted me," she said. Her eyes searched his, and as creases formed at the corners of his eyes, his face yielded to a huge smile. He enveloped her in his arms and they sat on the edge of the sofa, rocking back and forth with joy.

The next day, Carrie excitedly called her mother to tell her all that they had accomplished for the wedding.

"Oh, Carrie, that sounds wonderful,"

"I am so excited. Maybe you and I can go out this weekend and take care of some of the smaller details that Billy rolls his eyes at."

"I would love that. Your dad said that he wanted Billy to

come over, anyway. He has a project he is working on that he would like Billy's help on."

"Perfect!" Carried exclaimed. "The guys can do that and we can have a full day for ourselves. Maybe we can work in a pedicure too, while we are out."

"Of course we can."

Mother and daughter continued to chat for the next hour. She had called her mother first thing the previous night to tell her about the exciting news about acceptance into the OSBI. Her mother was always her first call, even before Billy. Neither could ever seem to exhaust their conversations with each other. They were as much like best friends as anything.

"Carrie, I am so thrilled for you. You have your career started. You got accepted to the OSBI, and you are marrying a wonderful man. All your dreams are coming true. Your father and I are so proud of you."

"Mom, I could never have done it without you. You and Dad have supported me the entire time with your love and encouragement. And money too." Carrie chuckled. She knew the great sacrifice her parents had made for her.

"Carrie, we wouldn't have it any other way. You are the light of our lives."

Hanging up the phone, she realized her dreams were all truly coming true. She had applied at the OSBI, but didn't know if she would indeed be accepted. The waiting had been excruciating. Waiting had never been her strong suit, but she had been resolved to wait and keep trying until she did make it. But she had, and she overflowed with excitement.

A knock at the door revealed Billy as it swung open. "I

just got off the phone with your dad. He wants me to come over this weekend to work on a project. Do you mind?"

Carrie snorted. "No. I just got off the phone with my mom and she and I have plans, anyway. We are going to go shopping for some of those small wedding details that bore you to tears. Then maybe get some pampering while we are out."

Billy moved closer toward Carrie and slid his arms around her. "Oh, yeah? Do I not pamper you enough?" His face held a large sloppy grin and Carrie couldn't help but shake her head. But in all the silliness, she felt an overwhelming love for the man who held her. She loved her parents, but this love was greater than anything she had ever known.

Their smiles faded and their embrace became passionate. Billy kissed her long and hard and Carrie welcomed it with her own fervor. She closed her eyes and walked slowly backwards by memory to her bedroom, never breaking their embrace as they made their way to the bed.

Hours later, after a few moments of passion and a long nap, Billy rolled over and tickled Carrie's bare shoulder. It twitched, and she mumbled. He pulled his finger away, but then began the silent torment again.

"Stop," Carrie whined sleepily.

Billy chuckled. Their romp and the nap had invigorated him. "Get up. The day is almost over."

Carrie huffed. The bed felt wonderful with Billy next to her, and she didn't want to get up. When she sensed he was moving to get out of the bed, she quickly rolled over and grabbed his arm. "No. Come back here."

He did as requested and they snuggled back in together, face to face. Carrie looked into Billy's eyes. She knew he loved her deeply. Not just because his eyes shone when he looked at her, but because of how he considered her first in everything he did. He deferred to her when making plans, always wanting to ask her opinion. They didn't always agree, but he often compromised because he loved her enough to not quibble over trivial things.

"What do you see our life like after we are married?" Carrie asked him.

"What do you mean? It will be more of the same, only better, right?"

"Yes, but we really haven't talked about whose house we will live in or all the logistics. Maybe a little here and there, but not concretely."

"Your house is a little bigger, not much. Mine is closer to my work, but the same for you. What do you want to do?"

A sly smile stretched from cheek-to-cheek across Carrie's face. A sparkle in her eyes paired it. "I say, we sell them both and buy our first house together."

Billy shut his eyes and smiled. "With all that money we will save on the wedding?" He laughed and looked at her. "Yeah, Peanut, I think we can do that." His voice was gentle and soft and fell on her ears just before his lips fell to hers.

Chapter Three

"So, you got in," said Tommy. His face was beaming. He was so proud of her.

"I did." Carrie was still in shock. Her life seemed like a fairytale, but was it all too good to believe? She had prepared herself for them to say she did not yet have enough experience under her belt and to apply again in a few years. She had only been on duty three years.

"I am excited, but nervous as well," said Carrie. "I have no idea what to expect. I have gotten so used to riding with you, and I feel so comfortable with you. Now, I will have all new people and procedures. I hope I can do it." Her face couldn't hide the anxiety she was feeling.

"You'll do great," said Tommy, patting her hard on her back. "When do you start?"

"Two weeks. I'll start on the first of February."

Tommy hated to see her go. She had been an excellent partner and there was always an adjustment period when riding with someone new. "I will miss you." His face had lost its smile and a look of sincerity had replaced it.

"I'll miss you too, Tommy," said Carrie as she reached to hug him. He had been the best mentor she could have had, and she meant it.

It had been a sunny morning, but the afternoon weather had turned back to being bitterly cold. There was no snow falling down, but the streets were still covered in remnants from the previous night. Melting rivulets from the day before froze over the pavement at night and turned them into treacherous black ice. The bright sun fooled many into thinking that the streets were safe.

The radio had been relatively quiet for the last few days, and Carrie hoped it would stay that way for her last two weeks on the OKCPD force.

On patrol, they did not do investigative work. There was a slight element of inquiry on a day-to-day basis, but for serious crimes, the detectives would step in and they were relegated to doing the grunt work for them. She was glad that she had experienced that. Having experience as a patrol officer would help her appreciate that type of work and those who did it.

Her mind flitted between nervousness over what to expect in her new job and the anxiety of getting everything done for the wedding. When interviewing at the OSBI, she had made sure they knew of her upcoming wedding and that they would give her time off for her honeymoon. Their wedding plans were already made, and they didn't want to change them. The OSBI had agreed, but it would consume her first allotment of vacation time.

"Can we stop and get some coffee? I am still cold even in the warm car. I can't feel my toes in my boots," said Carrie.

Tommy chuckled. "Sure. I could use a cup too. I can't believe how quiet everything has been on the radio."

"Hey now, don't go jinxing it," Carrie laughed, but actually felt her life was so charmed at the moment that nothing could change that.

The remaining frozen snow from last night's storm crunched under the tires as they pulled to the curb in front of the diner. Having signed off for a quick break, Tommy and Carrie exited the car and were met with a harsh blast of icy wind.

"My ears are going to flat fall off," said Carrie as she ducked her head further into her coat.

The diner was almost empty. Few ventured out in this kind of cold. Tommy and Carrie had a favorite booth near the front window where they could watch their patrol car and the street. As Carrie pulled off her gloves and rested her hand on the table, her fingers stuck.

"Hey Janet, our table is sticky. Can you toss me a wet rag?" Carrie bellowed out in a jovial tone to the waitress they knew so well.

Carrie caught the flying damp white dish towel with a splat, wiped the table in a quick swoop, and hollered, "Incoming," back to Janet. The familiarity comforted Carrie. She often loved the excitement of new things, but the old and the routine was a greater comfort to her.

Two steaming hot cups thumped onto the table, and Carrie leaned over to let it engulf her face. One of her favorite smells, coffee. But the steam did little to thaw her ears.

Two dollops of cream and one packet of sugar. The other cops ribbed her that she wasn't man enough to drink her coffee black, but she didn't care. A wave of emotion washed over her. She would miss them.

Watching Tommy drink his coffee, she wondered what life would be like with her new partner at the OSBI and if they would work as well together as she and Tommy did. What if they hated working with her? She shuddered and decided they would appreciate her as much as Tommy did, in time.

A crackle came through Tommy's mobile radio. Carrie took a gulp of her coffee as they both jumped up to go. They were needed.

The night patrols were the worst, Carrie thought as she bundled for her shift. They were once again facing rapidly-freezing roads, which would be filled with people who thought that they just had to be out, and were confident that they knew how to drive on them.

Just as she tugged on her last glove, her phone rang. Frustration spurred her to grumble that she would have to remove her gloves in order to answer it, and why hadn't it rung before she had put them on.

She didn't recognize the number coming from her little flip phone. She loved this technology, but wished each call that came through would automatically indicate where it was coming from.

"Hello," Carrie said irritably.

"Is this Carrie Border?" It was a woman's voice coming through the line, and it chilled her to the bone. The voice was warm, but Carrie froze in response just like the wind on the icy streets outside. She'd heard those four words many times before, but tonight a foreboding spirit ushered in fear with their delivery.

"Yes, this is Carrie." She found herself holding her breath, acutely aware of each syllable that came from the woman's mouth. Her heart pounded and it resonated in her ears.

"Your parents have been in an accident. We need you to come to the hospital as soon as possible," the woman said.

The phone clattered to the floor as Carrie sank to her knees. Somewhere in the distance, she could hear the woman asking if she was still on the line.

Nausea threatened her, but her trained mind kicked into gear and pushed all else aside. Her parents needed her. They were in the hospital, so they weren't dead. She grabbed the phone, confirmed their location, and told the woman she would be right there.

As she ran out her front door, she skidded and nearly fell to the ground. The small rush of adrenaline from the near fall barely registered. Her car engine roared as she turned the key, and she reached to crank up her heater. Then she dialed Tommy.

"Don't tell me. You can't get to work because of the ice," Tommy said as soon as he pressed the button to accept Carrie's call. He was laughing.

"Tommy, my parents have been in a car accident. The hospital called and they need me. I'm headed there now." Tommy had never heard Carrie sound so afraid. It was almost as if she was in a tunnel and her voice was a distant vapor.

"I'll meet you there."

"No, Tommy, it's time for our shift. Call our lieutenant and tell him what's going on. I'll update you later. I promise." She clicked the call closed before he could reply. She was now operating on auto-pilot.

Billy, she needed Billy. At a stoplight, she fumbled with the flip phone to scroll down her favorites list to find Billy's name. The ringing didn't stop until she heard Billy's voice come over the line. But it wasn't him, only his voicemail.

"Billy, call me now. I need you." Tears threatened to blur her vision, but she pushed them back.

She felt her tires struggle to find traction on the ice. She chided herself for not rolling at the light instead of stopping completely. Sliding sideways, she heard her tires spin on the ice, then catch. The car lurched forward and then slid in the other direction.

Finally, she was moving forward again and navigating the black ice. Everything within her urged her to hurry, to rush to the hospital, but the roads were not playing fair. She knew if she didn't take it easy, she would wind up in a ditch, unable to get there at all.

Panic washed over her in wave after wave. *What if they were dying, and she got there too late? What if they were already gone, and she hadn't been able to say goodbye?*

But they could be fine, right? She tried to think positive thoughts, attempting to calm herself and think rationally. But something inside of her knew when she'd heard the woman's voice on the line. She just knew. The car skated over another sheet of ice, fishtailing before straightening again. Each time, her stomach would tighten in a knot before her car would once again regain traction.

The parking lot of the hospital was nearly empty, but in the back where the emergency room was, there was barely a parking spot. Too many out on a night like this ended up here.

The automatic doors whooshed and the semi-warm air cushioned her entrance into the emergency room. The smell of antiseptic and sickness that was all too familiar in hospitals lingered, even in the lobby of the ER.

She was still dressed in her uniform and the nurses were courteous immediately as she walked up to the desk. But when she told them who she was and why she was there, she saw something unrecognizable flitter across their faces.

One nurse came from around the desk and ushered her back into the recesses of the emergency room, not saying a word. The ER doctor, a resident who had worked thirty-six hours straight, met her. He wanted to deliver the news in a respectful and kind manner, but his exhaustion, combined with a lack of experience, simply led him to say, "Your parents are gone. They didn't make it." Carrie felt the doctor catch her as the room faded to black.

Last week Carrie's world had ended, leastwise the world she had known and loved for her entire life. Being an only child, her parents had loved only her. They had been wonderful parents. Normal, boring, wonderful parents.

Memories pounded her, slamming her mind like the waves of the ocean, and she was unable to escape. Laughter rang in her mind as she pictured her parents playing board games, cooking treats for the holidays, sitting in awe of the fireworks display in summer, delighting over her opening mountains of presents on Christmas morning, and so much more. It was all gone now, and Carrie wanted to be gone with it.

Had it just been a week ago that she had wallowed in her charmed life, her perfect life? She could not have felt so high only to sink to this, the deepest depths of sorrow. The emotional fall had been crippling for Carrie. She struggled to function.

The day of the funeral was a blur. A doctor had prescribed some sort of pill to help her maneuver through the next few days, but it had only served to cloud her memory, not dull the pain. Being an only child, the enormity of the responsibility for making funeral arrangements and other similar decisions fell to her. Her mind had difficulty thinking though, it was numb.

Billy was there, and he had been wonderful. Each step of the way, he had been there to help, while not smothering her. The wedding. Sobs wracked her body as she once again realized her father would not be walking her down the aisle and her mother wouldn't be there helping with the last minute details. It seemed to be more than she could bear.

She had gotten the call exactly one week before she was to start her new job at the OSBI, her dream job. But now she had no dreams, only memories as sharp as glass that filled her mind and her heart. The trauma of losing her parents cut and dismembered every beautiful memory she had.

Everyone was sympathetic. The OSBI had graciously offered her time for bereavement. The OKCPD had released her with paid time served. Tommy had called and been there as often as he could, but he found that he had no words to ease her pain. No one did. How could any of them understand?

Her parents were her support system. They had been on her side, loving her and encouraging her for her entire life. They had been the driving force that fueled her fierce drive and determination. It had been them who had convinced her she could do anything that she set her mind to do.

Today she would have started with the OSBI. It had thrilled her parents to hear about the letter of congratulations, and now she had one more week to pull herself together. Entering her new position at the top of her game had been her utmost priority, but that would not happen now. She still owed it to them and her new partner to do the best that she could, but how could she promise that now?

The knock on her front door pulled her from her thoughts. As she walked to the door, she realized it was requiring all her energy just to move. It was Billy. She opened the door and seeing it was him, turned back to the sofa without even uttering a greeting. She was so caught up in her own world of grief that it never crossed her mind to greet him with any type of affection.

Billy was experiencing a genuine loss regarding what to do in order to help the love of his life. He knew his words rang hollow, and the loving touches and caresses he had offered were often rejected. He had never seen Carrie like this. Not one day that he had known her had she not been strong and capable, ready to tackle life and all that it brought her way.

A few years ago, her grandmother passed away, but she had been ill a long time and it was a relief to see her suffering end. The grandfather on her mother's side had passed away the year prior to her grandmother's death, also from a long-term illness. Her father's parents lived out of state in Michigan, along with a few other distant relatives that Carrie hadn't ever really known.

It was her parents' loving support and their knowing just the right words to say in every situation that had seen Carrie through those challenging times. Billy had been there with her, but it was truly her parents that she had leaned and relied on. At twenty-six, Billy was ill-equipped to be her emotional support.

"How are you doing today?" Billy asked as he followed her back to her sofa, where she had lain since the funeral several days prior. He was also quite sure she had worn the same pajama pants and t-shirt the entire time as well.

"How do you think I am?" Carrie snapped at him. She didn't want to speak to him that way, but she just couldn't seem to help it. Crawling out of this emotional hole that she was in was more than she felt capable of doing. She was angry. Angry at the entire world, and that included Billy.

Billy sat in the chair next to the sofa. He was leaning forward with his arms on his knees, gently rubbing his hands together out of sheer nervousness. The sun glinted through the gap in the curtains and bounced off of his college fraternity ring, catching his eye. The pressure to say the right thing had been with him day and night for the past week, and he had failed almost every time.

"Why don't I take you out to get a good meal?" He held his breath to see what her response would be, hoping for the best this time.

"I don't want to go out."

"You need to eat and I think it would do you good to get some fresh air. How long has it been since you took a nice hot shower?" Billy asked.

Carrie looked at him from over the edge of the quilt she had pulled up to her eyes. She was curled up in the fetal position on the sofa and had snuggled down deep into the quilt. She shut her eyes in response without saying a word.

"Carrie, please, let me help you. I can't even imagine how painful all this is, but I do know that your parents wouldn't want you to let this consume you. You have to move forward for your own sake."

"I can't."

Billy moved to sit on the edge of the sofa. He pushed down the quilt just enough to kiss her on the cheek. Her hair was matted from days of not being washed and was falling in clumps across her forehead. He brushed it back with his hand, still trying to generate the perfect words that would magically bring her back to life.

"It is only one week until you start your new job. You have to start making an effort so that you can do your job well."

Billy's words flushed through Carrie with vile heat. She knew she had to start her new job in a week. She knew she had to be okay by then. She knew all of this, and his reminding her didn't help her do that. It only added more pressure to do what she didn't think she had the strength to do.

He could sense her anger even though she had not spoken it. She had pressed her eyes tighter together and her cheeks were flushed red. He removed his hand from her hair and sat looking at the floor. "What do you want me to do Carrie? How can I help you?"

"You can't. Just leave me alone and let me be and try to heal the best way I can."

Billy nodded. Leaving her alone did not seem like the healthiest thing for her. He feared the isolation would breed even more toxic emotions and send her spiraling even further emotionally, if that were possible.

"Okay, but I want to sit here with you while you rest. If you need anything, I'll be here." He got up and returned to the chair.

She nodded just before falling into a fitful sleep.

Chapter Four

The past two weeks had been the hardest weeks of Carrie's life. Billy had been right when he had said she needed to get up and start working towards getting better, but everything within her had refused.

Billy had come back as often as his work would allow. Each night he would bring one of her favorite foods, hot and tantalizing. The smell of her favorite pizza and pastas awakened her senses somewhat, and she began to gradually eat again.

About three days before she had to start her new job, she had agreed to go out to dinner with him. She had showered and dressed, and realized how much weight she had lost. He had taken her to her favorite restaurant and had planned for a movie afterwards.

Carrie's heart was broken and heavy, and she didn't know that time would ever mend it. She didn't enjoy being out around people, seeing them laugh and enjoy each other's company. Even when she looked at Billy, who had been the love of her life, she felt an immense wall between them.

Then it was here. The day she had longed for. She should have felt excitement and eager with anticipation, but she didn't. She dressed in her tan khaki pants and navy polo shirt with the OSBI logo, and donned her own jacket since her company jacket was still on order.

On the ride to work, her mind flitted between wondering who her new partner would be and if he, or she, would measure up to Tommy. She arrived twenty minutes early, concerned about arriving late on her first day.

It was the second week in February, and the ice was gone for now. The sun shone high in the sky, deceiving one into thinking it was warm. As soon as Carrie stepped out of her car, she was hit with the brutal reminder that the wind chill was barely above freezing.

Standing on the step in front of the glass door, Carrie took a minute to take a deep breath in an attempt to gather herself. She hoped her mom and dad knew that this was her big day, and that they were pleased. The lump that formed in her throat was difficult to dislodge, but with a deep breath and firm resolve, she was able to move forward.

She was ushered quickly to the second floor and introduced to Special Agent in Charge John Bracket. Orientation meetings and paperwork filled most of her morning. Everyone had heard of her parents' death and they were sympathetic, expressing their condolences and shaking her hand in a heartfelt manner. She had yet to meet her partner. He had been called out and was not yet back at the office.

SAC Bracket asked her to lunch, and she accepted even

though she didn't feel her knotted-up stomach could accept one bite of food. They arrived at a noisy sports bar alone, but soon, along came a few of the other agents. Carrie was thankful that they seemed to be a welcoming bunch, and she felt like her fears of not fitting in were unfounded.

While they were sitting waiting for burgers and fries, a handsome man of around thirty walked up to their table and sat down. It was obvious he was OSBI, since he was dressed the same as the rest of them.

Once in his seat, Bracket introduce her to Randy Jeffries, her new partner. He had thick, dark hair and deep brown eyes. Had Carrie been in the market for a man, he would have done nicely, except for the fact that she knew from SAC Bracket that he was recently engaged.

He had an easygoing demeanor and the way he laughed and joked with the others, she could tell he was well-liked and respected. He grinned at Carrie while shaking her hand. It was firm, but not overbearing.

Lunch was good. Carrie observed from the sidelines as she picked at her food. She didn't feel she knew anyone well enough to enter into their easygoing banter. Her burger was good, but her appetite had not fully returned, so somewhere in the midst of the first third, she laid it down unfinished.

Bracket suggested Carrie ride back to the office with Randy, and so she did. He was polite and their small talk was superficial. She could feel the barrier she had put up between her and the rest of the world sitting solidly between them.

Randy showed her around the office and introduced her to several other agents and support staff. Her desk was positioned facing his with a short cubicle-type barrier separating the two desks which were near the rear of the large open room. They could see each other over the short wall while still maintaining a modicum of privacy.

Carrie looked over her sheet of logins and passwords and proceeded to get oriented with the agency network. Randy helped from time to time to show her how the system was set up. Carrie was a fast learner, and by the end of the day, she felt she was ready for more action. This is what she needed, to get back to work.

Billy was coming by after work and they were supposed to talk more about the wedding. Their shopping and planning had been put on hold abruptly the day her parents had died. She wasn't sure she was yet up for that, but she felt she had put Billy off long enough.

At six o'clock, he bounded through her front door with a big smile and hug. He loved her deeply, of that Carrie was sure. As she stood in his embrace, she pondered how she could still feel so numb inside. Shouldn't she be feeling better by now? Shouldn't she be able to once again feel the love she knew she had for Billy?

His patience was enduring though, and he had not pushed her in the least to recover more quickly. She knew she would never find a better man to spend the rest of her life with. Knowing this created yet another struggle within her.

What if she could not recover? What if she could not resurrect the emotions that she had had for Billy? Didn't he deserve better, deserve more? He did. She knew he did. So now, in addition to the numbness Carrie felt, it was joined by a horrific sense of guilt. The fact that she could not return the kind of love that Billy deserved weighed on her.

She would never win an Oscar, but she felt that during the last few days she had put on a pretty convincing performance. She nodded at the right moments, hugged and kissed on demand, and kept conversation flowing. All the while, her heart felt like a stone.

The drive to the restaurant was quiet. And then after ordering, Billy brought up their wedding plans. Carrie thought she felt dizzy. She dipped her head to prevent him from seeing any possible sign of what she was feeling. Then from out of nowhere, but with certainty, she looked Billy in the eye and said, "I can't marry you."

The pain in her eyes belied her words. For a moment, Billy didn't think he had heard her correctly. When she didn't continue, he asked, "What?"

The air around their table seemed to have dropped by ten degrees. Silence stalled time and nothing seemed to dislodge it. Carrie looked away and out into the restaurant, then down at her lap. She couldn't control the tremble in her hands as she twisted her napkin. Their silence was interrupted by their waiter bringing their plates of food.

They had welcomed these very dishes so many times in the past with laughter as they dove in and relished every bite. Today, those very dishes sat growing cold as Carrie fought for words.

Billy just sat and looked at her. His mind was sifting through threads of rationale. He was convinced that he hadn't heard what he thought he had heard. *She is just hurting and lashing out. She just needs more time. It was too soon to bring up the wedding. She doesn't love me anymore. She's found someone else.* Billy knew the last two weren't true, but how could those thoughts not dance through his mind?

"We don't have to talk about the wedding tonight. We don't have to talk about it at all until you are ready. We can even postpone the wedding until you are ready. I know how it must hurt knowing your parents won't be there," said Billy.

Carrie's head jerked up, and she said, "Of course you don't know. How can you know? Just how can you even imagine that you know my pain." The other patrons in the restaurant looked at them as Carrie's harsh words flew head-long at Billy.

Glancing around, she realized what she had done and ducked her head again. Billy sat still like someone had punched him in the gut. Neither one spoke for several minutes, their food growing even colder. The server avoided asking if there was anything further they needed, having witnessed her onslaught.

Carrie thought about getting up to go home, but didn't have the strength. Billy didn't know what to do either. He shut his eyes, took a deep breath and said, "Carrie, I'm sorry. I know I can't even begin to know your pain."

Billy motioned for the server and asked for to-go boxes and gave him his card for the bill. Carrie had not looked up from her lap and tears slid onto the knotted-up napkin in her hands. When the server brought their boxed-up food, Carrie woodenly slid her arms into her jacket, grabbed her purse, and walked towards the door.

In the car, Billy started the engine but left it in park. "Carrie, I am so sorry." His voice was quiet and sincere. He didn't know what else to say.

"I know Billy. I'm sorry too," said Carrie. "I just feel so broken and numb. I don't feel anything at all anymore. I'm afraid I'll never feel anything again." Then sobs that she had been holding back for two weeks burst forth.

Billy pulled her to himself and just held her, letting her sob. He didn't think he had ever loved her more. He didn't know the pain she felt from losing her parents, but if it was anything close to the pain he now felt seeing her this way, he knew he could truly understand.

Carrie and Billy had left the night before with things unsaid. They had both felt it best that way. Billy had held her, then taken her home. She realized lying in bed alone that night that she had needed to have that cry. She hadn't cried since hearing the news, not like that anyway. Even though she had shed some tears, she had not had those cleansing, heart-wrenching sobs that she had had last night. *Was it a step towards healing?* She hoped so.

The bit of emotional cleansing from the night before caused Carrie to be able to look forward to her second day at the OSBI. Now familiar faces greeted her at the office. Randy was in with Bracket when she arrived, so she went to her desk and logged onto her computer. She hadn't been involved in a case yet, so her email inbox was limited to two office notices, which she quickly read through.

Her desk was bare. She hadn't brought any pictures or other personal items. As a patrol officer, they rode in a car, so there was no need for personal items. As she looked around the room, there was little on the mens' desks, only an occasional family photo here and there.

"Good morning," said Randy. He was suddenly standing next to her desk, and it startled her. Her mind had betrayed her again, wandering off to entertain other memories. She jumped and quickly stood.

"Sorry, didn't mean to startle you," said Randy. The smell of coffee and donuts tickled her nose as Randy held out both to her. "We have a case. Come with me to Bracket's office and we'll talk about it."

"Shut the door behind you, Carrie," Bracket said as she walked into the room. She did as asked and then sat in the empty chair next to Randy at the front of Bracket's desk.

"Just got a call from the OKCPD. They have a body in northeast OKC. It is in a derelict part of town with very few residents. Most of the remaining houses are boarded up and abandoned. Several lots have been cleaned of everything. A body was found in an old small concrete structure.

"This isn't your normal death." Bracket paused to pull photos from the file. He laid them on the front edge of his desk for Randy and Carrie to see. Carrie wasn't sure what she was seeing at first. Then the abnormal images began to take shape.

"I know this is your first case Carrie. Do you feel strong enough to handle it? If not, I can give this to another team." asked Bracket with a concerned look on his face.

He knew this would be a big case, and one that would need to be handled with kid gloves. Media tentacles would need to be held at bay, and he suspected this would also be a dangerous case as well. He wasn't sure it was best for her first case, but he felt Randy was the perfect choice and now Carrie was Randy's partner, so...

Carrie nodded while looking at the pictures, then looked up at him. "I can." Her words were strong with confidence that she wasn't sure she felt.

"Ok, then. I gave Randy the packet when he arrived. Good luck," said Bracket. Then, almost as an afterthought, "I don't have to tell you to keep a tight lid on this. Don't talk about it to anyone. If the media gets hold of this one, there is no telling what will happen. Keep your eyes open out there too."

"Will do," said Randy as he shut Bracket's door behind him.

On the drive to the crime scene, Randy filled Carrie in. She would learn department procedure along with on-the-job detective work. There was no doubt that she had the book training and diplomas to prove it, but that didn't usually translate into field training. This case would plunge her in deep for the first time.

A dry, biting wind hit Carrie full in the face as she exited their SUV. Her eyes stung and teared up in response. She barely noticed though, as she focused on the old concrete building before her. It had been painted many times, with all but the most stubborn scraps of paint now gone.

The wood surrounding the windows, which used to hold glass, was equally bare and void of paint. No light shone from them to the outside.

Grass surrounded the small building but was beat down and even though dormant, Carrie could see that it would be mostly weeds in the summer. The doorway did not have the usual stoop and doorframe. There was a concrete ledge protruding upwards as if to keep water from coming into the building.

As she stepped over it and into the room, it reminded her of the feeling of walking into the old cellar on her grandparents' farm. The familiar smell of dank concrete reinforced her memory. The walls inside were also bare and void of paint. The building consisted of only one room with two tiny windows.

The odor attacked Carrie just as the wind outside had done, but this she could not ignore. Her wrist flew to her upper lip between her mouth and nose.

"You okay?" asked Randy.

Carrie nodded and lowered her hand. "I'm fine," she said trying not to breathe the foul odor in as she spoke.

Inside the dark concrete building, it took Carrie's eyes a moment to adjust to the room. There were two forensic techs and an Oklahoma City Police Department detective.

"The coroner is waiting for you to see the body in situ so they can take it to the morgue. He has already noted body temp and all other data that he could determine here," said the detective, turning to Carrie with an outstretched gloved hand. Then, before she had time to take it, he pulled it back and stripped off the glove, "Hi. I'm Rick Morris, OKCPD." His smile was welcoming.

Carrie shook his hand and replied, "Carrie Border."

"Agent Carrie Border," said Randy and smiled. "It will

take a bit to get used to your new title. What have we got here Rick?"

Rick stood with his hands down at his sides. His suit coat was riding slightly high on his ample middle, with the single button straining to hold. He was a large man, but not what one would call fat, merely plump.

He stood looking at the body, shaking his head. "I have never seen anything like it in my life. I have been trying to make sense of it since I got here. We have a young adult male, I would say early twenties. It appears he has died from some kind of poisonous toxin."

Rick donned clean gloves and pointed with one gloved hand. "See those strange woven pockets on his hands?" He turned to look at Randy and Carrie for confirmation. "They had a few large ants caught in them. His hands have swollen so large that they are protruding through the weave. We are going to wait until he is back at the morgue to remove them.

"We think the ants bit him until he died from anaphylactic shock. Either that, or the ant toxin was so poisonous that it killed him. Or... it could have been something else entirely, and the ants were meant to distract us."

Carrie was trying to make sense of what she saw. The young man had only a strange leather type loincloth on and the woven gloves. They looked like the cane weaving in an old chair she had once had, obviously handmade, with the two sides lashed together with the same type of cane.

He was lying down on his back, but she could see restraint marks about six inches up from his wrists. "Was he tied up when he was found?" Carrie asked.

"No. But the restraint marks seem to indicate that he was

tied to something. See these voids here?" Rick looked up at her. "I've never seen it look like that when the two hands are tied together."

Carrie looked around the room. It was empty. "Was his body dumped here?"

"Not sure about that yet."

As the two crime scene techs left, Randy moved around and squatted down close to the body. The boy's entire body was swollen as if the toxin had permeated it entirely. He could see through the woven gloves that the hands were a fiery red, with countless punctures.

As he was leaning closer to look, one of the trapped ants moved. Randy sucked in a shocked breath and jumped backwards, landing against the wall. He looked up at Rick. "I thought they were all dead." Randy hurriedly stood, brushing off his backside while looking around for more ants.

"Are there more ants? Were there more when you got here?" asked Randy.

Rick chuckled. "There were a few. It appears those left were caught on the gloves. The techs were able to catch a few for testing."

One tech came back in with large bags and covered each hand, tying it so that all forensic matter and the ants would be contained. They had a gurney waiting outside, but had to wait until the agents left the small room so that they could get it in.

Once outside, the agents and Detective Morris stood pondering what they had just seen. "We called you because of the bizarre nature of this. Figured there wasn't much else going on." Rick smiled as he looked at Randy. "I also have the feeling this isn't the last of this." His smile faded.

Carrie just stood wondering what the meaning of the gloves and ants were and why anyone would do this to another person. "That must have been pure torture. You know, to have those ants sting you repeatedly."

Randy nodded. "Yes, and he was tied to something, so he couldn't do anything about it."

"Do you think they intended to just torture him or to also kill him?" Carrie asked.

"Hard to tell," said Rick. "They may have had no idea that he would die. The ants may not be that toxic on their own. He may have had an underlying condition that caused him to die when someone else wouldn't have."

They moved aside to let the gurney roll past on its way to the van. Rick shivered, and Carrie looked over at him.

"I keep feeling creepy crawlers on me," Randy said, and Carrie couldn't help but smile.

Carrie noticed the wind had died down as they all three walked back to their cars. She looked at their surroundings. They were in a part of town where most of the houses were vacant and in shambles, and many of the lots had been completely razed with nothing but bare ground and little grass to cover them. She could tell that this was a sparsely populated area.

"Well, we have a lot of research to do," said Randy. "We need to find out who owns this lot and what this strange setup is all about. I am sure Rick, that you have the patrol canvasing to see if anyone saw anything."

"Yes, but they only found one person home. It looks like

most of the homes left here are abandoned. I'll have them wait until early evening and come back. Who knows, maybe there will be more residents here at that time to talk to."

They all shook hands and got back in their cars. Randy turned on the key but seemed in no hurry to leave. They were sitting facing the small, strange concrete structure.

"Any thoughts?" Randy asked Carrie after a few moments.

Carrie sat shaking her head as she thought. "I have no idea."

Randy looked at her and smiled, with only one side of his mouth turning up. "Great first case, huh?"

"Outstanding first case."

Chapter Five

The remainder of the day was filled with doing research. Their OSBI database seemed limited. She could not find any cases that were even remotely similar to this one. She would have to talk to Randy about whom to consult.

"Just got off the phone with a professor at the University of Central Oklahoma who teaches anthropology. He said this sounds like a ritual that the Satere-Mawe group in the Amazon rainforest often conduct. They believe it gives the men strength and courage," said Randy.

"They make these woven gloves and then fix these huge ants to them with their fangs facing inside. It is incredibly painful. One bite is said to feel like a bullet going through you. That is why they call them bullet ants. Their technical name is tucandeira ants, and they live in nests at the base of the jenipapo tree in the Amazon. The pain from the bite is said to last up to eighteen hours."

Carrie had been searching the internet when the OSBI database had come up short. She had found an article which seemed similar to what they had found at the crime scene. "Here, read this." Carrie gave him a printed article with a highlighted section, which Randy read aloud.

"They have a full day of various rituals surrounding the event, when they begin to retrieve the ants and then anesthetize them with a natural sedative that renders them docile for a time. The ants are about an inch long. This makes it easy for them to attach to the woven mitts. They put eighty ants on each mitt with their pinchers pointing inward.

"They have dancing and musical rituals they conduct. Then, one of the young men will shove their hands in the mitts that are being held by other men, and the witch doctor of the tribe will blow smoke to wake the ants up and agitate them, making them incredibly aggressive.

"They hold their hands in the mitts from five to ten minutes before pulling them out. To distract from the pain, they dance in a circle with other tribe members. Needless to say, during that time they are bitten repeatedly. The hands and part of their arms are rendered paralyzed, which is only temporary, of course.

"The result of this ritual is that the young men may shake for days on end, there is often vomiting, even sometimes blood in their feces. They do cover their hands in a coating of charcoal that does somewhat inhibit their stinging, but of course, in my opinion, makes little difference."

Randy looked up from the paper he was reading from. They both sat for a few seconds, trying to take in the information. They were dumbfounded. "With hundreds of continuous bites, I can't imagine the pain," said Randy. "Dr. Randolph thought that whoever did this must have used a different type of ant, because bullet ants do not exist around here."

"Well, thank goodness!" exclaimed Carrie

Randy plopped into his desk chair, still stunned by what he had just learned.

Carrie slowly nodded. "Okay, so we need to figure out if this guy did this willingly, or if there were others who did this to him and why. His hands were tied to something, but was he complicit in this ceremony or was he tied because he was not?"

"We need an ID on this young man too," said Randy just as his desk phone rang. "Randy Jeffries," He listened and nodded in response. When he hung up, he stood and looked at Carrie. "They are doing the postmortem soon. Let's go." He was gathering his small pocket notepad. "This will be your first?"

Carrie swallowed and nodded.

"You'll do okay. But if you start to feel sick, step out of the room. It's common in the beginning."

Carrie grabbed her coat. She had a knot in her stomach, and memories of seeing her parents side-by-side in the morgue after their deaths flooded her mind. They were horrific memories and she couldn't dislodge them.

The call with the news of their wreck had been bad enough. Then the doctor saying that they were dead took her breath and shook her to her core. But when she had to walk into that morgue in order to make a positive ID, it became real. The trauma of losing both of her beloved parents at the same time was catastrophic.

In the car, Randy could sense Carrie's anxiety. Without thinking, he said, "Have you ever been to the morgue before?"

A tear slipped out of the corner of Carrie's eye before she could gain her composure and prevent it from betraying her struggle. Her voice carried a slight tremble as she said, "Yes, just a few weeks ago, when my parents were killed in the wreck."

Randy felt like a truck had hit him. *What an insensitive idiot! How could I have forgotten?* "I'm so sorry! I didn't think..."

Carrie smiled at him. "It's okay. Of course, you wouldn't have thought about it. I'll be fine. I need to do this."

"No. I think it's too soon. You can wait here in the car and go in next time. Unfortunately, it is part of this job that won't stop. But, you'll have plenty of times to be there in the future."

Carrie joggled her head quickly in a shake. "I need to do this as soon as possible. I don't think waiting will make it any easier. I need to rip the Band-Aid off."

Randy sat looking at her for a moment as if deciding what to do. Finally, he decided to take her lead. "Okay," said Randy. "But any sign of discomfort, and you are free to step out." His reply was barely audible to Carrie. The ride there seemed as though there was a layer of wet wool covering them. To Carrie, the dreaded anticipation of it felt as solemn as her first trip to the morgue.

In twenty minutes, they were pulling into the underground garage. Carrie felt a sense of disembodiment. She wasn't quite dizzy, but slightly on the verge. Once inside, she followed Randy as he made his way through and down the dimly-lit hallway. After several turns in the sterile cold hallway, they were at the right door.

"Wait here a moment. I want to make sure they are ready for us." Carrie simply nodded. Standing outside the door thrust her back to that day. Her stomach was knotted and even though she was cold, her hands were in a sweat.

When Randy went inside, Carrie closed her eyes to try to strengthen herself. *These are not my parents. There is a young boy in there who needs my help. I am capable and I can do this.*

The swoosh of the door alerted Carrie that Randy was back. He handed her a paper gown and mask. "Put these on."

The smell had followed him out into the hallway. It was the same as it had been at the crime scene, with a hefty dose of antiseptic thrown in. Her hands were trembling, which made it difficult to put the gown on. She struggled with the booties and nearly toppled as one got caught on the toe of her shoe. Randy reached out to steady her and smiled. "You'll be fine."

Once outfitted, she followed Randy into the morgue. On the table lay the young man. He looked so much younger now that he was on this steel table, cleaned up and pale. Carrie forgot about her parents as she now took in the boy's face. He was a typical young man, not much younger than Carrie was.

Her eyes traveled down his arms to his hands, still both grotesquely swollen. There were multiple skin lesions where each of the bites were. She could not begin to count the number of bites on each hand, some trailing up the arms.

"Carrie, this is Dr. Henry Bloom, our coroner."

Both Dr. Bloom and Carrie gave a curt nod. "Call me Henry. I'm too old to put on fancies." Carrie nearly snorted at the word fancies.

"Okay, Henry it is." Carrie smiled in spite of their location.

"So, what have you got so far?" asked Randy.

"Well, we are still waiting on the tox panel, but I would say he died from the toxin in the ants. Maybe not directly, but by causing heart failure. These were fire ants, unlike the bullet ants in the Amazon."

"You know about those ants?" Randy asked, quite surprised.

"I'm an educated man, Mr. Jeffries."

Both men burst out laughing. Carrie just stood agape.

"So, do you believe there were others involved in this?" Randy asked.

"Oh yes, for a few reasons. See these ligature marks?" Henry pointed at the young man's wrists. "This area here causes me to think they tied him to a pole of some type. Maybe a large bamboo or other type of pole running about shoulder height parallel to the ground. Also, there were no ligatures found at the scene that I saw or am aware of, so someone had to untie him."

Both Randy and Carrie stood pondering this new information as they looked at the corpse. It seemed like such a bizarre thing for a modern young man to be involved in.

"I'll let you know if I find out more and when the tox panel is back."

"Thanks," replied Carrie and Randy in unison as they made their way out the door, ripping off the paper gowns.

Carrie was glad that her first week at the OSBI had plunged her headfirst into a challenging case. It helped to occupy her mind. Mists of thought would sometimes roll through without her realizing it, and soon her mind would float to her fondest memories. With those memories came wretched, stabbing emotional pain.

It took a concerted effort to shake the mist from her mind and refocus on the case at hand. Being an OSBI agent was a drastic shift from being on OKCPD patrol. This was what she had yearned for and dreamt about. It is why she had spent so many years at the university to gain as much knowledge and insight into serious crimes and their offenders as possible.

She had that knowledge now and had kept abreast of all new and emerging technology through the years. Now, being an agent, she was faced with having to take that knowledge and insight and apply it in a real-life scenario. These were real people, not just case studies. She felt an overwhelming personal pressure to solve this crime as soon as possible.

The paper before her came back into focus as she realized she had read it now multiple times and still did not know what she had read. Her recent trauma combined with the shock of this case kept preventing her from being able to zero in on what she was reading. *Maybe coffee will help.*

"You okay?" Randy asked as he approached from behind her.

"Yes... yes. Quite okay." Carrie nodded her head like a bobblehead doll in the back of an old car.

Randy was quietly looking at her. He could see how strong she was, but he also sensed that her recent trauma had created fissures in her soul that he could not see.

"Good. Did anything stand out on the missing person report?"

"Not at first glance." She hated to admit that little had soaked in while she read it at least five times over, and over again.

"Well, let's get some coffee and set up in a room with a whiteboard and lay out what little we have for now." Randy headed off, and Carrie followed. She was so thankful that he had spared her asking. She chided herself again for being so silly.

Armed with coffee and the thin case file, Randy and Carrie retreated to an empty gray room with only a table, a few chairs, and a large mobile whiteboard.

"Feel free to use any of these rooms when you need some peace and quiet and space to lay things out." Randy wrote on the board. "We'll have to call him John Doe for now. I've always hated that, but it is what it is. Now, let's write down everything we can think of that would describe this young man."

"Such as age, weight, and physical features?" Carrie asked. The certainty in her usually confident voice was lacking.

"Yes, we can do that, but I am referring to what we can glean from the situation he was in."

Carrie understood and nodded.

"How did he know about that ritual? This isn't something that most people just know. He would have had to have been in an anthropology class or watched a documentary on TV or..." Her words trailed off as she stopped thinking out loud.

Randy wrote college educated with a question mark out to the side. "He fits the common college age criteria. I would say he is about twenty or twenty-one, wouldn't you?"

Carrie nodded in agreement. "If that is the case, being away at college may delay a missing person report. His parents would assume he was at school. Friends might not miss him for a few days."

"True. Friends might not be so quick to file a missing person report, either."

"Particularly if those same friends had a hand in his death," Carrie offered. She was beginning to regain her confidence. She knew what she was doing. She just had to remember that.

"What I want to know is why would they do this?" Randy asked.

"So, both the professor at the college you spoke with and Dr. Bloom said that the Amazon tribe did it to gain strength and courage. That would fit for young men. Something could have triggered a need to show their virility." Randy wrote as Carrie spoke. "Could have been a dare. Show me who is tougher. Or, I'll do it if you do."

Randy stepped back from the board and pondered. "What we need is the crime scene and actual cause of death.

Was this young man susceptible to toxins in general, or were these ants so toxic they could have taken anyone down? He could have had a pre-existing condition that precluded his death."

"When should we hear from Dr. Bloom?" Carrie asked.

"Usually a day or so. Depends on how far the lab is backed up."

"Would that professor maybe know if he had any students who could be involved in this? Or maybe a student who is absent?"

"Good thought. We'll contact him again. I also wonder if there was any trace on the body that came from the original crime scene," said Randy.

"Could it have been the original crime scene, and they just removed the apparatus that he had been tied to?"

Soon, he turned back to the board and wrote several question marks as bullet points. Next to the first one he wrote - crime scene, identity, witnesses, accomplices, and 'cod' for cause of death. "That is a short list of what we need. I don't think the missing-person list is going to help much at this point. Let's call Professor Randolph and talk to him again. Maybe by then we will have heard from Henry."

Randy stepped over to retrieve a sticky note with Dr. Randolph's number written on it. He flipped open his phone and began dialing. "Dr. Randolph? This is Randy Jeffries again with the OSBI. Do you have a bit of time that I could ask you a few more questions?" Carrie could see Randy nodding in response.

For the next fifteen minutes, Carrie sat by and listened to the conversation between Dr. Randolph and Randy. He had confirmed that it was okay to put the phone on speaker so she could listen. Randy made copious notes as they spoke, shaking his hand out as he hung up, fingers cramping.

"Wow, that was a wealth of information. I'm not sure if he just liked to talk, being the center of attention, or if he genuinely felt that the information was helpful. Did anything stick out to you?"

"Honestly no. It seemed it was just a lot of random and general information that we already knew. He doesn't currently have any absent students, but he may after the next class session. He has had no students with excessive curiosity about this ritual either, or rather that have inquired of him."

Randy looked down at his watch and then back up at Carrie. "Well, I doubt there is much more we can do today. You have put in a full second day on the job. Let's go home and rest. I think we will need to be sharp and clear-headed tomorrow."

Carrie nodded in agreement as she stood and closed the file. She suddenly realized she was awash with the dread of going home.

"Hey, do you guys ever meet for drinks after work?" Carrie asked.

Randy's head bobbed from side to side. "Sometimes, but since we don't really work in shifts, we don't do it often."

"I just thought a drink might be nice before going home."

Randy checked his watch again. "If I hadn't made plans to meet my fiancé Sandy, I would. Let's plan on it another night."

Carrie forced herself to remain stone-faced as the word

fiancé slashed ribbons of pain across her heart. "Yes, yes, another time." Then a wide, forced smile crossed her face.

It was half-past five and Carrie sat in her car. She supposed she could go get a drink without any of the others going with her. She had never done that before, but she knew others did it all the time. She just didn't want to go home.

Her phone ringing startled her out of her thoughts. It was Billy. She didn't want to answer it, but knew she should.

"Hello."

"How did your day go today?" Billy asked. The bounce in his voice felt contrived.

"It was good. We got a case. Pretty bad one. It consumed the day, really. For all we did, it didn't seem like we made much headway." Carrie could not elevate the depressed sound of her voice.

"I haven't eaten. Thought you might meet me to get something." Carrie could hear the hope that bated Billy's voice. He was daring to ask and hoping she would say yes.

"I'm not very hungry." Then, almost as an afterthought, "Can we go somewhere that we can get a cheap drink too?"

"Yeah, sure!" The excitement in his voice almost sickened Carrie, and she didn't even know why.

They planned to meet at Caddies, a small local bar and grill near the golf course. It was a bit early on Tuesday night and there were very few at the bar. Billy had a table near the back and waved to her as she walked in.

As she approached the table, he popped up to help her

with her jacket. He moved to give a kiss to her cheek, but she moved just enough that it did not make its mark. The excitement Billy had felt quickly drained away.

As they ordered two draft beers and reviewed the short menu, the server walked away. The silence between them was excruciatingly uncomfortable. The early hour quiet in the bar resonated the silence between them. A slap and a sizzle behind Carrie told her someone had ordered a burger and the smell drifted through confirming it. Despite her emotional lack of hunger, her stomach growled.

Billy decided he would let Carrie take the lead in conversation. He had made too many blunders and he would just follow where she decided to go. When the silence became more than he could stand, he asked, "Are things going well at the new job?"

Carrie looked at him and smiled gently. She felt compassion for the man she used to love. Then it hit her. She had thought the words 'used to.' When had she stopped feeling that she loved him? She didn't know, but she didn't think she could ever love again, no one, ever.

"It's going great. The only awkward moment today was when I realized I didn't know where the coffeepot was."

Billy laughed and nodded. "That's a genuine tragedy."

The server brought the beer, and Carrie drank as though she had been in a drought. Billy didn't notice.

Soon, with the help of the beer, they began to relax and were coaxed along into the familiar rhythm of their old rocking boat. They chatted and laughed like they always had. Carrie told him as much as she could about her new job, about the differences in book facts and putting them to use.

Billy hung on every word. Around nine, Carrie looked at her watch. "I am so beat, and I really need to go home and get a good night's sleep. I haven't had many of those lately."

The hope of going home with Carrie faded, but Billy was encouraged by the breakthrough he had felt over the course of the evening. His warm smile in response assured Carrie that all was well and there would be no tension from her request.

Billy walked Carrie to her car with his arm around her. It felt good to Carrie, but there were no lingering sparks of passion that his touch would have brought just a few short weeks ago.

At the car, Billy faced Carrie close as she leaned against her door. With Billy only being a slight bit taller than Carrie, it put them nearly nose to nose. She didn't avoid his face and couldn't avoid falling headlong into those eyes that exuded rich, deep love for her. Her body tingled for the first time in weeks, but nevertheless, her heart felt as cold as a stone.

Chapter Six

"Everyone come on in here," SAC Bracket bellowed through the room. He was standing at the door of the conference room.

"What's all this about?" Randy asked a co-worker as they were walking to the conference room. A shake of the head and a shrug were the only response.

They all crowded into the conference room, standing where they could. On the long table sat dozens of small boxes.

"New toys!" Bracket said as he waved his hand to the table. "The old pagers are going away. They call these Black-Berry cellular phones. They should help us in the field to have more access to information and such that we need.

"I also have a new list of protocols that go with this toy. This is not your personal phone. We pay according to the data we use. And even though we have negotiated a great rate for law enforcement, the more we use, the more we pay. So, keep your flip phones!" His hearty laugh filled the room.

One agent reached to pickup a box. "No, not yet. I want to tell you about them before you get so distracted you don't hear a word I say.

"This device," he said as he held up the small dark blue rectangle, "cannot only make calls, but take photos, short videos, and its claim to fame is its ability to send and receive emails. We will have these synched with your company emails so that they will come to both your BlackBerry and your computer. If something important comes in when you are out in the field, you won't miss it.

"You can also send emails from anywhere. This should be a huge timesaver. Also, instead of pagers, the switchboard will push notifications to your phones now. They also have the ability to touch-to-talk, sort of like our radios. But we won't be replacing those. The touch-to-talk is still new technology and I'm not ready to trust my agents' safety to it yet."

The room was restless. Everyone wanted to get a look at the new device. "They also have advanced GPS. You can use the map program and enter addresses. We can also locate you, or rather, your BlackBerry, with that software. If you have it with you, then we can track you.

"We will have a training seminar starting this afternoon. We will host them on three different days at different times. You must complete the training before you can take your phone. Today, I want all of you to take this protocol packet and read it, memorize it, and then sign it. You will be tested on it during the training. The sign-up sheet for training is hanging on the board next to the coffeemaker. Sign up. That's all."

"SAC, you can't dangle a new toy in front of us and then not give it to us." one agent said.

"If I give it to you, you will not read the protocol manual, miss training, mess with it on your own, and then screw it up. Get signed up and read the protocol. Then we will have new toys."

Carrie and Randy had been two of the last agents in the conference room and were standing just inside the door. Randy turned and was gently pushing Carrie out the door and over to the list. "Let's get signed up quick."

The first class was that afternoon. They each wrote in their names. Just as they were finishing, they felt the throng of eager agents close behind them. They pushed their way out and laughed at how they had been first on the list. Randy raised his hand in a 'high-five' and Carrie slapped it with a grin.

"Now we have to get those protocol packets. While everyone else was doing that, we were signing our names to the top of the list." Randy was proud of his quick thinking.

The conference room was empty except for Bracket, who was standing at the front of the room fiddling with the new device.

"Have you signed the protocol packet and done your training?" Randy called out, startling the SAC.

"As a matter of fact, I have. I had to do it days ago before we even got them. They really are fascinating."

Randy walked over and looked on as Bracket showed him some features. Carrie held back and picked up two of the remaining packets on the table. She thumbed through, amazed at how a team of bureaucrats and lawyers could take a short list of simple instructions and blow them up into a document an inch thick. She wasn't looking forward to the paperwork, but the new phone intrigued her.

She walked up to stand on the other side of Bracket and watched while his beefy thumbs fumbled to type on the small, raised keyboard. He was growing somewhat frustrated at the auto-correct feature and the absurd creations it filled in when a head popped in the door.

"Dr. Bloom on the phone for you, Randy. Line two."

Randy looked at Sylvie and nodded. "Be right there."

Carrie and Randy reluctantly drew themselves away from the comical demonstration and convened at Randy's desk. He punched the speaker button and greeted Dr. Bloom.

"Randy, we have a mess here. The tox panel is back. We are finding drugs in this boy's system in addition to the fire ant toxin. These ants aren't your normal Oklahoma fire ants. They are referred to as imported ants, which started moving from Texas several years ago.

"They were discovered first at Ft. Sill years ago. Their toxin is somewhat higher, but the real danger is that they are far more aggressive than our normal fire ants. These will attack anything protein-related, whereas other ants often just go about their business climbing over this and that.

"We have two highly toxic psychotropic drugs in his system as well. I'll send you data sheets over on them. It is hard to know if he took them at the same time or actually, when it was. One was scopolamine.

"There is an urban legend surrounding it that says it is a mind control drug. It is not that simple and doesn't work the way often portrayed in movies and on TV, but in combination with bromo-dragonFLY it is anybody's guess."

Randy and Carrie were speechless, and both were deep in thought regarding what this could mean. "Thanks Henry." Randy was distracted when hanging up the phone. He turned to look at Carrie. "Henry was right. This is a mess."

"Was the scopolamine and bromo-dragonFLY the COD?"

It just dawned on Randy that Dr. Bloom had said they found those drugs in the boys' system, but he didn't say overdose. "I don't know. Contributing factor maybe?"

"No doubt we have more research to do. We have a ritual from the Amazon jungle and two nearly obscure drugs. Can this case get any more bizarre?" Carrie asked.

Randy pulled up his email with the emails from Dr. Bloom. He had included the autopsy report along with the data sheets.

"Here are the data sheets on the drugs. He has put suspicious death. Heart attack with contributing factors. Oh, I also have another email here from the forensics lab. There were no fibers on the body. In fact, there were traces of alcohol as though the body had been entirely cleaned prior to the incident. There were also no fingerprints or other recent debris in the building."

"The windows of that building had no glass and there was no door. There was nothing to keep the elements out. What we still don't know is if that was the crime scene or the dump site. He couldn't have been there long or the wind would have blown a ton of dust and debris in to cover him." Carrie was deep in thought about the crime scene.

"Okay, let's divide and conquer. Would you mind doing as much research on the two drugs as you can find? I will contact the anthropology professor at UCO again and see if either of these drugs are used as part of this ceremony. We still don't even know who this young man is. We need something to give us a direction. Right now we are flying blind." Randy was shuffling the papers he had just printed to put into the file before getting on the phone.

Carrie nodded. The enormity of her new job as OSBI agent was settling in. She had felt a great responsibility as a patrol officer, but this was somehow very different with new complexities. She hoped she was up for the task.

By the time the BlackBerry training rolled around at two that afternoon, Carrie and Randy were mentally exhausted. Neither one wanted to admit it, but they were somewhat regretting having signed up for the training so soon.

"So, Dr. Bloom is putting heart failure because of extenuating suspicious circumstances on the death certificate. Isn't that kind of vague?" Carrie asked.

"Well, it is accurate and leaves us a window and a reason to continue our investigation. We still don't know if the young man was a willing participant in this ritual or if it was murder. Dr. Bloom can, if need be, change the COD later."

The training for the new phone was interesting, but Carrie's mind kept wandering back to the case. Both she and Randy had just slightly skimmed the protocol sheets. It really was just an expanded version of common sense boundaries.

She had signed her copy, and they had handed them over once in the room.

The little shiny navy blue rectangle felt foreign in Carrie's hand. "I don't think this thing will fit in my pocket."

"I have a friend who has one, and he has a case on his belt that he slides it into."

"Just what I need, one more thing on my belt." Carrie snorted.

The training was helpful, after all, and they were given a new protocol packet with their logins and a place where they could put their passwords. There was also an instruction packet for help should they need it.

"It's getting late. Let's go back and update our whiteboard before we go home." Randy said.

They added the names of the two drugs found in the young man's system, COD, and an interesting fact that the professor had given them.

"Do you think it is significant that scopolamine is heavily used in South America? Could there be a link between that and the Amazon ritual?"

"Apparently, those taking part in the ritual in the Amazon had no drugs whatsoever in their system. That was the whole point, to be courageous enough to endure the pain on their own."

"It has been used world-wide, so I suppose I am just trying to stretch a link between the two. I found that it has been used for centuries in spiritual and magical ways. They would often pulverize the plants and combine them with animal fat, which would help it adhere to the body. Then the body would absorb it."

"With the body having been washed, and with only traces of alcohol, can we rule out a transdermal application of the drugs? The drugs would not have had to be ingested, would they?" Randy asked.

Carrie turned to study the board with the added information. The face of the young man stared back at her. It was a closeup taken in the morgue. *Can I still see the agony etched in his face, or am I just remembering the horrific scene in the old concrete building?* She didn't know.

She turned back to Randy and asked, "Have we found anything in our research or from the anthropology professor that there have been other rituals like this in the US?"

"None that I know of. He didn't volunteer that information."

"I still can't get around why he would willingly do this." Carrie pondered the motive of it all.

The room was quiet as they were both attempting to assimilate the information and organize it into some sort of sense.

"Where did they get the ants?" Carried asked.

"The ants," replied Randy. "Out of the ground?"

"It is winter. They are deep underground and dormant right now. They would have had to have known where an imported fire ant colony was, digging deep to retrieve it, or they fostered one of their own just for this purpose."

Carrie picked up the marker and put 'ants?' on the board.

"Is there a way we can tell if they kept them in a controlled environment or if they were living in nature?" Randy asked.

Carrie had no answer. "My brain is beginning to hurt."

"Mine too. We've ingested a lot with the new technology and this case full of closed doors and questions so far." Randy pulled out his new phone and tapped around on it. "Hey, I already have emails coming in." Carrie then looked at hers.

When Bracket walked into the room, both Randy and Carrie sat looking at their phones. "Good grief! I hope this isn't a sign of things to come."

"Hey, you want us to know how to use them, right?" Randy responded.

SAC's head nodded. "Yes, yes. I do. But we have another body."

He stepped into the room with a folder and laid it on the table. "I get the feeling they are connected," he said with a raised eyebrow.

Randy opened the file and there lay a picture of another young man, lying naked on the ground. The soles of his feet were burned black, nearly to ash in places.

Carrie sucked in a breath. "That must have been horrific! Brutal."

"Fire-walking," commented Randy.

Carrie's forehead pinched in consternation. "Why would anyone do that?"

"Why would anyone stick their hands in mitts of ants?" Randy replied.

Bracket moved to leave. With his hand on the doorknob, he turned back to Randy and Carrie. "Body is at the morgue."

Being so late in the day, they knew the body would sit in the morgue until Dr. Bloom did the autopsy in the morning. It was going to be dark soon, and the OKCPD had secured the crime scene, so they called it a day and decided they would come back fresh in the morning.

Carrie hated to ask Randy once again if he wanted to stop at the bar on their way home. She didn't want to appear as if this were a thing with her. Not knowing any of the other agents, she decided she would just go on her own.

She didn't want to go to the usual bar and grills that she and Billy had frequented. She wanted something to fit her mood. Something dark and hidden out of the way.

After driving around in a part of town she rarely ever ventured into, she came upon a brightly lit small building. The neon beckoned her. The parking lot was merely gravel, and it popped beneath her car. The winter wind was slightly receding from the wild thrashing it had caused during the day.

Once in park, she looked down at her OSBI shirt and gear and wondered about her decision. This didn't really look like the type of place that would welcome law enforcement. As the cold from the outside chilled the interior, Carrie lost her nerve and turned the key. A six-pack and a pizza would work fine.

Driving back home, a cold, drizzling rain began to fall. It drew her into the memory of the night her parents died. The pain was still so intense she could barely breathe. *Other people who have lost parents grieve and move on. Why can't I?*

The blaring horn of a passing car jerked Carrie's mind back to the present. A fleeting thought to call Billy was just that, fleeting. She just didn't feel she could pretend right then.

She called in a pizza order as she drove home and then stopped to get beer. By the time she pulled into her driveway, the pizza guy was also pulling in. The freezing wind and rain had stopped, and the night had cleared. Above her, the brightest pinpricks of light pierced the blackest night. *Beauty in the darkness*, she thought.

Her empty house was quietly loud to her soul. *I should get a dog. No. It wouldn't be fair to the dog with me hardly ever here.*

She ate the pizza and downed the six-pack, then fell asleep on the couch with the TV on. In the middle of the night, she stirred, realized where she was, and stumbled to bed. She had not gotten drunk, she didn't think, but she was mentally and emotionally exhausted for sure.

Starting a job that was such a drain on one's emotions was probably not the best idea when she was struggling to maintain an emotional quotient of zero so that she could stay above water. She was in emotional pain, but she could not fathom the physical pain these young men went through. *Maybe physical pain is easier.*

Once nestled in her soft bed, sleep eluded her. She lay looking out her window at the dark night and beautiful stars, and she cried over her memories one more time.

Carrie did not welcome the alarm. Once she had gone to bed, she had laid there awake for over an hour. She could barely stand the aloneness she felt. It was a feeling of complete isolation, and she knew that no matter how many people she surrounded herself with, it would not fill that void.

Slightly revived after a hot shower and a slice of cold pizza, she was ready for the day. The sun shone brightly and everything seemed to point to spring. But Carrie knew differently. This always happened. The promise of spring would be on the horizon and then another blast of winter weather would come out of seemingly nowhere. She would not get her hopes up.

She arrived at the office thirty minutes before her required check-in time. She decided she would take that time to do some research on her own. The internet was becoming an enormous source of information, but one had to be careful to distinguish between what was accurate and what was just slung out there to draw people to a website.

She typed in 'fire walker.' Several sites popped up in the Google search. One site read:

A widely practiced religious ritual the world over. Hindu communities in South Asia, Taoists and Buddhists, orthodox communities in Greece and Bulgaria, and places in Bali, Spain and Pakistan still practice this ritual today. It is believed that this ritual is a gesture of paying respect to God and has great religious significance. Those partaking of the ritual believe that it repels evil influences and purifies one's soul.

Carrie jotted down random thoughts on a blank notepad. On one page, she scribbled down everything she could think of after reading the article and seeing the crime scene photos. She wrote hurriedly, with little thought. If it came to her mind, she just wrote it down. Then, she did the same for the other crime.

The first page had little on it. They had not yet dived into the heart of the matter and truly begun to investigate. The other page, however, had several notations. She was rereading what she had written when Randy walked in.

"What have you got there?"

Carrie looked up, a little embarrassed by the juvenile exercise, and slid her hand nonchalantly over the top page. Her embarrassment showed as she responded. "Nothing really."

Randy reached down and pulled the notepad from under her hand and read. He flipped the page and read that one as well.

"What is this?"

"I call it a brain dump. I often find it helpful to just quickly write down everything that comes to mind, no matter what it is, when faced with a challenging subject. Most get crossed out later, but some can open new doors of thought."

Randy thought about what she was saying. He could tell she thought he would think the exercise silly. "I like it. Gets out all the data that we are unconsciously holding onto that might be helpful. Has anything surfaced that could be of use?"

"Not really. I just did it and haven't fully read through it again."

Randy once again looked at the top page. "Fire walker. Did you already know this, or have you been doing research?"

"I did some research. Here, let me send you this page. It is pretty succinct and seems to align with the other sites I've found."

Carrie emailed the site over to him and he sat for a few minutes reading it. Once done, he laced his fingers behind his head and leaned back in his chair, looking at her. "So, number one was a ritual to become more courageous, stronger. The second one was a ritual to purify one's soul, among other things. Do you see a link there?"

Carrie sat thinking. "All I can see is that they are two extremely bizarre rituals used only by a few groups of people."

Carrie's phone buzzed at the same time Randy's did. They looked down to read. 'John Doe #2 autopsy 9:00 a.m.' They had received the text from the receptionist, which she had forwarded from a phone message left by Dr. Bloom.

"Looks like we have an autopsy to attend. Let's grab the file," said Randy.

The second trip to the morgue was less traumatic than earlier in the week. Carrie realized this would soon become a routine part of her job and that she would be okay.

On the table lay the second young man, roughly in his early twenties. Once again, Carrie wasn't sure if she actually saw the agony he had experienced on his face or if she was just projecting how she thought the ordeal had been for him. A nightmare.

Dr. Bloom, Henry, was already deep in a discussion with Randy. "We've not been out to the crime scene yet. We'll head out there next," said Randy.

Henry raised the white sheet at the end of the table

where the young man's feet were. It was shocking. The limited research Carrie had done revealed nothing this intense. Those that suffered burns usually did so in a limited capacity. This boy had some spots burned nearly to the bone.

"How could you hold your own foot on a hot coal so long that it burned it like this?" Carrie could not comprehend how a person could do this to themselves. "Are there signs that they held him there, that someone else was forcing him to do this?"

"Not that I can tell," replied Henry.

"If we find him to have that same cocktail of drugs, could that cause the type of disassociations that would cause a person to do this?" Randy asked.

Henry contemplated what Randy had presented. "It is possible. Both are hallucinogens, each having a unique method of action. Combined, anything is possible. The key is determining what was the combined dose ratio and dose. Bromo-dragonFLY has an extremely long duration of action, up to several days. It could have been ingested days ahead of time, well ahead of the scopolamine."

"Would someone have given them these drugs and been able to coerce them to engage in these rituals against their will?" Carrie asked. "I know you said that the use of scopolamine as a mind control type of drug was simply urban legend, but what if combined with dragonFLY? Could that change things?"

"I don't know. You would have to ask a doctor of pharmacology, preferably one with years of research on class one drugs."

"Do you know who we could talk to?" Randy asked.

"Let me see if I can get some names together for you and I'll send them your way." Henry replied.

"What about the rest of the body? Any residue, or is it clean like the other one?" Randy asked.

"So far, it appears to be clean. I took a swab and there was a residue of alcohol."

Both Carrie and Randy were quiet when leaving the morgue. Their minds were each very far away, deep into the bowels of the cases. Each one probing in their own way with their own thoughts, trying to see links that would reveal what they could not see.

Chapter Seven

The drive to the second crime scene was further out east from the first one. They had left the metro area and were now amid farm and ranch land that sat on the edge of the city. Randy was finally able to locate the seldom-traveled red dirt road that led off through a wooded pasture. It was evident that it was not a public road, but one that was used primarily by the owner of the property. The lack of a gate though, did not prevent anyone from driving it.

The road was so rough that the SUV bounced and jostled them fiercely. "You would have to have a substantial vehicle to come down this road. An SUV, Jeep, or maybe even an ATV," noted Carrie. "A regular car would never make it down these ruts."

"That's for sure," said Randy as they topped a rise and could finally see the yellow tape, which marked off a small clearing in the brush.

"There really isn't anything here to see. Flat dormant grass in the middle of nowhere," Carrie said.

"Yeah... No doubt the techs have done all they can do." Randy reached for the door handle and moved to get out. "Well, let's at least have a look around and see if we can get a feel for the place."

The wind whipped Carrie's hair into her face and she kept sweeping it away as she turned a full three-hundred-sixty degrees to view the entire area. "Do you see anything unusual or out of the norm?" Carrie asked.

Randy shook his head. He stood with his hands on his hips looking first one way and then the other. His eyes squinted against the bright sun. "I'm going back to get my sunglasses."

As Randy turned back towards the SUV, Carrie squatted and looked at the ground where they had found the body.

"Hey Randy, this obviously has to be a dumpsite. There aren't any coals or signs of fire here. My guess is the other one was a dumpsite as well. These rituals are happening offsite and then when they go awry, the bodies are being dumped.

"Could that mean that they are actually performing more of these rituals than we know, and we are only seeing the ones that end in death?" Carrie's voice rose slightly as she continued.

"Could be. We need more information though to know for sure."

On the ride back to the office, they tossed around ideas regarding where to get the information they needed. Carrie took notes as Randy drove.

"What about clubs? Are there any groups or clubs that we could find that practice something similar?"

"Maybe. We have to talk to the anthropology professor again regarding this second death. He might help connect the dots for us," said Randy.

"So far, these are not typical actions or practices for North America. The drugs aren't even really used here according to the research we've read. South America, Europe, Asia, but not here."

"Could we be looking at recent immigrants?" Randy asked.

"Possibly, but the first one was tied to South America practices, and this one fits more in line with Asia."

Randy snorted. "Maybe they have a huge spinning wheel of weirdly dangerous rituals and they just spin the dial to see what they will do next."

"That isn't funny."

"I know. I just can't wrap my head around it."

Carrie looked down at her phone and scanned through her emails. She was really going to like the access this new device provided. One email stood out. "We have confirmation. The same drugs were in this young man's system as the first. They are definitely linked." Carrie read a little further. "Henry has sent us a name to check on the drugs. Dr. Amos Pinning. He is the director of pharmacology research at OU Medical Center Teaching Hospital."

"All right. Let's head that way."

It took a good twenty minutes to find the right building, park, and navigate the hallways. Finally though, they were in the right place.

"Do you have an appointment?" Dr. Pinning's research assistant asked.

"No, but Dr. Henry Bloom, the Oklahoma County Coroner, gave us Dr. Pinning's name. We're with the OSBI. We hope he can help us with our research regarding some obscure drugs found in our victims."

"Let me see if he can help you or if you need to come back." She escaped through a double swinging door.

"I hate hospitals," said Carrie so quietly that Randy nearly missed it.

Randy didn't quite know how to reply, so he just nodded in agreement.

It didn't take long before the assistant came back through the doors she had so quickly retreated to. "He said you can come on back."

As they entered the lab, a dark-skinned man with short cropped hair and small gold-rimmed spectacles was leaning over a microscope. When they approached, he stood to his full height and Carrie's eyes grew large. He must be nearly seven feet tall.

When Dr. Pinning saw her face, he chuckled. "I know. I'm tall. No, I didn't play basketball." He had a huge grin with perfect white teeth. His voice was wonderfully lyrical, with an accent that could only be Jamaican.

He ripped off his light blue gloves and reached to shake her hand. As he thoroughly shook, he covered her hand with his other one. Then, he turned to Randy and did the same. When introductions had been made, Dr. Pinning led them to the back of the lab and through another door which opened into his office.

"Please have a seat. How may I help you?"

First Randy, then Carrie, described the first two crime scenes and the drugs found in the bodies. Through the wonder of their new technology, Carrie pulled up the tox panels and emailed them to Dr. Pinning on the spot.

He turned to his monitor and pulled up the technical documents from the lab which Carrie had just sent. As he read, the smile on his face was replaced by a cloud. Once done, he leaned back in his chair and tapped his upper lip absentmindedly as he thought.

"What exactly can I tell you that you need to know?"

"We don't know if these young men acted on their own or if the drugs were instrumental in them being easily coerced to do this. I believe it is an urban legend that scopolamine can allow mind control. Is there any truth to that at all, maybe in combination with FLY?" Randy asked.

Dr. Pinning did not respond quickly, obviously contemplating the question. "All urban legend myths are birthed from a seed of truth. Scopolamine can render a person unconscious for twenty-four hours or more. When they regain consciousness, they have almost no memory of the time between when they first took the drug to when they become fully conscious again.

"During that time, when they are in a semiconscious state, they are suggestible to direction, but nothing close to a full mind control situation. Any inebriated or drugged person suffering under a psychotropic drug can be somewhat suggestible. In fact, even a person not under the influence can be impressionable. Just ask any marketing expert.

"Obviously, the degree to which they follow instructions

may be linked directly to the amount of the drug they took. More than mind control, we must consider that the drug is a hallucinogen. Both are. Combined, they could cause the victim to believe he was invincible and able to withstand the sting of the fire ants, or the coals of the fire."

"So they could have taken the drugs and then believed what they were doing was somehow good to do?" Randy asked.

"Yes, indeed."

"We know the victims did not die where they were found. So, we know that someone moved them. What we don't know is if this was murder, and they were disposing of their victims, or if they were jointly engaged in these rituals and when one died, they needed to dump them elsewhere to draw attention away from themselves," said Carrie.

"These are very dangerous drugs. The dosage for one alone is tricky. For someone to combine the two together and not have more deaths is the miracle here. In fact, I would be quite surprised that the combination of the two drugs were not the cause of death."

"Who would have this knowledge? They would need to know how to combine them, or even the thought to do so." Randy asked. "Someone in chemistry?"

"Hmmm... not just anyone. This would have to be someone who had access to a research facility and then specimens to experiment on, unless, of course, they were experimenting on themselves cand others randomly. But then I would think you would see more deaths come your way with drug overdoses."

"Can you think of any of your students or anyone you

may have come across who might remotely have an interest in this?" Carrie asked.

Dr. Pinning leaned forward and his brow pinched as he thought. "No, not at first thought. I will consider it more, and if anything comes to me about someone who might be involved or more information, I will contact you."

Since it was lunchtime, Randy and Carrie decided to stop and get something to eat.

"Where are your favorite places to eat?" Randy asked.

Carrie gazed out the window. She wasn't picky and would eat nearly anything, but she had had trouble getting her appetite back. "I'm not picky."

Randy glanced at her. He detected a note of sadness to her demeanor. He attributed it to her parents' recent death, but wondered if there could be more to it.

"I'm hungry for Mexican food. I've got a favorite little hole-in-the-wall place near here if that is okay with you."

Carrie looked over at Randy and smiled "Yes." She did like Mexican food. Loved it actually, and if anything would entice her to eat, that would be it, except of course, for pizza.

The lunch crowd was just beginning to arrive at eleven-thirty, so they had the pick of the place. They were seated in a torn red vinyl booth next to a bright orange and yellow wall on which hung pictures of several Mexican icons.

Carrie looked at the menu. It was pretty standard, but there were a few dishes she hadn't seen before. It didn't take long for her stomach to growl in response to the inviting food descriptions. The servers brought glasses of water, chips, and queso along with bowls of salsa. Randy quickly abandoned his menu and dove heartily into the chip bowl.

"Have you ever had the Tacos Pioneros?" Carrie asked.

"Yep. They're amazing."

Carrie snapped the menu shut and laid it on the table. At the request of her stomach, she too, reached for the chips. She could feel Randy watching her as she busied herself spooning queso and salsa onto her little plate.

"I think you are going to be an amazing partner," said Randy.

His comment surprised Carrie. She wasn't sure what she thought he had been thinking, but it wasn't that. She looked up at him and searched his eyes for sincerity. "Thank you."

"You have an instinct, an eye for what isn't obvious. It is incredibly necessary in this job."

The server took their orders, and they sat eating chips in silence for a time. "Carrie, I know you have just had quite the blow recently. If there is anything I can do to help you, please let me know. Or, if there is anything else that you need to talk about, please know I can be a good listener."

"Thank you. I appreciate that. It's hard for me to talk about me. If I don't, it isn't because I don't want to talk to you, it is just because I don't really talk to anyone."

"Not even girlfriends?" Randy asked.

Carrie looked down at the chip she held that was loaded with salsa as she thought. "I used to have a lot of girlfriends growing up. I guess you could say I was quite popular. During college, not all my friends went to the same college, some not at all. But..." She stopped. The day she and Billy met was the day he had become her best friend.

Randy waited patiently. If she needed, wanted to talk she would. If she didn't, that was fine too.

Carrie laid the chip down on her plate and looked at Randy. "Once I met my fiancé Billy in college, it seemed I didn't have time for anyone else. He was not controlling and didn't care if I spent time with my friends, but I just wanted to be with him or with my family."

"I didn't realize you were engaged." Randy's voice grew excited at the news.

At that moment, the server brought their plates, and Carrie was thankful. She didn't want to have to talk about Billy and their relationship. The rising steam from the sizzling beef and grilled peppers overtook their other senses, and the main focus became their meals.

Through that meal, they said little. Randy talked some about their co-workers, filling Carrie in on length on the job and some personality traits. He wasn't a gossip or derogatory about any of them, which Carrie admired. If he had issues with anyone, he didn't say.

When finished, they sat back and relaxed in the euphoria of satisfied stomachs.

"So, what is next?" Carrie asked.

"We need a starting point from somewhere. Neither young man had fingerprints or DNA in the system. Detective Morris is still searching missing persons. So far nothing."

"So, what happens if we can't find who these young men are and what happened? Does that happen very often?"

Randy took a deep breath before he spoke. "Sadly, sometimes it does. We are usually able to find who they are. Eventually, someone will look for them. We will work this as hard as we can, turning over every rock we can, but honestly, we need a break on this one or it will go cold quick."

"With two deaths from seemingly similar circumstances, there could be more coming. Those drugs are dangerous. I can't bear to think of more young men, and maybe women, dying from this silliness," said Carrie.

"We can search the national crime database to see if anything familiar triggers something. Other than that, for now, we have very little to go on." Randy slipped his card out and paid. Then they were back on the road.

After driving back to the office, they filled the afternoon with paperwork and updating their whiteboard. Even though it was challenging for both of them to generate hope regarding the case, they were resolved that discouragement wouldn't keep them down.

They still hadn't heard from the entomologist, but tomorrow was another day and would hopefully open new leads to further their investigation.

Carrie once again sat in her car, dreading going home, but having nowhere else to go. On the drive there, she decided she would change clothes and go out. She wanted loud music, bright lights, and drunken laughter, not necessarily in that order.

Carrie changed into tight jeans, a black tank top and then layered a form-fitting plaid shirt on top. She fastened only the snaps at her waist and left the others free. She wanted to feel sexy, and she did.

She found her favorite pair of worn cowboy boots in the back of her closet and slid each one on with a pop. The worn leather hugged her feet and the soles felt solid beneath her. The smell of old leather added to the feeling of familiar comfort. She had loved those boots since she began college and they had taken her on many nightly excursions.

She shoved a thin fold-over wallet with only her driver's license, debit card, and some cash into her back pocket. On her way out the door, she grabbed her old leather coat off of the hook and snuggled into its warmth.

For a few minutes, she sat in her car while it grew warm, contemplating where she wanted to go. At first nothing came to mind. She wanted to avoid the places she had gone with Billy. Then she remembered that about a year or so ago, there was a bar she and Tommy had been called out to. It seemed like just the place she needed for the night.

The night was clear and crisp, but just as cold as it had been. A bit of nerves tickled her stomach. She had never gone to a bar on her own before, but she knew she didn't want to be home and sensed that the rowdiness would drown out the voices of pain in her mind.

As she was pulling into the parking lot of the Blue Tiger, her phone rang. It was Billy. Her finger hovered over the answer key as she battled with the uncertainty of wanting to talk to him. Before she could decide, the call ended, sending him to her voicemail.

Guilt threatened to turn her around and send her back home, but she set her jaw and opened the door. The unknown driving force that propelled her into this new dark world was foreign to her, but one she couldn't seem to resist.

The moment she walked in the warmth of the bar, it clothed her in comfort. There were a few empty barstools and more empty tables. Rubbing her hands together from nervous tension, she walked towards a booth in the back. From there, she could watch the room inconspicuously and take the occupants' measures, ever the cop.

The server was quick to request her order, and Carrie was quick to give it. Tonight, she would just have a few beers and then go home. She mentally set her boundaries, believing she was in control.

The beer tasted good, and the music was exhilarating. There was a small dance floor in the far corner and two couples were taking advantage of it. As she watched them dance, she couldn't help but think of Billy. Was her heart melting? Was she wanting to love him again? She wasn't sure.

A shadow fell across her table, and when she looked up, a heavy man around fifty years old was standing there.

"Hey sweetie," he slurred. "Care to dance?"

"No, thank you," Carrie clipped, and went back to watching the dancers.

"Oh, come on. I dance real good."

Carrie was feeling agitated. "No. I am not interested. I just want to sit here in peace and drink my beer." The level of her voice had risen slightly from her first response.

He slid down on the seat across from her. Now she was really pissed. She looked him squarely in the eye, sat up straight, and leaned toward him. "I said that I am not interested. Get up from my table and don't bother me again." Her tough demeanor and demanding voice did the trick. Being the perfect target for her pent-up rage, he shook his head and skulked off with his defeat trailing behind him.

The server came back and chuckled. "Good for you, girl. Another beer?"

Carrie smiled and nodded yes. She would not let the world take advantage of her. Guarding herself had become her priority, and she would use any means available to do that. She could be as tough as she needed to be, and find as many distractions as possible to survive.

She spent the next hour enjoying three large draft beers, one beer over her previously determined, but now forgotten, boundary. Not having had anything to eat since she and Randy ate an early lunch at the Mexican restaurant, the beer hit her empty stomach and immediately landed its mark, anesthetizing her emotions. The alcohol, warm bar, bright neon lights, and engaging music took Carrie to a mental place that she needed to go. It felt good, and she knew she had found a new home.

When the server came around for the fourth round, Carrie agreed. "You are new here. Glad to have you."

Carrie nodded. She liked the server. Her guess was that she was around thirty-five, and not yet beaten down by life. As she worked, she smiled and got along well with the clientele. She made Carrie feel welcome, but did not probe into her life.

"Thanks," said Carrie. "I like it here. I'm sure I'll be back."

"There are some nights it isn't very busy at all. If you ever come in and need to unload, sit at the bar and we can chat while I work."

Carrie thought that sounded great. "Thanks. So what nights are you not busy?"

"Well, the busy nights are Friday and Saturday. Tonight is a little busier than a normal weekday, but you are welcome to sit at the bar anytime."

"Thanks. I will." Carrie watched the server walk away with the empty glasses. The vibrating of her phone for the third time caused her to simply turn the phone off. She did not know what to do about her relationship with Billy. She just wanted to avoid it all.

A handsome cowboy type popped over in front of Carrie. "Want to dance?"

He was smiling and seemed easygoing, and Carrie agreed. Her inebriated mind convinced her that he would be a pleasant distraction. The beer had taken away her inhibitions, and this guy seemed like he was all fun. He wasn't bad on the eyes either.

"My name is Andy."

"I'm Carrie," she replied over the din of the music.

Carrie was a good dancer, and so was Andy. She found herself filling the evening with dancing, laughing, and drinking.

About thirty minutes before last call, Carrie made her way to the ladies' room. On the way out, Andy was waiting for her in the hallway. At first, it startled Carrie.

"Hey, I was just wondering if you might want to finish our fun at my house." He could feel the mood in Carrie change. "But hey, if not, that's okay." He had raised his hands and was backing away.

"No wait, that's fine. Just not tonight. Maybe some other time," Carrie replied. She looked at him with pleading eyes hoping to convey her sincerity.

Andy moved back closer to Carrie and slid his arms around her waist. He bent down to give her a kiss, and she met his lips and gave herself over to him, just for a moment.

Chapter Eight

It was three a.m. when a bright light blasted through Carrie's bedroom window which faced the street. She had been so exhausted when she arrived home from the bar that she had failed to close the curtains on her windows.

The enormous size of the light and its penetrating beam startled her awake. She fumbled around for her phone with one hand while she attempted to press the numbers of her gun safe with the other hand.

Her nerves were in tatters, and a hangover was clouding her senses. Just as she was about to get the safe unlocked, the phone in her hand rang. It startled her, and she dropped it to the floor.

She was quickly down on her knees, groping for the ringing phone. She swiped wildly, attempting to find the device, only to scoot it further away. The ringing stopped, then began to ring once again.

Carrie lay down prone on the floor and reached as far as

she possibly could under the bed, finding the phone. The caller ID said, 'unknown'. Just as she answered the phone with a breathless, "Hello," the bright spotlight extinguished.

A deep, surly voice pushed terror through the phone line with a slow, evil-sounding tenor. "You don't know what you are dealing with. Drop the case now or risk death. Your death or someone you love." Then the line went dead.

Carrie was grasping for air. The terror she felt was palpable and her entire body trembled in response. Coming to her senses, she finished retrieving her gun from the safe, only to find it shaking erratically in her hand.

She ran to her front door to verify that she had indeed locked it when coming home, then to both the living room and bedroom windows to pull the curtains shut.

Her mind was racing, and she dropped to her sofa to relieve her weakened knees. She dropped her phone on the coffee table and grabbed her head with the empty hand. Her breathing was slowing, and she realized she was gently rocking back and forth.

After a few moments, she took one long-deep breath and sat up straight. *Who should I call first?* She dialed 911, gave them her name and OSBI badge number, then explained that the threat was no longer imminent, as far as she could tell.

Once that call was complete, she called SAC Brackett. Hearing his voice and explaining the situation nearly caused her to break down in tears. She choked back sobs and forced herself to try and maintain her composure.

Brackett and Randy arrived separately just before the OKCPD. Carrie led them into her living room. Her bedraggled hair created a wild halo around her face, and her sweatpants and tank top hung awry on her thin frame. She hadn't thought to change clothes or even throw anything over what she had gone to sleep in.

She had not released her service weapon since grabbing it out of the safe. As Bracket entered, he gently reached for the weapon, verified the safety was on, and laid it on the kitchen bar.

Randy gently ushered her back into her living room. He draped the throw from the sofa around her shoulders and sat her down. "Tell us what happened one more time."

Carrie had told them over the phone about the ordeal she had just experienced, but now she was able to relay the details in a much slower, succinct manner. Randy reached for her phone and noticed that the caller ID did indeed say 'unknown.' He pressed to redial the number back, but was met with a disconnect signal and canned message.

"Who could that be?" Carrie was exasperated, and still in shock.

"I don't know. But my guess it was to rattle you. They may know you are new, or because you are a woman, or some unknown factor that we may never know," Bracket said, looking at his newest agent with concern.

The next couple of hours were spent with the OKCPD exploring Carrie's front yard for footprints, or other evidence that someone had been on her property. They questioned her thoroughly, many times, rephrasing the questions repeatedly in order to hopefully jog a recessed memory loose.

By the time everyone had gone but Randy and Bracket, it was five thirty and the sun was casting a golden morning glow across the sky.

"Take the day off," Bracket insisted.

Carrie was shaking her head before the sentence had barely begun. "No! I'm fine. I need to work. If I don't go in, they will think they succeeded and got me off the case."

They both looked at her, knowing she would shower and be dressed and at the office before they were.

"Okay, but take your time getting ready. You are still in shock and need to recalibrate before getting to the office."

Carrie agreed. She was desperately shaken, even though she hated admitting it.

The room was dark, lit only by candlelight scattered around the room. There was a chill in the air because of the thin, uninsulated walls of the old structure.

Marta huddled close to Garrett. She didn't like being there, but Garrett had become increasingly obsessed with this new group of people. She was the only female, and could tell that she was not welcomed, merely tolerated because she had come with Garrett.

She didn't see the allure, but the men were eagerly discussing the rituals. The rumors of deaths had greatly alarmed Marta, and she continually urged Garrett to not go to their meetings. She didn't know if they were true or merely rumors.

"In this day and age of dwindling masculinity, we must confirm our masculine power while also increasing in it. We must reclaim our roles in dominating society. Religions the world over have practiced these rituals, knowing that they lead men on a path to strength and to God. Those that endure and survive will see God. They will be like God. Strong and courageous."

A man she didn't know seemed to be the main influencer in the group. His eyes were open wide with excitement and the men were enthralled when he spoke. He was strikingly handsome and charismatic. He exuded an electric energy which drew the men.

Marta tugged on Garrett's sleeve and whispered. "Let's go."

Garrett merely glanced down at Marta's tug and disregarded her frown. It barely registered as he focussed on the man speaking.

Marta quietly looked around the room at the men who were hungrily soaking in the hope of courage and power. They all felt diminished in life somehow. None were athletic, and all had been ridiculed by their lack of physical prowess. They yearned to be superior and were eager to become the strongest of them all. She could see the desperation in their eyes.

To Marta, Garrett was different from them. To her, he was strong, powerful, and courageous. Maybe that was because she loved him. She had come to see that even though what women thought about a man was important, what was more important to them was how another man saw him.

The men in the room began to rustle as they passed around the hollowed out wooden vessel, each taking a drink in their turn. "Garrett, don't drink that. You don't know what it is," Marta pleaded.

Garret responded by pulling his arm from Marta's grasp

and taking the vessel. He turned it up and sipped. *Marta is right. I don't know what this is.* He only took the tiniest of sips.

Marta did not drink. She was not allowed to do so, and she was glad. Being clear-headed, she was able to watch the effect the drink had on the men. They saw things. Things that must have been crazy, and some even vile. They became disconnected from the present. Several gazed into an unseen distance with glazed eyes.

Garrett had not drank the last time they had come to a meeting, and she was thankful. This would be his first time, and she was dreading it. Her hope in coming was that she could prevent him from doing something stupid, but she soon saw that her attempts to persuade him were fruitless.

The atmosphere in the room felt dark and evil to Marta, and it felt like the man before them was the devil himself. She didn't know what to do or how to save Garrett from this evil he had fallen into.

Suddenly, a shrill scream from the far corner of the room caused terror to course through Marta's body. Her entire body shook, not from the cold, but from fear. She drew her knees up to her chest and grasped them tightly, laying her forehead down. As she gently rocked, she tried to block out the surrounding sounds while she cried silent tears of desperation.

Billy slammed his phone down on the table. His patience was running thin. He knew Carrie had suffered a devastating blow when she lost her parents, it would have been like that for anyone. But he had been as loving, caring, and considerate as he knew how to be. He loved her to his core and wanted to help her through this. Right now, though, he had no idea how to do that.

"She still isn't picking up?" his friend Jack asked, as he sat two beers on their table.

Billy shook his head and reached for the glass. Tired of sitting at home, he had asked his friend Jack to go eat and maybe play some pool. He had readily agreed.

"I just don't know what to do."

Jack sat listening. He had no advice for his long-time friend. He had known Billy since middle school and was his closest friend. When he had been introduced to Carrie, he had also thought she was amazing. He honestly felt like Billy had hit the jackpot when they had met. He didn't understand why she was acting this way and could offer no rational advice.

The server soon brought their food, and even though Billy was hungry, he didn't know if the lump in his throat would let him eat.

"Hey man, you got to eat. She'll come around. Just give her some space."

Billy picked up a fry and dunked it in the catsup. "I've given her enough space. I don't call during the day when we used to talk two or three times a day. We used to be together every single evening. I've seen her one evening this week, and it was strained. It felt like I was with a stranger. Now she won't even answer her phone."

They both grew quiet as they ate. Billy's mind was

assuming the worst. He couldn't believe it was over between them, just like that. He had done nothing but be supportive. There was no reason for her to not want to see him.

"Okay, let's play some pool. Maybe when I take all your money, you'll have something else to dwell on." Jack laughed.

They played pool and Jack did well because Billy was so distracted. At somewhere around ten p.m., they called it a night. On the way home, Billy drove past Carrie's house and her car was not there. *Do OSBI agents work this late? Maybe that is why she hasn't called.*

He drove home, vowing not to call her again. He would wait for her and see just how long it took for her to call. She surely knew he had called multiple times tonight.

At home, he changed clothes and sat down in front of the TV, but all he succeeded in doing was flipping from one channel to another. He got up and paced the floor, looking at his phone call log to see if he had missed a call.

The more he paced, the angrier he got. He wanted to vent and scream, but he still felt too much compassion to do it directly to her. He grabbed another beer from the fridge and sat back down. By two in the morning and no returned call from Carrie, he had finished a six-pack and fallen asleep on the sofa.

Randy and Carrie both arrived at work at the same time and nodded greetings as they entered the building. Randy noticed the dark circles under Carrie's eyes, but said nothing. He knew she'd had a long night and he didn't want to elaborate on the events.

Coffee in hand, they both retreated silently to their desks. Carrie wasn't in the mood for conversation. Both Randy and Brackett had been wonderful to her, but she had gone from shaken to stirred-into-a-fury by the time she had settled into her car for the drive to work.

Randy opened his email and saw a message from Detective Morris. "Oh, look. Rick thinks he has a possible match on the missing persons list." Randy stopped to read the details.

"White male, twenty years old, attends college at UCO, didn't return parents' phone calls over the weekend, but because he attends college, the police department didn't file an official complaint for twenty-four full hours. In the meantime, the parents took it upon themselves to go to the campus and look for some of his friends. They realized then that none of his friends had seen him either. Then, checking with his professors, he had been absent from class on Friday as well."

Randy looked up at Carrie, who was hanging on every word. "Finally, we have a name, a real person. This will help a lot, right? We can talk to those friends, family, and professors."

"It will." Randy dialed Rick's phone. "Hey, just got the possible ID on our vic. How certain are you?"

"I just talked to the parents. I've arranged to meet them at the morgue. I hate this part of my job, but we all have to know for sure," said Rick.

"Let me know if they do ID him, then we can set a time to meet with them." Rick agreed, and Randy hung up the phone.

"He may be a friend of the other victim, too. We can ask his parents if they know him, can't we?" asked Carrie.

"Yes, we can, and we will.

"Rick didn't mention what he was majoring in at UCO. It will be interesting to know if he had any anthropology or chemistry classes."

"Dr. Pinning didn't think a person taking chemistry would have enough knowledge to concoct a tolerable dose of those two drugs."

"That doesn't mean they wouldn't try. He might have thought they had the knowledge, even though they didn't," Randy replied.

"Sure, but don't most college kids have to take at least one chemistry class?" Carrie asked.

Randy conceded reluctantly. "Yeah, you're right."

Randy's phone buzzed with a text from Rick. "The parents are meeting Rick at the morgue for an ID in an hour."

"Should we be there too?"

Randy considered Carrie's question. He was thinking of her recent ordeal when she visited the morgue to see her own parents and the heartache she had to experience. This would be the same for the parents of this young man. *Would this cause her to have to relive her recent trauma? Maybe it is too soon.*

"Not this time, since Rick has already set it up. Let's plan on visiting them at their home this afternoon."

They made arrangements to visit Travis Davis' parents for that afternoon. Randy and Carrie hoped that they could gain some insight regarding why he would do this, and who with.

They felt fortunate to have learned so much about the ritual and the ants, but as of yet, they still had no idea how this wealth of knowledge helped their case.

The Davis home sat in an elite area on the northeast side of Edmond. The sunlight flickered through the bare trees as they drove down the wooded road that led to their housing addition. The flickering light cast strange shadows in the cab of the SUV, as if the sun were refusing to allow the cold shadows of the day to take control.

Once they arrived at the correct street, an elaborate gate that restricted entrance to all but the residents halted their turn. While Randy fiddled with the call buttons on the speaker, Carrie looked at the massive houses sitting just beyond. They seemed to be at home in their heavily-wooded environment, as if they knew their own beauty and felt they belonged there.

"Sir, this is Agent Randy Jeffries with the OSBI. We have some questions that we would like to ask you that could help with our investigation regarding your son."

There was no response other than a loud beep and a hum as the large gate swung open and offered them entrance. Having lived in modest means, although very nice modest means, her entire life, Carrie absorbed the grand nature of the homes they were driving past. She tried to imagine the daily lifestyles of the people living inside. Were they different from what her's had been, or the same, only in a much more lavish environment?

"Here we are," said Randy, breaking her mental escape into a world of luxury. Carrie looked to her left at the house whose drive they had entered. It too was beautiful and very large. It had an attached portico over the driveway that led to two double car garages further back. The combination of cream stucco and red brick was stunning. The black decorative shutters appeared as though they were really working, with hammered black shutter dogs that added to the ornate feel of the home.

Carrie could only imagine how the well-designed flowerbeds and trees would enhance the feel of the home in spring and summer once the plants broke their dormancy. However, as if to detract from those plants that were in deep sleep, bright yellow and purple violas bobbled their tiny heads in the icy breeze. Someone had planted them in massive sweeps of color on each side of the front porch.

Before Randy could even ring the doorbell, one side of the large glass and metal doors swung open. They were expected, if not welcomed.

The inside of the home mirrored the outside in attention to detail. It was indeed grand, but also welcoming and homey. Carrie could smell the woodsmoke from the fireplace that burned beyond them.

Mr. Davis led Randy and Carrie to the rear of the home, where Mrs. Davis sat bundled on the sofa, soaking in the heat of a roaring fire. She had tucked a colorful quilt up close to her chin. She did not get up to welcome them. The shock and grief of learning her son was dead took precedence over normal hospitality decorum. She barely acknowledged the agents' entrance to the room.

Mr. Davis directed them to sit in matching leather chairs adjacent to the sofa. He then took his place beside his wife.

"Mr. and Mrs. Davis, we are truly sorry for your loss. We hate intruding so soon, but time is of the essence. We need to learn as much as we can, as quickly as possible, so that we can find out the situation regarding Travis' death.

"How they found Travis leads us to believe he was involved in some type of ceremony that may have led to his death. All signs point to his willing participation, but he did not do this alone. Can you give us a list of Travis' friends and any contact info that you may have?" Randy asked.

Mr. Davis nodded and rose to retrieve the information, while Mrs. Davis continued to be transfixed by the fire. Her soul seemed lost there, just as her heart had been lost by the death of her son. Carrie knew this, and as she watched, her heart grieved for Mrs. Davis.

When Mr. Davis returned with a few sheets of paper he had printed off of his computer, Randy thanked him as he glanced down at it. "I had made that list a few months ago when we had a party here at the house for Travis. My wife mailed out written invitations as well as sending out a few emailed ones. I still had the list on the computer."

"Thank you. This is a tremendous help," Randy replied.

"Mr. Davis, what can you tell us about Travis?" Carrie asked. "What type of things did he enjoy and what was he pursuing at college?"

Tears threatened to spill from the lids of his eyes as he spoke. The texture of his hands rustled as he nervously brushed them together. He was attempting to draw the strength he needed to talk about his son. "Travis was a wonderful son. He started college not really knowing what he wanted to do, but he soon found that he really liked history and literature. He was getting a double major in those subjects and was planning on teaching after college."

Mr. Davis didn't seem aware that he had stopped speaking, having become lost in thought.

"Was he involved in any clubs on or off campus that you know of?" Randy asked. He had withdrawn a small notepad from his jacket pocket and had started to take notes.

"He didn't like sports too much. He did when he was younger, but the older he got, he gravitated more towards the arts. He was involved in one or two clubs at college, but I'm trying to remember what they were. I think one was just a general club for history majors, but I can't think of what the other one was." Mr. Davis looked up at the agents with pain in his eyes.

"Where did they find my boy?" Mrs. Davis' voice was gravely from the trauma of the crying that it had endured.

"Mrs. Davis, we found Travis in a concrete building on the east side of town. It doesn't appear that it was where he died," said Randy.

Her hand flew to her mouth as a sob wrenched forth. A fresh torrent of tears broke loose and her body shook with pain. Mr. Davis put his arm around his wife and drew her close.

This raw pain was almost more than Carrie could bear. It pricked her own personal pain, which she had fought hard to lock away somewhere safe. She sucked in firm resolve and hardened herself to withstand this emotional onslaught.

Randy and Carrie waited to allow the Davis' a moment to

recover. "Have you ever heard of Travis talking about obscure rituals such as those from Amazon tribes or ancient religions?"

Mr. Davis shut his eyes as he laid his head on top of his wife's. There was a quick shake of his head as tears slipped free.

Randy looked at Carrie and indicated with a swift eye movement that they should go. Both stood. "Mr. and Mrs. Davis, we will go for now. I am sure we may have additional questions as our investigation continues, but I think we have enough to go on for now." Randy stepped towards the door and Mr. Davis stood, wiping his face.

He reached out and grabbed Randy's hand to shake it and looked straight into his eyes. "Find out what happened. Find out if someone did this to my son. Please, find out the truth."

"We will work hard to find out what happened. The information you have given us will help greatly. When we find out, we will let you know. If you need anything from us, please call." Randy slipped one of his business cards from his pocket and handed it to Mr. Davis.

The icy blast from the winter wind greeted them as they stepped out onto the front porch. They carried with them the heaviness of the pain this couple was enduring.

Chapter Nine

Back at the office, Randy and Carrie began research on the list of names. There was no sign of whether these were friends from college, high school, or both. They decided the most efficient way was to divide the list and start making phone calls.

There was a mix of cell phones and land lines. They left more messages than they made actual contact with a real person. Several were parents or siblings of those they were calling. The parents wanted information. It alarmed them that maybe their child, too, was in danger. And as human nature often was, they wanted the scoop. The full scoop, with all the details, which they were not given.

It was close to five o'clock when Randy's phone rang at his desk. "This is Agent Randy Jeffries." A bit of wavering between silence and uncertain syllables came through from the other end. Then finally, "You left a message for me."

Randy looked up at Carrie, then grabbed his pen and

notepad. There was an immediate surge of electricity in the air. "Thank you so much for returning my call. What is your name? We made several calls."

"Joe Daniels. I am a friend of Travis'. Was... a friend of Travis'." The voice trailed off as he spoke when realizing the reality of what he was saying.

"Thanks for calling me back, Joe. How well did you know Travis?" Randy's voice was crisp and alert.

"I've known him since junior high school. We've been friends a long time."

"When was the last time you saw him?"

"Well, honestly, I haven't seen him much lately. I guess the last time was at his parents' Christmas party. They invited my parents and me. Early December."

"Why haven't you seen him much lately?"

"Uh, well, we just kind of don't hang out much anymore."

"And why is that? Did something happen between the two of you?" Randy could sense hesitation from Joe, so he continued. "It's okay, Joe. Whatever you tell us will help us. We need you to fill us in on what was going on in Travis' life."

"He just started hanging out with a bunch of new people and I didn't really fit in. I'm not sure they wanted me there either."

"Who were these people? People from college?"

"Yeah, some were. I only remember that one was named Beau and one was named James. I don't remember their last names."

"When you say 'hang out,' exactly what were you all doing when you were hanging out?"

"Just sitting around, drinking and talking."

"Where did this happen?"

"Well, when I was there it was at an apartment, but I don't know whose. I just went there with Travis."

"Did you ever hear any of them talk about obscure rituals or ancient practices?"

"Like what?"

"Rituals that give warriors courage?" Randy didn't want to give too much away or lead him to answer, but he wanted just the right spur to jog his memory.

Silence hung over the line for a few seconds while Joe was thinking. "Not specifically. They laughed at how they were tougher than some jocks they had had a run in with. They were scheming up ways to get even with them and show them just how tough they were."

"Sounds like a lot of bluster to me."

"Yeah. But, there was one guy, I don't know his name, who was really mad, and it seemed like he had a chip on his shoulder about it."

"We found Travis with objects that have led us to believe that he was involved in a ritual that a tribe in the Amazon used to gain courage. Does any of that ring any bells?"

"No. None that I can think of."

"Can I get your cell phone number to put here in my notes? I may need to call you back."

Joe gave Randy his cell phone, and Randy jotted it down. "Is there anyone else you can think of that we should contact?"

"No, not really. If I do think of someone, I'll call back."

Randy ended the call and sat looking at his notes. Carrie

sat watching him, allowing him to mentally process the phone call.

Randy relayed the conversation to Carrie since he had not put the phone on speaker. He looked down the list for the two names that Joe had given him. There was no one on there with either of the names Beau or James.

"I can see that leading to something," Carrie said.

Randy nodded, deep in thought.

"They may think these rituals would show just how tough they were," Carrie added. "Or maybe they really believed that the rituals would make them tough."

"True. But they weren't really that tough, were they?"

"What do you mean?" Carrie asked.

"The drugs. They wanted to do the rituals, but they needed the drugs to give them courage in order to prove courage." Randy shook his head.

Carrie wrinkled up her face. "Not sure that rings completely true, but I think we are making headway. I think that other drugs would have been safer, easier to get, and would have done more to give them courage."

"We need to talk to the DEA about these drugs, and see if either of those two are crossing their paths. I've had that on my mental to-do list, but we've been too busy." Randy picked up the phone while searching his computer for a contact name and number.

"Ralph Jenks, DEA," the bold voice bellowed through the line, along with the distinct sound of a creaking chair.

"Hey Ralph. It's Randy Jeffries over at OSBI."

"Randy! How's it going? I haven't heard from you in a

while." The voice immediately transformed into a jovial greeting.

"Good. We have a strange case. I was hoping you might help us." Randy had casually leaned back in his chair, comfortable with the familiarity between him and Ralph.

"Sure. I'll do what I can."

"We have two victims who have died under suspicious circumstances, each having a cocktail of scopolamine and bromo-dragonFLY in their systems."

"Whewww." Ralph blew out his reply. "That's dangerous stuff."

"I know. Have you seen either in any of your circles?"

"No, not in anything I've had a hand in. Those are not recreational drugs. People who take either of them have said it is not a fun ride. Years ago, scopolamine was mixed with morphine for a type of pain relief. Gave the person what was called 'twilight sleep.' It's a psychoactive drug and often causes hallucinations, but there are much easier ways to do that. LSD being one."

"What about bromo-dragonFLY?"

"Well, again, if a person wanted the high, LSD would be a more reasonable choice. FLY is about one third as toxic as LSD, but way more potent than mescaline. And it takes awhile to take effect. Most junkies want an immediate high. FLY may take up to six hours or more before any signs even emerge to show it has been taken, but then it often lasts from two to three days, sometimes even longer."

"Why would anyone combine them?"

Randy could tell Ralph was working this over in his mind. "Were they taken at the same time?"

"We don't know."

"If they did, then scopolamine could have worn off before the FLY even took effect. FLY is highly toxic to humans. It is dangerous. I've never heard of anyone taking it."

"Have you seen any of either of these out on the street lately?"

"No. None. I never have here in Oklahoma."

"Where would someone get them?"

Ralph snorted. "On the internet!"

"Are you serious?"

"I am. With a click of a button, you can get them shipped from a foreign county."

It stunned Randy. "Thanks Ralph. Hey, would you put your ear to the ground and see if you can find us a lead on this? Any talk at all will help."

"Will do. If you have people taking this toxic concoction, you are going to see many more bodies. I hope this was an isolated event and that those two are the only two," Ralph said.

When the call was over, Randy was sick to his stomach. He had had the phone on speaker and Carrie had heard every word.

"What do we do now? We can't wait for more bodies," Carrie said. She was suddenly aware of her lack of experience and expertise in detective work, and it was overwhelming.

"Let's go fill in our whiteboard and see if we can make any connections."

By the time they had gone over the little they knew, achieving no new results, it was seven-thirty that evening.

Randy's phone rang, and it was Sandy asking where he was and when he was going to be finished. The sound of their loving banter made Carrie feel uneasy. Did she miss that type of casual rapport she had with Billy? She didn't know.

They called it a night, and Carrie was left once again with a feeling of dread. *This has to stop. I can't keep dreading going home.*

She didn't know how to fix her feelings. All she knew to do was avoid them. As she was clearing her desk and gathering her belongings, she thought of calling Billy. She hadn't talked to him in a while, and even though he might distract her from her pain, he was also a reminder of it.

With no other idea of what to do, she dialed Billy's number. There was no answer. It went to voicemail, but not knowing what to say, she simply hung up.

She decided she would go home and spend the evening there alone. As she drove there, she realized that in the past few weeks, she had developed a habit of avoidance. She would never be okay if she didn't face things. Her home had always been a place of refuge, a place that was uniquely hers, and she felt comforted there. She was determined it would be that again.

Knowing her fridge was empty, she stopped to pick up a few groceries. Cooking didn't sound fun this late in the evening, but maybe something from the deli would be okay. The grocery store seemed nearly abandoned since most shoppers had stopped in early in order to get home and out of the cold. She figured she was one of the few who waited until nearly bedtime on a cold winter night to get groceries.

Her cart was partially full of milk, eggs, and a few other necessities. The whole roasted chicken in the deli case looked good, and it was cooked, so she had grabbed one of those as well. She meandered through the store and found a few more items, mostly junk food, and tossed them in her cart.

About halfway through checking out, her cell phone rang. Thinking it might be Randy, she grabbed it and answered before looking. It was Billy.

"Hey."

"Hi."

"You called me?" Billy had lost his cheerful demeanor.

"Yeah. I'm sorry it was so late. I had just gotten done with work."

"What did you want?" His surly tone made Carrie sad. She had done this to him, and he didn't deserve it.

"I hadn't talked to you in a while. I wanted to see if you wanted to come over."

The long silence stung as she waited for his reply.

"I don't know Carrie. I'm tired of being strung along. You are hot and cold and everything in between. I never know what you are going to say or do next and honestly, you have been outright mean to me." Carrie could tell he was growing angrier the more he talked.

"I know. I'm sorry."

"I know you have suffered an enormous loss, but at some point you have to get back to living life. I love you so much! I've done everything I know to do to help you get through this and you've done nothing but throw it back in my face as if I haven't been hurting too."

For the first time, it dawned on Carrie in all her selfishness that Billy had been in pain too. He had loved her parents. Billy and her dad had spent many weekends hunting and fishing and working in her dad's workshop, while her mom and she had prepared elaborate cookouts for them all to enjoy together.

Billy had been grieving too, but had given way for Carrie to heal over himself.

She stood in the grocery's vestibule and juggled her phone as she pushed her cart back into place. "Billy, I am so sorry! I've been terribly selfish. I just couldn't cope. I still don't know how to cope."

The air between them hung pregnant with uncertainty. Neither one knew what to say or how to get past this.

"I got a roasted chicken," Carrie finally said from lack of anything else coming to mind.

Billy snorted at the absurd comment. "Are you inviting me over to share your roasted chicken?" She could hear the smile in his voice.

"I am."

Billy arrived soon after Carrie had tossed a bag of salad and poured some ranch dressing on it. They ate, watched TV and talked a little. The air in the room was trying to heal. It vacillated between feeling as though it always had, and feeling as though they were strangers.

In the end, Billy stayed the night. The touch of their bodies felt familiar and comforting. But in the middle of the night, as Carrie lay awake listening to his gentle breathing, she wondered why her heart felt so lost. She pondered how she could ever get back the joy and love she had experienced in their relationship, wondering if she ever would.

Randy and Sandy sat by the fire nursing a bottle of Chardonnay. Sandy's pale blonde hair glinted in the firelight, and Randy couldn't resist running his fingers through its fine silkiness.

Sandy laid her head over onto Randy's shoulder. She was so thankful that she had found someone who fit so well with her. She loved him dearly and knew he loved her just as much. It made her feel safe and secure.

"How is the new partner?" Sandy asked, sitting her glass on the table and snuggling up even closer to Randy's side, as if to remind him she was his one and only.

Randy looked into her blue eyes. Loving her had been so easy for him from day one. He believed in love at first sight because he had experienced it with her. He didn't want to talk anymore. He leaned down and kissed Sandy, and felt a surge of passion tingle through his body.

Sandy indulged him for only a moment, then pulled back slightly and grinned. "I said... how is your new partner?" Sandy's dimples accentuated her broad smile.

Randy sighed and shifted into conversation mode. He knew he would have to engage in conversation in order to get back to where his mind had parked itself, on Sandy's firm body.

"I think she will be an excellent partner and someday, an

incredible agent." Hoping he had satisfied Sandy's curiosity, he leaned back in for another kiss.

"What does she look like?" Sandy asked.

"What does she look like?" Randy repeated back to her, quite confused. "I don't know. She is average and has a blondish brownish curly-ish hair."

"Hmmm."

"What does hmmm mean?" Randy was getting a bit irritated. *Is Sandy jealous? Surely not.* He needed to satisfy her curiosity or it would be a long night.

"She is a few years younger than I am. She has a degree in criminology and worked for the OKCPD for three years prior to coming to the OSBI. She has a fiancé," Randy sounded as though he were reading facts from an encyclopedia. "Oh, and her parents died two weeks before she came to the OSBI in a tragic car accident. I think she is struggling to cope with it all."

Sandy turned from playfully jealous to compassionately concerned. "Oh, that's awful. I'm sorry. I'm not jealous, Randy. Really, I'm not."

Randy smiled and kissed the tip of her nose. "That's good. I like having Carrie as a partner, I believe once she settles in and has begun to heal from her parents' tragedy, she will be a huge asset.

"But as for being attracted to her, no I'm not, and cannot see myself ever feeling that way. She is completely different from you. You are my ideal and you are mine. I look forward every day to coming home to you."

Randy pulled her closer to him and tucked her in close to his side, wrapping his arms around her. They sat quietly, watching the glow of the fire dance. Each were lost in their individual thoughts. Sandy couldn't imagine how horrible it would be to lose both parents at the same time.

Randy, too, was thinking about Carrie. He had noticed her strength during this strange case despite its taxing nature. He hoped it wasn't more than she could take. Would he see the signs that it was affecting her, or would she be able to hide it until it was too late?

Brandon Ames sat on the bench in the cold room. He shivered and wished he had more clothing on than just the leather loin cloth. It was his time and he hoped that he could muster up the courage to go through with it. Whatever they had been giving him over the past week had helped. But it caused him to feel disassociated with reality, and he was experiencing hallucinations.

It had all become more than just a way to prove they were courageous to the outside world, and particularly to those who often taunted them. Now, they needed courage inside the group to prove they weren't the weakest of the weak.

A few weeks ago, they began to understand that this was about much more than courage. It was also about coming to know God, to even possibly become one with God, and the purpose had gained a loftiness to it that merely being coura-geous had never had.

None of them had ever gone to a church, synagogue, or temple. None of their families had ever talked to them about a god of any kind. Not only were they lacking courage, but also a sense of divine belonging and understanding of something beyond them spiritually.

The more their discussions escalated, the more their passionate desire to engage in the rituals grew. That newfound passion gave them the beginnings of the courage they needed, and fueled their momentum forward so that they were receptive to participation.

The door to the room swung open and he was motioned forward. The large old barn was empty, except for those in their group and the random lamps placed sparsely around the room which barely shed any light.

In the center of the room was an elevated galvanized pipe which spanned the distance between two of the barn's support beams. In the background, there was some type of tribal music playing low. It felt rustic and dark in mood.

Brandon walked to the center of the circle of onlookers, those in their group, and stood beneath the pipe. He knew what to do. He held up his arms, which were then strapped to the pipe with leather strips. His arms were tight and high, and there was no flexibility in which to move.

What no one could see was the fine mist that had begun to fill the room. It was slight, odorless, and invisible. Even though it was not noticeable to their ears and eyes, they felt its impact, and soon began to mentally drift away.

What none of them knew was that the mist they were now breathing in would wipe their memory of the ritual that was about to occur. They would appear cognizant and aware, but as the drug wore off, so would any memory of their time there.

The ends of the bamboo rods had been sliced at an angle,

and were fashioned to be incredibly sharp. They knew from experience though, that the rods would not pierce skin the way they needed to with clean precision. The best way was to first make incisions in which to insert them.

Now it was time to cut those slits into Brandon's skin. First one, then another. The drug he had taken several days ago and the one he had just unknowingly inhaled were hallucinogens and did not prevent pain.

They tied his feet to half-round steel rings that protruded from the floor of the barn. He could not retreat, even if his mind registered that he needed to do so.

The first slit just above his left shoulder blade was about two inches in length, and made with a sharp scalpel. It was only superficial, slicing only through the skin and not the muscle, but still excruciatingly painful nonetheless.

Brandon's screams filled the barn, but not one person there was mentally able to come to his aid. Nor were they fully comprehending what was actually taking place.

So the cutting continued, and when each pair of cuts were made, a bamboo rod was slid underneath the skin and pushed through to the matching opening, pulling the skin away from the muscle as it slid through.

By the time they were ready for the final cuts in his cheeks, Brandon was hanging as limp as possible within his constraints. He never knew when those final cuts were made. With Brandon no longer screaming in agony, the cuts and bamboo insertions went easily.

Finally, it was done. Those attending the ritual stood and saw the aftermath of what had just occurred. Brandon's eyes were closed, and he was still.

Now they just needed to wait for the drugs to wear off. The room was cleared of occupants, who would have no memory of what they had just participated in.

A feeling of pleasure with what had been accomplished took hold. They were proving that not only could they control susceptible minds to take part in absolute atrocities, but they could also control the memories of those looking on. Their experiments were coming along nicely, with only a few casualties. Those that survived were truly the strong.

When they re-entered the barn and looked up at Brandon, they realized that unfortunately he was not one of those.

Chapter Ten

"Good mornin' sunshine," Randy bellowed the next morning as he approached Carrie.

Carrie winced. The ibuprofen she had taken had done little to ease her excruciating headache. She had laid awake next to Billy for most of the night. She resolved to herself to be more diligent in getting sleep. Focusing on her job would come first from now on, ahead of even Billy. It had to.

"You don't look too perky this morning," Randy said.

Carrie wrinkled the corner of her mouth. "Yeah, I was up late, I couldn't sleep."

"Hey, that reminds me. I was talking to Sandy, and she suggested that the four of us get together and grab dinner and a movie or something." Randy had a huge big sloppy smile on his face. He didn't know the challenges she was having in her relationship with Billy. She didn't want anyone to know either.

She looked down at her desk and started shuffling paperwork. "Yeah, sure, that sounds nice. We will have to do that real soon." Carrie got up to get some coffee and a donut, and hopefully to avoid more discussion of double dating.

Randy was completely unaware of her awkward demeanor. "Cool. We'll plan something," he said as he was logging into his computer. There was a message waiting for Randy. It was from Detective Rick Morris. The urgent note said to call him.

"Hey Rick, this is Randy. What's up?"

"Well, early this morning, we found a body. It isn't dressed in a loincloth like the other two and there are no signs of ritualistic behavior, but Henry thinks it is an overdose, and all signs point to the same drugs. There are no track marks and there is no sign that it is meth or heroine, or any other common junkie drug. He was a strong healthy male in his early twenties.

"I'm just calling to let you know that I got your email regarding your discussion with Ralph. I don't know that this will be an overdose from those drugs, but I just wanted you to be informed just in case."

"Where was he found?" Randy asked.

"Out in a vacant lot on the north side of Midwest City, close to where the first one was found."

"I'm assuming he was dumped there," said Randy.

"It looks that way. He is out in the open, no coat, but otherwise fully clothed," said Rick. "That's all I have for now. I'll let you know if Henry determines they were the same drugs."

"Have they washed him like the others before putting his clothes back on? His clothes might contain some forensics we could use."

"It looks like that could be the case."

"Well, keep us posted. Thanks."

Randy stood and went to see if Bracket was in his office. He tapped on his door. "Got a minute?"

"Sure. Have a seat." He motioned to one of a pair of chairs in front of his desk. Bracket frowned in response to the look on Randy's face.

"I just got a call from Detective Rick Morris." Randy proceeded to go over his call with Rick. Bracket nodded his head, deep in thought. "I skimmed through your updated file last night. It seems like things are going slowly."

Randy leaned forward and rested his elbows on his knees. "They are. I was hoping you could help me brainstorm to try and find a new rock to look under.

"How is the list coming together that the Davis' gave you?" Bracket asked.

"Slow. We've left several messages and only a couple have called us back. Mostly parents digging for information. One guy called back. A Joe Daniels. He had been friends with Travis, but when Travis started hanging out with a new group of friends, Joe backed off.

"Why is that, you're going to ask?" Randy continued. "He said he didn't feel accepted, and he got a weird vibe."

"Well, keep working that list. You want people, and those are all the people you've got right now. Have you talked to any of Travis' professors at college?

"No, we need to do that too."

As Carrie walked by the windows of SAC Bracket's office with her coffee, he waved her in. "We are just discussing the case. Randy got a call about a possible overdose. We were just trying to brainstorm."

Carrie slowly sat in the chair next to Randy. "Oh, wow."

"Keep working hard at the list. If you need to visit them in person, then do that. While you are out, visit the college and talk to Travis' professors. Keep pounding the pavement and something will turn up."

They both rose to leave and headed towards the break room. "What are we going to do first?" Carrie asked.

"We are going to get our coffee to go, grab the list, and hit the road," Randy replied.

Once in their SUV, Carrie worked to group the addresses into some sort of order, so that they weren't driving back and forth all over town. Many were in Edmond, which made sense since Travis lived there.

"We have a few in Oklahoma City. Shall we hit those first before we head north?" Carrie asked.

"Sure. Are they close by?"

"No, not really," said Carrie as much to herself as to Randy, checking the list.

"Let's get Edmond done and then see what time it is."

An hour later, they had knocked on four separate residences and no one had answered their door. "I guess they are all at work," said Carrie as they stood in the driveway of the most recent house.

"Let's head on over to UCO and see if we can find any professors who will talk to us."

Parking was a nightmare. They finally pulled up near the front door of the closest building to the history department and put their law enforcement tag on their mirror.

Carrie had called on their way over and was able to have a list of Travis' classes and professors emailed to her. The intent was to start at the top and work their way down.

"Room 254 is World History & Civilization of the First Century, Professor Jill Bates," Carrie read from the email. The door was open, and the light was off. They scanned the hallway and found a class in session down and across the hall.

Randy lightly tapped on the door frame. Having their attention, he said, "Sorry to interrupt, but we are looking for Professor Jill Bates."

"Her office is on the third floor, room 350, I believe."

They found her office easily enough, and Randy was relieved to see her there.

After they made introductions and Randy and Carrie sat down in front of Professor Bates' desk, Randy pulled out his notepad and pen.

"Travis Davis was a student in your class, correct?"

"Yes. Being a history major, I've had Travis in a few classes now." Professor Bates was an attractive woman and not someone Carrie would have pegged as being a stodgy professor, particularly in history. She chided herself for having entertained a stereotype.

"I am not sure how much you have heard, but we found Travis deceased under strange circumstances. It appears he was taking part in a ritual similar to the one," Randy paused to flip through his notes, looking for the correct name. "The

Satere-Mawe tribe in the Amazon. Was that ever something that was discussed in one of your classes?"

A shadow fell across Professor Bates' face. "Yes, I believe I brought it up in my Uncivilized Tribes of the World class. It is a well-known ritual and not lethal. The tribe has done this for centuries, and each member repeats it multiple times throughout their life."

"True, but these young men weren't using bullet ants. There were using imported fire ants and a cocktail of extremely toxic hallucinogenic drugs," replied Randy.

Professor Bates drew in a sharp intake of breath, and her hand flew to her chest. "Oh, my!"

"Can you think of any students that Travis associated with that he might have discussed doing this with, and any other rituals they learned about? Who did he hang out with in class?"

Professor Bates sat and thought. "I'm not sure, but I believe that he and a student named Beau Barrett had a few classes together. They seemed to be friends."

"Do you have any idea where we could find Mr. Barrett right now?"

"I'm not sure I am supposed to give you that information." Professor Bates seemed uncertain. She was wavering between helping and violating Beau's civil rights.

"Ma'am, we have two dead bodies and a possible third. The sooner we get to the bottom of this, the sooner the death count stops. Beau could be the next in line. So, rather than worry about protecting his civil rights, think about protecting his life," Randy's adamant tone hit home, and he was soon presented with contact info for Beau.

"Now, let's talk about fire walking."

Randy and Carrie sat watching from the warmth of their SUV as students changed classes.

"She didn't give us anything new about the rituals that we didn't already know. But, we have a last name for Beau now," said Carrie.

"Yes, and that is critical. We have someone who may have very well been involved in the rituals."

"You know, just because Joe said Beau was in this new group of friends, doesn't necessarily mean he was part of the group that did the rituals," Carrie added.

"True, but he might know who they were. If he was a new friend, odds are they had something new in common."

Just as Randy shifted their SUV into gear, his phone buzzed. It was Rick. "Yeah?"

"It's Rick. Henry said the overdose was due to FLY, but not scopolamine."

"So, he took one drug and died before he could take the other and be in the ritual? Does that sound right?"

"Seems that way."

"I wonder if he was about to do it and died before he could, or if he was just curious and took the drug for a high."

"I don't know. Just wanted to let you know. Oh, and we have no ID on that vic either. He had no wallet or anything else in his pockets or on his person. I am sending over all we have via email. It's yours now," said Rick.

Randy navigated out of the parking lot midst all the

students leaving campus. Feeling overwhelmed, he suddenly dialed Rick back. "We have a list of all of Travis Davis' friends. His father gave us a list that was from a party they had several months ago. We are hitting walls finding people. If I shoot it over to you, could you coordinate that? I'll make notes on who we have contacted and the results."

"Sure, I've got some good people to help me with that."

When Randy hung up, Carrie said, "That will help us a ton. What do we do next?"

"Let's stop and get more coffee and see if we can put a plan together. I am tired of feeling like Don Quixote jousting at windmills."

They stopped at a local coffee shop close to campus. Once they had ordered their coffee, Carrie laid her large notepad on the table. She breathed in deep the smell of the rich roast, and soaked in the familiar sounds of the beans grinding and the milk frother. She had many good memories while in college studying for exams and spending time with friends tied to those senses, and she allowed herself to soak in them.

"Okay," Randy began, "we have drugs and rituals. The drugs seem incidental, as if they are part of the rituals and not an independent occurrence.

Carrie nodded. "These young men would have had to have gotten the information from someone. My money is on the college link. They could have used the internet, but that doesn't feel right.

"Professor Bates said she talked about some of these rituals in her class. Could she have taught about them in class in such a way that it made them seem noble?" Carrie asked.

Randy gently blew on the surface of his black brew before taking a sip. As he sat the cup back down, he said, "Were all of these rituals religious in nature?"

Carrie tried to think back to what she had learned so far. "The fire walking was. The drugs were, in some cases, but not these drugs. Nothing about the ants, but for the Amazon tribe it was carried out in a way that seemed religious to them. Are we stretching or trying to make something out to be something that it isn't?"

"What are these boys looking for? Courage seems paltry considering the gravity of the rituals. Something else is propelling them to feel the need to risk their lives," said Randy.

"Maybe they don't realize the risk. Particularly if someone is urging them on, the risks are probably downplayed, if mentioned at all."

Carrie wrote at the top of her page 'college education,' 'obscure drugs,' 'young men - courage.' Under college education she wrote, Dr. Amos Pinning - Pharmacology, Dr. Mark Randolph - Anthropology, Dr. Mitch Reynolds - Entomology, Dr. Jill Bates - History.

Under 'obscure drugs,' she wrote, scopolamine, and bromo-dragonfly - FLY.

Under 'young men - courage,' she wrote the two victims' names, Travis Davis - ants, John Doe 1 - fire, John Doe 2 - FLY OD. Beside each of those she put an asterisk, adding a question mark next to John Doe 2. Then she wrote Joe Daniels, Beau Barrett, and James with no asterisk, denoting those that had participated in a ritual and leaving the ones that were not confirmed yet.

~

<u>College Education</u> <u>Obscure Drugs</u> <u>Young Men - Courage</u>

Dr. Amos Pinning - Pharmacology Scopolamine Travis Davis - ants *

Dr. Mark Randolph - Anthropology Bromo-dragonfly - FLY John Doe 1 - fire *

Dr. Mitch Reynolds - Entomology John Doe 2 - FLY OD *?

Dr. Jill Bates - History Joe Daniels
Beau Barrett
James

~

"We need to find where all of these intersect," said Carrie. She wobbled her pen in the campus' direction. "And I believe it all intersects there."

"What if there is a professor behind all of this?" Randy asked.

"Oh my! That would be horrible!" Carrie was genuinely shocked at the thought.

"Students usually look up to professors. They have the power to inspire their students in many circumstances. What if that power has gone to their head and they are leading these young men right off the edge of a cliff?"

"They would have to be psychotic, wouldn't they?" asked Carrie.

They both sat in silence as they drank their coffee and contemplated what Carrie had written on her pad, as well as all that they had learned. A cold gust of wind rushed in with a new customer, and Carrie shivered and wrapped her hands around her rapidly-cooling cup.

"We have no forensic clues so far. This person, or group, has been careful to eliminate all forensic matter. I can't see anyone who is on these hallucinogens having the ability to think and act clearly enough to make sure there is nothing to link back to them," said Carrie.

"Good point. So, there is at least one clear-headed person in all of this. One leading and controlling the pack."

"We need to talk face to face with the anthropology professor. I want to sit in a room with him and look him in the eye," said Randy.

"I can't see Dr. Pinning having anything to do with this. He was such a nice man," said Carrie.

"No, I agree, but you can't let that fool you."

"He is also at OU Medical Center, not here at UCO. It seems to me that this is our hub."

"Could be. But, I don't want to get tunnel vision and miss something. For now, everyone we talk to is to be held in question until we have concrete evidence ruling them out."

Randy pulled out his phone and scrolled to find the number for Dr. Randolph. "This is Agent Randy Jeffries. We spoke a few days ago regarding the ritual using bullet ants..." Randy paused for the professor to remember their discussion. "My partner and I want to come by and visit with you in person. We are about five minutes from the campus. What is your office building and number?"

Randy ended the call and looked at Carrie. "He was not real keen on us coming by. He has a class for the next hour, but then he can see us. In the meantime, let's see if we can find Beau Barrett."

Carrie used her BlackBerry to enter the address that Dr. Bates had given them to see if the GPS would pull it up. As soon as she hit enter, the screen swirled and focused in, stopping with a red teardrop that located the spot. She looked up and grinned at Randy. "I've got it. Let's go."

In less than ten minutes, Randy and Carrie were standing in front of Beau's apartment. A knock on the door revealed a young man in his early twenties. "I am OSBI Agent Randy Jeffries, and this is Agent Carrie Border. We need to speak to Beau Barrett. Are you he?"

The young man standing in front of them had a sallow complexion and his eyes had dark circles around them. His dark hair hung on his forehead in damp clumps. It was clear that their appearance at his door was causing him distress. His eyes darted back and forth and he licked his dry lips.

"Uh, Beau ain't here." The door swung shut, but Randy had planted his foot on the threshold.

"Then we will come in and speak with you. How's that?" Randy said as he walked in.

The boy didn't seem to have the wherewithal to resist, so he swung the door open and stepped back for them to enter.

The space was a typical small college apartment. Empty beer bottles and takeout wrappers were littered about, common for this age. Then at the same time, both Carrie and Randy noticed the bookshelves on the far wall. Ancient artifacts. Hand hewn reeds resembling large needles, small woven baskets, crudely hewn hooks with cords made of sinew, among several other items that appeared to be ancient relics.

Randy walked closer to the shelves. There were also books. Randy read the titles out loud. "Ritual, Heka: The Practices of Ancient Egypt, The Book of Unusual Knowledge, The Craft of Ritual Studies." He turned and looked at Carrie. "I think we have found the right place."

Chapter Eleven

It turned out that the young man in Beau's apartment had just stopped by to recover from a recent drug bender. It appeared he knew nothing at all about the books or antiquities on the shelves. He also claimed to not know where Beau was, maybe in class.

They spent the best part of an hour trying to pull as much information out of him as they could. The more they talked, the more it was clear he was coming down from something.

Carrie looked at Randy and whispered, "What do we do with him? Do we arrest him?"

Randy stood and walked into the kitchen for some privacy. He dialed the local Edmond police department, explained who he was and the situation. They said they would come check things out.

Soon, they were passing the baton off to the EPD and heading back to the campus to meet with Dr. Randolph.

Carrie had used her new phone to take photos of the books and artifacts on the shelves. They wanted to know exactly what this anthropology professor had to say about those items.

Walking into Dr. Randolph's office was like walking into a room filled to the brim with the exact same books and artifacts that they had seen a small sampling of at Beau Barrett's apartment. Carrie stood stunned as she looked around the room. An involuntary shiver rippled its way from the top of her spine down.

Randy noticed the room, but was focused on Dr. Randolph himself. He was a small man, maybe five feet eight inches, and thin. His hair was thinning on top and unruly, as if he didn't care to comb it. Dark-rimmed glasses perched on his nose that he had already pushed back up twice since they had entered the room.

Dr. Randolph seemed eager to talk with them. It was clear he loved the subject of anthropology and sharing it with anyone who would listen. This had been evident from the first time Randy had spoken with him on the phone.

"Dr. Randolph, you had said that you had no absent students, but that you hadn't had a class since we found our victims. Have you had any since then?"

"Victims?" Dr. Randolph was quick to pick up on the plurality of the word. "I thought there had only been one when we spoke."

"That was then, but now we have more."

"Oh, I see." Dr. Randolph's face folded into a frown as he looked down at his desk. "Do you know who they are?" He seemed genuinely sympathetic and sincere.

"We know that the victim of the fire ant gloves was Travis Davis. Is he one of your students?" Randy asked.

"No. I don't think so. Let me double check." Dr. Randolph turned to his computer and began tapping the keys. He stopped and scanned the scrolling screen before him. As he neared the end, he began shaking his head. Then turned back to the agents. "No, I don't have a Travis Davis in any of my classes, and I don't remember him from any previous ones."

"Can you check for any new absentees?" Carrie asked.

Dr. Randolph returned to his computer screen. "Yes, there was a Beau Barrett absent from my last Anthropology of Development class."

"Beau Barrett." Randy quietly mumbled Beau's name, thinking.

"Dr. Randolph, I'm going to be very blunt with you. We believe we have a group of very misguided young men who have somehow gotten it into their heads that they can increase their courage and strength by participating in these deadly rituals. Someone somewhere is orchestrating this. We need to find them now before any more young men die."

Randy was working to hold down his temper. He was tired of this feeling of chasing their tails. He sensed that Dr. Randolph had more information that could help them if they could just get him to disclose it.

"We need any thread in this vein that you can give us, whether or not it leads us anywhere. We need names, friends of Beau's and Travis's. We need possible clubs or groups that they might be involved in or have created. These rituals come straight from an anthropology text and we know that someone integral to this chaos had to have passed through one or more of your classes."

"Dr. Randolph, we have two young men that we haven't even been able to identify. Their families don't even know yet that they have lost a loved one. We need your help. Can you give us a list of students who have taken your classes in the last few years?" Carrie asked. She looked at Randy and asked him, "How far back should we go?"

Randy shook his head and looked at Dr. Randolph. "Give us at least the last five years." At that, the professor became busy with his computer and soon pages were spitting out from the tan box on the corner of the bureau behind him.

"Right before we came here, we went to Beau's apartment. He was not there, only a friend of his. But we noticed he had several anthropology books on his shelf, as well as some small ancient artifacts. We feel his part in this may be greater than first realized."

"Ancient artifacts, or antique?" Dr. Randolph asked quite interested.

"What does it matter? What is the difference?" Randy's frustration was showing.

"Well, everything. A matter of centuries versus decades." Dr. Randolph's eyes were round behind his glasses.

"Okay, well, I don't know how old they were or even what they were."

"I have pictures." Carrie suddenly remembered and pulled them up on her phone.

Dr. Randolph eagerly received the little blue device with curiosity and looked at the pictures as Carrie hovered over his shoulder moving them across the screen with the arrow button.

"These artifacts are not ancient. They are really just a few decades old." Dr. Randolph sounded disappointed. "Really not what we would call artifacts at all. Just random, although interesting, pieces of antique junk. Beau must have thought they were intriguing." He reluctantly handed the phone back to Carrie.

Randy looked down at his notes to see if there were any other thoughts he wanted to discuss with the professor. He filled the pages of his small notebook slowly to stall for time. He was searching his mind to come up with another question, the right question that would unlock the information they needed.

Carrie took the pages from the printer that Dr. Randolph was handing them. *Maybe we can cross reference these to the list Travis' parents gave us.* She thumbed through the pages in search of any other names she had on her list. None were there.

"Dr. Randolph, are you yourself a member of any anthropological groups or societies? Even if just for academic purposes?" Randy asked.

"Yes." He opened a drawer and pulled out a trifold brochure which advertised meetings for anyone interested in anthropology, ancient cultures, sociology, and archeology. "We meet once a month. This brochure will give you all the information I have about our group. We are academics, but welcome anyone with interest. We meet again on Friday night. You are welcome to join us."

"Do you have a membership list?" Carrie asked. *This more lists I have, the more I can cross reference.*

"Uh, no I don't." He grabbed a page from a notepad and wrote, then handed the paper to Carrie. "This is the organizer of the group. She may have something." Carrie took the paper and, as she did, she noticed the light had gone out of Dr. Randolph's eyes. The possibility of sharing wonderful anthropological insights with them no longer excited him. *Maybe the seriousness of the situation had sunk in.*

"Dr. Randolph, our only goal is to gather the necessary information we need to find out who is doing this before more people die. Thank you for your assistance with this. If you can think of anything else that could help us, or if you can think of anyone else that we should talk to, please let us know." Carrie's plea was passionate, and she could tell it hit its mark with Dr. Randolph.

"I will Ms. Border, I will."

"Agent Border," Carrie corrected him.

"Excuse me. Agent Border."

By the end of the day, Carrie was mentally exhausted. Their lists were growing, and she had worked during the afternoon to cross reference them to see if there was any overlap. Beau Barrett was the only name that came up on all three.

He was on the list that Travis' father had given them, he was a student of Dr. Randolph's, and therefore on the student list he had given them, he was the only absent student Dr.

Randolph had had the last week, and he was on the list they had gotten from the organizer of the academic group. He was looking more and more like a primary instigator in these rituals.

Randy walked into the room they had come to know as their war room. They had several files now, and their whiteboard was in there. They also had moved a department laptop in as well.

"Beau Barrett's only living parent lives in Detroit Michigan. He moved from there to Oklahoma four years ago to attend college at UCO. I spoke with his mother and she hardly hears from him, maybe a few times a year," Carrie began the minute she saw Randy.

"How long has it been since she has heard from him?"

"He went home for Christmas, so a couple of months ago." Carrie stood and walked to the whiteboard to pin the most recent photo of Beau that they had received from his mother via email.

"I feel like we wasted a lot of time on the ants and that first ritual, but we had no way of knowing that there would be more various rituals. I think we can cross out the entomologist and his students. Don't you?" Carrie asked Randy.

"Yes, I agree. But I don't think it was a waste of time. All knowledge we gain is good, even if it is for elimination. They still had to get the ants from somewhere, so they had to have at least a limited knowledge of them."

A tapping on the door caused both Randy and Carrie to turn in that direction. It was Detective Rick Morris. "Can I come in?"

"Sure," said Randy as he stretched out his hand to welcome Rick with a handshake. Right behind Detective

Morris was another detective. As she stepped through the door, Carrie was immediately taken by how stunningly beautiful she was.

Carrie assumed she was her age, or maybe a couple years older than her. Her blonde hair lay in lazy curls that salons feverishly tried to replicate. Carrie suspected this simply came naturally to her. But what struck Carrie the most, were her eyes. They were large and painted in a crisp blue hue.

"I'd like to introduce you to Detective Jacobs. As you know my last partner retired and I've been working solo for a few weeks."

Carrie reached for Detective Jacobs hand and was immediately drawn to her. "Hi. I'm Carrie Border."

"It's a pleasure. And you can call me Molly." When she smiled at Carrie, her face lit up with a glow that seemed unnatural in this world of crime and degradation.

There were very few female agents and detectives, so it was a genuine pleasure to be able to work with one. But there was something else about her that was simply compelling. She seemed, to Carrie, quiet and borderline shy, or maybe it was just that she had a quiet confidence. Whatever the case, her posture was assertive and self-assured.

Rick's voice interrupted Carrie's analysis of the detective. "We've had patrolmen, as well as us, working that list you gave us. Here are our notes. I've also emailed it to you so that you can update your internal records."

Randy took the papers Rick handed over. "Anything stand out?"

"No, not really. Either they didn't know anything or were good at hiding it." Detective Jacobs walked over beside

Randy. "This guy here stood out initially. He is a grad student that works for a history professor at UCO. He works for a Dr. Jill Bates. We can't eliminate him, but he didn't seem to know anything."

"We spoke to Dr. Bates. She seemed startled and alarmed that any of her students might be involved," said Randy.

"I think we can eliminate him. You can follow up, but I didn't see any red flags."

Randy scanned through the list of notes Rick had made. "What about this one?"

Rick leaned over to look. "He has been out of town for a couple of weeks. He went to visit his parents and became ill while he was there, so he missed the last two weeks of school. He said he just got home. We need to verify with his parents, and receipts and such."

While Randy and Rick talked, Detective Jacobs took noticed of their whiteboards and began thoroughly absorbing what had been organized there.

"Who is this?" Molly asked as she tapped the picture that Carrie had just attached. She turned to look at the others with a questioning look on her face.

"That is Beau Barrett. So far he is our prime suspect. We've been trying to locate him to bring him in for questioning," said Randy.

"I can tell you exactly where to find him," said Molly. "He's in the morgue."

~

Carrie felt the entire room deflate. They had worked so hard to get to that one prime suspect, only to have it disappear in a slick moment.

They all stood looking at each other. Randy met Carrie's eyes. They both had the same discouragement reflected there.

"He must be the OD. We hadn't seen a picture of him yet." Randy said.

"Correct. We still don't know who the firewalker is," said Rick.

"Damn!" Randy hit the table and then leaned on it with both arms. "Back to square one."

Carrie didn't know how to respond to Randy's outburst. She had not seen this side of him since becoming his partner. He had always been high energy, upbeat, and optimistic. She stood still with bated breath, waiting for a sign that would indicate how she should react.

Fortunately Rick, who knew Randy well, had seen this before. He slapped Randy's back. "No, you aren't back to square one. You've gained an ID on another vic and look at that whiteboard and the piles of info you have laying on this table. You're getting closer."

Carrie moved to erase the large question mark where John Doe 1 was, and repositioned Beau Barrett's picture there, writing his name underneath.

"It's been a long day. Let's all go get a drink," suggested Rick.

Randy looked at his watch, assessing whether he could carve an evening away from Sandy. "Yeah, I think I can do that." He reached for his phone to call her and tell her where he was going. After hanging up, he looked at Carrie. "You in?"

"Hell yeah!" Carrie replied, then internally scolded herself for sounding too eager.

Randy laughed and tilted his head towards the door. "Let's go."

The four of them braved the cold and traffic to reconvene at a sports bar called Beers 'n Balls. Carrie had never heard of the place and sat staring up at the neon sign from inside her car. A bright neon outline of a glass of beer complete with suds bubbling over, next to a lower case 'n,' then a bright orange basketball layered over a brown neon football, was as tall as she was. "Beers 'n Balls. Who would have thought?" Carrie mumbled to herself.

The sun was behind the horizon but was radiating its final glow of orange and red. It's promise that it would be back soon to light the day. Carrie held her coat tightly around herself as she fought the wind that was trying to gain control.

Once inside, she saw a bustling crowd. A hand shot up from the corner where the team sat at a round booth. The mood was jovial, the floor was sticky, and the air was filled with the tantalizing smell of food. She felt right at home.

The only available seat was next to Molly Jacobs, so she pulled off her coat and slid in.

Carrie followed the lead of the others and ordered draft beer. The conversation was directed to Molly. Randy was curious about her experience and personal life.

Molly smiled slightly at Randy's inquiry. Her head dipped and a blond curl rushed forward.

"Well, I've been with the OKCPD for about five years,"

she said looking up through the curl. "But, I am a brand new detective. Only thirteen months under my belt."

"She is way too modest," belted out Rick. "She has been in law enforcement her whole life. Her father was chief of police in a small town east of here. Her mother worked there too. Then fifteen years ago, he accepted a position as chief of police at the Edmond police department. Molly has law enforcement running through her veins." Rick smiled proudly, as if he were her father and not just her partner.

"Wow, what a legacy!" said Randy. "I know you haven't seen all our research, but do you have any thoughts?" He was eager to hear what another detective thought. He knew with this case they needed as much insight as they could get.

"I honestly don't know. It looks like you are swimming in data. I would think that could be good and bad. I suppose I would try to dial it back to the simple basics and see if it brings any clarity.

"What is their motivation? Honestly, it appears they are accidents that happened during some sort of ritual. If they are participating willingly, then you aren't looking for a perpetrator, but the group who is participating in these rituals.

"The one thing that sticks out to me is that the motivation to continue is so strong the deaths haven't stopped them from participating."

The table grew quiet as they all sat mulling over what Molly had said. After a few minutes, Rick broke the solemn mood and said, "So Randy, when's the big day?"

A huge grin broke across Randy's face. "June. Sandy has a date circled on the calendar. I mean yeah, we have a place and all, but we might just elope." He laughed.

"Oh no you won't. Sandy won't let you!" Rick loved teasing Randy. They had worked cases together for years.

Carrie had sat quietly looking out at the crowd when the word 'day' had come up. The truth was, she and Billy had a date too. They had put money down on a venue, the flowers were ordered, and so was the catering. The very thought caused a nuclear jolt of anxiety to explode within her.

Carrie got up from the table to look for the ladies room and stood on wobbly legs. Her eyes searched through the crowd for any indication of which way she should go. "Hey, are you okay?" Molly asked.

Without turning back towards the table, Carrie said, "Yes, just looking for the ladies room."

Molly quickly gave instructions and Carrie immediately headed that direction. Once inside a stall, she sat down and lowered her head into her hands. The reality of her upcoming wedding, even though months away, and her emotional numbness came crashing down as a reality for the first time. She could not reconcile the two.

I have to officially end it with Billy. I can't go forward like this. It isn't fair to him. Maybe if we end it now, we can get refunds on our deposits. Tears slid down her cheeks. She had longed her entire life to find the perfect man who would love her dearly, and then have the perfect wedding and marriage. She had found that in Billy, but now she knew she was so damaged that the marriage would never be perfect for either of them. That very fact broke her heart even further.

I have to get out of here, but my purse is back at the table. Clean your face and pull yourself together, then go get your purse and make your excuses. She got up and stepped out of the stall. The face that stared back at her in the mirror seemed so much older than it had one month ago, and she didn't even care.

Back at the table, she reached underneath and grabbed her purse, then her coat from the hook. "Where are you going?" Randy asked.

"Honestly, I'm not feeling too well. I think I better call it an early night."

"You are the one who has been pestering me to go drink after work and now you are crapping out on us?"

"I'm sorry. I really am. You are right. I have been bugging you for us to go out, but I really don't feel well."

Randy frowned. She was right. She didn't look well. "Okay. Well, go home and get some rest."

Carrie nodded and said goodbyes all around. Just as she was unlocking her car, her phone buzzed. When she looked down and saw that it was Billy, she leaned over and vomited on the ground.

Chapter Twelve

She had not called Billy back from the previous night. She went home, drank to forget, and tossed sleeplessly in bed. The day at work had been filled with more phone calls, seemingly endless phone calls, mind-numbing phone calls. They had been in the office all day and it felt to Carrie that they had learned very little.

Once again, people wanted to turn the tide and ask for juicy bits of gossip. If they knew anything, they were slow to release it. Carrie found herself drifting to daydreams of happier days in her past, both with her parents and with Billy.

The night before, seeing his name on her caller ID right after falling apart in the bar restroom, had nauseated her. *Why did it affect me so much? I've loved Billy for so many years. He was my dearest friend. What has happened to me?* The voice message left by Billy had confirmed to Carrie that she needed to deal with her feelings, or lack of feelings, towards Billy and their pending wedding.

Usually her mind was consumed by the case even when not at work, but today as she drove home, her mind was on Billy. Once home, she kicked off her shoes, retired her firearm, and cozied up on the sofa.

Her hands were trembling ever so slightly as she held the ringing phone to her ear. She had made the brave choice to call him and try to talk through everything. When she heard his voice come across the phone, she realized that she had only reached his voicemail. Disappointment met her unexpectedly. She had been avoiding him on purpose and now that she wanted to talk to him, he wasn't there.

She stammered as she left the message. "Hi there. I'm sorry I missed your call. Please call me back. I plan on being home all evening. Well... bye."

Melancholy worked to engulf her, and she tried to self-analyze her thoughts and feelings over the last few weeks. Weeks? Yes, it had only been a couple of weeks, but had seemed like years.

She rehashed the pain of losing her parents, and tried to understand why in all of that, she had pushed Billy away rather than lean into him and allow him to comfort her. The answer was elusive.

Her forehead rested on her knees which she had pulled up close to her body, a typical protective posture. When the phone rang, she was so deep in her own thoughts that it startled her. His name filled the small screen.

Still trembling, she pressed the answer button and said

hello with a shaky voice. At first, only silence drifted into her ear. Then, Billy's familiar voice followed.

"You called." There was no noticeable emotion in his voice, so Carrie wasn't sure where she stood.

"Do you have time to talk?"

"I do."

"Would you like to come over?" She had planned only a phone conversation, but something had shifted when she couldn't reach him. Her failed self-analysis softened her heart even further.

Billy sensed her softened demeanor and agreed. One hour later, he was at her door with food and beverage in hand. As Carrie answered the door, a new awkwardness filled the space between them and she didn't quite know how to cross it.

They tried to make small talk as they retrieved plates and utensils, and filled glasses, but the heaviness in the room pushed back against their efforts. Neither one knew what to say when they both knew that so much needed to be said.

Billy felt that the ball was in Carrie's court since she had been the one to push him away. Carrie couldn't come in touch with any definitive feeling, so she had trouble navigating the conversation.

They ate in the living room just as they always had, Billy in the overstuffed chair and Carrie at the end of the sofa nearest to him. They ate in deafening silence with only an occasional word or two between them.

Carrie leaned forward and reached to dish out more food at nearly the same time Billy reached for another drink. His hand brushed across hers and that familiar electric touch triggered a tearful outburst in Carrie.

Billy jumped up from the chair as his tender love for her took over and he sat next to her, cradling her. She let him. It felt good and familiar and she thought she was once again feeling the love she had once known for him.

The emotional outburst exhausted Carrie, and Billy's arms felt so good. She had lost the power to resist and somehow she felt the wall around her heart that she had been working so diligently to build, begin to crumble to the ground.

Neither one was sure how long they sat on the sofa, with Billy holding Carrie in his arms. It didn't matter to them, because the troublesome void that had been between them seemed to have completely dissolved.

The moment they moved from the sofa, with Billy carrying Carrie in his arms to her bed, quickly became a faint memory amid their pent-up passion. The lovemaking didn't prove to be aggressive as it had sometimes been when they were so hungry for each other, but this time was gentle and tender.

Billy couldn't take his eyes off of the beautiful face of the one he loved. His fingers traced her tear-stained eyes that glistened from her crying. He smoothed back her damp disheveled hair and kissed her forehead. And Carrie held him tight the entire time.

When Carrie arrived at work the next day, her face carried a slight smile of satisfaction. Randy was already at his desk fingering the brochure that Dr. Randolph had given them the other day.

"Find anything of interest in there," Carrie asked as she walked up.

Randy looked up at Carrie and smiled. "I see you are feeling much better. Over your bug?"

Carrie was caught off guard, forgetting that Randy thought she had been ill. "Oh. Yes, much better."

"Good." He looked back at the brochure and opened it up for Carrie to see. "It looks innocuous enough. I have decided that I am going to go to the next meeting."

"Do you want me to go with you?"

"No. I don't want them to think that we are ganging up on them. I want it to appear that I am personally interested. Being male as well, there might be an inroad there somewhere."

He laid the brochure down and looked across his desk to where Carrie had just sat down. She looked much better and Randy hoped that she was moving through the grieving process.

"Okay. Let's talk about the two different drugs. Why would two drugs with such varying degrees of action be used? What is the purpose?"

Carrie was thinking. "Well, not knowing anything about who or what is involved in the rituals makes that reasoning difficult."

"Okay, then let's talk more about how they are possibly conducting things. We have only ever found one body at a time. What if there is only a single participant, and the others are onlookers who will participate themselves at another time, in another ritual?"

Carrie considered what Randy had said. "Sounds like that might be the case, but I can't imagine onlookers watching one of them being tortured, standing there doing nothing."

"The two drugs can be ingested differently. The scopolamine works immediately. The bromo-dragonFLY takes up to six hours but lasts for days. There must be separate reasons for the two. What if once a person has decided, or is maybe just picked, to do the ritual. Then they take, or are given the FLY to prep them. You know, to keep the fear suppressed. Then at the time of the ceremony, they are all given the scopolamine.

Carrie sat for a few moments considering what Randy had said."That makes sense. Maybe the scopolamine is used as much for memory loss as mind control? They participate in the ritual, but then forget afterwards," said Carrie. It made sense. "But then this becomes more of a perpetrator scenario where they are orchestrating this, not just young men voluntarily participating."

"It could be some of both. They are volunteering because they have no memory of the horror of the events. But there is a perpetrator who is instigating all of this. They also didn't stop with the first death, so on some level it doesn't bother them that men are dying, if they even know."

"I'm having a hard time envisioning a normal person knowing what drugs to obtain, then obtaining them, and then knowing how they need to be administered," Carrie replied.

"Maybe we should try and narrow down who could be obtaining these drugs, then using their chemical or pharmaceutical skills to prepare proper dosage. We need to know everyone who has imported that drug," said Randy.

Carrie frowned. "What is it," Randy asked.

"We also need to look at what drug interactions might cause death. If the perpetrators are being careful to administer correct dosage, then maybe the ones dying have another drug already in their system that caused such a severe reaction that they die when no one else does."

"Excellent. Let's talk to Henry first, then maybe we should revisit Dr. Pinning again."

About an hour later they were able to get Henry on speaker phone. "We have some questions about possible drug interactions between scopolamine and FLY. We were wondering if a person was taking another medication and it was in their system, would that trigger a reaction that would cause death, and maybe that is why the deaths seem random?" Randy asked.

Henry was mostly silent on his end of the phone thinking, except for a few hmms. "There were no noticeable drugs in their systems other than those two mentioned. If there were other chemicals, it is not anything that would pop up noticeably. Our tox panel is set to reveal the most common drugs. I saw indicators during the autopsy that led me to check for hallucinogenic drugs such as scopolamine and FLY. There were no others in there like those."

Silence sat on the phone for a moment, then, "What about food allergies? If these men had food allergies, would that cause an interaction?" Carrie asked.

"Possibly," responded Henry. "I just think that is a long

shot. There was no anaphylactic shock noted in their systems."

"Thanks Henry," Randy ended the phone call with more questions than answers.

"I think, now that we know a bit more, we should reach out to Dr. Pinning again. Maybe he can shed more light on these drugs and their interaction that he didn't before," said Randy.

Carrie dialed Dr. Pinning's office phone. The line rang several times and just as Carrie was about to hang up, Dr. Pinning's research assistant answered. "Dr. Pinning's office."

"Yes, this is Carrie Border with the OSBI. I would like to speak with Dr. Pinning if he is available."

"Well, unfortunately, he isn't."

"I see. Well, you are his research assistant correct?" When she affirmed Carrie's question, she continued. "We are researching the effects of drug interactions with someone who has taken scopolamine and bromo-dragonFLY. If someone was taking another medication or drug could that have been the reason for their death?"

The assistant stuttered around a bit before answering. "That is hard to tell, I can send you over a list of drug interactions listed in the PDR, the Physicians Drug Reference. We don't really deal with those drugs and I've not studied them personally."

"I understand. Yes, that would be great if you would email that list over." Carrie gave the assistant her email and terminated the call.

"Find something?" Randy asked as he entered the war room and saw Carrie standing, looking over everything.

"No. I was only able to talk to the assistant, but she is sending me a page from the PDR that shows known drug interactions for both of those drugs," Carrie replied never taking her gaze off of the board.

Randy noticed her concentration. "What are you thinking?"

"Kids couldn't pull this off. Young men I mean. They just couldn't pull all of these components together. Even if they knew about those drugs, I think it is a long shot that they would know the exact timing of when to administer them.

"I also don't think they would have the wherewithal to keep a clear head to clean up the body in such a way as to eliminate any forensics. I can see them getting together and complaining about being bullied, but not to go so far as to concoct and carry out this elaborate plan."

Carrie turned towards Randy, dropping her arms which had been wrapped around her waist. "What do you think?"

Randy studied the board and sat down on the edge of the nearest table. "I see where you are going with this. Educated adults, extremely educated adults working in unison, are reasonably the only ones who could do this.

"Possibly they became aware of the younger men bemoaning their weakness, said as much in class, and a discussion ensued between the educators or professionals later."

"And they chose to seize the moment?"

Randy was nodding while still looking at the board. "An experiment?" Randy asked.

A shudder rippled through Carrie's body. "Oh, how bloody awful!"

On the way home from work, Carrie stopped at the local liquor store and got a bottle of tequila and tequila mix. She knew that when she had thrown up the other night, it was not from an illness, but from anxiety. She intended to fix that tonight with as many margaritas as it took. She didn't want to think about her feelings for Billy, that were continually see-sawing back and forth between affection and numbness.

She peeled off her coat and work clothes and climbed into the hot shower. It was therapeutic. Her soft pajamas continued the flow of comfort she needed. She started with a margarita glass and the correct ratio of tequila to mix. She carried the glass to the sofa and flipped on the TV.

By midnight, she was forgoing the mix and drinking straight tequila. By one a.m. she no longer felt any anxiety. She was passed out on her sofa, sound asleep.

Sometime before the sun kept its promise to rise with light for the day, Carrie's phone was a distant annoyance somewhere in the bowels of her house. However the throb in her head was much louder. Through force of sheer will, she pulled herself up and finally found her jacket pocket which held the vile little device.

"Hello," came Carrie's raspy voice across the line.

"Oh my. Are you sick again?" Randy was alarmed that she might be really sick.

Guilt pricked her conscious and she dug deep to find her solid work ethic. "No, I'm fine. I wound up watching TV on the sofa way too late and fell asleep there. I'm sorry. I should have gotten more sleep." It wasn't a real lie. She had watched

TV way too late on the sofa. She just left off the part where she was drunk out of her mind the whole time.

"Well, we have another body. Are you up to it? Do I need to tell Bracket you aren't well?" Randy asked. No matter what she said, she didn't sound okay to Randy.

"Let me get a shower, I'll be fine." Actually, the fact that they had another body sent adrenaline surging through her and was even now pushing aside the fog of a hangover.

She met Randy a mere thirty-five minutes later back out on the east side of town. Once again, it was on the edge of town in a sparsely populated area. There was a pile of rubble where a small house had been, and three nearly collapsed buildings of various sizes. Randy was standing just outside of one.

He paid little attention to her appearance. She had showered, then blown her unruly wavy hair dry, and confined it into a tight ponytail. She hadn't taken the time for makeup. "Tight squeeze again," he said as he nodded toward the door.

The wind had decided to take a rest for once, and even though the air had a bite, it was nothing like the previous days had been. The air was tinged with a trace of alcohol and decomp.

Carrie was snapping on blue latex gloves as Dr. Bloom was exiting. He was shaking his head in bafflement. "The entire body is full of extreme piercings. Not rings, but long bamboo shoot-type rods. One that goes through his right cheek, through his mouth, then out through the other cheek, and one through his upper back. Also, there is one through each side of his upper chest."

Carrie stood fixed on what Henry was saying, her mouth

open. The thought horrified her. *What kind of mental state would one have to be in to subject themselves to such horror?*

Randy and Carrie entered the small shack, hanging back near the door in the darkness so that their eyes could acclimate. The young man in his early twenties, was bathed in the bright light of the portable spotlights which the team had set up prior to their arrival.

Henry was right. This young man was riddled with bamboo shoots that were about one half inch in diameter piercing his skin. None seemed to enter muscle or other deep tissue, only folds of skin.

"There's no blood," Carrie said as she squatted down to get a closer look. "He didn't die here, or at least the piercings weren't done here, unless they were done postmortem." Just like all the other young men, this one was lying flat on his back with his arms down at his side. They had all been laid out to rest after dying. "Another ritual. It has to be," Carrie said turning to look at Randy.

He nodded in agreement. "Has to be." He stood and glanced around the room. "I can tell there will be nothing here either, but let's go so the techs can do their due diligence. Maybe there will be a fingerprint or trace DNA on the bamboo shoots."

"At the first crime scene, they left the woven mitts on, here they left the bamboo shoots in. Why not remove them? Do they want us to know what they are doing? Leaving them seems risky." Carrie was searching Randy's face for answers.

"You are right. Maybe they are proud of what they have done. Maybe they hope the rituals will take us to false leads. They must be confident that there is no trace or fingerprints.

"Who found the body? Do you know?" Randy asked Henry who then thumbed through pages on his clipboard. "Looks like the call came through the OKCPD switchboard via 911 at three fifty-nine this morning. Anonymous." Henry looked up at the agents.

"Could be whoever dumped the body left an anonymous 911 call for us to find him. Shows they care?" Carrie asked. Her face pinched in a question.

Randy's brow was furrowed in deep creases. "I don't know. Let's get back to the office and make some calls. Henry, give us a call when you know anything."

"Will do."

Chapter Thirteen

On the way to the office, Randy and Carrie had called in a large order of breakfast burritos and pastries. They drove through, picked them up, and arrived at the office with a large bounty.

They made their way into the conference room and laid everything out. Randy had called Bracket on his drive in and had presented a suggestion to him, which he had agreed to. They got their whiteboard from the back room and rolled it into the conference room. Then Bracket called all available agents into the room.

"We bought breakfast for everyone. But while you eat, we want to present our case to you and see if you can think of something we haven't," said Randy.

Interested eyes searched the whiteboard while they picked up their food. The available seats were filled and soon the only sound was full mouths chewing. While they were getting settled, Randy pulled in another clean whiteboard and added their next victim and the little that they knew.

Randy gave the group a succinct summary of their case while they ate. He ventured into only a few details regarding the rituals, and drugs. It had become clear to them that the individual rituals were of no consequence, merely a means to an end, so he didn't elaborate there.

"Does anything stand out to any of you, or have you come across anything that might help us?" Randy asked.

"I'm assuming forensics has nothing to go on," an agent from the back of the room asked.

"Nothing. The bodies arrive at the dump site washed clean and then bathed in alcohol. The three that participated in the rituals wore leather fashioned into a type of loin cloth. The OD had jeans and a flannel shirt on. Forensics has those clothes, but has not found anything yet."

"What type of alcohol? Liquor or rubbing alcohol?"

"Rubbing alcohol from what we can tell, but we've not confirmed that yet. There was no smell of liquor, and Henry indicated only alcohol."

"How far apart are the deaths?"

"We are finding them about two days apart. It seems their TOD has been consistent with that," answered Randy.

"What is their official COD?"

"Henry is leaving that a bit open-ended. He is putting heart failure with contributing factors under suspicious circumstances."

"So the drugs did or didn't play a part?"

"Yes, the drugs are highly toxic and dangerous, so a person could OD on very little. Henry believes the toxic drug cocktail combined with the physical trauma of the ritual is what lead to heart failure."

Randy could see by the looks on their faces that they were deep in thought, but no one was coming up with anything new.

"Were both young men you've identified going to college at UCO?"

"Yes. We feel the connection is there. We have interviewed the professors and they seem to be alarmed at the news and have appeared very cooperative."

"Have you interviewed all their classmates?"

"No, we haven't. We have a couple of lists and the only intersecting name was our second body, Beau Barrett. No other names appear on more than one list. But, we do need to finish that as soon as possible. It just feels like about the time we make a little headway, we get another body.

"John Doe 1 was only identified a couple of days ago by Detective Molly Jacobs who just happened to see his picture on our whiteboard. We've not interviewed his family or friends yet."

Randy fielded a few more questions and when all the food was gone, he could tell the room was feeling restless. They all had their own cases to work on and were anxious to get back to them.

"Well, thanks. Just keep our case in the back of your mind in the event something comes across your desk that might lead back to this," Randy said.

Carrie began clearing the table once everyone had filed out. "It was worth a try. You never know when or if they might come across something that can help," she said.

"Let's call Rick and Molly and see if they can come in. We need help interviewing all the people on the lists," said Randy.

The call was made, and within the hour Rick and Molly were walking in the door of the war room. Randy had made copies of lists with the few notes they had regarding where they had obtained the lists and the few they had talked to.

"Dr. Mark Randolph is the anthropology professor. He knew about the rituals and they had been mentioned in one or more of his classes. He has had both Travis Davis and Beau Barrett in class," said Randy as he presented a photo and synopsis of the professor.

"Dr. Jill Bates," he said as he handed over a synopsis of her as well. "She is the history professor and knew both Travis and Beau. Travis was a history major so he had been in most of her classes. You will find attached to each professor's page a list of Travis and Beau's classes and the names of those also enrolled," said Randy.

"We checked and the only crossover we can find is Travis and Beau," said Carrie.

"What about the entomology professor?" Rick asked.

"We've visited with him on the phone, but neither Travis nor Beau took any of the classes he has taught. We only initially reached out to him on the first case since it involved insects. The others have not."

"Notification has been made to Beau's parents in Michigan?" Molly asked.

"Yes," confirmed Randy.

The detectives stood still reading through the lists. "Okay.

We will get started. If we find anything of interest, we will let you know asap," said Rick.

Randy called Henry, but he had nothing revelatory for Randy and Carrie. The tox screen would take another day or so, but they expected it to come in the same as the others. As they had thought at the body dump, the reeds were all superficial and did not penetrate any muscle, only flesh. But as many as there were, it had to be excruciating.

The bamboo reeds might be a legitimate line to investigate. I wonder where they bought them. Are they common or hard to come by? Carrie's mind was jolted back by Randy's question, "Are you surprised that they didn't find any fingerprints on the bamboo rods?"

"Yes. Someone must have worn gloves. Doesn't that tell us that even before they inserted the rods, they wanted to make sure that there would be no trace left just in case there was a death?" Carrie asked.

"Yes," Randy replied. "And Henry did however reveal one very interesting thing. The FLY was taken in by drinking. He found liquid in his stomach, a tea that seemed common."

"What about the scopolamine?"

"He was still working to determine that."

This information added an entirely new slant to the cases. When they arrived back at the office, Carrie began doing research on the ritual presented by the most recent body, the bamboo shoots through the skin.

"Randy, I was sitting here doing some research on the

piercing ritual, but is it even important? If we dive too deep into the rituals themselves I think it will just be a rabbit trail. What do you think?"

"Well, we should try to do some research while resisting the rabbit hole. Get the gist of them and then leave the details for another time should we need them.

Carrie sat reading an article by the BBC about a band of Hindus called Thaipusam, who practice a religious ritual each year to worship a huge statue of Lord Murugan, one of their many gods.

"Randy, listen to this."

"The devotes fast for 48 days prior to the ritual, then carry a kavadi, which is a kind of ceremonial burden. It is usually some type of frame festooned with feathers and flowers. They carry the kavadi by inserting hooks and spikes into their skin, then hooking it to the kavadi.

Even those that do not carry a kavadi often insert hooks and spikes and carry smaller vessels. Then there is the vel, which is a cosmic spear which pierces both cheeks. They do not use any type of painkillers as an act of devotion to Lord Murugan.

The pain serves to intensify spiritual devotion putting aside their ego, anger, and other human frailties causing them to concentrate on a closer relationship with Lord Murugan."

"I just can't believe this." Carrie looked up and over at Randy. He could tell by her face that she was in genuine shock over what she had been reading.

Carrie briefed Randy on more details of the Thaipusam ceremony. "It sounds exactly like what we saw with the last victim. These boys are suffering excruciating pain. But unlike those who practice these rituals in earnest, our victims take drugs, either for the pain or to gain the courage to participate.

"Part of the ritual is to not only show devotion to this god..." Carrie searched the page for the name. "Murugan. But partaking in this ritual also shows courage."

They both sat looking at each other for a bit while they mentally processed the information.

"Really, these rituals are all the same in the respect that those who participate are, in essence, proving their courage," said Randy.

"And devotion to God?" Carrie asked.

"Yes, it seems there is some element of that as well."

"Dr. Bates said that the fire-walking ceremonies rarely resulted in any injuries because wood and our feet are poor transmitters of heat. When a foot steps on the wood, it puts the flame out. Kind of like when someone pinches a candle flame," said Carrie.

"So why were Beau's feet so burned?" asked Randy.

"Well, if a person is not aware of what is going on because those drugs have them so impaired, they may not feel the burn of the surrounding flames. Somehow, he stayed on the hot coals or in the flames too long," Carrie continued. "It was as if he, or someone, held his feet in the actual fire, not just walking on burning wood coals."

Carrie shuddered. "I just can't imagine subjecting myself to that kind of self-harm on purpose."

"As a young man, there is often a need to prove oneself. It

is part of our internal desire to be stronger and more courageous than anyone else. As boys and young men, we have all done things to prove our courage. Most, I would assume, not to this degree."

After a few more moments of thought, Carrie said, "We may be looking at several perpetrators, a group of possible students who study those subjects."

"Well, we already know there is a group of them because those boys didn't wind up where they were washed and laid out by themselves after death."

Jason wouldn't look the detectives in the eyes. Molly had sat down directly in front of him on purpose, but had yet to lock in eye contact. He was noticeably nervous, rubbing his hands together as he leaned forward, elbows on thighs.

The small college apartment had two bedrooms and a shared bathroom. The kitchen was almost non-existent, but with the amount of cooking that college kids did, all it really needed was a fridge and a microwave. The trash bin was overflowing and a pungent odor floated past from time to time.

"Jason, classmates of yours are dying. If you know something and don't help us investigate, you automatically become an accessory, or at the very least, obstruction of justice which is a felony."

Molly stopped to let that sink in. He grew paler, but still said nothing.

"What part do you play in this group?"

Jason's head jerked around and finally she could see the

fear in his eyes. "What are you so afraid of, or should I say who, are you so afraid of?"

His mouth opened and closed like a fish gasping for water. Sweat began to drip from his hairline despite the cool feel of the room. And again, he looked away.

Molly looked over her shoulder at Rick. "I think we might have a more forthright conversation down at the station, don't you?" Rick was already nodding his head. "Yes, I do."

They meant it, but it was also a ploy to get Jason to open up. They didn't want to have to take the time to haul him to the station, fill out the paperwork, and then conduct the interrogation. They had many more people to talk to and didn't have time to spare.

Molly made a show of standing. Jason reached out touching her sleeve indicating for her to sit back down. "Okay. I know your tricks, and I don't have time to go anywhere. I have class in thirty minutes." His eyes were large and pleading.

"Okay," said Molly as she sat back down. Behind her, Rick pulled up a kitchen chair and placed it to the side, quietly sitting down.

"Tell me what you know, and you'll get to class right on time."

Jason huffed in resignation and sat back on the sofa. He looked to Molly as though he were defeated. "I am not part of the group. But I've heard the rumors." When he stopped, Molly raised an eyebrow to prompt further explanation.

"There is a group of guys who were fed up with being bullied by the football team. At first, it was just drunken banter while hanging out. But some of them couldn't let it go. You know how it is, you keep talking and things fester and before long they were plotting to prove just how tough they were."

"We assessed that much. Now, tell us something we don't already know." Rick was getting impatient.

"Can you give us names of those in that group? When and where do they meet?" Molly was more patient than Rick, but her voice was unmistakably firm.

"Yeah, maybe a couple. I don't know them all and I could be wrong. Like I said, I'm not part of the group, just heard rumors."

Molly reached into her pocket and pulled out a small notebook and pen. Never breaking eye contact, she slipped it across the coffee table towards Jason. "Write them down. All of them that you even suspect might be in the group."

As Jason began writing, Rick and Molly made silent eye contact ending with Molly giving a simple shoulder shrug.

When Jason slid the list back across the table to Molly, she immediately noticed how short it was. "This is all?"

"It is all I know." He continued to fidget. There was more he was holding back.

"What is it you are so afraid of?" Molly insisted.

He leaned forward again with his hand rummaging through the back of his hair as he looked to the side. "Nothing."

"Bull!" The forceful delivery of that word changed the ambiance of the room. Suddenly, Jason knew Molly was not just another beautiful lady playing detective, but that she was tough as nails and meant business.

"I didn't join the group, because after they started talking smack, I stopped hanging around them. It was funny at first, but then I didn't want any part of it."

"So you do know who they are and what they were planning beyond just rumors. Correct?"

"No. It was just silly talk. Nothing like what I think is happening. The rumors were afterwards when they started dying." Jason's voice trailed off and stilled.

Molly picked up the notebook and looked at the names. The first two were already dead, Travis Davis, and Beau Barrett. Two names remained. "This isn't a very long list. How many were there when you first heard them talking about all of this? Were there others there that you didn't know?"

Jason slightly shook his head. "No. That's all. Like I said, it was just a few of us hanging out."

"Have you ever heard of the drugs scopolamine and bromo-dragonFLY?" Rick asked.

Jason looked at the detective. He seemed to think of something, but then shook his head once again. "No. Is that what killed Travis and Beau?"

"No, stupidity killed your friends." Rick stood to leave and Molly followed suit. "We will probably want to talk to you more later. If we call, you better pick up. And, if you remember anything else or hear any more rumors," Rick emphasized with air quotes, "call us immediately!"

Jason stood, still rubbing his hands together as he walked the detectives to the door. "I will. I promise."

Once outside, the detectives were individually deep in thought. It was a beautiful day after having had so many cold and blustery ones, but it was difficult to enjoy with this case hanging in the air.

"What are you thinking?" asked Rick once they were back in the car.

Molly looked over at him as she was formulating her thoughts. "How many of these guys have we talked to? And they were all either very nervous just like Jason or seemed completely in the dark. The ones who were nervous were extremely uncomfortable about talking to us at all. They are afraid of something, but I'm not even sure that they know what."

Rick reached down and turned the key, resulting in a blast of air from the vents. He quickly turned down the fan as he thought.

Rick's forehead creased. "Well, we already know that if they had anything to do with this group, then they feel weak and bullied. That would translate to what we are seeing. They don't want the group to know that they are talking to us. Fear of the group finding out?"

Molly nodded as she buckled her seatbelt. "Possibly. I can't imagine that level of fear against a group of peers. In fact, Jason said he just quit hanging out with them. It seems to me like there is much more to it.

"What if there are adults involved that these guys either look up to, or those adults are holding something over them?" Molly asked.

"Like grades?"

Molly turned to look at Rick. "Like grades."

Chapter Fourteen

Carrie had been battling her conflicting feelings since the night Billy had stayed and they reconnected. It had brought her back to a more innocent time when everything seemed good and right and true.

But the next day, grief settled over her again. It occurred to her how she doubted she would ever heal from grief when working a case so horrid as this one filling her days. She felt sad and overwhelmed. It was taking too much energy to be what she thought Billy needed.

Yes, that had been a wonderful night, but she couldn't see how it would last, could last.

They had chatted briefly on the phone and exchanged a few texts. Truth was, during the day she was so engaged in the case that she barely had time for anything else, and she felt she didn't need anything distracting her mind in another direction.

The lack of interaction was unsettling to Billy. She could

tell. Their intimate reconnection had led him to believe that they were back to business as usual. How could she try and explain to him that she was still emotionally damaged, and not sure if she could be all he expected her to be?

She had needed him and their evening, or rather their night together. It was truly therapeutic and healing in one sense, but in the light of day she had realized that it was just a Band-Aid over a severely deep wound. A wound she felt every moment of every day, regardless of where she was or what she was doing.

Billy deserved more. She loved him enough to know that. Their night together had brought something she needed, and Carrie felt incredibly selfish that she had allowed it to comfort her, knowing that she may never be what he remembered her to be. A throb in her head told her she was using him, and that it was not right.

The turmoil she was attempting to sort out made her think of the offer the bartender presented the other night at the Blue Tiger. Carrie thought tonight would be a good night to go sit at the bar and engage in bartender therapy.

She went home from work and changed into jeans and a t-shirt. As she pulled into the parking lot of the bar, she saw that it must be a light night, as there were only three cars in the lot. Carrie parked and sat in the car a moment, resting her head back on the headrest with her eyes closed.

How have I gotten to this place? The entire world feels so foreign to me. My life doesn't feel like my own. But I can't stop hurtling down this alternate path that I feel so compelled to travel on.

As her thoughts subsided, her body moved and soon she

was in the bar and perched on a stool. The darkness of the bar accentuated by only the bright neon lights scattered on the walls was feeling more and more like home to Carrie, a womb of sorts. Maybe a womb of healing, she hoped. Or was it a womb of decay?

The bartender smiled and walked over to Carrie. "Good to see you again. What can I get you?" Carrie thought she might need something a bit stronger in order to bare her soul, so she responded, "I think tonight I'll have a Jack and Coke."

The bartender raised an eyebrow, but moved to fill Carrie's order. "Tough one today, huh?" As she placed the drink in front of Carrie she added, "I'm Sarah, by the way."

"Hi Sarah, I'm Carrie. But I guess you know that because you've seen my debit card." Carrie chuckled. Sarah nodded and smiled as she wiped the counter where she had just made the drink.

"It has been a particularly tough day. I was going home and remembered how you offered an ear should I ever need it. I always thought that was just something people said about bartenders but wasn't really true."

"Well, I don't know about most bartenders. I would think in those busy bars that are loud and crowded and the bartenders are rushed to keep up, that wouldn't be the case. But even I've gone to a busy bar and had the bartender offer an ear."

Carrie felt like the 'cat had her tongue' once she was at the bar in front of Sarah. "Is it guy or work troubles, or family?" Sarah prodded.

A deep breath filled Carrie's lungs as she looked up and met Sarah's gaze. "I suppose it is some of all those."

The depth of pain that Sarah saw in Carrie's eyes saddened her. "Sounds like a lot to carry. The three over there will be here for hours and I doubt many more will come in tonight. I'm all yours."

The whiskey burned as Carrie tipped to empty the glass. She then immediately pushed it toward Sarah, who promptly made another. A little liquid courage was necessary in order to talk to a stranger, to anyone actually, Carrie realized.

Two sips into the second drink, Carrie began. "I'm not sure where to start." But she did, and soon had given Sarah a succinct history of the tragedy of her parents' death, her immediate job at the OSBI, then how she had pushed Billy away with her newly hardened heart.

Sarah let out a low whistle. "I was right, you are carrying a heavy load. I know grief is tough, and in your case, extra tough. I know the only thing for that is to just let yourself feel the grief and let time heal the pain.

"The new job is a dream come true for you. Could it be that you feel a bit guilty that your parents are gone and you have nearly simultaneously been given your dream? Do you feel that in some way you don't have the right to enjoy your life since their lives were taken?"

Carrie rotated the glass on the bar robotically as she thought. "That could be some of it. Why do I get this charmed life when they have no life?" She looked up at Sarah through liquid eyes.

Sarah gave a pinched smile and tilted her head as she reached out to hold one of Carrie's hands in hers. "No one's life is charmed, even though it may seem that way. But you are on a great path. I suspect these are not just your dreams, but the dreams your parents had for you as well. Wouldn't it be a shame to fold in on yourself and see all of it crater? They wouldn't want that for you."

Carrie emptied her glass again and Sarah filled it. "I do love my job. I think I am good at it too. They supported me every step of the way and I feel like I am doing it for them as well as for me."

"But..."

"I'm struggling with my relationship with Billy. I feel like my emotions have gone dead and when anything that tries to draw on them, it feels like a violation. Like I just don't have anything to give to anyone emotionally." Carrie downed the remainder of her third drink. As she sat it on the bar, she could tell the room was slightly distorted and her thoughts had gone hazy.

"Let's wait a bit on the fourth drink. Here is a glass of water."

Carrie looked at the glass of water Sarah had sat in front of her. She didn't want anything to steal this feeling of comfort from her. But she acquiesced and took a good sip.

"I just don't know what to do about Billy. We have been hot and cold for weeks. He is so good to me. I doubt I'll ever find anyone to treat me so well and love me so much again. I just feel that I can't give him that right now and it isn't fair to him. I walk around all day feeling more guilt over how I feel about Billy than anything."

"You say you are hot and cold, so I believe you do still love him. To me, it sounds like fear. Maybe you are afraid of being close to him, loving him, and then losing him. It may seem easier to distance yourself than having to go through the pain of loss once more.

"In those moments when you are hot and in the good place with him, what takes you to that cold place?"

That question surprised Carrie. Her eyebrows showed her concentration. She looked up and into Sarah's eyes. "I don't know. It just seems out of my control."

The night before had been somewhat refreshing. Sarah had been a good ear to unload on and she had helped to moderate Carrie's drinking. She had historically just drank beer or an occasional Jack and Coke, but felt driven last night to indulge in something far more potent in order to mask her feelings. She had been thankful that Sarah was there.

The result was that she had not woken with a horrific hangover and even felt some emotional relief from having a friend to talk to.

When Carrie arrived at the office, she noticed that Rick and Molly were also there talking with Randy. "Hey Carrie, glad you are here."

"Am I late?" Carrie asked glancing at her watch.

"No, not at all. I just came in early and Rick and Molly stopped by before heading to their station."

"Have you got something?" Carrie was eager and hopeful.

Molly dipped her head to the side slightly and a curl bobbed in front of her eye, which she promptly brushed back. "Well, maybe." Rick and Molly filled them in on their previous interviews, discussing how the young men's reactions ranged from completely clueless to utter fear.

"Here is a list of those that were noticeably fearful. I think we can rule out the remainder. It's not much, but something." Rick paused before mentioning he and Molly's discussion the previous day. It had only been supposition without anything to confirm their thoughts.

Molly looked at Rick and noticed his slight nod in her direction. "We were talking after doing the interviews yesterday. This is only guesswork, but those that acted severely nervous seemed to be afraid of someone or something. We began to toss around suggestions between us as to what that could be."

"And..." Carrie urged.

"What if, now I sincerely mean if, they are concerned because the ones running this nonsense are their professors. Maybe they caught wind of the students' frivolous talks and decided to encourage it. Maybe they are running some type of sociological experiment. I know that may sound far-fetched. I can't imagine any professor doing anything like that, and then in this case maybe more than one. The odds of that seem astronomical, but a possibility."

The room fell quiet when Molly finished expressing her thoughts, each one contemplating the validity of them.

Carrie looked over at Randy. "I know this is my first OSBI case, but this idea just seems so bizarre that Molly could be right. It could be a group of professors conducting some kind of experiment instigated by these disenfranchised young men."

"It is definitely an option. The best we have at this point.

Just so happens that I've decided to go to their next scholar meeting consisting of those interested in sociology, history, and other such studies. I want to watch them closely and see if there is any indication that they may be involved."

"We need to go more in-depth in our interviews with each of them. I know there are several professors in each department. We were trying to interview the heads of departments or experts in their field to get the most information we could. But it could very well be other professors we've not interviewed that are involved," said Randy.

"Also, we checked with the parents and both sets confirmed that their sons didn't have any allergies. We were hoping that we could find something that triggered the overdose or interaction which caused heart failure," Randy continued.

"Can these drugs be made from a home lab, or do they need to be purchased from a manufacturer?" asked Molly.

"We've learned through our own research that scopolamine is a derivative of nightshade, a plant that can be grown nearly anywhere. It has been used for centuries for various things. It does have a medical usage and is often used for sedation.

"FLY, on the other hand, is a synthesis and is deadly compared to its predecessor 2C-D-FLY. There have been deaths due to someone thinking they were taking the 2C-D-FLY when in actuality they were taking 4B-D-FLY which is deadly at 700 milligrams." Carrie had studied until her eyes burned regarding these two drugs and she was eager to share what she knew.

"There is no known medial benefit to FLY, so research is

sparse. Those who have survived the 'trip' said it was straight from hell itself. It is a vasoconstrictor, which hinders blood flow, and some have had to have amputations days later."

The room sat silent. "So, if I get this right, the scopolamine works primarily on the nervous system and the FLY works on the veinous system?" asked Molly.

"Well, yes and no. The FLY is a hallucinogen, kind of like a combination of LSD and an amphetamine, but does affect blood flow. A side note, both have been used in occult practices," Carrie answered.

"That opens a whole new can of worms," replied Rick. "So do we need to switch gears completely and look for an occult angle?"

"It could be both. Let's just say for a moment that these professors are fostering these rituals, but they have an occult-like element in them. It still could be one and the same." Randy's hands accentuated his words. He, like the rest of them, was becoming increasingly alarmed.

"Where do we go from here?"asked Molly.

"There are still so many questions we need to ask and have answered. Maybe after the meeting Friday night I'll have more avenues to investigate. I feel like we are making headway, even though it is like walking through heavy fog."

For the next hour they discussed what they needed to know and from whom they needed to know it. They once again split up the tasks between them with a plan to reconvene later.

They all felt that heavy fog as they filed out of the room. Rather than gaining ground, it felt like more was being layered on with each new discovery, making the fog that much more dense and harder to navigate.

Carrie spent the rest of the afternoon attempting to study the two drugs in relationship to occult practices. She could find no instances where they were ever used together, even though they may have well been.

The truth was that very little was documented about FLY. It was so lethal that no one was making or distributing it within ten years after discovery. *So why bring it back now? There are so many other drugs they could have used or combined.*

"Any progress," asked Randy as he walked up.

"No. It appears the uses in the occult are just for mind alteration. They are psychotropic drugs and 'expanding' the mind is a component of the occult."

"So do we eliminate the idea that some type of occult ritual is part of all this, or not?"

Carrie just shook her head. Her face showed doubt and fatigue. "I've been wondering about what you circled on the board this morning, survivors. How do we go about finding if anyone participated and survived?"

Randy moved to his desk and sat down. He leaned back and scrubbed his face with his hands. After a few moments, he popped his chair forward and looked at Carrie over the divider. "Some of those young men that Rick and Molly inter-viewed may have been survivors. That may be one reason they were so nervous. They sure don't want to talk about it."

"What if we bring them into a more formal setting? That may tip them over to talking about it. Also..." Carrie looked down and shuffled through the file searching for something. "We still don't have an ID on the overdose victim. How do we pursue that? Is there an avenue at UCO where we could post it and ask for information?"

"We could start with the professors we previously visited with. We have their email addresses, why don't you email a photo and see if they recognize them." Carrie nodded and was immediately tapping her keyboard. At the sound of the whoosh, she turned back to Randy. "Done."

"What about the leather? Is there anything distinctive about that?" Carrie asked.

"Hmmm. Maybe, I'm not that familiar with leather, but there could be. Let's get with the forensics team and see what they can tell us." Carrie was making notes on the list she had made.

"There could have been fingerprints left on the smooth portion of the leather, right?" Carrie asked.

"One would think so. I'm sure the forensic team has looked it over well. Whoever left the bodies cleaned up thoroughly. I doubt they would have overlooked the leather."

Just then Carrie's phone rang. "This is Molly. I just had an interesting call from one of the guys we interviewed. He wants to come in and talk to us. I was thinking that we could meet at your office and have him come there."

It was just the surge of adrenaline that Carrie needed. "Let me check with Randy, but I am sure that would work." Carrie confirmed with Randy and they agreed to wait and see what time the young man would want to meet. It was already four in the afternoon, but both Randy and Carrie were willing to stay as late as necessary.

Sometime before the now confirmed five-thirty appointment, Rick and Molly arrived. "What can you tell us about this young man?" Randy asked.

"His name is Blain Griffiths, twenty-two, from Ardmore, Oklahoma, a junior in college at UCO and he is a sociology major. Those are the details that we have. However, when we were interviewing him, we thought he came the closest to talking. On that day though, there was nothing we could say that would push him over the edge. So, why he finally decided to talk, we just don't know."

Just then, Sylvia approached the group to let them know that Blain had arrived. He was sitting in the vestibule waiting for them. His left knee was bouncing up and down as he rubbed his hands together between his legs. He was clearly nervous.

Randy reached out, offering to shake Blain's hand. He stood and limply shook it. Instead of ushering him into the interrogation room, they took him into the empty conference room. They had all agreed that since he came in voluntarily and was so jittery, the change in rooms might set him at ease. They also agreed that it wasn't a good idea for them to all gang up on him.

Randy, since he was the senior OSBI agent, and Molly who had been able to establish some rapport with him, as well as being the one he had called.

Once in the room, Randy asked Blain if there was anything he needed, a soft drink, snack, or anything else.

Blain indicated no and stood waiting to be directed on where to sit.

"Blain, thank you for coming in today. We value any information you have to give us," began Randy.

He nervously nodded and looked around the room, not saying anything. Randy gave the tiniest nod in Molly's direction.

"Blain, we could ask you questions and probably will, but why don't you start us off by telling us what you know and why you decided to come in today."

The young man looked at Molly. She made him feel at ease and she was the only reason he had decided to call. "I was there. I mean, I don't remember being there, but I know I was there." Blain stopped and his face crumpled in on itself. He sat staring at the table for a few moments trying to find the words to explain.

He looked back at Molly who was patiently waiting. "I... I... I just don't know how to describe it to you."

"Okay. Well let me ask you a few questions to see if it will help jog your memory. You say you know you were there. Where exactly is there?"

Blain looked at Molly with a blank expression. "Well, I don't know exactly. You see, we all met at Hafer Park and were then taken to a secret place, none of us were told where. Then we got out and that is all I remember." He looked at Molly, his eyes pleading for her to understand.

"Okay. That's good. Do you remember the date?"

Blain turned introspective as he tried to remember the date, then slowly began nodding. "It was last Friday night."

"Is that the only time you participated in this?"

Blain nodded.

"How did you know to meet at Hafer Park? Had you gone to meetings before or by word of mouth?" Molly continued the questioning as Randy made notes. They also had a video recorder monitoring as well.

"I went with a friend. He told me about it. I think he had gone before. He seemed pretty chummy with the others as we waited."

"What is that friend's name?"

Blain hesitated. He felt like he was throwing his friend under the bus. Finally making a decision, he shrugged his shoulders and said, "Jason Anderson."

"What did they talk about while you waited?"

"Actually, they all seemed excited, maybe a little nervous. But honestly, I think they were just trying to make it look like they weren't terrified. I don't think they knew any better than I did what was going to happen, and that made us all nervous."

"Had any of them done that before? Could you tell?"

"Yeah, I think most of them had, but they didn't seem to remember any more than I do now."

"What was the purpose in meeting and doing this? What did your friend tell you it was for?"

"Courage mainly. Like it would help us toughen up. He also said it was a path to finding God."

"And that was what attracted you to go with them?" Molly was trying to set her personal feelings about God and religion aside. There had never been a time when she had not known God, and she was sincerely sympathetic for those who had not.

"I've never gone to a church and I don't think any of those guys there had. My friend talked about it some. He had read some books on Buddhism and another type of religion. He dabbled in it some, but said he never felt like he had found God. I know he wanted to, and thought this was possibly the way. That made me curious. It sounded cool."

Molly and Randy continued to talk to Blain for the next hour. He didn't know anyone's name except for his friend.

He remembered nothing except them meeting, the van ride in the dark, and getting out. He said it was pitch dark where they arrived, but he thinks they went into an old barn. After that, he woke up in his own bed the next morning and thought it had all been a dream. A bad, bad dream. And he didn't even know why it had been bad.

That was all they had gotten from Blain. They asked the same questions over and over in different ways to only get the same answers. It appeared he knew very little and had told them all of it.

Chapter Fifteen

Carrie had a date with Billy that night and was anxious about it. *Why am I so wound up? It's just Billy.* As she drove home, her thoughts carried her back to a much happier time. The last really good memory was when they were wedding shopping. She knew that this limbo state she was in had to end one way or another. She needed to cancel the wedding or continue to move forward with Billy and get married.

She felt so numb as she thought about it all. There was something still inside that drew her to Billy, and since some of the anger over her parents dying had passed, she no longer felt that emotion towards him either. But could she say she loved him the way she had in the past? She didn't know. And she didn't know if she should just give it time, or face the fact that it was over.

There was fear, she realized after Sarah had pointed it out to her at the bar. Fear of loving him so deeply again, and then losing him the way she had lost her parents. No love, no pain, right? But she hated the hollowness this state-of-being left her with. *I don't want to feel so numb. I just don't know how to fix how I feel.*

Billy was waiting in his car in her driveway. When she pulled in, he opened his door and got out. Carrie's heart skipped a beat. He was so handsome and the late afternoon sun glinted off of his blonde hair. She also noticed he hadn't skipped his routine gym visits either and her body responded.

They greeted each other with a hug and a kiss and went inside. The mess inside slightly embarrassed Carrie and she began nervously picking up. "Let me just take a quick shower and change."

Billy smiled a silly grin. "Need someone to wash your back?" He bobbed his eyebrows up and down and Carrie found herself feeling a little bashful. "No. I'll be right out." But she did return his grin with a smile.

In the shower, she felt nervous like she had on the first date. *How silly! We've been together for years. It does feel good though to look forward to being with him. Maybe I am turning a corner.*

Carrie hurried to dress and get ready, each moment keeping Billy in mind as she made her clothing, makeup, and hair decisions. It paid off too. When she walked out of her room Billy's face shone with all the compliments she needed.

He stood and pulled her into his arms, breathing her into himself deeply. "You smell so good." For Billy, and Carrie too, it felt so good to just linger in that embrace and neither wanted to rush through it. Finally, Billy pulled back. "So, where do you want to go eat?"

"Surprise me." Carrie felt happy. Not as happy as she had a few months ago, but the beginnings of happiness.

They rode in Billy's car. "Tell me about the case you are working on. I know there is some that you can't, but you know I won't tell."

The slight smile Carrie had worn on her face faded. She looked at Billy with pained eyes. "Billy, this case is so tragic." She began to give him the basics of the case and the little they knew. "As a man, can you see any benefit to participate in these rituals?"

Billy sat frowning as he thought. It was hard for him to imagine wanting or needing to engage in such a thing. But then again, he had been a star athlete and had even grown up in a family who had gone to church from time to time. He felt courageous and knew where to find God should he wish to.

"Carrie, I don't know. You know growing up there were a few guys in class that didn't fit in. They weren't athletic and on the smaller side. Well, there was one who was very large. He didn't play sports either, so he hung out with that crowd. Some were book nerds, made great grades, and liked science and stuff.

"I tried to never be one of those who teased them, but there were many on the football team that gave them hell. I could see how those guys could feel compelled to find a way to prove their courage. It is hard growing up as a guy when there is a brutal pecking order.

"As for the God thing, I don't know. I suppose they may feel having courage could prove something to God? I don't know." He looked over at Carrie to gauge her reaction. She was sitting quietly thinking.

"I know it is rough for the guys growing up, but it is the same for girls. Maybe not with being tough or in sports, but with beauty and social status. Money. Money is a big one. Having the expensive clothes, best purses and shoes. Those things just aren't important, but as kids we obsess about them as if they genuinely raise our statuses and make us happy, which is untrue.

"I always felt sorry for the girls who were just barely fed when they came to school, much less with nice clothes. Kids can be so cruel. I didn't really help either. I noticed, but didn't do anything about it. I never had the best stuff, but I didn't really care either. But I saw how those girls treated the others. It makes me sick now. It has to have shaped their whole life."

"True. My parents didn't really talk about it, but they should have. They should have taught me to have been kinder and stand up for those less fortunate and those being teased so fiercely. Now, I wonder what happened to them? Did they go to college, get good jobs, or just barely make it."

Carrie nodded. Many of the girls she hung out with had their sights set on college and wanted to make as much money as possible. They hoped to be doctors and lawyers. Carrie always wanted to solve crime. She loved the mystery, the problem solving of it all.

She wanted to do the best she could do and go as far as she could. So, she set out to arm herself with as much information as possible. That is why she went to college and kept going. The pay didn't really match her degrees, but that isn't why she continued. She just loved learning.

"You are lost in thought," said Billy. Carrie looked over and smiled.

"Yes. My thoughts ran off to college and how I was hungry to learn as much as possible about criminology and law enforcement. I was convinced that the more I knew, the better I would be, and the easier it would be for me to solve crime."

She snorted and shook her head. "I think I thought that I would hop on the scene and just instantly deduce the who - what - where - and why of every crime. That certainly isn't the case with this one. I feel so lost most of the time. The puzzle is so complex. I don't think I ever anticipated anything like this."

"You are so smart and intuitive. You'll figure it out. And don't be so hard on yourself. The other agents and detectives haven't figured it out yet either."

"True."

"But I know how competitive you really are. You always want to be the first and the best. You've always been that way. I can see how it doesn't matter that no one else has solved it, you are upset that you haven't solved it."

"True again."

Billy pulled his car into the parking lot and they entered the restaurant and placed their name on the list with the hostess. He slid his arm around Carrie's waist as they stood in the vestibule. It felt good and comfortable for both of them. They were enveloped in the hope that they were finally healing and moving forward.

Billy pulled out Carrie's chair at the table, and Carrie smiled. She still had a bundle of nerves knotting her stomach, and sadness still encroached on her heart. But maybe...

Somewhere in the middle of appetizers, Billy mentioned

the wedding. "I know you may still not be ready to move forward on the wedding, but we need to talk about all the arrangements we've made. I love you and am ready, but I want to be considerate of your feelings. I may not fully understand what you are going through, but I want to do whatever it is that you need."

Carrie looked up to see compassion in his eyes. Her throat closed up and she couldn't speak, so she nodded. "I... I..."

Billy slid his hand over and covered one of hers. "It's okay. It really is. I love you Carrie and I'll wait. I'll give you time."

She laid the dip-loaded chip down onto her plate, no longer able to eat it. "Thank you. I know we need to do something. Do you think we can get our deposit money back?"

The disappointment that Billy felt didn't show on his face. "Yes, maybe. I'll make some calls tomorrow and see."

They worked to regain the comfort they had experienced earlier, but sadness had taken up residence at their table.

Billy had spent the night again, but their lovemaking had not held the passion of their previous encounter. No matter how they had tried, Billy's disappointment and Carrie's sadness at disappointing him lingered. Both wondered where things truly stood with them.

When offering to wait for Carrie, Billy had thought it was a noble gesture that she would swat away, but instead she had grabbed onto it without hesitation. Billy's disappointment had not shown visibly, but Carrie knew him well enough to know that he had been crushed. She should have at least put on a show of debating and discussing the pros and cons.

Carrie welcomed work the next morning. Her mind shifted quickly back to the case and she hoped the day would bring new insights.

Randy greeted her heartily. "Tonight is the academic meeting. I am going to go. The number on the brochure was answered by a Rodney Grapple. He is Dr. Jill Bate's grad student. He gave me the address of a Dr. Micah Severs. He is the sociology chair at UCO. Meeting starts at eight p.m.."

"Why so late?"

"I don't know. Maybe it is an after-dinner thing."

"Hmmm." Carrie mused.

Both were soon lost in paperwork and follow-up. As Carrie was checking her email, she opened one from Rick.

"Randy. They have an ID on the OD. Silas Berry - 20 - UCO student. OD from FLY, but no sign of scopolamine in his system."

Carrie looked up to gauge Randy's reaction. "So, that makes some sense. We know that in all probability they are taking the FLY first, then a few days later the scopolamine. My guess is they gave him the FLY and he died before the ritual, so they dumped him."

"Whoever is doing this, and we assume it is more than one in order to pull this off, is relatively intelligent in order to prevent forensic contamination." Randy leaned back in his chair and, as usual, linked his hands behind his head. The chair squeaked as he gently rocked in place.

Both Randy and Carrie were once again deep in thought,

attempting to put all of the bizarre pieces into place. "Is Rick going to meet with the parents?"

Randy's chair popped forward. "Yes. He said he will forward any notes to us as soon as possible."

"Have you been able to reach Jason Anderson yet? I have a feeling that right after we interviewed Blain, he called Jason and warned him we would call. He is probably avoiding us. Does he live in the student housing or in an apartment?" Carrie asked.

Randy shuffled through the file on his desk until he found what he was looking for. "He lives in an apartment, but I don't know if he lives alone or with others. We are kind of at a dead end. Let's go visit Mr. Anderson and see what we can find." Randy stood and Carrie did likewise.

It was a quick trip to Edmond up Broadway Extension. Jason's apartment was close to UCO, just south and to the east. It was midday on Friday and there was little activity. The parking lot was only half-full.

They parked quickly and were soon standing in front of apartment 2307. Randy rapped soundly on the door with no result. After three separate attempts, Carrie walked over to the window and peered in. "It's dark in there. I see a small bit of light from another window, but there are no lights on that I can see."

As they stood by Jason's front door gazing out across the parking lot, a young woman came walking up the stairs with two large bags of groceries. Randy hurried to help her with her bags. "Let me help you with those." He reached out and the woman, tired from walking up so many stairs, readily relinquished the bags.

She dug for her keys and pointed to the apartment door next to Jason's. Randy waited patiently while she unlocked and opened her door. As she reached for her bags, Randy said, "Do you know the guy who lives at 2307? We wanted to talk with him."

The woman nodded and looked over at the door. "He's not home?"

"No, we knocked a few times and there was no sign of him."

"Hmmm. He should be there. He doesn't usually go home very often."

"We are agents with OSBI, could we come in and ask you a few questions?"

There was a flash of uncertainty on the woman's face, but it was fleeting. "Sure," she said with a shrug and led the way into her apartment.

"Have a seat on the sofa. I'll put away the frozen items."

Carrie and Randy perched on the edge of the tan fabric sofa and Randy pulled out his trusty notepad and pen. The apartment was simple, but tidy. A female influence was evident, but not overly done.

The woman walked to her front window and opened the drapes flooding fresh light into the room. As she sat on the opposing chair, she said, "I'm Rhenda Ames."

Randy began with simple questions, such as how long had she lived there, and how well she knew Jason.

"I've lived here for about two years. Jason moved in last summer, I think, right before the fall semester began. Could I ask what you are investigating?"

"There have been some murders recently and we just

wanted to talk to Jason. He may be a witness or just have some information that will help us."

"Oh, I see. Should I be alarmed?" Rhenda tucked her body tighter into the chair on impulse.

"No. The murders have all been young men so far. We see no reason you should be alarmed."

"Do you know what Jason's major is?" Randy asked.

Rhenda looked away as she thought, struggling to remember her previous conversations with Jason. "I think he said he was currently a chemistry major. Said he wanted to do something in pharmaceuticals possibly." She looked over at the agents for affirmation.

Both Randy and Carrie sat quietly, hoping it would prompt Rhenda to continue, which it did. "I asked him why he hadn't gone to SWOSU to be a pharmacist major, or OU for a pharmacology major. It seemed odd to me that he would study something like that here."

"What was his reply?" Carrie asked.

"He said he would probably wind up at OU for his master's degree, but for now, wanted to stay in a smaller school."

"Oh," Rhenda suddenly remembered. "He was minoring in criminology and that was the main reason he was here. He was a chemist major and a criminology minor."

For several moments, the electronic buzz of the refrigerator was the only sound filling the room. Randy and Carrie were individually placing this new, and incredibly impactful, information into what they already knew.

"Do you know any of Jason's friends?"

Rhenda tilted her head and wrinkled her mouth. "I've

met a couple. He invited me over one night for drinks. My girlfriend was here and we were coming home when they just asked us over. Very spontaneous.

"There were three other men there, all about our age. They were nice. I'm trying to remember their names. I think there was one named Gary, and one named Silas. I can't remember who else. Sorry."

"Do you know their last names?" Rhenda was shaking her head before Randy had finished his question.

"It was a casual thing and I just barely got their first names."

"Are you a student at UCO?" Carrie asked.

"Part-time. I work full-time during the day and then attend a few evening classes. I have to work to pay my way and this was the best way I found to do that."

"What is your major?"

"Nursing. I hope to be a nurse, but at the rate I'm going, I may be eighty!"

Carrie smiled. "It will go faster than you think. Just keep plugging away and you'll get there."

Randy pulled out one of his cards and handed it to Rhenda. "If you see Jason, will you give us a call? Don't mention that we were here. We don't want to alarm him. Just call and let me know."

Rhenda leaned forward and took the card. She saw no reason not to comply, so she nodded yes. "Of course."

The agents stood and moved towards the door. There was a moment's hesitation as they wondered if there was anything they had failed to ask. When nothing surfaced, they said their good-byes and left the apartment.

Once in their vehicle, Randy looked over at Carrie. "There can't be two young men named Silas in this town?"

Carrie shook her head. "Nope. That has to be our OD."

Randy struggled over what to wear to the event. He didn't want to stand out from the crowd. Blending in would best serve him to infiltrate and observe the group. He finally chose a pair of casual pants, a polo-type shirt and a navy sports jacket.

"Well, you certainly look handsome," said Sandy, as Randy walked out into the living room. Sandy had come by and made them a light dinner and was now on her way back to her place.

She walked up and straightened his shirt collar, then smoothed down his jacket shoulders. "Do I look okay?"

Sandy nodded. "Oh yes. You look quite nice."

"My goal is to blend in. It is a university crowd. I don't think it will be formal since there was nothing in the brochure about that."

"You look university administrative casual." Sandy grinned.

Randy raised one eyebrow. "Is that a thing?"

"Sure." Sandy laughed outright. "One can only imagine that professors dress pretty much the same all the time, right?"

Randy looked at his watch and gave Sandy a quick peck on the cheek. "I've got to go. Be safe and I'll call you when I get home."

"No matter how late?"

"No matter how late."

Randy's personal car was a bright red Nissan Titan pickup truck. Hopefully, it would not stand out since he could park away from the house and walk in if he needed to. But then, in Oklahoma, even professors often drove pick-ups.

It was already past dusk as he drove to the east side of Edmond. He merged onto I-35 traffic and headed north. At the Waterloo Road exit, he left the highway and headed east. Homes were present only sporadically in the somewhat densely-wooded area. After about two miles, he came to a property with an ornately-grilled electronic gate.

There was a keypad with a call button to his left. "Hello?" came the voice over the speaker.

"Yes, I am here for the meeting." The only response from the speaker was silence, but the gates began to open with a low buzz. Upon opening, they revealed a very large two-story home made of both brick and rock. The home was awash in skillfully-designed landscape lighting which enhanced the luxury of the home. *I'm in the wrong profession. Who knew college professors made so much money?*

The drive was long and ended in a large circle. To the right, the drive divided and appeared to lead to the back, possibly to the home's personal garages. Several cars were parked on that wide drive. Randy followed suit. He parked and turned off the engine. He wasn't prone to nervous reactions, but at that moment, his stomach was in a fitful ball of nerves.

He made sure he had his phone and keys and locked the truck. No one else was outside, so he felt late in his arrival.

The ringing doorbell quickly produced a young person of about twenty, if Randy were to guess. He greeted him with a broad smile and an outstretched hand. "Welcome. Everyone is already in the back room."

Randy nodded and tried not to gawk at the lavish surroundings as he made his way toward what he thought was the back of the house. The house was dimly lit overall, so he followed where the brightest light was leading him.

He stepped through a large arched opening and down into a massive room. The walls were lined with several custom built-in bookcases and expensive art, or anyway it looked expensive to Randy. There were approximately twenty people or so, milling about the room in small groups. They all had drinks in their hands and were very engaged in conversation. So much so, that Randy's arrival was of no effect.

Randy moved to his right along the wall, while watching the room. He noticed Dr. Jill Bates, and Dr. Mitch Reynolds. They were the only two professors that he had actually met face to face. The average age of the guests was mainly forties and fifties, with a few outliers on either end of the age spectrum.

In Randy's estimation, the younger ones had the look of students. The guests were largely dressed as he was, while the younger ones were either in pants or jeans and a nice shirt with no jacket. This caused them to stand out somewhat from the others.

A server came by with a tray of drinks and offered Randy a glass of what appeared to be some type of white wine. He accepted it, if only to hold the drink for appearances sake.

"Randy!" A voice called over the din of the room. Dr. Reynolds walked toward Randy with a pleased expression. "I'm so glad you made it! Let me introduce you around."

Anonymity promptly out the window, Randy settled in to try and remember as many names and faces as possible. He was introduced to Dr. Mark Randolph, who they had spoken to on the phone, and who was the chairman of the Anthropology department at UCO. Then to Dr. Micah Severs, the chair of the sociology department at UCO and the owner of the home.

He decided to sip on the wine slowly, making sure to guard himself against drinking too much. He wanted his full faculties about him while in this group.

The tinkling of a wine glass caught the attention of the crowd and all eyes turned toward the person making the sound. Randy didn't recognize the man who looked to be about forty, and dressed as the other professors were.

"Welcome this evening." Clapping filled the room, but quickly subsided.

"Tonight, we have a guest bringing us a short dissertation on his topic of interest. Make yourselves comfortable and I will relinquish the floor to him. Professor Jim Blankenship, professor of sociology for the University of Oklahoma." The speaker lifted his hands applauding fervently, encouraging the others to do so as well.

Randy noticed for the first time that the room was filled with cloisters of decorative hard back chairs set about the room. The guests each began to find a seat to face the speaker for the evening. Randy found a chair near the very back, with an excellent vantage point in which to observe the others in the room.

"Good evening. Thank you for allowing me to speak to everyone this evening. I have enjoyed being a member and am excited to now be a featured speaker."

The speaker rambled on about various sociological topics which bored Randy to tears. Nothing spurred him to believe that the content had any relation to their case, and it became very difficult for him to stay awake. He had been up since five that morning and was past ready for bed. Tomorrow was Saturday, so he intended to sleep in. He just had to stay awake for a while longer this evening.

After what seemed to Randy like hours, but was actually only about forty-five minutes, the speaker took his bow and exited the area designated as a makeshift stage. Randy began to stand, when Dr. Severs stood to address the crowd who was still seated.

"Thank you all so much for attending our monthly meeting. And thank you Professor Blankenship for your informative soliloquy." The room once again broke out into a short applause session. "Next month, we will feature Dr. Amy Gravenue, an anthropology professor with Oklahoma State University. In the meantime, we will have the fundraiser for Dr. Severs' project. If you wish to attend and make a donation, I'll be emailing out that information this coming week."

Attendees began to stand as the speaker exited the room. Randy turned to look for Dr. Randolph or Dr. Bates before leaving to thank them for welcoming him, but neither seemed to still be in the room. He slowly made his way back towards the front door, still surveying his surroundings.

Most attendees had gone out ahead of him. He was following behind the others, taking in the beauty of the spectacular home, which he had wanted so badly to do when he first entered. *Dr. Severs or his wife must have come from money. No professor could afford this on a university salary.*

Once in his pickup, Randy felt disappointed. He was the lone remaining car in the side drive and there was no one left outside escorting guests to their cars. There were, however, a few remaining cars in the circle. All the lights in the house had gone dark except for one window which shone brightly at the very back of the house, but not positioned where the great room had been.

Randy sat for a moment assessing all that he had seen that evening. He jotted down names and positions of those he could remember. Once done, he continued to sit. Something gnawed at him, but he couldn't figure out what and he just couldn't make himself leave.

Curiosity about the remaining cars and the light at the back of the house drew him to leave his truck and quietly make his way to the window. He stood to the side of it and leaned in slightly to see who occupied the room.

Before Randy could see who was there, a sharp pain sliced through his head and he plummeted to the ground unconscious.

Chapter Sixteen

It was a Friday night and Carrie should have agreed to a night out with Billy, but she just couldn't make herself go. Their last date had ended so awkwardly. She really thought Billy would be fine with waiting. He asked her as though he appeared to understand, but when she had said she would like more time, she could see his internal collapse from disappointment. The pressure from that, combined with all else she was going through, was more than she thought she could endure.

The Blue Tiger's parking lot was full and it was only seven o'clock. Inside, the crowd was high energy and it disengaged Carrie from her tormenting thoughts. Sarah waved from the bar and pointed to a hidden empty barstool around the side of the bar. Carrie smiled in acknowledgment and headed that way.

"Good to see you tonight. What'll you have?" Sarah was wiping the bar in front of Carrie to make sure she hadn't missed anything when cleaning it earlier. The noise was much louder than it had been the last time she'd been there, and it made conversation difficult.

"Let's start with a beer. Michelob Light if you have it."

Sarah nodded and moved away to fill her order. Carrie rotated on the barstool to view the crowd. She didn't know anyone there, which wasn't a surprise. Most were her age, but a few were older. All appeared to be having fun. Upon hearing the beer settle onto the bar, she turned around. "You guys are busy tonight."

Nodding, Sarah held up a finger for Carrie to wait. She moved down the bar to another customer who was tapping an empty shot glass on the bar. Carrie wrapped a hand around the cold wet bottle and lifted it. She tilted it and let the pale amber liquid slowly slide down her throat. Closing her eyes she enjoyed the taste and the thought of the buzz it would eventually bring.

Carrie kept her back to the crowd and sat alone with her thoughts as she nursed her beer. Sarah remained busy with other customers and filling waitresses' orders. That was fine with Carrie. She enjoyed Sarah the other night, but wasn't sure she was ready to talk to anyone about anything personal right then.

After three beers, Carrie was feeling soft and tranquil. She had forced herself to not drink quickly like she had the other night. The result was a slow, but pure fade unhindered by food since she hadn't eaten since lunch.

It was eight thirty. Sarah had popped over from time to time to not only bring her another bottle, but to toss in a bit of conversation here and there. "Hey, can you watch my stool? I need to make a trip to the ladies' room."

"Sure! I can't promise to keep it warm, but I can keep it empty." Sarah winked as Carrie vacated the stool and focused on walking to the back of the bar. Right as she reached for the door handle, out popped two giggly young women who didn't look much older than twelve. Carrie knew that wasn't the case, or Sarah wouldn't allow them in. But their vibrancy caused Carrie to feel old.

Carrie used an empty stall and then moved to the sink. The lighting was poor and the purple walls had been a horrific choice. But as Carrie looked at herself in the mirror, she didn't think there was any lighting or wall color that could enhance her appearance at that moment.

She was sad inside and it showed on the outside. She hadn't felt sad the other night with Billy, until... maybe she should call him. There was still time to see him tonight. Maybe he had recovered and would want to see her. She didn't want to feel sad. She wanted to feel that joy she had always felt before. Transfixed to her own gaze in the dark mirror, she convinced herself that calling Billy right then was a bad idea.

She shook the water off of her hands and left the ladies' room. Just as she stepped back into the bar area, she saw Andy. Nervous ripples skittered up her spine and the hair on her arms stood up. Part of her wanted him to notice her and the other, more rational part wanted to hide from him.

He stood with a group of three men laughing, his back partially turned toward where she stood. She made her way back to her seat which, as Sarah had promised, was still empty. Her bottle was empty though and ready for another.

Just as Sarah was bringing her one, she felt a presence close behind her and she instinctively knew it was Andy.

"Hey there. Remember me?"

Carrie didn't turn around, only nodded. "I do."

Andy slid in between Carrie and the stool next to her. She could smell his cologne and her body responded against her will. She looked up and smiled.

"How about a dance?"

Carrie sat studying Andy's face. He was handsome. His eyes were blue, a light blue that seemed unnatural. His face was tanned from the sun and was showing some signs of wear. She could tell he worked outside, but it added to his allure. He had a pierced ear, but no earring. A regretful rebellious moment as a teen she guessed.

She smiled and reached out to take his hand. The music filling the room had transitioned to a slower song and Andy pulled Carrie close. She could feel his toned and muscular body underneath his starched shirt. It all nearly made her weak in the knees.

The beer had vanquished her inhibitions, so she leaned into him and laid her head on his shoulder. He was about eight inches taller than she was, and she fit just right. When she closed her eyes, she didn't see Billy. She saw herself enjoying this man with abandon, knowing that was where the night would end.

Andy could feel Carrie responding to him, so he moved his hand along her back and onto her bottom, his hand resting there, pulling her in. The slow song had only lasted long enough to tease them both into a precursor to passion.

Carrie didn't want to let go, but the song was over. She needed this man tonight. It wasn't an emotional need, but a base physical need without thought or feeling. Emotions had only served to wear her down and she couldn't bear the weight any longer. Still holding him close, she looked up to his face and said, "Come home with me."

Andy smiled and gave a slight nod. Carrie moved to the bar to pay her tab with Andy in tow. Sarah gave a slight smile but said nothing. It was not her place to do so.

Carrie insisted she was fine to drive, but Andy had arrived late and had only had one beer, so he drove them both to her place. Once they were just inside the front door, their hunger which had only intensified with the wait, burst forth and clothes ripped and dropped onto the bare floor.

In the midst of a deep kiss, Andy picked Carrie up and she wrapped her legs around him. They bumped and stumbled their way to Carrie's unmade bed and fell onto it.

They quickly satiated each other's need, then collapsed breathless in each other's arms. Carrie looked at Andy in the dim light. She had been correct in her assessment of his fitness earlier at the bar. She ran her hand down his hard chest and taught muscular stomach, and her fire flared yet again.

Andy rolled over to her and held her wrist in his hand. "In a bit." He kissed her fingers one by one and tucked her hand under his jaw.

They lay there in the quiet looking at each other. Nothing was said, only unspoken communication. Just looking, gauging each other, and learning the rhythms of their temperament.

Andy let go of Carrie's wrist and enveloped her in his arms, pulling her close. He could sense what she needed most, and it wasn't more passionate physicality. No, he knew... could sense, that more than anything else, she needed to be held.

Outside the night was pitch dark. The only light seen from where Billy sat in his car was the small bedroom lamp that Carrie often kept on.

She hadn't answered her phone, and he had had no idea where she was, maybe working late. So, he had decided to drop by her house and wait for her, surprise her. He had bought her a bouquet of red roses, and two tickets for next month to a concert to see her favorite band.

The longer he had waited, the more anxious he had become. But he loved her, and he wanted her to know that he would wait for her as long as she needed. He regretted the wash of disappointment he had experienced the other night when her choice had been to wait. He knew she needed time, but he had hoped nonetheless.

He had been sitting in his car across the street for over an hour when the new F-150 pulled into her driveway and out stepped Carrie and another man. He had also seen the fire of passion that raged between them as they had gone to her bedroom and then expressed that passion.

Billy was shocked by what he had seen, and then became so broken he couldn't move. Once the shock had worn off, he became furious, then he crumbled and died right then and there. He should have driven home then, but he felt so completely devastated that he couldn't even move to start his car.

Finally, he could sit no longer. He started his car and drove down the dark street with tears silently escaping down his face. There was no mending this now. There was no going back.

The five remaining attendees sat in the private study of Dr. Micah Severs. They were nestled in an overstuffed brown leather sofa and chairs, nursing expensive whiskey and cigars, that is all except Dr. Jill Bates. She did indulge in the whiskey, but could barely abide sitting in a closed room with the cigar smoke, much less actually smoking one.

The room was a miniature version of the much larger great room where the meeting had been held. It was Dr. Severs private office and study. The walls were richly paneled in walnut wood and nearly wall to wall bookcases filled with a vast array of books on all topics.

The room always smelled of expensive cigars. It was an indulgence that Dr. Severs unapologetically experienced every day. The room was also designed with inconspicuous speakers which allowed his extensive collection of classical music to flow, creating a feeling of being immersed in music no matter what part of the room one were in. At that moment, Adagio for Strings by the London Philharmonic was playing. A soothing rich compilation that was perfect for rest and contemplation.

No one spoke for several minutes while they reveled in

their elements. The men were taking deep breaths of the cigars and then slowly releasing the smoke above themselves at an angle. They would often look at the object of their pleasure, holding the cigar first one way, and then another as if admiring the plump brown sausages.

The five of them routinely met after the meetings. They had been colleagues for many years and enjoyed each other's company. A couple of other professors had come and gone through the years, but this was the core group and that had remained steady in attendance and friendship.

"The meeting went well, don't you think?" asked Dr. Bates as she fanned the smoke from her face.

The others were deep in thought. Eventually, a nodding consensus was achieved. "What did you make of that OSBI agent attending?" asked Jim Blankenship.

"Oh, I invited him," replied Dr. Randolph. "He came about when investigating the death of a student."

"Yes. Yes. I've heard of those suspicious deaths. Rumors or facts. Which is it?" asked Jim.

The occupants of the room were slow to respond. Some made inconspicuous eye contact, which Jim noticed immediately.

Upon noticing, he leaned forward placing his arms on his thighs. "I can see something more is going on here. Are you involved in the deaths?" His voice was incredulous.

"No, no. Not at all." Dr. Randolph was quick to respond, making a symbolic wave of his hand as if to dispel the suspicion. Almost too quick and fervent in his response.

"Well, what is it? Do you know something about who is doing this?" Jim persisted.

"Honestly, we don't know," began Dr. Bates. "It is suspect that the rituals have been discussed in one or more of our classes. We don't know who is behind it all, but there is a possibility that they have attended one or more of our classes."

"A student you think?"

"We really don't know." Dr. Randolph was once again quick to interject.

Jim looked from first one to the other attempting to gauge their demeanor. He could tell there was more that they weren't saying, but wasn't sure how far to probe. It was probably wise that he keep his distance.

The lack of discussion in the room hung heavy in the air. No one knew how to segue from the awkward conversation to something more benign.

Suddenly, a muffled noise just outside their window caught everyone's attention. When there was no follow up noise, they relaxed back down into their whiskey glasses.

"What will be the topic of our next meeting? Dr. Gravenue is an excellent speaker. I am looking forward to hearing her once again," said Dr. Reynolds.

"I believe she will be discussing how religion has evolved socially throughout the classic and postclassic eras of Pre-Columbian America," said Dr. Randolph.

"That sounds intriguing. Is that her specialty?" asked Dr. Bates.

"I'm not really sure. I believe it is a recent fascination of hers."

They sipped their whiskey slow. They all knew they had to drive home, and yet none were in any hurry to leave.

A tap at the door interrupted their thoughts. "Yes?" Dr. Severs responded.

The double-doors opened to reveal his grad student Mark Plainer. "Everything is tidied up. Is there anything else that you need me to do before I go?"

There was something in Mark's eyes, but Dr. Severs wasn't sure how to interpret it and hesitated to inquire while in the presence of the other professors.

"No. That will be fine. Can you give me a call in the morning so that we can make arrangements for next week?"

"Yes, that will be fine. Around ten?" A bead of sweat inched its way down Marks hairline. He was eager to leave.

"Yes. Ten will be perfect."

As Mark turned to go, Dr. Severs thought of something. "Oh, Mark."

Mark turned back to Dr. Severs. "Yes?"

"There was a loud noise outside just a bit ago. You don't have any idea what it was do you?"

Mark remained stone faced and attempted to feign ignorance. "Why no. I didn't hear anything out there. What did it sound like?"

"Oh, I don't know. Just a loud bump of sorts. Probably just some animal out prowling."

"Yes, that is probably what it was."

Sandy hadn't stayed long at Randy's house. He had said not to wait up for him and she knew she could use the time to grade papers and enjoy a night of what Randy called, 'girl TV.'

When eleven o'clock rolled around, she began to watch the phone. *He should have called by now.* The papers had long since been graded. It was easy with kindergarten. They were letter formation pages and crayon drawings of birds. She had been snuggled in her bed with a glass of wine since nine-thirty.

Watching one of her favorite movies had distracted her from the fact that Randy had not yet called. Then, as the movie began rolling the credits, Sandy was reminded of the time.

He had promised he would call, so she did her best to not be a worrywart and call him. She picked up the novel off of her night-stand that she was well into and resumed her reading. It was difficult to focus however, because her mind kept drifting to Randy. After reading the same paragraph three times, she popped the book shut and swung her legs over the side of the bed.

As she tipped the wine bottle to drain out the last drops of liquid, she realized she was physically frowning. Her frustration compelled her to tip her glass straight up, draining the last of the wine.

Back in the kitchen, she sat the glass into the sink and paced the floor. *I have to call. Something is wrong. I just know it.* The silence in the house was unnerving and reinforced her fear. She walked over and blew out a candle she had left burning. The pungent change from floral scent to burnt cotton prickled her nose.

She could wait no more. Her fingers flew across the

phone keypad, and she nervously twisted the phone cord while waiting. Each unanswered ring created a greater sense of urgency within her. When the call ended, she pressed the hangup switch and redialed. Before a third attempt, she retrieved another bottle of wine and poured yet another glass.

As she paced her living room with one arm wrapped around her middle and the other holding her wine, her thoughts began to spiral out of control. It was too late to call her parents. They would have been in bed since nine.

She could call Bracket, but was it really necessary? Carrie was another choice, but she didn't know Carrie well enough to call her, even if she had her number. Finally exasperated, she dropped down onto her sofa. She tipped her glass, draining it once again, and laid over on the sofa to rest her eyes for a bit. She pulled the throw she kept on the sofa up over herself, and soon drifted off to sleep.

Waking with a start the next morning as the sun came up, she realized she had slept on the sofa all night long. Her body was rebelling from the awkward position in which it had laid during the night while barely moving. She had also been tormented in her sleep from the alcohol-induced dreams.

Her head was throbbing so hard that she felt she could hear each and every throb as if it were a banging gong. Sitting on the edge of the sofa, she cradled her head in her hands. She looked up and over at her answering machine. There was no blinking light and tears slipped down her cheeks. Where could he be?

Sandy shuffled to the kitchen and located the ibuprofen. She poured out three capsules into her hand and downed them with a glass of water. She forced herself to drink the entire glass knowing it would help her recover quicker.

It was time to call Randy once more and if he didn't answer, then she would call Bracket. She dialed the familiar numbers and waited. Crestfallen, she pressed the hangup button and dialed Bracket's number from the emergency list she kept by the phone.

A woman answered the phone, who Sandy knew to be Bracket's wife Diane. Bracket was soon on the line and Sandy instantly broke into tears. "Randy didn't come home last night after the meeting."

Sandy's words brought Bracket to high alert, but he was slow to respond. There could be a thousand reasons why he had not yet contacted Sandy. "Now, now. It's okay. There is probably a very good reason you haven't heard from him. You don't sound well. Did you get any sleep last night?"

"Yes, some." Sandy sniffed. "I think I drank too much wine and then I fell asleep on the sofa. I feel pretty rough."

"Okay. Well then, you need to go take a long hot shower and you will feel better. Once you've done that, fix yourself some breakfast. That will help. I promise. Then rest if you can. I will follow up and see if I can find out why you haven't heard from Randy."

Sandy knew she couldn't stomach breakfast, but Bracket was right that a shower would feel good. "Okay. Do you promise to call me as soon as you know anything?"

"I promise. I'm sure he just stayed there late and then fell asleep as soon as he got home."

The sobs started all over again. "He always, and I mean always calls me when he has been out late."

"Okay. Calm down. I know it is just something silly that we will all laugh about later. Please take care of yourself and get a shower and some food in you. I'll call you soon."

As soon as Bracket hung up the phone, he looked at Diane. "Something is wrong. Randy went to a meeting last night of college professors and other academics, and Sandy has not heard from him since."

Bracket was hurrying around to ready himself to leave. "I'm going over to Randy's house now to see if he is there. Then I'll contact Carrie just in case he contacted her and she knows anything. If he is at the house there is no reason to alarm Carrie."

Diane's face was filled with concern. Randy was one of the most stable and predictable agents John had. If he hadn't called Sandy, then something was surely wrong.

"Keep me posted?"

Bracket pecked Diane on the cheek. "Yes. I'll keep you posted."

Chapter Seventeen

Carrie's night had been filled with emotional breakthrough, but not in a good way. She had allowed her body to lead her and drive the night. And she had known that crossing that line was the end of her emotional wavering over Billy.

Whether she loved him or not was irrelevant now; she had severed any emotional tie she had with him, and she wondered if she had done this on purpose. Hurt him first in such a devastating way that he would never want her again, which would end her continual wavering.

But she hadn't done it on purpose. It had all been an unconscious defensive maneuver ushered in by her inebriated mental state. And the morning light questioned her. The morning's clear mental focus had returned only to show her as the despicable person she felt she was. She was ashamed, but was hardened to shame's regret. Her resolve refused to regret it.

Andy lay sleeping beside her, and she smiled thinking of what a considerate partner he had been in bed. The air was still filled with the smell of physical passion and release.

Her thoughts of Andy and the previous night were suddenly interrupted by her phone. She rolled over to her nightstand and answered the little blue Blackberry.

"Carrie," it was Bracket. His voice carried alarm across the line.

"I received a call this morning from Sandy. She said Randy never came home after the academic meeting last night. I drove over to his house to see if maybe he was home and had just fallen asleep or something before calling Sandy. But his car isn't there and there is no answer to his door.

"Have you heard from him? I thought maybe he had let you know more about what he was doing."

Carrie tried to assimilate the information from Bracket, along with trying to recall the exact words that Randy had said to her before leaving work. "The only thing he said was that he was going to go to the meeting and check it all out. It is a monthly meeting for anyone interested in those academic subjects. It appeared that anyone interested was invited. They had brochures and everything. I thought it was purely harmless."

Carrie was standing and holding the phone under her chin while pulling her robe on. Andy was now awake and also dressing. "What do you need me to do?" Carrie asked.

"Meet me at the office and we will get a game plan together. I'll call OKCPD and let them know we have an agent missing."

"Will do."

Carrie turned to see Andy half-dressed and searching for his remaining clothes. "Sounds like you have something urgent to attend to. I just realized I know nothing about you, like what you do for a living."

"I am an investigative agent for the Oklahoma State Bureau of Investigation. I just started a few weeks ago. Before that I was a patrol officer for the OKCPD. My partner is missing and my boss needs me to meet him at our offices to develop a plan."

Andy smiled. "It fits you. I sensed that last night may have caught you off guard, but I would like to see you again. Not just for this," Andy motioned his full hands toward the bed. "I'd like to get to know you better."

Carrie saw hope in Andy's eyes and felt herself shut down in response. She couldn't deal with anyone else's hope. Not right now anyway, when she had no hope of her own. "Andy..." Carrie began while nervously fidgeting with her robe tie.

"I get it. I'm sorry. No worries." Andy looked away and began frantically gathering his things and dressing.

"I really am sorry. Really, I am." Carrie felt bad about having brushed him off so quickly. "I would like to see you again too... sometime. Maybe just to talk. You don't know me and what I have been going through. If you knew, it might change your mind about me."

Andy, finally dressed, looked at Carrie. "It really is fine. I would like some time to just talk and get to know you. I doubt anything you have to tell me will change my mind about you, though." Andy smiled.

As he turned to go, a glint of sunlight ricocheting from a

small shiny object in a dish on the end of Carrie's dresser stabbed him in the eye. He stopped and reached down to pick it up. An engagement ring. Beautiful and expensive, and barely worn. He stood with the ring in his fingers, and gently laid it back down in the dish.

He looked over at Carrie with a sad smile, tipped his hat and left. Maybe she was right. Maybe he wouldn't like her if he knew her better.

Andy was halfway down the street when Carrie realized that her car was still at the bar. She could have done without the morning drama and chided herself for what she had allowed to happen the previous evening.

She dressed furiously, which mirrored her internal struggle, all the while thinking of Randy and wondering what could have happened. Soon, a taxi dropped her off at her car and she was quickly on her way to the office. Bracket was there waiting for her.

"I have the file. Can you help me understand who might have been at the meeting last night? We can begin calling them to see if he even made it to the meeting. There were no alerts on his car or accidents that could be him. Nothing at the hospitals either."

Carrie took the file from Bracket and turned to the list of university professors they had been in contact with. "I don't know if all of these professors would be in attendance at the meeting. I know that Dr. Randolph is the one who invited Randy. I think that maybe Dr. Bates would have been there too. Other than that, Dr. Pinning is in pharmacology at OU and Dr. Reynolds is in entomology at UCO.

"The meeting seemed to be more about sociology, history,

anthropology and such things. I don't know if those other two things fit or would be of interest to them." Carrie looked up at Bracket. He nodded.

"I'll call Reynolds, you call Bates."

"Dr. Reynolds, this is Special Agent in Charge John Bracket with the OSBI. I have an agent who possibly attended a meeting you invited him to last night. He has not come home. I wanted to confirm that he did indeed attend the meeting."

Dr. Reynolds paused before answering. This sounded serious and he didn't want to say anything that would lead the agent to believe he had anything to do with his missing agent. "Yes, he did attend the meeting and was there for the entire presentation. I stayed later with a few of my colleagues to have a drink and a cigar. There were no other cars there when we all left."

"Can you give me the names of the others who were in attendance?"

"Well..."

"Also, where did this meeting take place?" Bracket's demeanor was clear that he wanted cooperation, and quick.

Dr. Reynolds gave him the address of Dr. Severs' house, where the meeting was held, and the names and phone numbers of those he knew.

At her desk, Carrie was talking with Dr. Bates. "So, Randy did make it to the meeting. How was he? Did he seem fine?"

"I don't know him except for our one meeting, but he seemed fine. Seemed interested. He stayed until the end."

"Did you see him talking with anyone else there?"

"I wasn't watching him the whole time. I did see him talk to Dr. Reynolds, but honestly I don't remember anyone else."

"I need a list of all the names and phone numbers of those in attendance. I know a group like that keeps a record of attendance. And I need the address of the meeting."

Dr. Bates began to object, but Carrie made it clear that with a missing agent, she did not have a choice.

Upon hanging up her phone, Carrie looked up to see Bracket coming her way. "I have a short list of people that Dr. Reynolds knew that attended the meeting along with the address where it was held."

"Well, I hate to one-up my boss, but I have the entire list of attendees from last night. Dr. Bates just emailed it to me." Carrie looked up at Bracket hoping he would be pleased, and he was.

"We need to go through the list and do interviews, but I believe we need more to go on. You and I will go to the address where the meeting was held." Bracket paused to look down at his notes. "The home of a Dr. Micah Severs. He is a professor of sociology at UCO. We'll tackle the list later today."

Carrie stood and gathered her things, preparing to walk out with Bracket while he phoned Rick.

In just five minutes, Bracket and Carrie were in his SUV headed toward the northeast side of Edmond.

Carrie and Bracket pulled up to the massive private gate of the home of Dr. Micah Severs. Bracket rolled down his driver's side window and pressed the call button. It was nine a.m. and someone should surely be awake. But even if they weren't, it didn't matter, Bracket would keep pressing the button until someone answered.

A cool breeze drifted through the open window and Carrie shivered. The organic smell of dried leaves and earth carried on the breeze. It was still early enough in the spring that the mornings were quite cool, and she regretted rushing out of the house without her heavier jacket. She wrapped her arms around herself and rubbed her upper arms, hoping the friction would generate some warmth.

Finally, after several attempts on the call button, a groggy sounding man answered. "Yes?"

"This is John Bracket. I am special agent in charge of the OSBI. I need you to open the gate so I can come in and speak with you."

"What is this about?"

"One of our agents, Randy Jeffries, attended a meeting here last night and did not return home. Open the gate so that we can come in and speak with you."

No answer came across the speaker, but in just a few moments the ornate metal gate split in half and began to slowly open inwardly. Before them was a long wide driveway leading to a large and beautiful home. Carrie's mouth hung open. Not even the homes in the neighborhood she had recently visited with Randy compared to this one.

Bracket had raised the window and Carrie was beginning to warm again. They pulled into the large round drive and stopped in front of the substantial double front doors.

Carrie stepped out of the SUV and began stepping up

the semi-circular stone steps that led to a shallow portico over the front door. The sporadic breeze whipped up and once again chilled Carrie to the bone. She shivered and her arms responded with pimpled skin.

She deferred to Bracket and stepped aside as he rang the bell, taking note that there was a security camera to allow residents to see who was at the door.

When the bell was not immediately answered, Bracket balled one of his meaty fists and banged abruptly on the door. Before he could bang again, a latch clicked and the door slid open and inward.

Bracket stepped into the large foyer and was face to face with Dr. Micah Severs. He was dressed in slacks, a white undershirt and a silk dressing gown in deep red and black.

The first thing that Carrie noticed about the man, other than what he was wearing, was how much shorter he was than Bracket. Granted, Bracket was six feet two inches tall, but she had never seen him next to a much short man like Dr. Severs, whom she guessed was around five foot eight.

Dr. Severs was reading the wallet badge that Bracket had held out for him to read, then nodded and motioned for them to follow him to a side room. He pressed a button, and the tall draperies hummed to an open position revealing the dappled light from the morning sun, which was fighting its way through the trees.

"Please have a seat." He motioned for the agents to have a seat on the sofa facing the newly revealed window. He sat to the side in an artfully done brocade chair in a soft peach and coral pattern.

The agents sat near the edge of the seat unwilling to

appear casual in their purpose. Bracket flipped out a small notebook, not unlike the one Randy always carried. He also pulled out a department photo of Randy and held it up for Dr. Severs to see.

"This is Randy Jeffries. He is one of our agents and attended a meeting here last night. He did not arrive home and his car has not been located. What can you tell me about the meeting last night, and what you remember about Agent Jeffries." Bracket's pen was poised to write.

Dr. Severs tossed his hands out as his elbows rested on the arms of the chair. "I only briefly met the man. Dr. Randolph introduced us, but then I needed to speak to other guests, so I left them. That is the only interaction I had with him."

"Did you see him leave?"

"No," he said with a slight shake of his head. "There were about twenty or thirty guests here last night."

"Twenty-eight to be exact." Carrie interjected, then sheepishly deferred once again to Bracket who smiled over at her and gave her a wink.

"Please continue."

"Well, with that many guests leaving, it is hard to notice who went at what time. For the most part, they all left at about the same time."

"For the most part..."

"Well, there were a few of us who retired back to my private smoking room. We have been close colleagues for years and always enjoy a drink and a smoke after the meetings."

"Who were those who stayed behind with you?"

Dr. Severs gave him the names of the remaining guests, their professional designations, and the universities where they worked.

Carrie peered over at the names. She knew a couple, but there were also a few, she was not familiar with, Dr. Severs being one.

"So, tell me what this meeting was all about."

"We have a monthly academic meeting in the sociological and anthropological studies, but there are others in various studies that enjoy it as well. Such as Dr. Reynolds, whose specialty is in entomology. He attends occasionally. Each month we have a speaker that gives us a talk on something new they have learned or discovered, or have developed a particular interest in.

"Some months it is an oration from the speaker, and some months it is more of a Q and A where the speaker welcomes audience interaction. Last night was a talk from Professor Jim Blankenship. He is a professor of sociology at OU."

"What did he speak on?"

"The relationship between culture and the structure of welfare recipients. It was quite enlightening."

"Did you notice anything unusual about last night? Anyone you did not know? Any confrontation? Anything abnormal at all?"

Dr. Severs was shaking his head as he thought. "No. Not anything that I can recall. Might you indulge me for a moment, Agent Bracket? What was your agent investigating here at our meeting? I'm sure he wasn't here for purely pleasure."

"I would expect you have heard about the recent deaths

of young college age men. Deaths in very suspicious circumstances. They seem to be related to ancient rituals. When Agent Jeffries and Agent Border," Bracket's hand indicated Carrie, "spoke with Dr. Randolph, he gave Agent Jeffries a pamphlet regarding your group and invited him to attend."

"I see."

"What do you and your colleagues discuss, or more importantly, what did you discuss last night in your private meeting?"

"Nothing of any consequence. It is usually just a time to enjoy good whiskey and fine cigars. We sometimes reflect on our opinions of the evening's speaker, sometimes not. It is a very casual relaxing respite from the week."

"Were you the only ones in the home at the time?"

Dr. Severs didn't respond immediately. His eyes darted back and forth in their sockets. Both Carrie and Bracket noticed his indecision. "Well." Bracket insisted.

"My graduate assistant was here. He comes to help set up and clear away after the meetings."

"What is him name?"

"Mark Plainer."

"I'll need his contact information."

"Yes. Yes. Of course." Dr. Severs voice was soft as he spoke. He got up to go get the information that was needed.

Bracket looked over at Carrie. "Did you notice anything strange about him just then?"

"Yes. He didn't want to tell us about his assistant, and he sure didn't want to give us his information."

"He's worried about something. It could be nothing, but it could be everything."

Dr. Severs returned with a small slip of notepaper with Mark Plainer's name and number on it.

Bracket stood and took the paper from Dr. Severs' hand. "Now we need to look around your house on the inside and the outside."

Alarm struck Dr. Severs. "Not at all! You must have a warrant."

Bracket's face moved into a half smile with a glint in his eye. "We will wait."

He sat back down and made a phone call on his new mobile device. "Yes, this is SAC John Bracket with the OSBI. I am in urgent need of a search warrant. We have a missing agent and we are currently at his last known location. I will send you the details via email and then if you could respond the same, I will wait here."

Bracket looked up at a worried Dr. Severs. His attempts to look calm and confident had long since vanished. The depths of his flustered state rendered him speechless.

From an adjoining room, a woman they assumed to be Mrs. Severs, peeked through the door. "Mark is on the phone for you. He said you had an appointment to talk with him this morning."

"Can you please tell him I will call him back?"

Bracket's half smile spread across his face, and he gestured to the chair that Dr. Severs had been seated in. "Why don't you have a seat while we wait for our search warrant.

With such a large house and surrounding property to search, it took most of the day. Bracket had called for a forensic team of six to come and help. Bracket and Carrie began their search in the office.

After about an hour of searching through reams of papers, they had found nothing leading to any suspicious behavior. Carrie plopped a handful of documents down onto the desk in exasperation. "I feel like there is so much we need to go through, that we may miss something important that is too small to notice."

Bracket nodded without looking up. He too was exasperated, but knew that these types of searches had to be done meticulously while maintaining a keen eye. "I know that it feels like we aren't making any progress. But you need to be alert, knowing that at any moment some seemingly small item can break everything loose. Don't get frustrated, that will only hinder your focus.

They continued to work in the office, searching each desk drawer and file drawer in the credenza. Bracket felt along the inside of each drawer and underneath the desk for a trigger which might reveal a hidden compartment or drawer.

Carrie left the desk with its mounds of paperwork and began to examine the perimeter of the room which was flanked by massive bookcases. She let her gloved hand drift over the books, many of which were leather bound.

Some titles she recognized from mandatory reading in college, and others she had never heard of. "Do you think there is something hidden behind a bookcase?" Carrie asked Bracket spurred by his meticulous search of the desk.

He stopped reading through the document in his hand

and looked over to where Carrie stood. "Possibly, but we can see where the two walls of windows are and know that the cases are not deep enough for that. That wall where you are standing has the large great room on the other side. The only ones that could hide something are on that wall there." He gestured to the wall with no windows or doors.

Carrie walked over to it and Bracket went back to reviewing paperwork. She moved along the wall searching as thoroughly as she possibly could to find any indication of a false doorway or a trigger to open a bookcase.

She popped out books at eye level and then slid them back in. None seemed to be a lever disguised as a book. The search revealed nothing and she stood looking, still not convinced that there wasn't more to find.

"We've done a lot in here. Let's go outside and check the perimeter of the house. That will give us a break," said Bracket as he placed the last of the documents on the desk.

Bracket and Carrie stepped out of the front door and stood surveying the massive driveway. The circle portion of the drive could accommodate two cars side by side, and possibly eight in total. The side driveway was equally as wide and long enough to accommodate six to eight vehicles.

"They are certainly set up for parties," Carrie observed.

"Yes they are. Let's start by making a tight loop around the house. Then we can move out and make a larger loop."

When they came to the back window on the side where Randy had been attempting to peer into the window, the flowerbed was obviously disturbed. Carrie squatted down and gently used a gloved hand to move dormant plants from side to side.

"Bracket, look here." Her blood pressure spiked when she saw what she thought was a minuscule drop of blood on one of the plants.

Bracket bend down and looked. "Hmmm. Could be. Let's bag it. Clip the entire stem that drop is on. It is a rosebush and that may be old blood where someone pricked themselves on a thorn."

Carrie carefully retrieved the branch. Pulling it to her face for a closer look, she observed what she thought was fresh blood. "It could be old, but look." She stood and held the branch closer for Bracket to see.

"Yes, it does look fresh," Bracket agreed. "Let's keep looking."

Just past the house and slightly down the hill in back, there was a storage building that matched the house.

"I know you want us to keep making a perimeter of the house, but I am dying to check out that building." Carrie looked at Bracket, hoping he would also be anxious to do the same.

He smiled and nodded. "Let's go. Keep a watch along the way for anything we can use."

The grass was still dormant from winter, but some new shoots of green were pressing their way through. "There are footstep depressions. But that doesn't really mean anything. Anyone going to the building would leave footprints." Carrie again deferred to Bracket for instruction.

"Take a photo. They aren't deep enough for a mold. Really just a disturbance of the debris and old grass. But I don't want to discount it."

Carrie wanted to run to the out building, but she knew

that being thorough might be the thing that could save Randy's life, if it were even in danger.

Carrie took the camera she had remembered to sling around her neck and adjusted it for outdoor photography. She took an adequate number of photos from various angles using the ruler for scale.

A twenty-minute walk of careful observation and debris gathering brought them to the door of the building. Carrie reached out and attempted to turn the knob. "It's locked." She looked up at Bracket for direction.

Bracket pressed the button on his radio and sent word to the lead tech in the house. "I need the key to the building out back. Can you get it and bring it to me? Thanks."

While they waited, Carrie and Bracket carefully made their way around the building, peering into the windows as they went. It was dark inside and the well-built structure prevailed against random slivers of light as an old structure might not have done.

Carrie tapped loudly on a window, black with lack of light. "Randy, are you in there?"

There was no answer or sound, and yet she tried again.

A tech soon brought Bracket the key and he quickly unlocked the door. Once just inside the door, he flipped on the interior light to reveal storage of lawn and garden equipment, tubs of Christmas decor, and other stored but rarely needed items.

Bracket and Carrie looked carefully around the room, but didn't delve deep. The room was covered in a slight layer of dust that showed no disturbance. "No one has been in here for a while," said Bracket. He finally shut the door behind them as they exited and relocked the door.

Both stood in front of the small building looking back towards the huge home. From the lower vantage point, the home appeared even more imposing.

Carrie felt a knot in her stomach and rubbed it absentmindedly. Noticing the anxiety on her face, Bracket reached out and patted her on the shoulder. "We'll find him. We won't stop looking."

They made their way carefully back to the point where they had found the drop of blood and resumed their detailed search of the home's perimeter. After two hours, they had circled the home twice. They had done both the tight and wide search perimeters and found nothing beyond the small drop of blood.

Re-entering the home, they snapped off their old gloves and donned new ones. They were met in the foyer by the lead tech. "We found something that I'd like you to come look at." He turned as he talked, and walked back towards the rear of the house.

Near the large great room, he turned towards the kitchen and stopped at an open door in the hallway that led to a basement. They followed the tech down the steps to find a labyrinth of various types of rooms. Many were storage rooms.

There was a workbench with carpentry tools in one room. In another was a small apartment suite that didn't appear to have been used since it was built.

But there was one room near the back of the basement that had a deadbolt. "I've retrieved the key from the owner, but haven't entered yet. I thought you might want to be the one to make initial entrance into a locked basement door." The tech smiled at Bracket whom he had known and worked with for many years.

He turned the key in the deadbolt which held no resistance, then stepped back allowing Bracket to make entrance. The knob slid easily and the door glided open.

At first the room was totally black except for the small bit of light that encroached from the room behind them. Bracket flipped on the light and stood as the fluorescent lights buzzed and flickered to life. As the flickering lights held steady, Bracket and Carrie stood looking at the room before them, neither one saying a word.

Chapter Eighteen

"What in the hell are we going to do with him?" Jonathan Park was livid. These fools had not thought this through.

The three of them stood around. They knew they had crossed a line and had no idea what to do about it.

"Why did you take him?"

"He was looking in at our profs. I didn't want him exposing anything they might be involved in," said Mark Plainer.

"We don't even know for sure that they are behind the rituals." Jonathan looked down at the unconscious OSBI agent and he felt nauseous. "Although, it seems likely that they are. But it isn't our job to protect them." He looked back at Mark and Rodney Grapple.

"If we let him go, we will be charged with assault and kidnapping." Rodney fidgeted and rocked from one foot to the other.

"So, what... we murder him? This is an impossible spot you have put us in." Jonathan turned and began pacing the floor. His mind was searching and discarding one random idea after another.

"No one knows we did this. We can take him out somewhere while he is still unconscious and leave him. He didn't see us." Mark was hopeful.

Jonathan sat down on an old cinder block to think. He held his head in his hands. "The further we go into this, the more dire the consequences if we are caught."

"If... we are caught." Mark nudged.

Randy could feel the scratchy substance that felt like hay under his cheek long before his stiff and sore body could manage to open his eyes. Voices drifted in like a dream. *That's it*, he decided, *I'm dreaming about the case.* Randy faded back off into the darkness.

"He's going to wake up soon. We have to make a decision." Rodney was getting more anxious by the second.

Jonathan was the unofficial leader of the little clan of grad students. He had to think of something quick.

"What if we tell our profs. They can help us." Jonathan spun around to look at Rodney.

"You've lost your mind. If they are involved, we will be complicit in their mess of rituals and deaths. If they are not involved, we will get expelled at best, and they could very well turn us over to the authorities. We can't take that chance!" Jonathan was nearly screaming by the time he was done.

"We have to make sure he stays out. We have to put something over his head so he can't see us."

Mark hurried to look for something to put over Randy's head, but could find nothing. "I'll go get a pillowcase and some NyQuil to keep him asleep."

"Hurry."

Mark drove off to the nearest Walmart. He wanted to get a new pillowcase so their DNA wouldn't be on it. He grabbed the first package he came to and hurried across the store to get the NyQuil. He decided they needed zip ties too.

His heart was pounding and he was having trouble focusing. It seemed like it was taking him forever. As he was heading to the checkout stand, he rushed past an aisle with foam earplugs and grabbed a pack.

When he returned, Jonathan and Rodney were still standing over the agent. They made quick work of dosing Randy by dribbling the medicine slowly into the side of his mouth and then tilting his head slightly so it would drain back into his throat. They didn't want to choke him.

They were equally as careful pulling the brand new pillowcase out of the package. They knew better than to touch it, so Jonathan had put on a pair of gloves that were on the workbench in the barn. Before pulling the pillowcase down, he pushed the foam earplugs into Randy's ears.

Jonathan stood and pulled off the gloves and shoved them in his back pocket. His DNA would be on the inside and he didn't want them found. He would dispose of them somewhere else. "Now what?"

"I say we just take him and dump him way off somewhere. I can't be part of killing him." Rodney's face was tied in a knot with worry.

"I agree," said Mark.

Jonathan nodded. "Let's put him back in your car trunk and figure out where to go. Then the car has to get detailed, then messed up a bit so it doesn't look freshly cleaned." The other two nodded as they reached for Randy's legs. They were thankful that Jonathan had a level head. They were both beyond reason at this point.

"Mark, you drive his truck and follow us so that we can leave it somewhere out wherever we take him. Not close enough for him to easily find it, but nowhere near here."

They loaded Randy into the trunk without incident and were soon heading north along the country road outside the barn. "Where are we going?" Rodney asked.

"We have a full tank of gas and we are going to drive as far north and east out into the country as we can and find an isolated place to leave the truck. Then we are going to dump him somewhere else. When he wakes up, we will be long gone." Jonathan was hoping his plan would work.

They decided on an overly-wooded piece of land that was several miles down a dirt road after driving for an hour and a half. They drove on two-lane paved country roads, then located the winding dirt road. They all agreed that this was their best shot.

The bumping of the old roads, along with traveling up and down the roller-coaster type hills, had jostled Randy awake. His head hurt worse than anything he had ever experienced. He was extremely groggy as if he had been drugged and kept losing the battle of consciousness.

The trunk was small enough so that he was wedged in. His hands were tightly bound behind his back, and he couldn't remove the cloth over his head, nor the foam earplugs. He had no idea who had taken him or why.

When the trunk flew open and sunlight flooded in, Randy, having lost the battle to stay awake, was not aware of his surroundings. He moaned loudly as the three young men reached in to drag him out of the trunk.

"Shit, man. He's awake!" Rodney had once again lost his composure.

"Pull him out and lay him on the ground." Jonathan pulled on the old gloves and grabbed the bottle of NyQuil. He pushed the pillowcase up just enough to reveal Randy's mouth. "Hold him down."

Jonathan tilted Randy's head to the side and once again dribbled in the NyQuil. He stopped from time to time to allow the sedative to drain back down into their captive. He wanted to make sure that he slept for a good long time.

"Are you giving him too much?" Rodney asked. "Don't kill him."

"I'm not. He'll just sleep for a while."

When Jonathan was certain that he had given Randy enough, he capped the bottle and stood up. "Let's take him as far back in the woods as we can."

Randy was heavy and unwieldy, even with three of them. He was a limp burden to carry, which made him seem even heavier. The tangled brush underneath the thick trees made their progress that much more difficult.

"How far do we need to go?" Mark asked, half complaining, half asking.

"As far as we can." Jonathan didn't want to take any chances.

Finally, they were so deep into the dense woods that their progress was stilled and they rested Randy down in the brush. Jonathan felt around to see if they had missed anything earlier. Mark had removed Randy's phone, broken it, and hid the remains way back in the woods around the other side of Dr. Severs' property.

Only the agent's wallet and wallet badge remained. They would leave those in his truck. "Okay. We need to get rid of his truck now." Jonathan led the way back out of the woods.

"What if he doesn't wake up or is bit by a snake or something and dies?" Rodney worried aloud.

"Shut up! I'm sick of hearing you." Jonathan wanted to be done with this. He had been dragged into it and for some reason felt compelled to help these idiots. Why, he didn't know.

Jonathan turned Mark's car around and Mark followed in Randy's truck. They drove several more miles east and then south, still on old country roads in a remote area. After about thirty minutes, Jonathan found another old dirt road that looked rarely traveled and took it.

He pulled off to the side and instructed Mark to keep going and find the most hidden spot available, then to clean up any fingerprints or other such evidence so that it couldn't be traced to them.

Mark drove down the dirt road and then turned into a break in the trees that led to a small clearing. He didn't think anyone would see the truck from the dirt road. It was well hidden.

He frantically wiped down all that he could remember

touching, twice for good measure. By the time he walked back to Jonathan and Rodney, he was exhausted.

"We still need to wipe your car and get rid of the other pillowcase, NyQuil, and pack of earplugs." Jonathan got back behind the wheel of Mark's car. He turned the car towards Tulsa to finish the last steps.

By midnight, Mark's car had been thoroughly cleaned and they had new fast food wrappers and sacks in the floor-board, as well as a spilled Coke and chip crumbs. The car was now clean, but not too clean.

Bracket and Carrie stood in the doorway of a massive wine cellar. To calculate the number of bottles, it would take a Rhodes scholar. Both had set their minds to witness the key to their investigation at the opening of the door. Truthfully, they also hoped to see Randy held in there so they could rescue him and take him home.

But that was not to be the case. At that moment, after a day of hard searching, they felt disappointment draw exhaustion down upon them like a thick cloud.

"Well, we still need to search the room. Maybe, just maybe, there will be something here," commented Bracket with little excitement.

Carrie only nodded and moved forward. As with the building out back, a slight layer of dust covered everything. Rather than touch every bottle, Carrie walked slowly down the rows looking for any anomaly, anything out of place.

Not every slot was filled and it appeared that the wine

was organized strategically so that a sought-after bottle could easily be retrieved. There were two aisles with metal wine racks about six feet high, with bottle slots on both sides of the racks in the center.

The forensic team was called and they dusted the two random bottles that were found to have no dust on them. Everyone knew however, that they would only have the homeowner's prints on them.

It was late Saturday and when Bracket finally called it quits, they had nothing to show for their time except the small drop of blood. Carrie was not only disappointed, she was deeply concerned for Randy.

"What next?" she asked, furrows deep in her forehead.

Bracket looked down on their new agent. Her shoulders slumped from exhaustion and he knew she would be useless if she didn't take a break.

"Go home. You have to get some rest so that we can start fresh in the morning." He held up a finger as she started to object. "Rest for Randy's sake. He needs us both to be at our best. Otherwise, we will never be sharp enough to see and find what we need in order to find him."

Carrie knew he was right, but she didn't want to go home. She wanted to go find him. But where? Where on earth would she even start?

"Okay." She nodded and turned to go to their SUV. A breeze floated through the still dormant woods and the scent of decaying leaves drew Carrie's attention out beyond the house. Woods surrounded them everywhere and they had found no footpaths or prints at all.

The soft leather-like seat felt like heaven as she sank back into it. Her mind began to scold her for not going with him on Friday night. It would have kept her from making a colossal mistake with Andy, and she could have been there for Randy.

Her thoughts shifted for just a moment from Randy to her liaison with Andy. She felt shame in the light of day and hoped and prayed that Billy would never find out. She resolved to get her head on straight and be what Billy needed her to be. She hated that she wavered in her feelings for him, feeling love one moment and then nothing the next.

Bracket's door opened and shut with a thud. "I want you to promise me you will go home and rest." He gave her a stern father-like warning with his eyes, and Carrie nodded.

"I went out last night and didn't get much sleep. I am truly exhausted. I know I need to listen to you."

"Good. I am going to call Sandy and talk with her as soon as I get back to the office. She will be frantic by this point. It is a job I always dread, but feel is necessary for their sake. Diane went over to her house earlier today so she would have someone there with her. I've touched base with Diane a couple of times so that there would be something besides just abject silence all day. Getting no word at all is the worst kind of torture.

"I'm going to go home, eat, and get some rest myself. Then I will put a solid plan together so that we can hit the ground running in the morning." He looked over at Carrie. "Unless you feel like you need the day off. I will understand."

"Oh no. I will be there."

"Well, sleep in as long as you can and then come on in."

Carrie nodded and turned to look out her side window. After a few minutes she looked back at Bracket.

"Are all our cases like this? I came into OSBI on the tails of my own trauma, then was thrust into one of the most horrific cases I could have ever imagined. Now while we are still trying to stop bodies from falling, my first partner turns up missing. I have to admit, my mind is spinning."

Bracket looked over at Carrie. "Bad luck of the draw. No, we have many cases where the forensics are simple and lead directly to the perpetrators. Most criminals are just dumb, which makes it easy for us. Technology is growing every day and that is on our side.

"We'll get through this. We will find Randy and we will solve this case. Then you'll have time to take a breath and get more settled in."

Carrie continued to study Bracket's profile as they drove. She could tell he had been a very attractive man at one time, still was if you discounted his age, maybe mid-fifties.

But, Carrie could see the lines in his face and the tiredness that had settled into his eyes. Eating various fast food fare on the run and at his desk had expanded his waistline. She knew that no matter what he said, this job was and always would be very stressful.

The day had grown overcast and was reflective of their mood. As soon as they pulled into the parking lot, Carrie looked over at Bracket.

"Thank you."

His eyebrows shot up. "What for?"

"For everything. You are a good boss, and I just wanted you to know that I appreciate it."

Bracket smiled. "I know you are still getting your sea legs, but you are a good agent Carrie, and you will only get better with time. Now go home and get some rest."

Carrie's own car was cold from sitting all day, but the cold served to revive her just enough to make the drive home. The weather was turning, and it seemed like a late spring cold front was moving in.

As she drove, she scoured her mind for any trace of information that was there yet untethered to an actionable clue. She could find nothing. Nothing at all. She wished she had the case file at home so she could work on it that evening. Well, tomorrow would come soon enough.

Walking into her home, she felt its emptiness and her mind briefly went to Billy. She was too exhausted to call though. The drive from the far east of Edmond to the office and then home had allowed the day's remaining bit of adrenaline to seep out.

She dropped her keys in the bowl by the door and went to turn her heater back on. She needed to eat and when she opened the refrigerator door, she shivered. Nothing, as always. She resolved to do better about grocery shopping.

Warmth and comfort were her present priorities, so she changed into her comfy pjs and curled up on the sofa under a thick throw. Once again, her mind went... not to Randy, but to her own life.

The house felt colder and emptier than it ever had. It felt different somehow, but it wasn't anything she could put her finger on. Something in her life had changed that she herself wasn't even aware of, but she felt it, and it frightened her.

At ten p.m. she woke from a hard sleep on the sofa starving, so a pizza was called for and soon filled her stomach. If only it could fill her soul and the deep hollowness that resided there.

Carrie's bed had enveloped her thoroughly and had caused her to sleep until nine-thirty the next morning. At first waking it felt like any other day, but as her mind focused, she remembered. Randy was missing. That memory brought an instant surge of urgency and she was quickly up, showered, and dressed.

When she arrived at the office, the room of agents was buzzing, and Bracket was in his office. She instantly felt ashamed that it was her partner missing and she was walking in well past everyone else.

She tapped on Bracket's doorframe before entering. He was looking only slightly better than when she had last seen him.

"Excuse me if I am too forward, but it doesn't look like you took your own advice. Did you rest at all?"

Bracket sadly shook his head. "I slept for a while. Diane and I spent several hours with Sandy. She is understandably a wreck. We just couldn't bear to leave her. Finally, a friend of hers came over and was going to spend the night with her."

"I am sorry I came in so late. I slept without an alarm to wake me."

"No worries. I'm glad you did that. We may have a long haul in front of us and you will need to be at your best."

"Any news at all?"

"We did find his truck, but he wasn't in it. I have all our

available agents on various assignments that may help us locate him."

"Where was his car?" Carrie slid to the edge of the chair and rested her elbows on her thighs.

"Several miles north and east of Wellston. A very wooded area. Forensics are there now going over everything. They are going to load the truck and bring it back to UCO to put in their garage. That way they can thoroughly go over every inch."

"So..." Carrie pondered out loud. "Someone drove it way up northeast to get rid of the truck. They must have been followed by another car to bring them back. Is there any chance that they will find Randy up there unconscious or..." Carrie couldn't bring herself to say it.

"The county sheriff and his deputies are doing a grid search all over that area. But so far, there is no sign of him or anyone else at all. My guess is that it is just a dump site for his truck."

"What do you want me to do?"

"I have a list of all attendees for that meeting on Friday night. It includes several of those professors' grad students. Apparently, they are joined at the hip. They want their professors' approval so badly that they almost appear to be their lackeys." Bracket shook his head. "I'm tired and angry. I shouldn't be so derogatory."

He reached out and handed the list to Carrie. It was complete with addresses. "I want you to go out and interview each of them. Detective Jacobs will be going with you. Her partner Rick is away in Michigan. His father passed away over the weekend.

He is an only child and his mother is already gone. He will be handling all the funeral arrangements, his father's estate, and whatever else is needed to empty the house and get it on the market for sale. He has taken a three week leave of absence."

"Oh, wow. When will all the tragedy stop?" Carrie's voice was barely a whisper, but loud enough for Bracket to hear.

"Soon Carrie, soon."

Just then, a melodic voice tempered with respect greeted them. Carrie turned to see Detective Molly Jacobs enter the room. She was still caught off guard by her beauty. What on earth was she doing as a cop? She could be a model or an actress.

Carrie rose, smiled, and took Molly's outstretched hand. "Thank you so much for helping us with this. I'm so sorry to hear about Rick's father." Carrie could relate and she commiserated as the last few weeks rushed through her memories.

"I am more than happy to help in anyway I can." Molly's smile was genuine, and Carrie continued to marvel at this woman, an enigma to her.

"Yes, thank you Molly, very much," said Bracket. "This is urgent as one of our own is missing and, of course we assume, in danger. Carrie has a list of people that I want the two of you to interview. I trust both of you to be thorough and I want you to use your cop's intuition to read between the lines."

"Certainly."

Bracket had given Carrie two copies of the list and she handed one to Molly, who read over it carefully.

"I recognize a few of these names. None had anything to

contribute when Rick and I interviewed them earlier. Some were very stoic and some very nervous. We can look back at my notes before we approach them again."

Once in Carrie's SUV, Molly pulled her notebook out and thumbed back through the pages. She cross-referenced the list with her notes. "I'm going to put a star by the ones that I felt were hiding something at the time. They should be the easiest to get to talk, hopefully.

"Then we can work on the others. Some that seemed like they didn't know anything may have just been good at lying about it. Of course, your list does not completely correspond with our first list. This time we are interviewing only those that came to the meeting. It appears that the students who came were all grad students of the professors, and not just underclassmen."

"Yes. But I like your idea. If you've already talked to them, they may be more prone to break and tell us what we need to know."

"If you don't mind, let's go talk to Jason Anderson too. He isn't on the list, but he was the friend who invited Blain Griffiths to come to the ritual meeting. We tried to contact him, but were unable to reach him. We got busy with other aspects of another case we have and never followed up."

Carrie deferred to the more seasoned detective. She was thankful she didn't have to do these interviews on her own. She knew at some point she would easily be able to, but her confidence had been shattered and she now questioned everything, including her ability to be a good agent.

"It is Sunday. I would guess that most college students are home asleep from being out on Saturday night, unless of course they have to work or go to church. I don't want to call ahead. Let's just surprise him at home."

"Sounds good." Carrie pointed the SUV north on Broadway extension. She wanted to take the opportunity to ask Molly some questions, but didn't know if it was appropriate. She didn't want to appear nosey, but she was extremely curious about her.

Without looking up from the lists she was working on, Molly asked, "You seem a little edgy. What's up?"

"Uh... well..."

Molly looked up from the papers and over to Carrie.

"I am feeling a little subpar today. I feel like I should have been a better partner to Randy. And I was just wondering about you. I would love to know more about you and your path to becoming a detective."

Molly laughed. "Well, I've had quite the life." A momentary sadness settled in, but Molly quickly brushed it away. "How about we work hard to get through this list, then we can sit down for dinner and chat?"

"Sounds good. I don't mean to pry. There are so few female detectives and certainly not ones that are beautiful enough to be a model. I guess I just want to know why you chose to go into law enforcement."

"Well, the short answer is that my father was chief of police, and my mother worked in the police station. I was constantly surrounded by it. I grew up playing at the station. There is so much more that we can discuss later. But I suppose law enforcement is in my blood."

"Makes sense. Are your parents still alive?" Once again that momentary air of sadness tried to move in, but Molly refused to let it. She pondered the quickest way to honestly answer Carrie's question. "Yes, and no. My adoptive parents are. My birth mom died when I was six. I never knew my birth father."

"Oh, wow. I'm sorry." Carrie felt the sting of her own parents' death still so fresh in her heart and mind. It took her back to the life they had given her which was so precious to her now.

"My parents died just a few weeks ago." Carrie's voice was soft and thoughtful as if she were really speaking to herself.

"Yes, I was told. I'm so sorry you had to go through that. Are you doing okay?" Molly was genuinely concerned. Even after all the years since her birth mother had died, that memory still held a painful edge that was fresh every time it appeared.

"I honestly don't know. I guess overall I am coming through it. But I am probably not handling it as well as I should be."

"I know that everyone has probably told you this a million times, but give it more time. And reach out when you feel overwhelmed. Holding in the pain won't help you heal. You can always reach out to me." The look in Molly's eyes told Carrie that she could genuinely reach out to her.

"Thank you."

Molly smiled one of those engaging smiles and Carrie felt just a bit lighter. It had been a long time since she had had a close female friend and maybe, just maybe, this was the beginning of that very thing.

Chapter Nineteen

Jason Anderson shuffled to the door barefoot and bare chested. His hair was a messy mop and he squinted from the light as he looked at the women at his door. "What? You just woke me up."

"We need to speak with you. It's urgent and we won't take no for an answer."

Carrie was secretly amused at the fortitude of this woman, who to an onlooker, might appear outwardly soft. Jason had no defense against her, so he swung the door open wider and stepped back so they could enter.

Jason ambled over to the sofa and flopped down, resting one foot up on the coffee table. He was about five feet nine and thin.

Molly sat in the chair nearest to Jason. Carrie took the opportunity to gaze around the room for any sign of participation in the group. She wandered over to a bookshelf and took note of each item placed there. A few books, but mostly random items. It looked to be a catch-all sort of place.

Carrie pulled out one of the books. She didn't recognize the title or the author. It appeared to be a novel of some sort, and she slid it back in line.

"I know you know why we are here. I feel as though you have been avoiding us for days." Molly got right to the point.

Jason just stared back at her silently. There was no nod or any other physical sign that he agreed or disagreed with her. Except for his eyes. They were no longer fogged from sleep, and they pierced right through her. They were hard and unwavering.

"Tell me about the group that meets at Hafer Park and goes out to a barn to conduct courage rituals." Molly was unrelenting.

Jason continued to stare at Molly, not saying a word. Molly didn't flinch and stared right back, but Jason didn't seem the least bit phased by her staunch persistence.

"We know you were involved. We have had several deaths that are linked to the rituals so if you do not comply here, we will take you in to the station."

There was a momentary flicker in Jason's eyes.

"Carrie, let's get him cuffed and down to the station." This time Molly wasn't bluffing. She was ready to haul him in. Molly stood and Carrie moved to her side. "Get up."

"No. Wait." Jason seemed suddenly willing to speak.

"Get up. I'm done with your nonsense. Let's go." Molly motioned with her hand for him to stand and come towards her.

"No, seriously. I don't know what you mean by deaths."

Jason was visibly alarmed. "Seriously. What are you talking about?"

Molly looked at Carrie, who gave a slight shrug. Both women sat back down.

"Tell us about the rituals. Everything you know."

Jason sucked in a deep breath and let it out in an exaggerated huff. Removing his foot from the coffee table, he leaned forward with his arms resting on his thighs. He looked away from the women and out the window. *What can I say? What should I say?*

He looked back at Molly and began. "I guess it all started when a bunch of us were hanging out and were pissed at how we felt bullied by the jocks in football. They think their sh.." He paused considering his present company. "Their stuff doesn't stink."

Molly and Carrie nearly burst out laughing from his new consideration of them, but both held straight faces. "Please continue."

"So, we were hanging out and bitching. One of the guys started talking about a ritual that they talked about in his sociology class. It was to prove bravery for those participating. I guess we wanted to prove we were brave, but we didn't do anything about it.

"It seemed, though, that every time we got together, someone would bring up the ritual and then people would add stories to the mix about others. Honestly, the thought of going through them scared us to death." He looked back out the window. "I guess we really were cowards."

The silence in the room echoed his statement. It resonated with sadness and a sorrow that was deeply penetrating. Both Carrie and Molly waited, not wanting to disturb his memories.

Jason looked back at the women, this time with a brokenness in his eyes. "I'm not exactly sure how it all got organized, but all of a sudden someone said that someone had set up a ritual for us to participate in. We were to meet at Hafer Park. I don't know why it was such a secret where we were going.

"We got in a couple of old vans and rode way out in the country. By the time we got to where we were going, it was very dark and there were no lights outside on the property. I do know there was a huge old barn. We unloaded and went inside.

"Apparently, there was only one person set to do the ritual. I don't know who. Only one person did the ritual each time. The rest of us just stood around waiting. But then each time, I didn't remember anything after all of us were standing there waiting. The next thing I remembered was waking up in my own bed the next morning.

"Each time I was fine. I woke up with no hangover and feeling fine. So, I kept going."

"Why did you keep going back if you couldn't even remember what happened? And why did you not volunteer to participate in a ritual?" Molly asked.

"I just kept waiting. I thought if enough others did them and were fine, then I would take a chance. I don't know why I kept going back. It never felt wrong to not remember. Actually, I was thankful."

"We have four dead young men. How could you have not known about them? Were there men who participated in the rituals that survived?"

"There were rumors about guys dying, but I thought it was all just BS, something to add to the fear factor of it all. I've been out to the barn six times. I didn't know there had been any deaths.

But if you say four have died, then that would leave two who might have survived. Even though they did it one at a time, there could have been several individuals each night, which would mean more survivors. I just don't know."

Carrie and Molly sat quietly looking at Jason, and he in return looked at them. They had broken him. He had confessed all he knew. They were pretty sure of it.

"We need a complete list of everyone who was in the group talking about being courageous and everyone that met at Hafer Park. Everyone." Jason knew that Molly was sincere and that he needed to comply, just as his friend had when he had ratted him out.

"This is serious, and you could have been one of the ones. You may very well be one of them if you continue to do this. The drugs are lethal. The rituals are heart stopping."

"Wait! What drugs?" Jason had scooted to the edge of his seat. "We never took any drugs. I never took any drugs. That was never part of the deal."

"All the bodies had both FLY, which is bromo-dragon-FLY, and scopolamine in their systems. FLY is horrifically lethal. That alone could have killed them."

Jason was stunned. He looked directly at Molly and with a slight shake of his head said, "I promise. I know nothing about any drugs."

"You are a chemistry major, correct?"

"Yes, but..."

"So then, you know exactly how lethal those drugs are. And you know exactly how to calculate dosages accordingly." Molly sat back in her chair and narrowed her eyes thinking. "As a chemist, how would you see someone incorporating those drugs into what you were doing, the rituals?"

He rubbed his hands together and looked down and away, thinking. With a shrug of his shoulders, he said, "FLY is a hallucinogen, and scopolamine is a sedative that often causes one to say and do things they wouldn't normally do with no memory afterwards."

Molly let what he had just said sink in. And it did. His eyes grew large. "But I never took anything."

"How could someone in a group like that administer a dosage of scopolamine without them knowing?"

Jason's mind began to work with intense focus, in an attempt to figure out what had happened. Then suddenly he looked up. "Vapor. I would vaporize the drug and gas the area where someone would breathe it in. It is odorless and tasteless. We would have never known."

His heart was beating rapidly as the realization of what had been done to him and a host of his friends occurred.

"Write the list and anything else you can think of. If anything else occurs to you after we leave, please call us. We don't want any more young men to die." Molly slid her card across the table as Jason diligently began writing on a yellow tablet.

Molly looked up and over at Carrie. They were both relieved and shocked by what they had just learned. But, where should they go from there?

Back in the SUV, Carrie said, "That felt like a rerun of the other interview we had with his friend. We can continue to interview more on that list of friends, but I think we need to shift our focus somehow. I think we will just get more of the same."

"I agree. And I think the whole point of the scopolamine was so that they wouldn't remember what had happened."

"So, why do this to someone else? I can see that the boys wanted to participate in the rituals to prove their courage, but what would someone else get out of doing it to them?" Carrie asked.

Molly sat contemplating what the driving factor could be. She gazed out the front window as she entwined a curly strand of hair around her finger. "To me, they are sadists that enjoy seeing the pain they are inflicting on others, but this is too complicated to be doing it just for that. They have to be conducting these rituals for another reason. Right now, I have no idea."

Carrie looked over at Molly. Her brows were pinched together, and her eyes reached across to her colleague with pain. "I am so worried about Randy. It will soon be forty-eight hours that he has been gone with no sign of him."

Molly dropped her hand, leaving the hair strand sticking out to the side adrift, and turned fully to face Carrie. For a moment she didn't speak, she only analyzed Carrie's concerned countenance.

"I know. I've been thinking about him all day too. Let's put our heads together and see if we can come up with a plan to combine what Bracket asked us to do with finding Randy."

"What do you mean?"

"Well," Molly looked at their list. "We know that if we interview more friends like the one we just interviewed, we will get more of the same." Molly was marking a blue 'x' by each of those names with her pen. "Let's take this list and separate out the grad students only, and particularly the ones who were at the meeting."

She then put a small circle by each of those names. "Let's concentrate on these here," she said holding the list over to where Carrie could see. "We will be working on the list, but also maybe gaining ground on finding Randy as well."

"Yes!" Carrie once again felt renewed energy. "I like that." She put the SUV in gear and began driving toward the first grad student on the list.

"We are talking about a group of academics who love experiments, whether social, mental, or medical. I believe it is inherent for them to want to try things just to see how people or society will respond." Molly looked at Carrie and smiled. "It would make one hell of a doctoral thesis if so many hadn't died."

Carrie huffed out a laugh. "True, write the world's greatest thesis and then go straight to death row. No, if that was what they were trying to do, they failed. But I can see it being some type of experiment."

Carrie pulled into the driveway of the first grad student on their list. "What do we know about this one?"

Molly flipped a page to read her notes. "Rodney Grapple. Grad student for Dr. Jill Bates, professor of Anthropology at

UCO. He is twenty-three years old and has a grade point of 3.4. He was born and raised in Ardmore, Oklahoma." She looked up from the page and over at Carrie. "That's all I have."

"Okay, let's do this." Carrie had a knot in her stomach. With each passing moment that Randy was still missing, she feared the worst. As she stepped out of the SUV and looked around, it appeared to be a nice quiet neighborhood. That was usually the case though. The most normal neighborhoods hid the worst atrocities.

It took three knocking sessions for the door to crack open. "Yes?" A quiet voice slid through.

Carrie and Molly held up their badges. "I'm Carrie Border with the OSBI and this is Molly Jacobs with the OKCPD. We would like to speak with Rodney Grapple."

There was a moment's hesitation. "He's not here."

"Ma'am, can you open the door wider so we can speak with you more clearly?" Molly asked. She was always aware that when someone was hiding, they were usually dangerous.

The woman inched the door open a little further. It revealed a woman about forty-five years old. Her hair was short, almost boyish. She was slight of build and wore no makeup.

"Are you related to Rodney?" Carrie asked.

The woman's brow furrowed, as if the question presented to her was a difficult one to answer. "He's my stepson."

"May we come in and speak with you?" Molly continued.

The door swung open a bit more as the woman turned to survey the room behind her. "The house is in quite a mess."

"We don't mind. We just want to sit and talk with you for a while."

"Okay." The woman opened the door so that they could enter the room. It was a moderately-sized living area with unfolded laundry on the sofa, soda cans on the coffee table, and various other objects strewn across the floor.

Molly led the way and scooted the laundry over to the end of the sofa so she and Carrie could both sit. The woman sat in an adjacent matching chair. She had not lost the worried look that had greeted their arrival.

"Ma'am, could I get your name?" Carrie asked, ready to jot it down on the list next to Rodney's name.

"Yes. I'm Mary Booker."

"We know that Rodney is a graduate student for Dr. Jill Bates at UCO. Does he ever talk to you about his studies there?" Molly began.

Mary looked thoughtfully at the floor. "Well, I've overheard him talking to his father a time or two. But, he doesn't really talk to me about things."

"What can you remember that he has said?"

"I get the impression that he really likes it. He gets really excited when he is talking to his dad about it all. I can't remember anything specific. I honestly don't follow a lot of it. I never liked history"

"Has he mentioned what he wants to do after college?"

"Uhhh..." Mary was now looking upwards in an attempt to pull something out of her memory. "I don't know." She looked back at the women. "What does one do with a degree in history anyway? Teach?" It was as though that thought had just occurred to her, and both Carrie and Molly had to hold back a chuckle.

"There is always teaching, but many corporations hire for marketing research, government positions, politicians, and things like that."

"Ohhh..." The woman nodded. "Well, I don't recall him mentioning anything like that. Actually, I just don't remember. Maybe I didn't pay enough attention when he was talking about it."

Molly nodded. "I understand."

"Could you tell me what all of this is about?" The worried look was back on Mary's face.

"We've had some incidents that have an academic flair to them in the disciplines of sociology, history, and anthropology. We also want to speak to his professor, Dr. Bates, too." Molly didn't want to tell her exactly why they wanted to talk with Rodney. They had no idea what the woman really knew and what she would tell Rodney before they got a chance to speak with him.

"Do you know where he is right now?"

"I think he is at his friend Mark's house."

"Do you know his last name?" Molly nearly held her breath waiting to see if it was the same Mark they had on their list.

"Yes. Mark Plainer."

Pent-up air escaped both Carrie and Molly in large sighs. The connection of Rodney and Mark was forward motion, and they welcomed it. They had his address on their list, but asked Mary if she knew of a favorite hangout spot just in case they weren't at Mark's house. She wasn't aware of any.

Back in the SUV, Carrie was deciding the best route to Mark's house. "He lives out in the country."

"Does he live near Dr. Severs?"

Carrie took her pen and marked the map where he lived and then traced her finger to where Dr. Severs lived. "Well, not too terribly far, but not super close either. They both live on the northeast side of Edmond on the east side of I-35. But Mark lives further south than Dr. Severs." Carrie looked up at Molly. "What are you thinking?"

She shifted in her seat to look at Carrie. Her eyes narrowed somewhat as she was thinking. "Where would anyone do these rituals? We've heard twice that they were taken to a barn. It would have to be on a larger property than in town, and private. You wouldn't want anyone knowing what you were doing.

"If Mark didn't live far from Dr. Severs, he could have taken Randy to a barn on his property. He could be hiding him there."

Carrie began slowly nodding. She kicked the SUV into gear and sped off. Excitement filled the cab as hope rose that they could find Randy.

It took about twenty minutes to find Mark's house. It had a long gravel drive that wound through the woods on its way to the house. The house was a small white farmhouse. And there was a barn in the back. It was faded and old, but still standing.

Carrie parked and they looked at each other. A quick nod and they were out the door.

Once outside, they looked around at their surroundings. The house had a yard that was somewhat large, both in the front and the back. Surrounding the yard was a thick copse of woods. From the backyard, a grassy meadow strip meandered off and up to a hill in the distance.

It was quiet and there were no cars. "It doesn't look like anyone is home," said Carrie.

"No, it doesn't." Molly rapped on the screen door. After three tries and no response or sound, she gave up.

"Well, crap," said Carrie. "I want to go look in that barn so bad, but we don't have a warrant."

"No, and we need to follow protocol."

"Extenuating circumstances?" Carrie presented hopefully.

Molly smiled, "No. Sorry. We aren't quite there yet." Carrie nodded. She knew, but just wanted someone to push her over the line a smidge.

"Can we at least walk around the outside of the barn?"

Molly nodded and they trampled through tall grass surrounding the barn. Most of it was dry and had not been mowed down over the winter. The barn was weathered and grey, the paint long faded away. But it had been built tough and there were only slivers of gaps between the boards.

"I can't see anything through the cracks. It is too dark in there." Her shoulders slumped and she walked away from the barn. They had walked the perimeter and had found nothing unusual or suspicious. Carrie had called out for Randy, but there was no response.

"What now?" Carrie asked.

"We continue down the list. But let's focus on the grad students and look and see if any more live in the country."

They spent about fifteen more minutes going over the list and plotting the addresses on the map. "Jonathan Park lives over by Piedmont. Near the edge of town, but it looks like it is mostly rural there." Carrie looked up at Molly. "Should we go all the way there or try another one local first?"

"Who else is local?"

Carrie looked at her map. "No, not really, several live closer to OU and in Oklahoma City."

Molly looked back at her list. "You know there are several professors in addition to those that met privately. They will all have grad students as well. I feel like we need to sort through this list better. Why don't we drive out to Piedmont to find Jonathan Park, then we can get dinner and maybe spend some time getting a better feel for who we should target."

"Sounds good to me. I don't know where the day has gone."

They drove back to the west, through city and county streets. Piedmont was due east of them, but there were no highways to make their journey faster.

It was a pretty drive though, through countryside filled with pastures, fields, and woods. All were starting to turn green with the springtime warmth. As they drove, Carrie looked at all the barns they were passing. "We've passed at least a half dozen barns so far. Any of them could be where they have the rituals."

"True. We can't focus on that. If we stay diligent and targeted, we will not only find Randy, but our killers too."

Carrie pulled up to the address that was listed for Jonathan Park. "It's a duplex. It looked like it would be more rural from the map. There's no barn. Oh, well. Let's go."

After just one knock, the door swung open to reveal a young man about five feet ten inches tall. He had thick glasses with black frames, and a severe case of acne. "Are you Jonathan Park?" Molly asked.

The young man nodded. After introductions, the women were escorted inside. Molly sat in the nearest chair and Carrie once again meandered through the room. Jonathan stood by the coffee table, with arms crossed. "What is this about?' he asked.

"Please have a seat. We just want to have a talk."

"Do I need an attorney?"

Molly stood up straighter and Carrie turned to look at the young man.

"Now why would you think that?" Molly asked.

"I don't know. I've just seen too many bad cop shows where they twist things that are said. I don't want nothing I say to get twisted."

"We are just here to talk. We are talking with many people and you are only one of them." Molly watched Jonathan. He seemed nervous, but she suspected that might be his normal behavior.

"Okay," Jonathan said as he sat on his sofa.

Molly quickly went through the standard questions of name, work and school history. They already knew everything, but needed him to confirm. Then, she got to the heart of it.

"You meet with a group of students and grad students to engage in various multi-cultural rituals. Where exactly do those rituals take place?" She looked pointedly at Jonathan, unwavering.

His anxiety peaked. "Why, I don't have any idea what you are talking about." His knee was bobbing up and down slightly, and one hand was clutching his polo shirt collar.

Molly and Carrie quietly continued to look at him, waiting. Suddenly, Jonathan stood up and suggested they leave.

But instead, Carrie sat down in the chair next to Molly. Exasperated, Jonathan finally sat back down.

"You are making yourself look very guilty of something, Jonathan," said Carrie. We just want to ask you some questions. We haven't accused you of anything illegal."

He rubbed his hand backwards over his hair, shut his eyes, and took a deep breath. The women could smell a strong body odor they knew was caused from his stress.

"Okay. Okay." He took another deep breath and let it out slowly. He proceeded to tell them the exact same things that the other two had told them.

"So, you participated in the ritual?"

"No. I was going to, but I never could get up the courage. I hoped that if I kept meeting with them, I would work up to it. Then I heard one guy had died. I wasn't sure, but when I heard it on the news, it sounded familiar."

"So, explain to us the process. When someone wants to participate, what happens next?" Molly asked.

Jonathan sat quietly thinking. He didn't have a ready

answer. His eyes shifted around, as if he could find the answer somewhere in the room. "I don't know." He almost sounded surprised.

"Since I never agreed to go through a ritual, I don't know. It is all handled privately until the rest of us go to the barn to watch."

"Tell me anything at all that you can remember about going there and what you saw." Molly was pressing him as hard as she felt she could.

"It was just an old barn. We were standing around. There was some light, maybe candles, I'm not sure." Jonathan shut his eyes to try and remember, then opened them. "Nothing. I honestly don't remember."

"Jonathan, how many times did you meet with them and go to the barn?" Molly asked.

"I guess about three times."

"We need you to make a list of everyone that you know who went to the rituals and whom you met with initially to discuss starting all of this." They wanted to compare and see if there was anyone on his list that hadn't been on theirs.

"Jonathan, how do all of you guys know about these rituals?" Carrie asked.

He looked up from the pad he was writing on and shrugged his shoulders. "I don't know. Everyone knows about them, don't they?"

Chapter Twenty

Molly and Carrie were spent. "I was certain the grad students were the key to this whole thing, but now I am not sure. In the beginning, I thought the professors were responsible. Maybe they still are, but now I have no idea who is doing this or why," said Carrie. She was exhausted from attempting to mentally make it all fit together.

"Let's go get a bite to eat and regroup." Molly was equally as tired. She had handled a few murders and serious crimes as a detective, but this one was challenging. Nothing about it made sense.

"If we go to a busy place, it will be loud. How about we get something to go and head over to my house. It will be quiet there and we can eat and brainstorm," Molly suggested.

"Sure. Sounds good to me."

An hour later, Carrie was pulling up to Molly's quaint little home in the old part of Edmond. It had white clapboard siding, a pale blue front door and flowerbeds overflowing with what would soon to be a lavish abundance of plants, and blooms.

"Your home is so cute," Carrie felt its charm and anticipated an interior equally as inviting. And it did not disappoint. Molly's home felt like a home. Every piece of furniture and all the eclectic decor had been purposefully chosen to reflect who Molly was as a person. It welcomed them with the heartwarming scent of cinnamon and apple pie, certainly residual from a candle that Molly had often burned.

Molly blushed and took the takeout bags to her small wooden dining table. "Thank you."

They then quickly dove into their burgers and fries, famished.

When done, Carrie watched as Molly quickly tidied up the takeout boxes and bags and laid out their lists and other notes. As she watched, the previous questions she had about her resurfaced.

"You were going to tell me a little about yourself."

Molly smiled. "Yes, I was. What do you want to know?" The wooden chair creaked a sigh as Molly settled back into it.

"You mentioned you were adopted?"

"Yes, but I knew my birth mom. I lived with her for the first five years of my life." Molly's thoughts drifted away and a mist seemed to gather in her eyes. A soft smile of remembrance soothed her face.

"I suspect there is an interesting story there."

"There is." Molly began to tell Carrie the story of how her birth mom was kidnapped when she was eight months pregnant with her. And how she was in captivity with her mother for the first five years of her life. She continued talking about her path to Sharon and then Donna's death.

"I don't have any pictures of my mother, but I do remember her. It was just she and I alone all day everyday except when Buddy would come. She is my memory. While other children remember going places and doing things and playing with siblings, all my memories are tied to her." Molly's face held a sweet smile as she remembered, and her words were almost faint as she looked off somewhere into the past.

Carrie sat quietly as she allowed Molly those precious moments. When Molly finally remembered she wasn't alone and looked up at Carrie, she said, "My Momma Donna taught me everything in those first five years I would ever need in life. She taught me about love and positivity regardless of the circumstances. We read the Bible every day and I learned how baby Jesus loves us and was there with us. I grew up always knowing him. He was there taking care of us the entire time."

Molly looked down at the table and fingered the paper napkin she had left behind. Carrie was shaken. She could not reconcile being kidnapped and held in captivity for five years and God supposedly loving them. "I... I... just can't reconcile any of that. If God loved you, he would have rescued you!" The animosity Carrie held toward God for her own parents' deaths was thick in her words.

"Oh, but he did rescue us! What many people view as captivity was a special time to me, a sequestered time if you will. It was a time of concentrated learning to fully trust in him each and every moment of each and every day. We learned to see and be thankful for the positive things in our lives, and our days were sweet and precious. And it was quality time with her alone.

"Momma taught me scriptures and we let them transform our lives. In the worst of times, God was there with me. His presence was palpable. I learned very early to hear his voice and to follow his instruction. Had we been in the outside world, I may have learned about him, but not with that indelible experience which taught me in a way that the outside world never could have."

"But he let your Momma Donna die! How can you forgive him for that?"

"Carrie, we all die. Some sooner than others. He did free my Momma Donna. The day she died, she became freer than any of us left here on this earth. Yes, I miss her, but I have my memories, and I have her journals which she wrote in multiple times each day.

"She gave me something incredibly valuable. Something no one else has."

Carrie just looked at her, speechless. She could not understand, she could not comprehend. There was, however, a small part of her deep inside that wanted to. She wanted to forgive and let go of the anger and the pain, but she just couldn't, so she chose to cling tightly to it.

Molly gave one of those huge engaging smiles that welcomed one in. "I know it makes no sense, and without actually living it, it is incomprehensible. God allowed my Momma Donna to move to heaven, but he had already prepared my new parents. He never, ever took his hands off of me and he orchestrated my life in a profound and amazing way.

"Not only that, but him bringing me into my Momma Sharon's life freed her as well. She was bound up in hurt and pain from years of losing people, and from people betraying her. She wanted a child in the worst possible way and couldn't have one. She was the perfect mother to me after Donna.

"But, as she puts it, me coming into her life with my sense of knowing Jesus, led her to forgiveness and straight into the arms of God. Nothing about my life was random or by accident."

"So, you are saying that God orchestrated your kidnapping and captivity?"

"No, God never ever does anything bad. That is completely against his character. He does not bring illness or pain. But we live in a fallen world where the rain falls on the just and the unjust. It is because of all the imperfection in this world that we need him even more. I hope to live every day as if I am desperate for him regardless of how good or bad things are around me."

Carrie's mind was spinning. She wanted to hear more, needed to hear more, but at the same time didn't want to. She knew if she continued to listen to Molly she would let go of her anger, and she wasn't ready to do that yet. She deserved to be angry, and she refused to give it up.

Silence echoed through Molly's house. Molly knew that she had said what needed to be said and did not want to pour more on Carrie than what she could consume.

Carrie sat quietly because she had no idea what to say.

She knew in light of what Molly had lived through, she had not cornered the market on tragedy. She also saw the massive contrast between the two of them. Carrie defiantly chose to hold onto the anger and to feel like a victim, while Molly embraced the pain and thanked God in spite of it.

"Carrie, being in law enforcement has shown me the worst in people in this world. I feel the pain every day and I still often ask God why and how. But at the end of the day, even with so many unanswered questions, I choose to trust him and rest in his peace and love. It must be a choice I make, or the pain and the evil of this world would suck me down too. I get up every morning making the choice that will continue to feed me with God's life and love."

Carrie was slowly nodding. She knew that Molly was living proof that what she was saying was true. Maybe someday, that would be true for her too. "I believe you. I just can't quite get there in my heart, or in my mind. When the argument comes forward of, 'But I loved my parents, and they were my whole world,' I compare it to you and Donna and she really was your whole world. My experience pales in comparison."

"It was never just me and Momma Donna, but you are right. She was my whole world for a very long time. Then, God brought me Momma Sharon before my Momma Donna was ever gone. He eased me from one world into the other. That is the precious grace of our heavenly father.

"You know, I still have all my Momma Donna's journals. If you are interested in what our world, our life was really like, I'll let you read them. Her words describe it all much better than I ever could."

Carrie sat thoughtfully for a moment, then something in her compelled her to quietly say, "Yes, I would like that very much."

Billy's mind was still reeling after witnessing something his heart could not bear to absorb. His nights were filled with either insomnia or fitful dreams. In the quiet hours of the night, he questioned whether he really saw what he had, then it would all come back to him in vivid detail. There was no doubt. Carrie had betrayed him in the worst way possible.

He had not talked to her, but part of him wondered if there was any defense that she could present that would excuse it all away. He knew the trauma she had just faced, but the fact that she wouldn't allow him to help her through it all bore witness to how she must truly feel. He'd been too blind to see it.

Seeing her with another man was most assuredly what he had needed to finally break free. The last several weeks had felt as if he had been crossing a rickety old bridge across a deep crevasse. That night that rickety bridge had collapsed, and he found himself falling down, down, down.

How long had it been? The hours and days had spun, then slowed, then spun again. He had no concept of time. Tears began to flow again. He didn't know it was possible to be this broken.

He had called no one. A man isn't supposed to cry, right? The truth was, he didn't know what to say, and he was ashamed that he hadn't been able to be what she needed in her most traumatic moments. To try and tell someone, to convey the event in a way that captured how it sliced through him to the core, was impossible. There were no words, and there was no energy to attempt to pull them forth.

It was morning. He only knew that because a slight sliver of light was fighting to peek around his blackout shades and curtains. Finally, he swung his legs over the side of the bed and sat, slumped. That small amount of energy drained him, but it was Monday morning and he had to pull himself together and go to work.

He reached over and turned off the alarm that would soon ring out, and rose to go find coffee. He'd eaten nothing in the last two days, and his body was urgently reminding him of that very thing. He opened the coffee sack, the vibrant aroma awakening his senses. His taste buds tingled in anticipation.

As the coffee hissed and popped inside the coffee maker, he shuffled over to the cabinet to see if he had any bagels left. He did, but they were half green with mold. The trash in the can rattled as he tossed in the new contribution.

He poured a cup from the half full pot and tasted the dark liquid. With no energy left, he sat on the sofa. *Is this what Carrie felt like after her parents' death? Had I been too hard on her? No. I've given her everything she indicated she needed from me, and more.*

The weight of the heartache was suffocatingly heavy and he considered calling in sick. He just didn't know if he was capable of work right then. He also needed to cancel all their wedding plans and see if he could get their deposits back.

He'd put most of them down from a joint savings account they had formed just for the wedding. Each of their perspective paydays had a portion of their paycheck going straight to that savings. They had been doing it since they knew there would be a wedding, since he had proposed to her.

It had been a wise thing to do. It had built quite a nice fund and they had spent lavishly on the plans, which meant huge deposits. Now, he had to be the responsible one and see if he could get as much back as possible.

Had he not seen her, would she have ever officially called off the wedding or just left him hanging? He didn't know.

The coffee did have some effect and he knew what he needed to do for the day, what he had to do. His supervisor was not at work yet, but he called anyway and left a message on his voicemail that he was sick. He hated lying, but it was necessary. And truthfully, he was genuinely sick.

A hot shower added to the caffeine, and inch by inch, he was moving forward. Once everything was cancelled and over, how would he tell Carrie? Would he tell her? Maybe he would just wait for her to call him, just to see how long it would take.

With a full pot of black coffee in him and a hot shower, he sat down with their wedding planning notebook and began making calls. In every call, he found himself playing the sympathy card, explaining about Carrie's parents' death and how the devastation had affected her dramatically. They just couldn't move forward with the wedding at this point.

They all commiserated, while stating their strict cancellation policies. They did still have time to get a good portion of their deposits back in some cases, with only one being fully non-refundable.

He would need to go to each place though, and sign a

form stating that they were indeed cancelling, and pick up the refund check. He hung up the last phone call feeling like he had been hit by a truck, but still thankful to have the daunting process nearly over and done with.

His body still gnawed at him for food. He grabbed his keys and left to go finish the awful ordeal, and to eat.

The sun had come into its own. When he stepped outside onto his front porch, he faced its light and shoved on his sunglasses. He was determined to face the day and whatever else was to come. He felt harder, more jaded, and he knew this was the new Billy.

He ate a fast-food burger and fries from inside his car as he thought about the last time he had sat in it on the previous Friday night. His hurt was turning to rage. *How could she do this? Was there any excuse for the pain she was causing? Was she really that selfish? Had she always been that selfish?*

The grumbling in his stomach stopped after the first few bites. However, he forced the rest down, only because he knew he needed to eat. He dreaded going to each vendor and formalizing the cancellation. It was humiliating.

Each place expressed sympathy for what Carrie was going through, and hoped the couple would soon be able to come back to make new arrangements with them. They all wanted assurances that they had done nothing to warrant the cancellation and Billy confirmed that they had been great, fine, all the things a business owner wants to hear.

Checks in hand, he drove by his bank to make the deposits. As he sat in the drive-through line, he made a quick decision to go inside to complete the transaction.

"Hello. How may I help you?"

"I want to make a deposit and then close an account."

"Would you like the proceeds of the account in cash or a cashier's check?" the teller asked as she looked at her screen and tapped proficiently on her keyboard.

"Cash."

"That is quite a bit of cash." The teller looked at Billy for confirmation.

"Can you just transfer it into my checking account?"

More tapping and reading of various screens. "Yes, I can do that."

"Then can I get an updated bank statement for that account?"

"Sure."

He was thinking on the fly. A good portion of the money was Carrie's. He would go home and do the math and figure out just how much was hers and write her a check. Whether or not he would deliver it in person or by mail was still undecided.

The teller had him sign that he was closing the account, at which time she provided him with proof that the funds had been transferred. A quick trip to the credenza behind her produced an updated bank statement.

"Thank you," mumbled Billy.

"Is there anything else I can help you with?" The teller beamed at Billy eager to help.

He gave a lopsided smile and a slight shake of his head.

Then it hit him. A slight waft of fragrance thrust his mind into the memory of another person who often wore that same fragrance; Carrie. He gritted his teeth, ducked his head and turned to go.

He realized the hollowness in his gut was back as he sat in his car in the bank parking lot. He looked down at the paperwork and the finality of what it represented hit him one more time. He knew he couldn't deliver it to her in person. He drove to the post office, wrote out a check to Carrie Border, shoved a quick impersonal note of explanation inside the envelope and sent her money away.

As he turned his car toward his home, he wondered just how long it would take her to call, or if she ever would at all.

Molly and Carrie had gone over their lists in detail the previous night and had separated them out. There were the professors who came to the event. There were the grad students of those professors. There were the friends of those young men who had died. Then there was the short list of professors who seemed to be in a tight little clique.

Both women agreed that the tight little clique was suspicious. They had been at the event, along with all of their grad students when Randy had gone missing. None on the list of friends, all undergraduate students had been there.

"What if the short list is in cahoots?" Carrie looked at Molly to gauge her reaction.

"And then maybe Randy discovered something and they did something to him?" Molly looked back at Carrie.

Neither one wanted to admit such a thing, but from all that lay before them, it seemed the most likely. Molly looked at her watch. "It's late. Let's wrap this up and start bright and early in the morning. We'll focus only on the five professors and their grad students."

Carrie drove home exhausted. It was nearly eleven p.m. and she could barely hold her eyes open to drive. The last of her energy was spent entering her home and shuffling to her bed where she promptly fell into it. She only managed to strip off her clothes before she passed out.

Total exhaustion did wonders for getting a good night's sleep. Carrie slept hard and felt much better the next morning, though she had received no calls during the night regarding Randy. *I have to find him.*

It was seven fifteen when Carrie arrived at the office and Molly came soon behind. "I've routed out all five of the professors and their grad students so we can make the most efficient use of our time. Of course, we've already visited with Jonathan Park, so that leaves us four grad students and all five of the professors." Molly was fired up and ready to go.

"Bracket grilled Dr. Severs pretty heavily the day after. We spent the entire day there with our forensics team combing the house, shed, and adjoining area. I think we should put him last so that we can speak to some we've not spoken to. Maybe after that we will have a new vein of information to pursue with him."

"I agree. I have routed our list so we can visit with the OU professors and their grad students first. Then we can work our way back up north. I hope that we can get much more done than yesterday since we are starting early and have a firm game plan."

The women were barely out of Oklahoma City when Carrie's phone rang. It was Bracket.

"Hello."

"We have another body." Bracket's voice held more tension than usual.

"Is it... is it Randy?" Carrie was terrified to ask.

"I don't know. It is a male, but the dispatcher didn't know anything else. I need you and Molly to head over there now."

"Will do. Give me the location." Carrie motioned to Molly to pull over, then pulled out her ink pen and notepad. She was rapidly writing everything down as she held her phone between her cheek and shoulder.

"We were heading to Norman with a short list to follow up on. We think they are important interviews. If I give you the list, can you see if there are other available agents who can do them?" Carrie continued to explain to Bracket their reasoning.

"Yes, I will make sure they get done."

The moment she hung up, she looked at Molly. Distress creased her face. "We have another body. Bracket wants us there ASAP."

"Is it..."

"They don't know." Carrie gave Molly the address since she was driving her department vehicle that day. She quickly headed back out into traffic, finding the nearest exit.

A knot the size of a boulder sat firmly in the pit of Carrie's stomach. Her mind was racing and it felt as if every synapse was firing in her brain. She felt she could hear each one in her ears as they buzzed. She was close to passing out and needed to get control of herself and calm down.

Molly pulled her car up behind the coroner's van and the other patrol cars. She looked over at Carrie. "Take a deep breath. You can get through this no matter what we are about to see."

Carrie nodded and reached for the door handle. The thirty-yard walk to the shack, a.k.a. crime scene, seemed much longer than it was. As they neared, they could see Dr. Bloom through the doorway squatting by the body. His position obstructed Carrie's view of the victim's face.

They stepped inside and took a moment to allow their eyes to adjust to the darkness. Then Carrie stepped around Dr. Bloom and let out a gasp. "It's not him." Her hand flew to her stomach and she doubled over with relief.

"Not who?" Dr. Bloom asked. He had not been privy to Randy's disappearance. Molly filled him in.

He looked back down at the body to continue his examination. It was nearly naked, cleaned, and laid out as the others had been. But this time it was completely covered in snake bites. "I hadn't heard about Randy. That's disturbing, but I have confidence that you will find him before any harm comes to him."

As relief flooded her body, Carrie came back into full focus. "What kind of snakes? Can you tell?"

"I will have to test the toxin once I get him back to autopsy. I can tell it was multiple types of snakes. See here, the size of the bites are different. Some are further apart in width and some have a larger diameter of puncture wound. Of course, just like the others, he didn't die here, but was moved. I detect the smell of alcohol again."

"Why do these young men keep submitting themselves to this after so many have died?" Molly was speaking as much to herself as to those in the room.

Carrie came and stood beside Molly. "Where are we going wrong?" Carrie's question was sincere, and she hoped to gain new insight from the experienced detective. She had snapped off her blue gloves and shoved them in her back pocket.

Molly stood quietly thinking. She was well into her own mind, rolling things over one by one. Then something occurred to her. She looked at Carrie. "What is the most unique and rare thing about this case?"

Carrie looked at Molly as if trying to read her mind. But Molly was patient. She wanted Carrie to think of the one thing, that if followed and uncovered, would lead to the killer or killers.

"I..." Carrie was trying. She was doing what Molly had done, rolling each component over and over. "The most rare and unique thing I can think of is the FLY. No one anywhere that we have talked to has any idea why they are using that particular drug. It makes no sense since there are far safer drugs which can do the same thing."

"Yes. I believe that if we can find that out, we will find the perpetrators. There are other agents conducting the interviews. We will let them follow through on that and we'll attend this autopsy and then do more research on FLY."

Carrie nodded. It sounded good, and she wanted to believe that would be the key. "Okay. Where do we start? I have tons of research back at the office. I've interviewed people and asked about it. What else do we need to do?"

"I think we need to go to the FBI. They have more resources and may have had more experience with the substance."

"The FBI? Will they even help us?" Carrie asked.

"They will. I have a contact there." Molly smiled.

"Oh, do tell." Carrie was intrigued particularly because of the smile on Molly's face.

"Let's go. I'll tell you all about it."

Once back in the car, Molly turned the key so the AC could cool the interior. Then she turned towards Carrie. "Brandon Emerson. He is an FBI agent in the Dallas field office."

"Go on..." Carrie saw there was more to the story and couldn't wait to hear it.

"He's my ex-fiance."

Carrie's mouth fell open. She was not expecting that. She had wondered about Molly's love life, whether she had been married or if she was seeing someone.

"I grew up with him. He was my best friend's older brother. Our moms were best friends too. I developed a crush on him pretty early on, but in his estimate I was just his kid sister's friend. But as I matured, he began to see me differently.

"We dated in high school and then went off to college at OU. He was a senior when I started as a freshman. He proposed that year, but we agreed to hold off for a while to get through college. He had planned to stay and get his master's degree."

"Okay, so what happened?"

"Well, we were best friends, which we both agreed was the best part of a relationship and future marriage. But near the end of his senior year, instead of moving forward on his master's degree, he applied to the FBI academy at Quantico. He was just what they wanted, and off he went to Virginia.

"We will always love each other and have a very deep bond, but with our careers we know that marriage would not have been best for us."

"Did he ever get married?"

Molly gave a slight shake of her head and sent a blond curl hurtling across her cheek. "No. Neither of us ever married."

"How often do you see him or talk to him?"

"Pretty often, when our work allows it."

Carrie sat back in her seat. She smiled at Molly. "Well, what are you waiting for? Call him."

Chapter Twenty-One

Molly and Carrie were still sitting in Molly's car at the crime scene. Carrie could hear Molly's phone ringing even though it was not on speaker. When the voicemail came over the line, Molly smiled at the sound of Brandon's voice. "Hey there, it's Molly. I need to pick your FBI brain. We have a case here in OKC that has maxed out our limits. Give me a call when you can."

Molly ended the call and turned the key. She glanced at Carrie who was looking at her, and blushed. "What?"

"Nothing." Carrie reached for her seatbelt, smiling.

They drove from the crime scene they both knew was just a body dump, back towards Oklahoma City. "Let's go to my office and sort through the research I've done while we wait for Brandon to give us a call back."

"Sounds good."

As they walked into the OSBI offices, Carrie felt like it had been forever since she'd spent any time there. Since

Randy had gone missing, her days had been filled with interviews and crime scenes. Once at her desk, Carrie pulled out the file and turned to the section on FLY. She handed it to Molly. "You can start with this while I print off more information that I gathered but haven't yet put in the file.

The printer came to life and Carrie headed that way. "I'll meet you in the war room with the whiteboards."

Molly absent-mindedly nodded and headed that way. Soon, Carrie had retrieved a considerable stack of pages and joined Molly in the room. Molly looked up. "It makes no sense at all that someone would even attempt to use this drug. If they were trying to honestly conduct experiments in sociology they would have used a more stable drug. The volatility of FLY, along with the inconsistency of the outcome, would prevent any credible experimental results."

Carrie sat at the table across from Molly and looked at her. "So, the main question we need answered is why. Why would someone use such an unpredictable and dangerous drug? What is the benefit for them or for the experiment?"

Molly pursed her lips together as she thought. Then suddenly, she looked up at Carrie. "Unless they intended for people to die."

Carrie squinted. "Like someone wanted to kill on purpose? We were looking at this as sort of an accident, an experiment gone wrong. If they intended to kill, they are actually serial murderers. If that is the case, then why the elaborate ruse of the rituals?"

The two continued to sit while deep in thought, then Molly added, "Think about this. You have someone conducting rituals to determine who is courageous, but many are dying. What if in the mind of those conducting them, it is as if the deaths are culling out the herd. Only the truly courageous survive such a dangerous drug and ritual."

"What are they hoping to achieve?" Carrie couldn't wrap her mind around such a scenario.

Molly sat absent-mindedly flipping a pencil back and forth between two fingers as she went back to studying the file.

Carrie's phone rang and she looked down to see that it was Dr. Bloom. "Hey Dr. Bloom. That is pretty quick. Are you ready for autopsy?"

"No, but I got some results back from the tech lab, so I did a quick test on this body to verify. The alcohol used on the bodies to clean them was ethanol, not isopropyl. This body too."

Carrie had clicked on the speaker after answering the call and now laid it on the table between her and Molly. "The difference is, in a nutshell, that isopropyl is what is sold over the counter at your local drug store.

"Ethanol, or ethyl alcohol is used in labs. Ethanol evaporates slower and makes it more useful in a lab setting. For industrial cleaning and disinfecting, denaturants are added, which make it palatable for consumption."

"So, are you saying that the alcohol used to clean the bodies was from a lab or from a cleaning company?" Molly asked.

"From a lab. It had no denaturants in it."

"Is there a specific clearing house where only this kind of alcohol is purchased?" Carrie asked.

"No. You can get it anywhere unfortunately. And I would

venture to guess that every lab in town has ethanol. I don't know if that helps at all, but wanted you to know as soon as possible."

"Thank you, Dr. Bloom."

Carrie shut her eyes and let out a huge sigh, then asked, "That really doesn't help us much, does it?"

"Not yet. It may figure in down the road. We can circle those who work in a lab and have a higher access to ethanol. That would certainly be all the chemistry profs and students." Molly was still formulating her thoughts as she spoke.

"But let's face it, anyone near a lab would have access to it. I doubt it is a substance that would be locked up."

As they continued to sit there combing through the files and research material, Molly's phone rang. She smiled broadly as she answered her new phone, a Blackberry similar to Carrie's. She held it to her ear so she could warn Brandon that she was in the company of other law enforcement.

When the greetings were past, Molly hit the speaker button and continued. "Carrie Border with the OSBI is here with me. Have you got some time for me to quickly fill you in on this case?"

"I do. I am driving across the metro and it will take me about an hour and a half to get to where I need to be."

Molly tried to succinctly fill Brandon in on the case. There were so many outliers that seemed relevant and important, but no time to give him everything. "Why I called you, is that we have decided that the thing that stands out the most is the use of the drug FLY, or bromo-dragonFLY. It is highly unstable. There is no medicinal use. Its greatest claim is that it was sometimes, rarely, and I mean very rarely, used as a hallucinogen. It has a safer counterpart 2C-B-FLY, but they aren't using that one, only 4C-B-FLY which is the more volatile and dangerous one.

"We feel like if we can find who is synthesizing this drug, or buying this drug, then we will have our subject." Molly stopped, nearly out of breath for having laid out the entire case so quickly.

"Hmmm."Brandon's mental wheels were now in overdrive.

Molly explained to Brandon the details of their case and what they suspected was happening and how the FLY played into the scenario.

"I have never even heard of this drug. Let me see what I can find out with our resources. If we have a channel of import or sale that we can key you in on, that may help. Or if we have some research regarding illegal manufacturing of it here in the states. Also, I can check for any deaths here in the US from FLY."

"The only recorded deaths I've found, so far, have been in Scandinavian countries. There were five," Molly began. "It makes no sense for anyone to use FLY recreationally. Acid or mushrooms, yes, but not FLY. We just can't seem to see the reasoning why they are using this, and we were hoping you could help us."

"You mentioned you had one overdose?"

"Yes. One apart from the deaths from the rituals. But that drug was a contributing factor in the deaths. In all probability, if they had gone through the rituals without the drug, they would have survived. That overdose had no scopolamine in his system."

Molly explained how they suspected the drugs were being administered and when.

"It seems like you've uncovered quite a bit so far. I'll be back tonight and can dig into it. I'll call you as soon as I have anything."

Molly tapped the speaker button to send the call back to listen privately as she got up from the table and walked outside into the hallway. "It's been a while since we've talked. It is good to hear your voice."

"I miss you," said Brandon.

"Yes, I miss you too. When all this is over, I promise we'll get together."

Brandon took in a deep breath and let out an audible sigh. "How does the old saying go? Man makes plans and God laughs?"

"Shame on you. You know that isn't true, well not entirely I suppose. Sometimes I wonder what it would be like if we both didn't have such crazy all-consuming jobs."

"Me too, Molly Sue. Me too."

The heavy traffic lulled Carrie back into thoughts of Randy. *Where can he be? What can I do to help find him?* Her stomach tightened into knots each time she thought of him.

Molly glanced at Carrie. "You know, you wear your thoughts and emotions on your face."

Carrie looked over at Molly. "What do you mean?"

"When you are deep in thought or worried it shows on your face without you ever saying a word. I would guess that you were just thinking about Randy."

Carrie huffed out a short breath and her shoulders dropped. "I didn't know I was such an open book. You're right, I was thinking about Randy. I can't imagine where they have taken him or what they are doing to him. And... I have no idea what to do to help find him."

"It is terrible when one of our own is in trouble. The best thing you can do is to focus on finding the perpetrators. Once we find them, we will find Randy."

"It also concerns me that we still are having bodies turn up, which means that these deaths have not slowed the rituals. They are doing them anyway. I feel like what may have started as a group of young men simply wanting to prove their courage, has now become something akin to a serial killer type of situation."

"You are right. Maybe we have been looking at this all wrong. Maybe a psychotic serial killer has become part of the core element in these rituals and he likes it when they die."

Back at the office, Carrie checked in first thing with Bracket to see if there had been any word on Randy. Her hope was quickly extinguished when Bracket confirmed, "No, none at all."

They grabbed the files and made space on the whiteboards for a category of 'LAB' and listed all information they had learned, pertaining to what might be used in or made in a lab.

Molly stood with one arm wrapped around her middle supporting the other elbow. She tapped her chin with her free fingers, lost in thought. "I suppose scopolamine could also be included. For such small amounts it seems it would make more sense to just purchase it."

"This isn't just any lab. This is a lab that has approval to house the actual drugs that FLY is synthesized from. What labs would that be? Hospital, college, commercial?" Molly dropped her arms and went to the laptop they used there and began typing. She was reading the research one more time on FLY.

"I don't care how many times I've read this, it is still foreign to me. I passed the minimum chemistry classes to get my degree, but I have no ability to decipher any of this or formulate a hypothesis."

Carrie mentally replayed the conversation she and Randy had with Dr. Pinning, and realized there was much more they could learn from him, at this stage of their investigation. She looked over at Molly. "I think we need to go talk with Dr. Pinning again." She explained her concerns to Molly about the first interview. "We didn't know enough at the time to be able to ask the right questions and I feel, I could be wrong, but I feel that looking back he was a bit evasive."

"Sounds good to me. Let's go."

By that time, it was afternoon and they stopped to get a bite to eat while on their way. They drove through a fast-food burger place and sat in Molly's car to eat. "So tell me about your love life." Molly began.

Carrie was focused on the container of french fries in her lap. The request was another punch in her gut. She didn't want to talk about it. She hadn't talked to Billy since last Thursday. The entire weekend had been consumed with work, and now that it was Monday, she realized just how long it had been.

The way she had betrayed him on Friday night stuck in her craw like glass. She couldn't undo it, she couldn't ignore it, and she couldn't fix it no matter what she did. Maybe that was one reason that she hadn't reached out to him, but then it occurred to her that he hadn't reached out to her either.

The silence from Carrie at Molly's quasi-question caused her to feel as though she had stepped on hallowed ground. "I'm sorry. I didn't mean to pry."

Carrie gave a slight shake of her head while fiddling with a fry. "I was engaged to be married when my parents had their car wreck. But, I didn't handle any of it well. I fear that I have pushed him so far away with my bitterness and anger that our relationship is irreparable."

"Oh Carrie, I'm so sorry. What a lot to deal with all at once. I'm sure if he loves you, he will be patient."

"He has been. But I've been so hot and cold, and at times, cruel. I don't even know why."

Molly didn't have what she felt were adequate words, so she just sat quietly. She could sense that Carrie needed space.

Carrie wadded up the remainder of her lunch and stuffed it in the sack. Molly tossed down the last few bites and did the same.

Once at the office of Dr. Pinning, they were once again met by his research assistant. Carrie took a good look at her. "We need to see Dr. Pinning. And what is your name?"

A look of surprise popped up on her face. "Oh, uh, Laurel Wilson. Uh, I don't think Dr. Pinning is available."

"And why is that?" Carrie was going to use her emotion to do good. She wouldn't back down and let anyone shift her questions off course again.

"Uh, well, I'll have to see." Laurel disappeared behind the doors to his lab.

Molly looked at Carrie with a raised eyebrow. "I've learned a lot since I was last here. Now, everyone is a suspect that has access to a lab."

Laurel reappeared. "He is in a meeting with other professors. He can't be disturbed."

"Okay. We will just interview you." Carrie motioned with her hand for Laurel to have a seat.

"Me? Why me? I don't know anything."

"You work in the lab, correct?" Carrie asked.

"Yes."

"Well, we need to interview you."

They all sat in a grouping of chairs in the waiting area of his office. Carrie began to drill hard with all the questions she had concerning their case. She was now watching closely to see how Laurel responded.

Carrie pressed her for at least thirty minutes, or more. She ran out of questions and could see that Laurel was clearly shaken by the ordeal, but why, Carrie wondered. Was it because she felt threatened by Carrie's questions or because she was involved?

Molly had let Carrie lead this questioning. A part of her felt that she was being unnecessarily tough on Laurel, but then maybe Carrie knew or felt something that Molly didn't know about her.

When Carrie had asked Laurel all that she knew, to ask she said, "We must speak with Dr. Pinning as soon as possible. Do you know when he will be out of his meeting?"

"Uh, no I don't." Laurel was angry that the agent had pounded her so. The moment she had felt threatened by Carrie, she resolved to give as little information away as possible. She wouldn't say anything that would shed a bad light on Dr. Pinning.

Laurel knew about FLY. She had done a research paper on deadly and rare synthetic drugs. FLY had been included in that mix. She didn't, however, let Carrie know any of that, nor would she.

Carrie stood and Molly followed suit. "As soon as, I mean absolutely the moment Dr. Pinning is out of his meeting, have him call me."

Laurel nodded, taking the card from Carrie's hand. When Carrie made her way out of the office and down the hall, she was still angry. Angry in general, and maybe she shouldn't have taken that out on Laurel, but she couldn't help herself. There was such a long list of things to be angry about.

As they approached Molly's car, she said, "I suppose you know Laurel better than I do. What is it you suspect that caused you to drill her so hard?"

Carrie sat in the car seat deflated. "Nothing. Nothing at all."

The weight of this case, Randy missing, and her personal life was weighing Carrie down. She didn't feel rested after a fitful night of sleep. Her inexperience as an investigative agent frustrated her. Often, she found herself at a loss for what to do next and the few clues they had seemed to be a jumble in her brain.

Carrie combed the files from beginning to end once more. She was convinced there was something she had missed. An hour later, she stood to stretch her legs and get another cup of coffee. The office was quiet. Bracket had several agents working on Randy's kidnapping and many were out of the office for that reason. They were having to juggle their regular case load along with finding Randy. She wouldn't disturb the few who remained in the office. They would tell her as soon as something was found.

She herself would rather be out pounding the pavement, but she couldn't deny the gnawing sense that at this juncture, reading the files with fresh eyes would reveal something. Compiling case files, she knew, happens in bits and pieces. What is learned through the day, and of course all interviews conducted, go into them. It built a mountain of paperwork that was rarely revisited due to lack of time and forward momentum.

She came across the interview with Jason Anderson. As she read through, something occurred to her. She quickly searched for the interviews she and Molly had done. *We never followed up to find possible survivors of the rituals.* Things had gotten so crazy with Randy's disappearance and more bodies being discovered that she had become distracted and forgotten.

About noon, Molly called Carrie. "I am sorry if it seems like I have been MIA today. I had some departmental stuff that was mandatory, but I am done now so I thought I would see what you were doing and what you needed me to do."

Carrie began to babble about what she had realized, and additional thoughts that she hoped would lead them in the right direction. "But, I am forcing myself to continue to read these files until I am through them all. I'm just making notes as I go."

"Sounds smart. I know with so many involved in working the case, some things fail to come to the attention of everyone. Have you had lunch?"

Carrie was starved. Molly agreed to stop and get them some takeout and come help Carrie review the files.

By two that afternoon they had completed a linear review of everything. Carrie had a head start on Molly, but rather than dive in to where she was, Molly chose to also start at the beginning and read through them.

Carrie finished and went to get both she and Molly fresh coffee. She always felt greater fatigue from just sitting and handling paperwork than out being physical. This day was taking a toll on her.

She dropped off Molly's coffee and went to her desk to review any new emails. She had a few from the forensic lab.

There were no fingerprints or other substances on the leather. *Wow. How could that be? Even the retailer that it had been purchased from would have left some tiny residue or a few random fingerprints. They were lucid enough to clean everything they touched thoroughly.*

The next email was also from the forensics lab. There had

been no fingerprints at any of the body dumpsites. *This is so frustrating. The diligence that these people are operating under is thorough, but to not find anything is shocking.*

Then there was a third email. Randy's truck had been dumped deep in the woods under trees and brush. It was completely clean, no fingerprints or other residue. It had also rained for a couple of hours in that part of the state. There were no tire tracks or footprints. *Can we even catch a break on this?*

Carrie and Molly compared their notes and came to the same conclusion that they did indeed need to continue to focus on FLY, and also on finding survivors. They hadn't heard from Brandon but knew they needed to move forward with that as their focus.

They worked for the next hour on making lists and adding notes on the whiteboard. They checked their notes and added cross references where they could. Many had been interviewed, but with the probability of scopolamine in their system, they could not remember.

"We have a short list here. I believe these are a priority," said Molly. "Plus, we still need to get to Dr. Pinning."

"I agree. Why don't you call and see if we can set up an appointment with Dr. Pinning. Maybe Laurel will be more agreeable with you."

Molly sat thinking for a moment. "If we can find a survivor, maybe the trauma from the ritual, along with any physical injury caused will result in them remembering."

"I hope so. Honestly, I doubt it. But they should have wounds to deal with that should trigger their memory of the ordeal.

"So far, all the rituals have been different that we know of, but they have all produced some type of injury. If they 'woke up'," Carrie used air quotes, "and found severe injuries, wouldn't that have caused them to remember? Wouldn't they have gone to the hospital?"

Molly's face brightened. "We haven't checked any of the hospitals, have we?"

"No, but what would we ask for?"

"Any type of unusual injury. I know it is broad, but maybe..." Molly trailed off.

"Okay. You call Dr. Pinning's office and try and set us an appointment and I'll start collecting a list and calling hospitals."

Molly nodded and picked up her phone. Carrie headed back to her desk and decided to call those hospitals closest to where the bodies had been found and also nearest to UCO.

It only took Molly a few minutes before she came to find Carrie. "Laurel is still giving us the runaround. Do we have a direct number or email address for Dr. Pinning?"

Carrie shuffled through her computer. She finally found an email on the university's website under his profile. "An email is all I have, other than his office phone." Carrie jotted it down on a sticky note and handed it to Molly. "I can email him, but I suspect that Laurel screens his emails. Maybe you'll have better luck."

Molly took the paper and began to type an email from her BlackBerry. She was thankful for the technology, but she still wasn't used to the awkward typing on the tiny keyboard. It took her twice as long to formulate the email and send it compared to what it would have on her computer.

"Done."

"Here, let's split this list of hospitals." Carrie handed her half of the printed list of hospitals. It was nearly five o'clock, but they both felt the urgency to get as much done as possible and vowed to work through the list before going home.

Chapter Twenty-Two

It had been another long day when Carrie stepped up on her porch and retrieved her mail from the box attached next to her front door. She had not bothered the day before, and now there was a large bundle of mostly junk mail and newspaper adverts. She shoved the large bundle under her arm so that she could fumble with the keys and unlock her front door.

Once inside, she dropped the entire bundle on her countertop and retrieved a beer from the fridge. As best as she could remember, she had paid all her bills so she felt no urgency to go through the pile.

This was the first evening that she had gotten home at a decent hour. For the past several days she had come home late and exhausted, which resulted in a quick shower and bed. Each night as soon as her head hit the pillow, she was out. She did wake several times in the night and her sleep was fitful, but it was still sleep. In the morning, she was quick to jump up and out in a near run back to work.

As she sat on her sofa with the TV still off, the stillness of the room began to cloak her in emptiness. As it did, she thought of Billy and realized it had been days since she had heard from him. Guilt and shame welled up because she couldn't think about Billy without thinking of the night she'd betrayed him with Andy.

She had avoided calling Billy and used her heavy workload as an excuse, but normally he would have been calling or texting her at least once each day. Something was wrong and Carrie was suddenly terrified to find out what. Had he had enough of her avoidance? Was he injured? Had he found someone else?

Thoughts rushed through her mind like cars on a racetrack, each one weaving a heavy thread of anxiety through her mind. Dare she call him? She should. She knew she should, but just couldn't bring herself to face him. How she had treated him so badly by pushing him away, and how she had betrayed him with another man wasn't something she could reconcile in her heart. He had been so good and kind and patient with her and she had responded horrifically.

She rose and meandered to the kitchen to appease her gnawing stomach. She popped a frozen meal in the microwave and stood by her counter waiting. She began absentmindedly weeding through the mail pile, immediately throwing away the junk mail. When she was done, one lone letter remained. It was in Billy's handwriting.

Carrie became chilled to the bone, frozen and unable to open it. Sweat broke out on her forehead and her hands

began to tremble. The microwave began its beeping notification to alert Carrie her meal was ready, but she couldn't
respond.

Suddenly, in an effort to stop the noise, she reached
around and jerked the microwave door open, then turned
back to the letter she still held. She knew instinctively that it
was bad, really bad, and a tear slipped down her cheek.

She turned the letter over and began to open it. Her
fingers shook at the direction of her trembling hands and she
could barely conduct the routine maneuver. When she finally
managed to get the envelope open, she slid out the check and
handwritten note on a small piece of paper. It read...

*Carrie, here is a check for your half of the
wedding deposits that I was able to get
refunded. Billy*

That was it. She turned the notepaper over to see if there
was more on the back, but there was not. The air flew out
from her lungs and anguish pushed her emotions to the
brink, causing her to crumple to the floor. She had pushed
him away, permanently. She had abused his love for her,
testing it to the limit. He had loved her deeply and she knew
that. It was unlike Billy to do this without a final conversation, so the pain he must be feeling was deadly acute, and
Carrie knew it.

She had to call him. She had to face him, but she didn't
know if she had the courage to do so. As she sat on the floor in
the corner of the cabinets, she leaned her head over and

allowed the tears to fall. The smell of her microwave dinner drifted by and nauseated her.

For an untold amount of time, she sat numbly on the kitchen floor. Moving was not an option, her body would not respond even if she had the desire to will it so. She had done this to herself.

Had Sarah been right at the bar that night? Had she set out to punish herself, or had the utter fear of losing yet another person she loved drove her to this moment?

The last few weeks had spun past. The demand on her time from the frantic pace of her first case at OSBI was a nearly blur. Had it only been six weeks since her parents had passed? A mere month and a half. The bad choices stemming from her anger and corrosive attitude had sent her on a life spiral like none other. She knew in her heart she had chosen it, only making it even more painful to endure.

Looking down at the note that she still held in her hand, she realized that the lack of and sterility of the words could only mean one thing. He was done with her, completely and forever. Fresh pain sliced through her heart and she broke into a course of sobbing, not unlike the day she had lost her parents. Now, she had lost everyone who had ever loved her. She felt like a broken shell of a woman.

The ordeal exhausted her and she drifted off briefly, still sitting on her kitchen floor. Wild dreams of torment plagued her and she cried in her sleep.

It was nearly eleven o'clock when her phone began to vibrate on the counter. It woke her from her fitful sleep and as it buzzed, she wondered if she had the strength to stand and answer it. The buzzing finally stopped, but she knew if it had to do with the case, then she had to see what the call had been. Who else at this point could it be?

She pulled herself up onto her feet and looked at the now quiet phone. She felt hungover and wished it had been from an alcohol binge rather than the emotional upheaval that she had just experienced.

The light flickered on that a voicemail had been received. It was Molly and she pushed the button to return the call. She answered on the second ring. Before Carrie could even say a word, Molly rapidly spoke. "I found a survivor."

Adrenaline pushed away some of the fog that had settled around Carrie. But when she tried to speak, her voice was rough and gravely. She couldn't hide it or fake it and Molly knew that something horrific had happened.

"What is wrong? Tell me!" Molly had grown to care deeply for Carrie. She empathized with the tragedy she had experienced so recently with her parents. She knew this was a horrible case to have to deal with at such a time and she wanted to be there to help her navigate it all.

Carrie could only stutter. She tried to tell Molly, but the words jumbled and tied in knots. "I'll be right there. I'm coming to you."

Hearing the genuine care in Molly's voice reignited the tearful burst of emotion once again. "Okay," was all Carrie could squeak out. Molly hung up the phone and Carrie walked robotically to her sofa, but didn't sit down.

It would take Molly about fifteen minutes to get to her. She made it to her bathroom and splashed some tepid water on her face over and over again. Finally, she rose and looked herself straight in the mirror. Carrie gasped. She didn't recognize her face. Even after all the water, her face was puffy and red. Her eyes were swollen and they felt scratchy.

When the knock came at the door, she moved towards it with leaden feet. As soon as she opened the door and saw Molly standing there, she once again succumbed to an outburst of tears.

Molly stayed with Carrie until the early morning. They had downed a shared bottle of wine and sat on Carrie's sofa and talked. Carrie expanded on the little she had told Molly already about her life with her parents, their death, and how she had treated Billy so poorly, atrociously actually.

There had been many more tears and comforting words. Molly listened with empathy. It broke her heart to hear the depths of pain that Carrie was experiencing.

Carrie respected Molly not only as an excellent detective, but also as a good solid human being. She'd watched Molly and hoped that someday she could be as stable herself. During the night, Carrie stopped from time-to-time to ask questions of Molly, about her life and advice.

By two-thirty in the morning, both were spent. Their eyes were scratchy and their lids were heavy. "You can spend the night in my spare room," Carrie offered.

"That is so tempting, but I think I might as well go on home. I can get a shower and rest in my own bed for a few hours." Carrie nodded understanding.

At the door, Carrie stood attempting to formulate words of gratitude for Molly. Her eyebrows were pinched together and her mouth moved to speak but was void of sound. Another rogue tear tracked down her cheek.

"I know Carrie. I know." She reached out and patted Carries hand. "I'll see you in the morning."

Carrie slept fitfully for the little that she did sleep. She grieved over the loss of Billy, knowing that this time she had crossed the line and there was no going back. She questioned herself. Did she loath herself that much? The continuous barrage of questions was a pounding, berating drum beat through her soul all night and she couldn't make them stop.

She was awake when the sun slid through the blinds in her bedroom window. Even though she felt completely and utterly exhausted, she was eager to get to work and let the details of the case carry her away. Hopefully, it would stop all the self-hatred that had assaulted her all night long.

Carrie knew that Molly would feel nearly as bad as she did for staying up so late with her, investing herself so fully. Molly had sacrificed her own rest for Carrie. It was just another quality that exemplified Molly's virtuous character, and Carrie admired her even more in the light of morning.

It was ten minutes after eight when Carrie walked into the office. She checked in with Bracket to see if there had been any progress on finding Randy. There had been none. Carrie knew Bracket would call her first, even before calling Sandy, but she still had to ask. It was a disappointing start to the day.

At her desk, Carrie went through emails and other messages so her desk would be clear when Molly arrived. The previous night Molly had mentioned that she thought she had found a potential survivor of the rituals. With all the drama the note from Billy had created, they had not revisited that bit of information.

Molly had a quick departmental meeting first thing, but arrived shortly after Carrie had finished tending to messages. Carrie looked up to see a bright and chipper Molly at the side of her desk.

"How on earth do you look so wonderful after such a long night?" Carrie asked.

"Oh, I may look good on the outside, but my insides are already begging for a nap." They chuckled and headed to the war room.

"Okay," Molly began as she pulled out her notebook still standing, "I found a young man in the right age range that is in the hospital at Summit Medical Center. It is a fairly new physician-owned hospital that specializes in wound and surgical care. I searched in our system and found a corresponding police report for him as a 'John Doe.'

"He was admitted there several weeks ago due to some abnormal needs which have proved to be quite horrific. Unfortunately, he has been in a medically-induced coma for recovery reasons since soon after arriving."

"What are his issues?"

"He has gangrene in his limbs. Just like your research showed on others in the Netherlands who took FLY years ago. He has lost his legs and arms, and they have him in a barometric chamber. There was no ID on him when he arrived and they do not have a name for him."

"How did he get there?"

"Someone put him out in the grassy area to the side and back of the hospital, away from any surveillance cameras. It was very late at night. They then called the hospital from a burner phone to let them know he was there. The hospital staff quickly found him. His wounds were so critical they began treating him immediately, while a staff member called the OKCPD. They have been treating ever since."

Carrie sat back in her chair stunned and horrified. A few silent moments ticked by, then she looked up at Molly. "Is there anything we can gain from going there?"

"His fingerprints were not in the system. They were able to take them prior to amputation. He has already been through a couple of surgeries and his body was cleaned thoroughly in prep for both. His clothes were put in a bag and given to a patrolman who came by to take their statements. They are in our evidence locker. There might be something on there."

Carrie felt gutted. "We have to do something before more young men die or wind up damaged for life." Her fatigued eyes pleaded with Molly. "So many young men have died. I feel like I have failed them."

Molly sat down across from Carrie and looked her steadily in the eye. "This is not your fault. It is the perpetrator's fault. You have been working nearly non-stop to halt this madness. You are not to blame. You have to shut out the voices that tell you otherwise, for the victim's sakes. This part of law enforcement is new to you, but one that is crucial for you to learn."

Carrie gave a slight nod. She was an overachiever and had

always succeeded brilliantly at everything she had ever done. To her, she felt she was falling far short of where she needed to be. She felt like she was failing for the first time in her life, in more ways than one.

She sat up straighter and took a deep breath. "Okay. What do we do next?"

"I'll call and make sure his clothes get to the forensics lab for testing. Then we keep calling hospitals to see if others have found their way in with serious wounds. I was nearly done last night when I called you. How far did you get?"

"I have only about three more. We can get these churned out and then go from there." Carrie said.

For the next hour they finished calling the remaining hospitals. They found no other young men with strange or unusual wounds or illnesses.

Molly was on the phone with the last hospital on her list when another call came through. It was Brandon. As soon as her call ended, she clicked the voicemail he had left. "Call me."

"I just got a call from Brandon. Let's hope that he has something concrete for us."

Molly dialed Brandon with the press of a button.

"I'm going to get right to the point of the info you needed. I need to hop on a conference call but wanted to get in a call to you first."

"Okay, good." Molly replied.

"There are a few chemicals that are needed to make FLY. It is started with a base of n-butyllithium. It is highly unstable and flammable. It can spontaneously combust in air if not handled properly. It is odorless. Because of the danger, it is usually obtained as a solution and not pure.

"That base is then treated with hydroquinone, a chemical which is found in many cosmetics and dermatological creams for pigment bleaching.

"I have this entire process written down and have sent it to your email. There is more, and I may get the process wrong quoting over the phone, but there are other chemicals used. A nitropropene derivative is obtained by condensation with nitromethane. Nitropropene is used to manufacture Adderall, an amphetamine that is used for the treatment of ADHD and narcolepsy. Nitroethane is a solvent used in resins and waxes. It is an oily liquid.

"I've obtained a list of those chemicals that have been ordered and shipped, which I have also emailed to you. None of the quantities were outstandingly large, but then I've been informed it takes very little of them to product the product. Maybe the list will give you a place to start if you can cross it with suspects you already have."

"That is a lot. Thank you, Brandon. We appreciate your help more than you know. The killer or killers are not slowing down. It feels as if they may have even stepped up their game. This information will help us."

"Okay. I've got to scoot. Love ya, girlie!" Brandon chuckled and hung up before waiting for her reply.

Molly had had her phone on speaker so that Carrie could hear it all. Molly used the email app on her phone to forward Brandon's emails to the printer. They laid the printed sheets out on their table and began to review for recognizable locations that they could tie to any of their known suspects.

"I did okay in chemistry in college, but this is all beyond my knowledge." Carrie was reading the chemical process of creating FLY.

"I would guess that only someone with a doctorate in chemistry would be able to easily pull this off," Molly replied.

"He didn't mention scopolamine."

"When I talked to him before, he said that was a common drug used in hospitals and clinics. We thought focusing on FLY since it is the most unique one would make the most sense."

Carrie nodded in agreement and looked back down at the page she was reading.

"A doctorate in chemistry..." Carrie mused under her breath.

In his dreams, Randy sensed he was outdoors. The wind, the sounds of the birds singing, the smell of the earth. He had never had such vivid dreams before. But it wasn't a dream. He was indeed outdoors.

Before he could open his eyes, the pain in his head sent him reeling. Maybe it was the pain that had brought him to consciousness. His attempt to raise his hand to feel his head posed a challenge, as he felt he lacked control over his own body.

He had a syrupy feel to his mouth that was sickly sweet. He worked to open his eyes against their reluctance. The light pushed them tightly shut again.

His head. He had never had pain in his head like that.

Something was not right. He needed help. He opened his eyes just a slit to allow them to warm to the idea of light. He was now aware enough of his surroundings that he could tell he was somewhere deep in the woods.

He raised up on one elbow and scooted back to lean on a nearby tree. The effort drained him and the movement sent his head pounding in overdrive. He was instantly sick and leaned over to release whatever his last meal had been.

His pockets were empty. No phone, wallet, keys, nothing. He would have to walk out of here and get help. But just exactly where was here? By the looks of the sun, it was nearing the middle of the day.

He placed one hand on the tree and pushed to stand upright. Once done, he clung to the tree to allow a wave of severe dizziness to subside.

What did he remember? His mind tried to sift through memories of the last few... few what? Had it been hours, days, or weeks? And where had he been last? He felt his cheek. He remembered what had felt like hay. Had he been in a barn lying on hay or had it been a dream?

But before that. What had been before that? He couldn't remember. He couldn't remember anything else at all.

He glanced around him. There was no sign of a house or other civilization. There was only a small path the led out of the woods to an old dirt road. Well, that was a start.

The dirt road was difficult to walk on with ruts from rain and tire tracks. It was becoming hot too. He looked down and realized he wore dress shoes and trousers. How odd. Did he always wear dress clothes? His mind held no answer.

The dirt road went on for a very long distance, winding

first one way and then another. His head was screaming in pain the entire time. Finally, he heard noise. Machinery of some sort, and he tried to decide where it was coming from.

When he looked around everything became blurry and shifted so that he couldn't decide what was real and what was made up. Then there was nothing.

Randy slumped to the ground in the middle of the dirt road. He lay crumpled in a heap.

From up ahead, a man on a tractor was heading toward Randy. He had seen him fall to the ground and not get up. He put the slow tractor in park and jumped down. Then he ran towards Randy and reached to feel his pulse. He was still alive.

The man reached for his flip phone and attempted to dial, but there was no signal. He shoved it back into his pocket and ran back to the tractor to drive it closer to Randy. When he had gotten as close as possible, he jumped back down. He had to figure out a way to get Randy up in the tractor so he could get him to a hospital.

Randy was not a heavy man, but at six feet tall, it was difficult for someone to maneuver his dead weight. The farmer was tough though, having tossed large bales of hay and wrangled livestock his entire life. He worked to position Randy up and over his shoulder and carried him to the tractor. One step at a time, he climbed up into the cab with Randy in tow.

It took a good thirty minutes to get to a phone on the tractor. He called 911 and asked for an ambulance. He explained he was at a small rural convenience store and that he had found a man unconscious in his pasture.

Randy never regained consciousness during the thirty-minute wait for the ambulance and the forty-mile ride to the nearest hospital. No one knew who he was. By the time he was in a bed in the ER, it was four p.m.

An examination found that he had a hematoma from an impact to his head. It appeared someone had hit him hard enough to cause a slow brain bleed and it had swollen to the point of being critical. He needed immediate surgery, or he risked severe brain damage or even death.

At ten p.m. after awakening from surgery, Randy looked around at his surroundings. He was in an ICU at a hospital. A nurse saw that he had awoken and quickly came to his side.

"Welcome back." She smiled as she checked his tubes, monitors, and vitals.

Randy just looked up at her.

"Do you know where you are?"

"A hospital." His mouth felt dry and his voice was faint.

"Yes. Do you know why you are here?"

"No." Randy tried to shake his head, but it sent a round of sharp pain through his skull and colored lights skated across his eyes.

"Do you know your name?"

Of course he knew his name. What kind of nurse was this? But then he stopped. It didn't come quickly. "Randy. My name is Randy, I think."

"And what is your last name?"

He frowned as he thought. Then, slowly, it emerged. "Jeffries. I'm Randy Jeffries, I think. Honestly, I don't know if that is my name or just a name I remember."

"That is good Randy."

Randy reached out and grabbed the nurse's arm. "I don't remember much. But I do think I might be in law enforcement." His eyes pleaded with the nurse.

"Okay. The local sheriff is wanting to speak with you anyway. He's been waiting for you to wake up. I'll go get him."

The nurse left to go fill in Sheriff Pine on Randy's status, and he was soon heading into where Randy lay.

"I'm Sheriff Pine. It's good to see that you are awake. Nurse Reynolds says you say you are in law enforcement." He could see that Randy's face carried concern.

"I think I've lost part of my memory. It took me awhile to remember what my name might be. But I am pretty sure I am in law enforcement. I don't even know what or where." Randy's eyebrows once again pinched together and he searched the Sheriff's face for some type of answer, but none was there to be found.

The sheriff clicked his mic and gave instructions to a deputy to search for one Randy Jeffries, possibly in law enforcement. Soon, the deputy's voice came back over with the details Randy had been trying to remember.

"He is an OSBI agent out of Oklahoma City. He's been missing since last Friday night. Suspected abduction."

"Thank you, deputy."

Randy had heard the exchange and worked to fit the new knowledge into his mind, into his memories.

"You get some rest. We will let your people know."

"Thank you, Sheriff."

The nurse replaced the sheriff at Randy's side. "You need

to rest. You've just had major surgery on your head. Try and get some sleep. It is for your own good."

Randy gave a slight nod and closed his eyes. But his mind was working overtime to try and find any sliver of memory. He was an OSBI agent in Oklahoma City. Did that fit? Yes, he thought it did, maybe. Who did he work with? Did he have a wife? He looked at his hand. There was no ring, but then they would have taken that off for surgery. However, there was no indentation where a ring had been.

He closed his eyes again. Why had he been hit on the head? Who had hit him on the head? Was it because of a case he was working on, or just some thug?

Sleep came, but with disturbing dreams. There was a big house and a party. He didn't want to be there. Then, it was dark and people were taking him somewhere. A rough bumpy tractor took him away. Far, far away.

A rustling noise beside his bed caused Randy to awaken some time later. There stood two women by his bed. He should know them, right? Was one a girlfriend? No, he didn't think so. They were law enforcement too. They knew him, or were they there to arrest him for something? He shut his eyes and drifted back off to sleep.

Sandy had driven way too fast to the hospital. The moment she had been notified, she got in her car. She didn't even look in the mirror and she didn't care that she had her old sweatpants on. Her only priority was getting to Randy.

When she rushed into the ICU unit, Carrie and Molly were at his bedside. "Ma'am you can't go in until those two leave." Nurse Reynolds had come from around the desk to stop her. When she was confident that the woman would stay put, she motioned for Carrie and Molly to come out.

Sandy immediately rushed in and gently laid down onto Randy, sobbing. He opened his eyes and saw blonde-haired woman sobbing on his chest. He felt lucky that someone so beautiful cared. But, who was she?

Chapter Twenty-Three

Garrett didn't know that Marta had planned on following him that night. It was his turn to participate in the ritual. None of them ever knew which ritual would be conducted, even if it was their night.

It had been a few days since Garrett had agreed to be next. At that point, he had stayed with a person he didn't know, and rarely saw. His only instruction had been to stay indoors, and to eat and drink only what was served to him.

He had been told that in order for the ritual to be successful, his intake of food and liquid had to be closely monitored. There had been no access to television, phone, or other electronics, in order to purify his mind and soul in preparation.

The first day had gone slowly. The confinement and strict diet had been hard, but the lack of electronics was the worst. By evening, he was pacing the floor.

The second day was somewhat better. Without him knowing, they had put the tiniest bit of FLY into his water the previous day. Because of the earlier deaths, the amount had been adjusted to only add a minuscule amount each day. Getting the dosage of this component correct was crucial to the experience.

On the third day, Garrett didn't think or feel anything accurately. The feeling of floating and seeing other worlds carried him through the day. It was the spiritual awakening that had been promised. He knew he was getting closer to God and to proving his courage. As each moment passed, he became more convinced that he could.

The evening of the fifth day arrived and Garrett was taken with the others from Hafer Park to the old barn. He had a handler to help him navigate to the van and then to the barn. He knew he was no longer of this world and needed a contact from the other world to guide him.

At the barn, Garrett was separated from the others and taken to a back room to wait. It was closed off from the open portion of the barn by a sliding door.

Marta had been watching and waiting. She did not trust any of this and was terrified that Garrett would die. The fear of getting caught pressed her to be overly cautious. She had followed Garrett when he had gone to stay sequestered for five days. She watched and waited outside, only leaving for short periods of time to use the restroom and to grab some fast food.

She was there on the evening of the fifth day and watched as Garrett was led out the door and into the van. Since she knew they were going to meet at Hafer park, she felt comfortable following at a distance.

Entering the park, Marta veered off from the van to a

place where she could watch unseen behind a grove of trees. It appeared to her that there were about six young men waiting. It was a far cry from the number that had attended the first meeting. They were literally going to kill them all off. Would they stop when they were all dead or search for more?

When Marta saw them getting in the van, she hustled back to her car and turned it around so that she could easily pull out behind them.

It was nerve racking attempting to follow the van close enough so that she wouldn't lose them, but far enough back that they wouldn't notice her. It was dark long before they pulled down a tree lined road. A shiver ran up Marta's spine. The tension of the drive had pulled her tight up to the steering wheel and her fingers clutched the wheel with a death grip.

The van pulled into a large clearing with an old barn in the center. She didn't dare follow. The risk of being seen was too great. She stopped just shy of the opening, pulling over to the side into the tall weeds. She had shut off her headlights before turning onto the old dirt road, using the lights from the van as her only navigation.

Once out of her car, she crept up in a squatting position as far as she felt she could without being detected. Garrett was being led around the side of the barn and into another door in the back. The remaining guys were led into the main barn door. Once everyone was inside, Marta hurriedly walked hunched down in a near duck walk to the edge of the barn. The doors were all shut.

After a moment, Marta hurried back to the door where Garrett had entered. She knew that she was outnumbered, so was as quiet as possible. With each step, she could hear pounding in her head from the anxiety of the moment. At the door, she stopped and slowly turned to survey the area for anyone who might be watching. When she saw no one, she gently tried to turn the doorknob but was instantly met with resistance. "Damn," she whispered. *Now what?*

If she knocked on the door then anyone in there would be alerted. She had to find a way in. The barn was huge. Marta looked up to see that the barn appeared to be two stories and maybe about thirty feet or more tall. A hay barn. Someone had used this to store massive amounts of hay in it, which would mean there was a large loft above a main room. Garrett must be in some kind of storage or tack room.

There were no lower windows. The lower level had two huge barn doors, one on each end, with one on the top floor. Marta walked to the barn door in the back, which was opposite of the one the other guys had entered through. There was a haze of light where the doors didn't seal tightly against the barn and she was hopeful that opening that door wouldn't plunge her into the middle of the group.

She grabbed a handle, stepped to the side and began pulling backwards as she braced herself with her feet. She wanted strength to pull, but hoped that her stance could help her control the speed at which the door opened. It didn't budge. It too was locked.

That failure moved her around to the other side of the barn. A tiny glow of light eased out of a chink in the wood siding. It was only about the size of a small pencil and about level with her knees, but Marta would take it. It was her gateway to see what was going on inside.

It took several tries to position herself so that she could see with one eye through the tiny hole. Having done that, she could only see dimly. The barn was lit by just a few battery-operated lanterns. *At least they aren't stupid enough to use flame lanterns in a hay barn.*

The six young men who had arrived at Hafer park stood around nervously. Marta repositioned to see if she could see more of the barn. As she did, she stepped into a pile of something mushy and a stench rose up from the ground. Wet cow dung. As she tried to brush her foot off on some dry grass, it took her attention away from the hole.

When she had finally repositioned herself to see inside, the young men had moved to the side and there sat a large wooden cross. Marta felt lightheaded. She had to save Garrett. As she continued to peer into the hole, a nearly undetectable mist floated through.

Marta began to feel a bit dizzy and stood up. She took several deep breaths of fresh air and halted when the stench of the cow dung hit her nose. *I have to get Garrett out of there.*

Panic made it difficult for Marta to think. She bent back down to once again peer into the hole. She could only see the backs of the young men now. Movement from the side of the barn where Garrett had entered split the group to allow Garrett to pass.

He seemed nearly catatonic and was being led by someone with a hood on. Marta could see what appeared to be a gas mask peeking out below the hood, with maybe a strap or a buckle.

Garrett was led to lie down on the wooden cross. He did so willingly. Fear surged through Marta, but each time she peered through the hole she became dizzy. Suddenly, she didn't care about being caught, and she began to bang on the barn walls. She ran from place to place, banging as loud as she could.

No one emerged, so she went back to the hole and peered in. What she saw sickened her. She turned away from the hole, leaning back against the barn. She slid to the ground, sobbing uncontrollably. *How can they all stand around and allow that to happen?*

Marta pulled her knees up to her chest and rocked back and forth. *I don't know what to do. I don't know what to do.* Then, all of a sudden, she remembered the new cell phone her parents had bought her. She rarely used it because the plan they had purchased had so few minutes that she just didn't mess with it.

She stood up, wiped her eyes and took off running for her car.

Carrie picked up her phone. It was Molly.

"Dispatch had a 911 call come in. I'm going to swing by and get you. I'm almost there."

Carrie changed from her sweats and was ready to go in seconds. "What is it?" Carrie asked as soon as she was inside Molly's car.

"A young woman called in hysterical. She was somewhere in the country at a barn. Dispatch could make out very little. I was at the station when they transferred the call. Officers are heading that way, but I wanted to stop and get you.

"I'm glad you did." Carrie's mind was racing, and she couldn't make conversation. What would they find? She was so tired of all the deaths, and along with the drama in her own life with Billy, she felt like she might have a mental breakdown.

"You okay?" Molly asked.

Carrie gave a jagged nod without looking at Molly. She wasn't, but she couldn't let Molly know. She had to do her job.

Molly knew Carrie was tough, but with all she had been through with her parents' recent death, the tumultuous breakup with Billy, and this horrific case, she knew that it would test anyone's metal.

She also sensed that Carrie needed quiet to sort through her thoughts, so Molly just drove fast toward the crime scene. There was only one patrol car with lights still flashing as they drove into the clearing.

Molly had barely put the car in park and turned off the key when they both jumped from the car. In the barn, one officer stood back near the door as the other one stood by a young woman crumpled to her knees, sobbing hysterically. Next to her was a young man stretched out on a huge wooden cross. It was lying flat on bales of hay that elevated it up from the floor.

Blood dripped down from the young man's wrists and feet. He was stark white and his flesh had a barely visible sheen.

Molly and Carrie stopped short at the appalling site in the barn. They could barely assimilate the visual information that was assaulting their senses. They had slowed to a stop when entering the barn, then began to slowly walk toward the scene.

Molly saw his chest rise and fall ever so slightly. "He's still alive," Molly exclaimed. "He's still alive!" She whirled around to the other officer. "Did you call an ambulance?" He was a young rookie on the night shift and was struggling to function.

He shook his head with wild eyes. "No. I thought he was dead."

"Call now!" Molly barked orders.

The other officer looked at Molly. "We just got here ourselves and this is what we found."

Garrett's head fell to the side and a moan slipped out of his mouth. At that movement, Marta shrieked and crumpled into another round of hysterical sobbing. The officer had his hands gently on her shoulders to keep her where she was.

"Let me go," Marta screamed. "Garrett needs me!" Marta had little strength, but was using it to push her way to him. However, the officer's hands, even though gentle, were just enough force to keep her back.

Molly walked around the cross to get as close to Garrett's head as possible. She placed two fingers on his neck and held them there. Looking up, she confirmed, "He is still alive, but barely."

She leaned in and quietly said, "Garrett. Garret, stay with us now. We are here for you. We are going to get you help."

Marta shook uncontrollably. "Garrett, don't die. I'm here. I came for you." Her words trailed off with anguishing cries.

It seemed like it took the ambulance much longer to arrive at the barn than it actually did. The officer tried multiple times to remove Marta from the scene, but each time she erupted into greater hysteria, so they agreed that as long as she stayed put, they would leave her there.

The ambulance arrived along with two other officers and the forensic team. When the EMT's saw the young man nailed to the wooden cross with large square-cut spike nails that appeared to be about six to eight inches long, they stopped in their tracks.

"He's still alive," Molly said, still near Garrett's head. "But, barely."

They rushed over and felt for a pulse. The dilemma over stopping the bleeding and preserving evidence was in the balance.

"We need tools to get these spikes out. Right now, the spikes are staunching the blood flow. When we remove them, he could bleed out quickly. And, we don't have anything large enough to transport him as is." The EMT glanced over at Marta as more wails cut through the air.

The officer spoke gently to Marta. "We need to go now so that they can help him. They can't do their job with us right here."

It took more urging, but Marta soon gave way to allow the officer to help her up and out of the barn, all the while looking back at Garrett and the horrific sight she could not comprehend.

Once Marta was out of the barn, Carrie looked at Molly. "What do we do?"

Molly knelt down and with a gloved hand, grasped the end of one of the spikes. She gave it a slight push with her hand and found that it moved. She looked up at the EMT's.

"I think that these are put in so shallow that we can pull them out."

The forensic team held out a brown paper evidence bag and Molly slightly wiggled the spike back and forth until it did indeed slide out into her hand. Garrett moaned through the process, but had not regained consciousness. The EMTs rapidly attended the wrist wrapping it to stop the blood flow.

The next spike at his other wrist came out in the same manner as the other one. Each time, the EMTs waited to grab the wrist and wrap it to stop the flow of blood.

Molly moved to Garrett's feet. They had been placed side-by-side rather than pinned together as she had always pictured Jesus's crucifixion. Each foot was nailed just above the ankles rather than through his feet.

Molly once again took hold of a spike at the very top. The first one proved much more formidable. She didn't want to cause more damage to Garrett's leg than was necessary. She looked up to the forensic tech. "I can't seem to budge it. Do you want to try?"

He nodded, and with a little more strength than Molly had, was able to get both the remaining spikes out. With Garrett freed from the wooden cross, the EMTs were able to gently lift him onto the stretcher and tend to him. In a short time, they were off to the hospital.

Carrie looked up for the first time since entering the barn. High above them was an elaborate pulley system with thick ropes. It was attached to the top of the cross with a large metal ring.

"They had stopped minutes away from using that pulley system to stand that cross upright. At that moment, Garrett's full weight would have been on those spikes. He has Marta's concern to be thankful for. It is a good thing she followed and then disrupted the ritual." Carrie was aghast at the thought of what lay before them.

Molly and Carrie had slid blue booties onto their feet when first entering. They now did a visual sweep of the barn. After about fifteen minutes, nothing obvious had surfaced. "Let's let the forensic team do their job," said Molly as she popped off her gloves.

"Do you think the girl is in any shape to talk to us?" Carrie asked.

Molly stood at the door of the barn looking at the patrol car where the girl sat. "Maybe. We can try."

At the car, they found Marta nearly catatonic. Molly opened the door and squatted down beside her. "Is it okay if we talk with you a bit?"

No response came at first, but then Molly's words finally penetrated and Marta gave a slight nod. "I'm going to go around and slide in beside you if that is okay." Marta gave another nod, quicker this time.

Molly did as she said, and Carrie stood outside the open door next to Marta. "Can you tell us your name?" Molly began.

"Marta." Carrie jotted down her name and had her pen at the ready for more.

"Marta Bradford."

"And what is your friend's name?"

A sob jerked its way out of Marta and silent tears slid down her cheeks. "Garrett," she halted and closed her eyes. "Garrett Hyde."

"That's good, Marta. Very good. Now, we need you to tell us everything you can remember about tonight. Why did you come here, and everything that happened after you arrived. We need to get whoever hurt your friend." Molly paused. "Can you do that for us Marta?'

Marta gave a nod. She suddenly felt sick and leaned out the door causing Carrie to jump back. When she saw that Marta was sick, she quickly reached to help the young woman. This was only heaping more heartache on Carrie's already deeply wounded soul. *I can do this. I can do this.* Carrie forced herself to push her emotional wounds aside so she could focus on helping Marta and catching this killer.

Molly found a bottle of water in her car and helped Marta to a drink. It seemed that the bout of sickness helped her to regain some of her composure.

"It all started when..." Marta continued to tell the entire story, from the time of their first visit to the ordeal they had suffered that very night. Carrie was writing furiously to try and get it all down. Much they knew, some they suspected, but there was key information that Marta was giving them that would help them bring this case to a close.

Carrie's phone rang, it was Molly. She was sitting at her desk waiting for Marta to arrive so that they could get her statement on the record. "I am on my way, but traffic is backed up. I just received word that Garrett is stable. The doctors do not want any visitors quite yet, even law enforcement."

"Thank you for letting me know. When Marta arrives, I'll

make her comfortable and wait for you before getting her official statement."

Carrie felt that they were gaining momentum in the case, but it seemed that it had come at a high cost. The body frequency hadn't slowed, so with each passing day that they didn't solve the case there was a risk of one more person dying. It was Carrie's hope that today she could tease some additional critical details from Marta that would point them to the key person responsible.

When Marta arrived, Carrie helped her to get settled into an interrogation room. She treated her to coffee and a donut from the batch that had just been delivered. She looked haggard and worn out. Her eyes were bloodshot from having cried so much and she'd not bothered to apply any makeup over her mottled face.

"We are waiting on Detective Jacobs. She is stuck in traffic." Marta hadn't moved toward the coffee or donut. "I heard that Garrett is stable. That is good news."

Marta looked down at the donut. The ordeal had left her exhausted, yet sleep had been elusive the previous night. She reached over and picked a small piece of the donut off and placed it in her mouth.

The interrogation room door swung open and in stepped Molly. She smiled at Marta and sat down next to Carrie, who turned on the recorder.

Carrie began the interview. "Marta, thank you so much for agreeing to meet with us this morning. We know you've been through a lot. You did very good last night in telling us what happened and I know repeating it won't be fun. We are hoping though that we can get it on the record and maybe now we can slow down and get a few more details."

Marta nodded and reached for her coffee. "How did you and Garrett, or even just Garrett, first become involved with this group?"

Marta thought, roaming through her bank of memories. She wanted to arrive at the very first time she had heard Garrett talk about it all.

"Garrett came over to my apartment very excited. He had been with a group of guys and they were not happy about how weak other guys had made them feel."

Marta continued through the same series of events that she had given them the previous nights. She had only given them a couple of names and they were resting on their whiteboard, dead.

"Marta, you said that there was a guy who came into the barn with a hood on, but maybe had a gas mask on. Can you tell us more about that?" Carrie urged.

Marta sat thinking. That moment had been terrifying for her and to go to that memory pierced her heart with a deep pain, but for Garrett's sake she pushed forward. "He had some sort of cloak on. The hood was very, very large. It covered his entire head and whatever mask he was wearing."

"What color was the cloak?"

Marta looked up at the women and began to describe the red cloak in as much detail as she could remember.

"What color was the person in the cloak? Could you see their skin?"

"No. They had black leather looking gloves on and I couldn't see any facial skin."

"What about shoes or pants? Can you remember those?"

Marta shut her eyes in an attempt to see the person once again. "Tennis shoes. Just some white Nike tennis shoes."

"Did they look like men's or women's shoes?"

Marta once again shut her eyes, searching her memory. She wrinkled her brow and began to shake her head. "I don't know. I could see just a bit of jeans on the top of the shoes, but they didn't seem too small for a man or too big for a woman. I just don't know."

"How tall do you think the person was? Picture them against the others in the group. Were they taller or shorter?"

"About the same I think." A tear slid from Marta's eye. "I'm sorry. I feel like I'm not any help at all."

"Oh yes, you are. More help than you realize. Thank you for being patient with us to get as many details as we can. You are being very brave."

Carrie and Molly spent at least two hours with Marta gently teasing as many details out of her as they could. She had been very cooperative, but she was so wounded and weary that the interrogation was taking a huge toll on her. They finally called it at nearly noon.

Molly had excused herself for a bathroom break and Carrie had gone to the war room with Marta's statement in hand. For a moment she stood reading and shuffling a few items, all the while thinking. Thinking about what details they needed, but also about what details they had that could mean more than they had previously thought.

"Solved it yet?" Molly asked as she entered the room.

"We have so much information. There must be something in all of this that is the key to solving it."

Molly reached over and took the statement from Carrie's hand. "So, we know that when Marta first went to a meeting with Garrett, it was off campus in a house. It was dark and she didn't know where they were. Garrett had driven and she had been focused on asking him why they were going and what was going to happen.

"But she did say that it was a man speaking to the others, commanding the group. She couldn't verify, but let's assume that was the same man in the hood. Makes sense."

Carrie nodded in agreement, her mental wheels turning.

"As far as his age, she admitted she wasn't good with age, but knew he was older than the other young men in the meeting, maybe by a few years. So, let's say from twenty-five to thirty? Does that sound about right?"

Again, Carrie gave an affirmative nod.

Molly walked closer to the board. "We have no one on this board in that age range. The young men are all from nineteen to twenty-one. The male professors are all at least forty-five and above." Molly looked at Carrie. "We still don't have the perpetrator on our board."

Carrie sat down and pulled the tablet that Marta had used to write out her statement and began writing on the board. As she did, she spoke out loud. "Advanced chemistry knowledge, possibly doctorate of chemistry or pharmacology, male from twenty-five to thirty, medium stature, brown hair."

Carrie tapped on the board. "This is who we are looking for." She looked at Molly for confirmation.

"Who are the professors of chemistry at UCO? I believe they would all be too young, but their grad students might not be." Molly said.

Carrie thumbed through a file until she came to the correct list. The list was long and as she read each one from both the University of Central Oklahoma and the University of Oklahoma, she realized they had not interviewed any of them.

She looked up at Molly in shocked realization. "We haven't interviewed any of these. We got sidetracked with the rituals and the professors who attended that meeting. To my knowledge, none of these professors were there, or if any attended, they were not in the small private meeting afterwards."

Molly tapped the pencil she was holding against her chin, thinking. "But Randy was abducted while at the meeting. That is a glaring red flag that the attendees were part of this. If that was a detour, then why was Randy abducted?"

"We need to talk to Randy. Do you think he has regained any more of his memory?" Carrie's face was wrinkled with worry. She had been putting thoughts of Randy on the back burner. She had been so thrilled that he had been found in one piece, that she had moved on to more pressing concerns.

"The only way we will know is if we ask. Let's go talk to Bracket and see what he thinks."

Bracket was at his desk shuffling paperwork when the two women entered. "Your faces don't look like we achieved a major breakthrough, even with last night's ordeal. What do you need?"

Carrie went through the recent revelations that had surfaced concerning the chemistry portion of the case, and the need to talk with Randy about anything he had discovered while both at the meeting and afterwards.

Bracket thought about their request. "Randy has regained very little of his memory. The doctor said this often happens with this type of head injury, especially with what Randy went through and the time between injury and surgery. I honestly don't know if asking him will help or maybe even hurt."

"Can we at least try? We can just take it a bit at a time and if it appears he is getting distressed, we will stop. But we need to know what he found out, if anything."

Bracket gave a decisive nod and they were soon out the door and heading toward Tulsa.

Chapter Twenty-Four

The hospital floor seemed abnormally quiet when Carrie and Molly stepped off of the elevator. They had left Oklahoma City about three p.m. beating the rush hour traffic for those commuters who lived in Tulsa but worked in OKC. The drive usually took about an hour and a half, give or take, but they were in Molly's car with lights on.

As they turned the corner to the hallway where Randy's room was, they saw Sandy leaving his room. She looked weathered and they could tell that hovering under the surface was a sense of desperation.

"Sandy," Carrie said as they approached. "How are you?"

Sandy had been looking down as she walked and looked up at her name. When she saw Carrie and Molly, she burst out in a torrent of tears. They ushered her to a small waiting room and sat on either side of her. Neither wanted to say anything that might inflict more pain.

Sandy began to recover somewhat. "He is slightly better. Physically, he is improving by the hour. There have been a few things he has remembered, but the mass majority of his life is still a blank." A series of sobs jerked their way from her already exhausted body.

"I don't know if he will ever remember..." She couldn't utter the words. "I don't know if he will ever remember m... me." She crumpled in on herself as the pain those words inflicted charged into her soul one more time.

Compassion for Sandy was the commanding emotion for Carrie and Molly. But when hearing Sandy's words, thoughts of getting more usable information that would help them solve the case, dissolved. "Have you eaten?" Molly asked Sandy.

"I can't eat." Her sobs punctuating her words.

"You need to eat something so that you can endure this for you and for Randy."

Carrie remembered hearing those same words from Billy after her parents had died. He just hadn't understood how she physically couldn't force food into her body at that moment.

As Sandy continued to lean forward resting her elbows on her legs, Carrie gently rubbed her back. Words would not help her, but she still felt compelled to do something. She was gradually gaining an understanding of what others felt on the other side of her grief. Feeling compelled to do something to ease their pain, all the while knowing nothing could.

Carrie's mind drifted to Billy. He, more than anyone, had wanted to ease her pain, but she had refused to allow herself to feel any comfort. She felt she needed to hurt, needed to feel the pain of loss as a tribute to her parents. So, she would not be comforted.

When Sandy had regained some composure, and after no one had spoken for a while, Molly asked if it would be okay if they visited Randy. Sandy nodded wordlessly. "I was going to go for a short walk just to stretch my legs and get some more coffee. Maybe something will jog his memory when you two go in."

Randy lay in the bed looking out the window. He looked the same except for the tubes and bandages. But there was something missing from his eyes. The movement caught his attention, and he turned to look at the two women entering his room.

There was no recognition that they could tell. Carrie walked up beside his bed and laid her hand on his. "Randy, do you remember me?"

He looked over her face, then fixed on her eyes as if probing deep. Carrie realized without a word spoken that he didn't remember her. Molly stepped closer and stood beside Carrie. "Randy, what have you been told about what happened to you?"

Randy shifted his gaze from Carrie to Molly. He searched for the words they had told him and for what he could actually remember. "I woke out in a pasture or the woods or something. I had a headache, and I knew I had to get out of where I was."

"Do you know how you got where you were?"

His eyes moved slightly back and forth, as if reading or searching for internal data. He looked at Molly but said nothing. After a few silent moments he asked, "Why was I there?"

His voice was hard and terse. He wanted to know the truth and felt he was clear-headed enough to accept it. He was tired of everyone dancing around him since his arrival.

Molly looked over at Carrie who gave a slight shrug. "I'm Molly Jacobs. Do you remember me?" When no acknowledgement occurred, she continued. "This is Carrie Border, your partner at the OSBI. The Oklahoma State Bureau of Investigation." Randy shifted his gaze to Carrie. His memory flickered. There was something there, but he couldn't pull it to the surface.

"We have all been working on a case together. I am a detective with the OKCPD. The case involves horrific rituals where young men are dying. Through the course of the investigation, you attended an academic meeting of professors, students, and other individuals who are interested in anthropology, history, and other similar topics.

"You went to the meeting but didn't come home." Molly paused so the information could settle in. Randy shut his eyes. *There is something there, but what?* Faint shadows moved in his memory, ghosts of his past, but none that he could see clearly. He finally opened his eyes, which carried an air of distress, and gave a slight shade of his head.

"Keep going. I want to know."

Over the next hour, Carrie and Molly tag-teamed a slow roll of the entire case to Randy. They didn't want to overwhelm him, but he kept insisting that he wanted to know everything. Sandy had arrived back at his room, but when hearing on approach what was happening, she pulled back and sat in a chair outside his room to wait. She did not want to disturb the process that would hopefully pull him back to himself.

As each new event or fact was presented, the women hoped it would be the one to trigger a flood of remembrance. As they neared the end, where they were currently held hostage by lack of clues, they began to lose hope.

When done, they all three sat quietly. Randy once again shut his eyes. He could feel hay against his cheek and smell the musty scent of mildew. His eyes popped open. "Hay."

The women sat up straighter in the chairs they had pulled to the bedside. "Hay?" Carrie asked.

"I began to wake up and felt hay underneath my cheek." He paused and frowned. "I could hear them talking." The air in the hospital room was pregnant with the hope that Randy's next words would reveal what they needed to know, as well as show that his memory had returned.

Suddenly, he looked over at Carrie. "One was very mad that they had taken me and asked why they did it. The other two, yes, I think there were two, said to protect their... protect their..." Randy strained to pull it out.

Carrie took a chance and softly said, "Their professors?"

Randy's head jerked over. "Yes!"

"Did you see faces?" Molly asked.

"No, I never opened my eyes. I felt like I couldn't fully wake up, but I could hear them. Does it make any sense to you?"

"Yes, it does. It fits right in line with what we have been discovering. When we first started the investigation, we focused on the rituals which led us to that particular group of academics. None of that led us further. We then decided to focus on FLY, which has changed the perp investigation to someone who is a chemistry major.

"From what we can tell, there was no one at that meeting who is a chemistry major or a related field of study." Carrie tried to not let her frustration show, but it still tinged the edges of her words nonetheless.

"Do you remember us yet?" Carrie's eyebrows were pinched, and she gripped her hands tightly together. Randy once again focused on her face.

"There is something about you. It is in there, but I can't pull it out yet. I'm sorry."

Molly was quick to divert the mood. "It will come. I am certain of it. You have come a long way today." Her smile warmed Randy as he looked at her. She was not in his memory, yet knew she should be.

Sandy had been hovering just outside the door when she sensed that the conversation had been winding down. When she walked into the room and over to the other side of Randy's bed, he smiled. "Sandy, you finally came."

Carrie and Molly decided to eat before heading back to OKC. Neither had eaten well over the past few weeks and decided to splurge on a steak dinner. The ambiance of the restaurant was somewhat moody and cozy. The booth was lush and as they sat down, they felt an instant relief surge through their bodies.

As they waited on their orders, Carrie looked at her detective counterpart and hoped for answers. "What does that mean, his memory? Is he going to remember every-thing, or will it always remain spotty?" In the short time Carrie had worked with Randy, she already felt a cohesion in their partnership that she didn't want to have to start again.

"Honestly Carrie, I don't know. I have very little experi-ence with this type of thing. But, I felt we made great headway while there, and he recognized Sandy. What a relief that has to be for her. Maybe now that he remembers her as a person, he will begin to remember things about their life together."

Carrie silently nodded, focusing on her salad. "So, he heard one person ask 'why' and the others responded 'to protect their professors. That tells me they were grad students who might have thought their profs had a hand in the rituals and deaths. Which would say that they themselves are inno-cent. Are we back to the professors?"

"I wonder why they thought their professors might have been guilty, or needed protection." Molly pushed her salad around with her fork, unable to eat and think at the same time. "Assumptions can be based on facts or just supposition. The nature of the rituals was taught by those professors, so maybe they are just assuming they are involved. But they may know something concrete that we have not been able to pry out of them."

The sound and smell of sizzling steaks changed their focus, and they welcomed the wait staff. As they were settling into preparing their meals, a thought occurred to Carrie. "I feel like we are flip-flopping again between the two compo-nents of the crimes. From the rituals to the drugs and back.

There must be more than one person involved and they must each bring their own expertise."

Molly sliced a bite of her steak and began to chew as she thought. "I agree. Even though Marta only saw one young man leading them or spurring them on, there must be someone else helping him. It is a lot to pull off for one person." Molly said.

"So, what if one person is an expert in the rituals and the other person brings the drug aspect into it? That would be a complete package."

"That would make sense. So, what if Randy's abduction has nothing really to do with the case? The guys who took him were attempting to help their professors, who probably didn't need help because they didn't do it. And the guys weren't doing it for their own benefit because they didn't need help to cover it up."

Carrie let the words congeal in her mind. "But why would they think their professors needed help?"

Molly shook her head before taking another bite. "We found nothing in any interview or in the search of Dr. Randolph's home. We never had any of the student interviews lead back to the professors." Molly stopped to stir her baked potato to work the melted butter into the entire thing. "What if because the rituals were so unique and the only link they had to that type of information were their professors, they just assumed it was them?"

"So, let's put the professors from the meeting and their grad students on the shelf for now. We made the list of chemistry professors that we still need to go through. I say we tackle that first thing in the morning, what do you say?"

"I agree. The other agents in the OSBI are working on finding out who kidnapped and assaulted Randy. If there is something they feel leads back to our case, then they will let you know. I still think narrowing our focus to the chemical aspect will give us a tighter suspect pool." Molly looked at Carrie for confirmation.

Carrie agreed and they each became occupied with the wonderful meal they had before them. As they were slowing down due to expanding stomachs, Molly leaned back and considered Carrie across the table. "It has been a crazy few days. How are you doing since getting the letter from Billy?"

Carrie nervously fidgeted with the remaining items on her plate. She really didn't want to talk about it. "Honestly I've been working overtime to not think about it."

"Has that worked?"

Carrie snorted. "No. It is always lingering there in the back of my mind, no matter what I am doing. It is like a sad dark shadow that hangs over everything."

The wait staff came and cleared the remaining plates. With the drive home ahead of them, and a reluctance to leave the atmosphere of the restaurant, they each ordered coffee.

"You know, at some point you are going to have to deal with it. Now probably isn't the right time with the case and all, but soon. There may be hope for you and Billy. It sounds like he loved you dearly and this just may be a knee-jerk reaction. You should talk to him as soon as you are ready."

Carrie shook her head. "No. He's done with me. I pushed him too far. I've done horrible things and I don't deserve someone like Billy." Carrie looked out away from their table and swiped a rogue tear away.

"I know you feel that way now, but Carrie you do deserve someone who loves and values you. You made a mistake born of pain. Don't let that define your life. You are not the mistake you made."

Carrie looked down at her lap and gave a jagged nod. She felt shame and couldn't bear to look Molly in the eye.

"Molly, why did I do what I did? Why did I push him away when all he wanted to do was comfort me and take care of me? And why of all things, did I have such a driving need to go to the bar and then hookup with Andy?" Her eyes insecurely drifted up towards Molly. Her face was wrinkled by heartbreak.

"Carrie, it was the greatest pain you had ever experienced. Not losing just one parent, but both suddenly, is a horrific event to survive. Your heart was pure and light when it happened. You weren't experienced with trauma and you weren't guarded against it. When it happened, you weren't prepared and had no idea how to manage the trauma.

"But it will get better, and you can reconcile things with Billy. Even if as you say, he is done, you can't leave things unsaid. You have to talk to him and make amends. Whether you wind up with each other or need to move forward and forge a new life. You can't let it all sit and fester, for your sake as well as Billy's. Respect him enough to apologize without making excuses for your behavior."

Carrie knew Molly was right. It still hurt so bad that she just didn't know how she could bear to deal with it. But she would, someday.

The drive back to OKC was slower since there was no

need for lights to clear their way. They tossed around more ideas about the case, re-hashing already discussed aspects.

"I think we should make it a priority to go back to OU and try and talk to Dr. Pinning. Now that you've had a chance to cool down, maybe we can sweet talk our way past his research assistant." Molly grinned as she glanced over at Carrie.

"I am sorry I reacted that way. I just felt like she was lying and was blocking our way to him on purpose."

"Maybe she was. But, we are law enforcement and we will get in there one way or another. Tell me more about your first encounter with him. You said you really liked him."

"I did. He was unexpected. He was a very tall black man with a broad smile. He wasn't thin, but not fat either. He was very engaging and seemed lighthearted. His voice rang out with that Jamaican lilt."

"Afterwards though, you felt that he talked openly but never really gave you the information you had gone in to get."

Carrie ran their meeting over in her head from beginning to end. "No. No, he didn't. Not really. Of course, we knew so little at the time. Now we have so much more we could ask. Yes, I think we need to make it a priority to talk with him first thing."

The ride back from Tulsa started off as a pleasant ride home under the starlit night sky. Their conversation and full stomachs had lulled them into a lack of awareness of their surroundings. The traffic on the turnpike was light, as it was later in the evening.

Suddenly alerted, Molly looked up into her rearview mirror only to see bright car lights closing in on her. She sped up and turned on her lights to let them know she was in law enforcement. The car behind soon caught up with them. Then, they were thrust forward from the car ramming into them from behind.

Carrie swung around in her seat to see if she could tell what kind of car it was. When the lights blinded her, she snapped her hand up to shield her eyes and turned to Molly. "What's going on?"

Glancing from the road to the mirror, Molly said tightly, "I don't know." She focused on outmaneuvering the car behind her, her speed now up to one hundred miles an hour.

Suddenly, the car bolted to the left and moved up beside Molly. Realizing what was coming, Molly slammed on the brakes and let the car speed past her. She then darted in behind them, following closely.

Carrie began immediately calling in the license plate and the situation that they were facing. The dispatcher promised she would relay the message to the Oklahoma Highway Patrol.

The car swerved back into the right-hand lane, slowed so that they were nearly even with Molly, and lurched towards them. The car careened toward the center median barriers. Metal bent and whined as it tore and twisted.

When all was once again still and quiet, the only motion was the rocking of their now stationary car. The car that had attempted to kill them was long gone.

Carrie's neck hurt a little, but she realized she was in one piece. She looked over at Molly, who sat with closed eyes and lips silently moving.

"Are you okay?" Carrie asked.

Molly turned to look at Carrie with large, round eyes. "Yes. Yes, I am. How about you?"

"I'm fine, but the car isn't." She looked out of the shattered windshield to see the hood and front fenders crumpled like discarded aluminum foil.

"Carrie, we just experienced a miracle."

Carrie doubted that, but then to look at the car and how well they had come through, she had to believe that something had spared them.

Bracket came to retrieve Molly and Carrie. The OKCPD tow truck loaded the totaled detective car as Molly and Carrie watched from the back of the ambulance. The EMTs thoroughly examined them each and found only minor cuts and abrasions. By one in the morning, they were all back home and tucked soundly in bed.

Carrie thought she would sleep for days, if only she didn't have a driving need to talk to Dr. Pinning in the morning.

Chapter Twenty-Five

It had been difficult for Carrie to sleep once again. The adrenaline had worn off about halfway home. Once it did, her body began to feel the discomfort of having been tossed around violently in a metal box.

The most painful places were where her seatbelt had cut into her as she body was flung forward and then side to side. She was thankful for the seatbelt, but it would take a few days for the bruising to heal.

While her body reminded her that she had been physically hurt, keeping her awake, her mind was also awake. Molly's words from dinner kept drifting through, causing a flood of what-ifs that led to anxiety. What if she called Billy and he wouldn't speak to her? What if she called and he wouldn't even answer the phone? There were many others as well. Her body was also physically tired though, so it eventually won out in the end.

They had agreed to meet at Carrie's office at eight a.m. As

soon as she arrived, Carrie called Dr. Pinning's office to see if they could make an appointment. His research assistant was not yet in, so the department secretary checked his schedule and made them an appointment for ten that morning.

While she was waiting for Molly, she made some notes of important things she wanted to ask Dr. Pinning specifically so that he would not dance around the subject, hopefully. Carrie had done well in chemistry in college and in her forensic classes, but she was not a chemist and it was challenging for her to follow the method by which FLY was created.

This knowledge convinced her even more so that the person creating FLY knew what they were doing. She had traced some of the chemicals through her DEA source, and they were indeed common to most university, hospital, or commercial labs. But were they looking for a doctor of chemistry or a doctor of pharmacology. They were specialized, but probably either could create FLY.

She had also gone back through all of the young men who they had interviewed or had contact with regarding the case. Many of them were dead, and some didn't fit the description that Marta had given them. Jason Anderson did fit the description, but he seemed genuinely shocked when the drugs had been brought up. *Could he have fooled us?*

"Good morning," Molly was cheery as usual, if not somewhat subdued from the previous evening's ordeal.

Carrie quickly shared with her the thoughts she had written down.

"Do you think Jason Anderson fooled us? He seemed shocked about the drugs. But was that an act?"

Molly stood pondering the thought, remembering back to being with Jason. Suspects and witnesses had fooled her before, but not for long. It was a huge side effect of always believing the best in people.

"I don't think so. But thinking back, his statement and Marta's varied in that she mentioned going to a group meeting where a young man was speaking, and they drank something that was passed around. Jason never mentioned anything like that."

"Do you think it was on purpose?"

Molly sat on the edge of Carrie's desk and looked at the floor. She was replaying every word and movement that Jason had made. Had she seen deception? She looked up at Carrie and said, "If he was lying, he is one of the best I've ever seen."

"I wonder what was in the drink they were passing around."

"I don't think it was FLY or scopolamine. Acid? They could easily dose it down in a drink so that very little was ingested. Or it could be some form of CBD oil. Maybe just enough to make them feel good. A mood builder to entice them further into the rituals."

Carrie nodded as she thought. "Maybe so."

"Marta couldn't give us a location on where the first meeting was held. That would be a huge benefit for us if we could find that."

"Maybe she will remember later. She was still pretty traumatized, even the next day."

"And there is always Garrett to talk to when he recovers," Molly said.

Carrie nodded and looked at her watch. "Well, we can

head that way. We might be a little early, but that is fine. We can snoop around a bit." She grinned and looked up at Molly to see her reaction.

Molly grinned back. "We have to keep it on the up and up, but yeah we can snoop a bit."

The drive to OU Medical Center College of Pharmacy was uneventful and they did arrive about thirty minutes early. "You know," Molly began, "I just realized that Garrett is in the OU Medical Center hospital. It is just across the street over there. We can visit him after we speak to Dr. Pinning."

Carrie glanced over at her shoulder to the hospital and then back at Molly. "Oh cool. That will be great. We can just leave the car here and walk over. It is a massive complex. I sometimes forget how huge it all is."

The sun was immediately present on their faces as they stepped out of the vehicle. Its warmth felt good on their skin. "Wow, what a beautiful day," Molly said as she turned her face fully to the sun. A sudden gust of wind nearly swept her sunglasses from her face, and she jerked quickly to grab them. "That is except for the wind."

Carrie took a hair tie from her wrist and made herself a ponytail. "Yes, the wind is fierce today, but the sun does feel good." She tucked her folders tightly under her arm. She had brought one of the case files that pertained to the pharmacology and chemical aspects of the case, and her notebook folder.

They gradually made their way into the foyer of the College of Pharmacology building. Their heads seemed to be on swivels. They had no idea what they might be looking for, but didn't want to miss any slight clue that might present itself.

What appeared to be two students were waiting at the elevator and the up button was lit. As they stood there, Laurel Wilson, Dr. Pinning's research assistant, walked by. They had seen her coming with her head down, reading the papers she held. When she finally looked up and saw the ladies standing there, a look of horror crossed her face.

"Oh, hi. Why are you here today? Dr. Pinning has classes almost all day." Neither one responded quickly, as they were each assessing Laurel. To fill the awkward gap in conversation, Laurel kept talking. "You know Dr. Pinning is trying to wrap up the end of semester and probably won't have time for you for a few weeks." Laurel was not able to hide her nervousness. She fidgeted from one foot to the other and shuffled her papers about unnecessarily.

The bell signaling that the elevator had arrived sounded and the other two waiting moved forward. As Molly and Carrie walked in as well, Carrie said, "Well we have an appointment with him at ten this morning." She held the door open for Laurel. "Coming?"

Laurel walked onto the elevator and stood in front of Carrie and Molly. "I don't know how you got an appointment. I haven't spoken to you since you were last here."

"We called the department secretary. She made the appointment for us," Molly offered. The comment only served to cause more obvious stress for Laurel. "Oh," Was her only response.

Up one floor, the elevator stopped and the other two got

off before the door slid closed again. "Laurel, why do we make you so nervous?" Molly asked.

"You were so rude to me when you were here before."

Molly looked over at Carrie. "I was a little short with you and I apologize. I was very frustrated because we have young men being killed and injured. Speaking with Dr. Pinning will add critical information to our investigation and you seem to feel the need to be his stalwart gatekeeper."

"It is my responsibility to help him with his schedule and keep people at bay so he can do his research."

"Just what is his research right now?" Molly asked.

"Well... well, I can't really divulge that."

The elevator stopped at the correct floor and as soon as the doors opened, Laurel rushed out. Molly looked at Carrie and raised an eyebrow. They watched Laurel in a near run down the hall to Dr. Pinning's office and research lab.

Carrie looked at her watch. "Something isn't right here. It is ten to ten. Let's do this." Carrie pushed the door open to the outer office where Laurel usually sat. It was empty, but the swinging doors to the lab were still drifting back to their resting place.

"Let's find out what she is hiding." They moved forward in unison and pushed through the doors. Each had their hand on their weapon out of habit when entering a potentially dangerous situation. They didn't know that Laurel would be dangerous, but she was clearly acting strange.

At first glance, there appeared to be no one in the lab. There were two main aisles down each side of the center work table. It was filled with various types of equipment, beakers, and other random lab items. Molly motioned and

Carrie took the aisle opposite her, their weapons still at the ready.

They moved down the length of the lab, carefully on guard. As they continued, they still saw no one or anything out of the ordinary. The lab was completely empty. Once at the far end of the lab, the only place to go was into Dr. Pinning's office.

Carrie tapped on the door. "Dr. Pinning?"

They could hear movement inside the office. Dr. Pinning coughed. "Yes, yes, come on in."

Molly turned the office door handle and opened the door. Dr. Pinning sat at his desk. Laurel was nowhere to be found.

They stood looking at Dr. Pinning. The atmosphere in the room felt off. The absence of Laurel made it even more so.

"We were following Laurel and thought she had come in here."

"Why no, no, I am not sure where she is." He wasn't coming off as believable.

"Well, we had a ten a.m. appointment with you anyway. We just ran into Laurel and she seemed quite upset at seeing us, so we wanted to speak to her as well. When we began to talk to her, she hurried away from us, quite suspiciously," Carrie said.

They were still standing in front of Dr. Pinning's desk. At the moment, the need to be ready to react took precedence over the comfort of sitting. Dr. Pinning hadn't offered for them to sit anyway, which seemed out of character for the normally hospitable man.

After a few moments of uncomfortable silence, Dr. Pinning finally motioned to the chairs, indicating that they should sit. When Carrie had met him the first time, he had been so warm and welcoming, almost jovial. Now it seemed as though there was a dark cloud over his mood.

"Dr. Pinning, the last time we spoke, we discussed FLY and scopolamine. We have had considerably more deaths, and the victims had those two drugs in their system. Our coroner, Dr. Henry Bloom, has said that the drugs are the cause of death or a main contributing factor in those deaths. One died of a heart attack which he said was because of the trauma of the event plus the drugs.

"From what we have learned from you and in our own research, it is extremely difficult to replicate. The dosage for the combination of the two drugs is a balancing act that only a skilled pharmacologist could even attempt. We need to know who we should be looking at specifically. You are the head of this department, and you are very involved in the state as a whole in this field. Please tell us who we should be looking at?"

As Carrie was issuing her plea, something occurred to her. Dr. Pinning himself was the most likely suspect they had. He not only had access to a lab to create the drugs in, but he had the knowledge and skill to do so. Plus, his lab most certainly carried the type of alcohol that was used to clean the bodies. His easy-going demeanor had caused her to exclude him up until that very moment.

Dr. Pinning splayed his hands open, palms up. "I really

don't know. Yes, I have students, and even research students, but none with the skill to produce and administer those drugs. I also do know most high-level doctors in this field in the state, but I can't think of anyone who would do such a thing."

Molly had also come to the same thought as Carrie while listening to her speak. "Dr. Pinning, what about you?" She looked straight into his eyes and held her gaze there. She wasn't smiling and was attempting to notice every micro-expression that his face relayed.

He held steady in her gaze for a few moments, then sat up and back in his chair. "Me? How dare you accuse me of such travesty." He stood up, forming a formidable wall of human flesh as if to make a point. "I don't think that we can continue our conversation. If you have more questions for me, I will direct you to my lawyer."

The two women sat in their chairs nonplussed. They were used to this type of behavior. "Dr. Pinning, I was not accusing you. I was merely asking about your possible involvement because so far you are the most likely suspect due to your qualifications and skill.

"Point us to someone else who has the same ability and skill, and we will gladly research them and question them. We won't even tell them that you were the one who pointed us to them." Molly was pleasant in her delivery as she sat calmly waiting for his response.

"It is true that in my field, I am at the top. I don't believe that anyone has the same skill and ability that I do, none-the-less that doesn't mean that they haven't tried and been successful. But then, since there have been so many deaths, can we really say they have been successful?"

"True, but they have been somewhat successful. And very few could come to the level we've seen. There is a survivor in the hospital now, so you could say they were successful with him," Carrie said.

Molly cut her eyes over to Carrie. Surely she knew as an OSBI agent not to disclose such information, but then this was her first case. As soon as they made eye contact, Carrie realized what she had done. She had just put Garrett in danger.

"A survivor you say?" asked Dr. Pinning.

"Why would that be of any interest to you if you are not involved? But yes, there is and his room is being heavily guarded. We have other evidence and we are narrowing in on the perpetrators. We were just hopeful that you would aid us in our evidence gathering and help us further our investigation. But it seems that you are not willing to do so."

"We plan on waiting around for Laurel. She has acted extremely suspicious around us and since she has access not only to you personally, but also your lab, she has risen as a person of interest." Molly had locked in on Dr. Pinning's gaze. She had seen several micro-aggressions while watching him that concerned her. She had never met him before and what she witnessed did not fit with the jovial Jamaican that Carrie had described.

Carrie and Molly said their good-byes and loitered in the hallway just outside the office. "He is not the same as when we first interviewed him," Carrie began as soon as they were out of earshot.

"I assumed as much. He was good at being deceptive, but I noticed several small tells that indicated he either knew more than he was saying or was involved on some level. Let's hang out here awhile." Carrie agreed.

"One thing that really bothers me is that Marta spoke of a younger thin white male leading the group. That description could also fit the figure she saw in the barn with the hood and cloak. Also, Randy spoke of possible white males according to the voices he heard. How does a larger Jamaican male and a small white female fit into all of this?" Carrie asked.

Molly considered Carrie's thoughts. She too had tried to reconcile the facts with what they were seeing. Marta had no reason to lie about what she saw. She wanted the perpetrators caught. "We need to do a deep dive on Laurel. Who is she dating, what is her background, and such."

"That could be the key. She could be dating someone who is the leader."

"So lay out the scenario for me. How does it begin and evolve, and what was the true agenda and motive here?" asked Molly.

"We were under the impression that it started with the young men questioning their bravery and disconnect from God. But, that couldn't be the origin, could it?"

"I'm concerned about Garrett and Marta." Molly pulled out her phone and called her precinct. She explained the imminent threat and asked for twenty-four-hour surveillance to be posted just outside Garrett's room. Her captain agreed. "They will have a guard there within the hour."

Molly turned and leaned on the chrome rail opposite Dr. Pinning's office and looked out over to the first floor below.

People were coming and going on with their lives as if there was not a possible killer in their midst.

Back in Dr. Pinning's office, Laurel emerged from under his large walnut desk. Her eyes were wide and she looked to Dr. Pinning for instruction.

"It will be okay. They have nothing on us. They can't say we had anything to do with this," Dr. Pinning reassured her. Laurel looked at him doe-eyed and jumped towards him. Her arms stretched around him as far as possible. "Thank you so much Dr. Pinning. I am terrified, but I know you will protect me."

Soon outside of the office, as Molly and Carrie both leaned on the rail, they noticed a small young woman with hair like Laurel's exiting through the front door. "Molly look! That was Laurel. How did she get past us?" Carrie exclaimed as they both rushed to follow her.

"I don't know. Obviously, there was a door we were not aware of."

By the time they reached the front door and pushed their way outside, Laurel was nowhere to be found.

Molly clicked the radio on her belt and requested the car make, model, color, and tag on one Laurel Wilson.

Marta sat by Garrett's bed. She was exhausted and heartbroken. Garrett had briefly woken a few times and tried to mumble communication with her, but he just wasn't the same. He was sleeping now, and Marta held his limp hand.

She had only left the hospital to go speak with law enforcement, no eating or showering.

As she sat, she kept reliving those moments. Her hope was that she could recall some bit of information that she could give them to help with the case. To find the killer. It all played on an endless terrifying loop in her mind.

An officer had been stationed outside his door. They were obviously concerned that someone would harm him for what he knew. Or maybe Marta's mind was just fearing the worst. As she sat in a chair tucked close to Garrett's bedside, a nurse came in. She was flitting around the machines and tubes.

"You really should go get some rest. He is sleeping well and doing fine. You should be at your best when he wakes up fully."

Marta barely glanced at the nurse. She didn't want to leave his side, however, she was getting hungry and could use a shower. Would she really want Garrett to see her like this when he was fully alert?

"I need to bathe him and refresh his bed soon. Now would be a good time for you to take a break."

Marta stretched and yawned. Maybe the nurse was right, but still she hated to leave him. She stood and looked around the room. The nurse had gone. Sunlight filtered in through the blinds that were set partially open. The light strips were boldly staking their claim across the floor.

Garrett hadn't moved in the slightest when Marta had slid her hand from his. She decided he might need her more later when he woke fully than he did right then, so she began to gather her things to leave. She bent over to give Garrett a kiss on the cheek, never noticing her phone sliding out from her pocket to the floor.

She turned to leave, and looking back from the door whispered, "I love you."

The guard by the door rose from his chair as she exited the room. "I'm going to go take a shower and get a bite to eat. I'll be back soon. Watch over him for me." Her woeful eyes locked onto the officer's and he nodded assuredly. "Will do miss."

As Marta was heading toward the elevator, Molly and Carrie were arriving at the hospital. "We don't know that Laurel came in here," said Carrie.

"True, but I feel like we need to check in on Garrett while we are here."

"I feel horrible about revealing that information. He could be in grave danger because of me." Carrie's distress had brushed her face with concern.

"Carrie, we have all done something similar when we were new. It will be okay. We will be on guard and make sure Garrett is safe." Carrie only nodded.

They made their way to the floor where Garrett's room was. As they approached, the officer stood to greet them. "It has been quiet. His girlfriend Marta is in there now. She had left but forgot her phone. The nurses are also in there to bathe him."

"We can give you a break for a bit. Get some coffee and stretch your legs." The officer was relieved and thanked them, quickly walking off before they changed their minds.

It was true that Marta had left, but she had barely gotten to the elevator when she realized her phone was not in her pocket. She immediately turned around and hurried back to Garrett's room. As she opened the door, she saw the nurse at Garrett's I.V. preparing to inject something into it.

Just as she began to ask what she was giving him, a hand clasped her mouth from behind. It felt like a man. He was stronger and taller than she was, and was now dragging her backwards into the adjoining bathroom.

Marta knew the danger both she and Garrett were in. She had been merely curious when she saw the nurse injecting his I.V., but now she was convinced that it was meant to kill him, which would mean she would have to die as well.

She began to instantly flail about. She dropped her bag and jacket and began kicking and pounding the air with her fists, hoping to hit flesh. Her foot shot out and kicked a metal table holding his water decanter and Kleenex. It all toppled to the floor with a crash.

Outside the room, Molly frowned and looked at Carrie. "Did you hear that?" Carrie nodded and they moved to the door. Molly pressed the latch and moved the door open. She was in the door quickly with Carrie right behind her.

The nurse had stopped what she was preparing to do when Marta had entered the room and was standing stunned as the girl was being dragged away. Coming to her senses, she turned to finish what she had started as Molly entered, seeing the chaos.

"Stop what you are doing!" Molly commanded the nurse at Garrett's side. She was pulling her service weapon, when the nurse swung around and grabbed her around the neck. As Carrie entered, she saw Marta being dragged away and the nurse holding a hypodermic to Molly's neck.

"Don't move," the nurse threatened. Carrie had had time to pull her weapon and it was now aimed firmly at the nurse. Off to her side, she could hear Marta still struggling in the arms of her captor. Molly was in imminent danger though, and she was the priority.

Carrie was trying to stay calm. She had never had to pull her weapon in this type of situation before. Yes, as a patrol officer she had pulled it many times in anticipation of such an event, but had never had to shoot. She was terrified and hoped that no one noticed the trembling that was coursing through her body.

"Drop the needle!"

Laurel laughed. It hadn't been a nurse at all. The man holding Marta had to be the man at the meetings, or Dr. Pinning. "I'm not dropping the needle. Back out of the room." Her arm was so tightly bound around Molly's neck that it made it difficult for her to breathe, but she fought to hold onto consciousness.

In the struggle, Laurel accidentally pricked Molly's neck with the needle gouging out a small ribbon of flesh. A rivulet of blood ran down, and fear caused Molly's eyes to open wide. She knew, though, that to struggle would only serve to press the needle further into her neck. Whatever was in the hypodermic had oozed out and several droplets had entered the wound.

Molly could feel that something was wrong. Adrenaline, which usually brought clarity, was succumbing to another more powerful chemical. She closed her eyes and began to pray the best that she could. The words could not leave her mouth, but she knew that they were being heard nonetheless.

Carrie could see that something was critically wrong with Molly. She had to act, and act quickly. Looking at where they were standing, Carrie could see valves that she knew contained various flammable gases, such as oxygen. To fire a gun from that vantage point could kill them all.

Her mind was racing. The pressure to decide to do something immediately, whether it was right or wrong, pressed in on her. She began to step to her left, entering the room even further. Laurel was still threatening her to stop and leave, but she ignored the threats. She had already harmed Molly and Carrie had to act.

Behind her, now to her right, she could hear the other person pulling Marta into the bathroom and attempting to shut the door. Carrie knew if he was able to do that, then he would rush her. She couldn't wait.

Having moved to a better vantage point, she breathed in to steady her aim and fired. Laurel, with Molly in her grasp, slumped to the floor, neither one now moving. Carrie couldn't breathe. What had she done? Had she hit Molly too?

She rushed over, just as Laurel began sliding to the floor with her arm still around Molly's neck. A hole in the center of Laurel's forehead rested just above her still open and shocked eyes. Carrie took her foot and kicked the syringe out of Laurel's hand, which now lay limp.

Suddenly, Carrie felt a rush of movement from behind her as the man, now with Marta successfully contained in the bathroom, moved rapidly toward her.

Carrie whirled around to see him holding a heavy metal chair high above his head, ready to slam it down upon her.

She pulled the trigger yet again, and he stopped mid-air as the bullet entered his heart.

He dropped the chair, which hit Carrie and glanced to the side, then he fell to the floor dead. The door to the room burst open, as the other officer had just returned to his post and heard the gunshots. Nurses were rushing in behind him.

Carrie's head swam and white dots shot randomly behind her eyes. She felt cold all over, but sweat dripped in her eyes. She laid her gun hand on the floor and looked up at the officer in a panic. He squatted beside her and the tumbled pile of Laurel and Molly. "Are you okay?" He asked.

Carrie tried to speak, but the words didn't seem to form to communicate to the officer. She looked over at Molly whose eyes were still shut, and she could not hold back the flood of emotion that overtook her.

Tears distorted her vision, and she cried as though she were finally crying for all the pain she had pushed down over the past several weeks. It was all too much, and now Molly too. She had not acted quickly enough, and she couldn't bear the pain of it.

Epilog

andy's recovery had been slower than they had hoped, but with intense cognitive therapy he was finally remembering everything presented to him. Sandy was overjoyed, and Bracket was very thankful. He knew every day he put his agents in danger. It was the part of his job that was the worst and most painful should it all go awry.

Carrie had not only fired her weapon for the first time, but twice in the matter of a few moments. There had been a review board, but they found she had acted accordingly, and with a clear head in her movements to gain a vantage point that was the most advantageous.

Mandatory counseling for eight weeks, with a review at the end was required, not requested. Carrie complied, even if begrudgingly. She had never expected to feel the trauma of taking another person's life in the way that she did. It was good to talk to someone about it.

In the hospital room that day when she had seen Molly lying there so still, she had broken down. She had grown to love the detective as a sister and friend. Molly had been there for her when she had needed someone the most, staying up with her nearly all night long after receiving the letter from Billy. She knew she couldn't bear the loss of yet one more person she loved.

Sobs had wracked her body as she sat on the hospital room floor looking at Molly's still body, with blood still trickling heavily from her neck. Then it hit her: a dead body doesn't bleed. She had jumped up and directed the nurses and doctors to Molly, who was barely hanging on to life.

Hope sprung up in her chest as she backed away to give them space to work. They acted quickly to get Molly up and away to where they could care for her properly. Laurel and the other man lay lifeless on the floor. Carrie stood there stunned, looking up at the officer who had holstered his weapon and was calling in the incident.

Garrett never woke during all the explosive confusion.

It took Carrie several days to feel somewhat normal again. She had spent the next two days beside Molly's bed. The syringe Laurel had was filled with pure scopolamine. It was all she could get her hands on in such short notice. The drug had sedated Molly, just as it is designed to do during surgery. Carrie had feared it was FLY.

Molly was made from hearty stock though, and her prayers had been heard. She recovered quickly. "Thank you," Molly said the first time she saw Carrie sitting beside her bed.

"Thank you for not dying! I broke down when I thought

you too had died. I knew it would be the death of me, the final straw."

Molly smiled, that smile that was so captivating and hers alone. "It wouldn't have been, but I am glad I am still here. You saved me."

Carrie knew it was true, but couldn't receive the praise. Two others had died and she lay awake replaying the scene in her mind every night. Could there have been another way? But no matter how she tried, she was never able to make it turn out any better.

"Garrett finally woke up. It will be a long recovery for him. They are fighting every day to combat the damage the FLY has done. Marta has not left his side.

"Dr. Pinning is in custody. They have been grilling him non-stop for nearly twenty-four hours. His home and lab have been searched. They have found documentation of experiments on mind control.

Apparently, he hoped to be able to find a way to control others through mind control in order to do anything he wanted, even vile things like participate in the rituals. He was working to find the exact right combination of the two drugs. Using FLY was a difficult challenge and he wanted to conquer it. He felt it would show his superiority in pharmacology.

"Laurel was so enamored with him that she was a willing participant. They knew that they needed to get a young man on board to coerce the others to participate in the rituals. Laurel's boyfriend, David Smith, was a grad student for Dr. Amy Gravenue who is the department head in the OU anthropology department. David was well-versed in all the rituals that were conducted."

Molly pinched her forehead in concentration. "So let me get this straight. David would encourage the others to participate in the rituals. Then what about the drugs and where was the barn where Marta said they met?"

"They met in Dr. Pinning's old farm property outside of town. The process went, as best as I have been able to ascertain, that when one would sign up for a ritual, they would be sequestered away for five days prior. They would be given a regimented dose of FLY that would react in their system over time so that they would have the 'courage' to not back out.

"Then, when they went to the barn, that person would be taken in the back door, barely aware of what was happening. They would be undressed and put in the loin cloth. The others would go into the front of the barn. Then, scopolamine would be flushed into the entire barn with an air system developed by Dr. Pinning. Everyone, including the one participating in the ritual, would breathe it in.

"Once they began to breathe the scopolamine, they would have no memory of the event afterwards. David was the one in the cloak and hood. He did have a full-face gas mask on to keep him from suffering the effects of the scopolamine. He conducted the rituals since he was the so-called expert on them. Turns out he was a closet psychopath as well, and loved seeing the pain it inflicted on others."

Both women sat quietly for several moments, thinking over the bizarre nature of the events that had sent them on the wild roller-coaster ride. Molly looked up and smiled at Carrie. "What a first case, right?"

"No doubt. Oh also, since David was the only one at the rituals other than the young men participating, they had hidden video cameras all over the barn. They were so well hidden up in the corners that they were not found in our initial search.

"Dr. Pinning didn't want to miss out on all the fun, and of course he needed them for his research. The search team found tons of video on the hard drive in his home. He was always trying to perfect the drug cocktail so that the young men would not die in the process. It appears he didn't factor in the stress of the horrific rituals.

"David didn't carry them out exactly as they were usually done either. He got a thrill out of adding extra pain and trauma to them. The drugs weakened their hearts and then with the trauma, they would just die."

Carrie and Molly had many long talks during the two days she remained in the hospital. About a week later, Carrie went to see Garrett, who remained in the hospital. He was recovering, however slowly. As Carrie approached his room, she could hear Molly speaking to Garrett. She didn't want to disturb them and held back just outside the door peeking through the crack to watch them.

Garrett was looking at Molly with a pained expression. "I wanted to find God as much as prove I was courageous. I thought that if God saw I really wanted to find him, then he would know I was serious. I was willing to do whatever I had to do, go through whatever I had to go through. I was, I am, tired of feeling so empty and hollow."

Molly reached up and laid her hand on Garrett's. "Garrett, you don't have to prove anything to God. He is always here, right here and ready for you any time."

"You're talking about that Christianity stuff. I went to church for a bit." He was shaking his head in disgust. "They didn't want me there. And I knew some of them, they would talk and act one way while they were at church and then be the exact opposite when they weren't. I found no authenticity in it at all."

"I understand. But I'm not talking about the Christian religion. I am talking about the Christian God. The God who loves us all passionately no matter what. His love is unconditional. We as a people are flawed. We come to him with our flaws, and unfortunately that is all some people ever see of God, his flawed people. So, they turn away from him.

"And Garrett, when a person is in church surrounded by others who love and serve God, it is easier to do and say the right things. But when we get out into the world, and are surrounded by the challenges of everyday life, it is much harder. Everyone who comes to God experiences times of what others call being a hypocrite. It is a process. A daily process of growth toward him."

Garrett was drawn to Molly's words. He did want to know God, the real God. "You know Garrett, the ritual that you experienced was an old Roman ritual that they used to punish criminals. When Jesus, God's only son, came to Earth as a man, they said he was a criminal and hung him on a cross.

"The difference was that he was not a criminal. I'm sure if you have been to a Christian church before, then you have heard of Jesus coming and bearing our sin on the cross because of his love. I don't want to spend this time giving you the complete history of why we had sin and why we needed to be delivered of it. I would love to do that another time.

"But for now, just think about a God who, rather than make you go through painful and traumatic rituals to be close to him, HE goes through that pain so he can be close to you. He does not want anything standing in the way of you coming to him anytime you want to come. He does not ask anything from us other than to come to him with earnest sincerity."

"It seems too easy. Maybe that is why so many don't seem to be committed. If they had to go through that kind of pain then it would show their commitment, and many just wouldn't do it." Garrett was animated.

"But God loves us too much to put us through that. It is completely out of his character. And yes, many may not be fully committed, but they often become more so as they grow and come to know him even more. God loves them anyway. He made us. He understands us."

"But they give him a bad reputation. When people look at them being hypocritical, they assume he is that way."

"He isn't moved by what people think. He is the strong and solid creator of the universe. He can carry the weight of a bad reputation. And, he wants to love people to him, not force them to come to him. He knows that the ones who do choose him have come to him willingly and freely."

Garrett looked at Molly for a few moments. "I want to know this God. I want to know more about him and how he loves." Tears streamed down Garrett's cheeks.

Carrie felt a tightening in her chest as she listened. Suddenly, a sharp sob escaped. There was something there that she knew was true, yet she just couldn't reconcile the fact that a loving God had allowed her parents to die.

Strong emotion threatened to push a torrent of tears outward, but she forced them back. No. She wouldn't give in. Then as she listened, a softer moment emerged and she thought, "Maybe someday, maybe someday."

Author's Note

I am so excited to release this book, finally! It goes back to the beginning for Carrie Border and dives deep into how she became who she is. As I was writing, a wind of inspiration hit me and I included a grown-up Molly Sue. The combination of the two couldn't have turned out better!

The rituals, drugs, and other aspects of the book were researched in depth. I included more than is here because it all fascinates me so much, and I wanted to share. But, thankfully, my editor Andrea Hurst reined me in. Too much she said! So I whacked, and whacked.

There are still many questions left to be answered in Carrie's life. Many of those are answered in subsequent novels such as The Redemption Series, however a few still remain.

Also, if you have not read Choices Like Rivers, you absolutely must do so in order to hear the real, on-the-edge-of-your-seat story of how Molly Sue came to be.

I have plans for more Carrie Border and more Molly Sue novels. Who knows, maybe their paths will cross again.

But, for the near future, I have a burning desire to launch a new series completely different from this one. I promise you will love the new heroine and the suspense that surrounds her just as much as you do Carrie Border!

As always, I want to say that this is a complete work of fiction. I hold law enforcement in the highest regard and in no way want to diminish what they do by my fictional depiction of them.

About the Author

Nancy's love of writing fiction began in the seventh grade in literature class.

Through the years she has written magazine articles, newspaper articles, countless blog posts, and both fiction and non-fiction books. Many of those books have made it to the Amazon best seller ranking as well.

Nancy resides in Oklahoma in the state she was born.

Always a creative person, she has done more types of arts and crafts than you can imagine. Recently, she has found a love for watercolor painting in her spare time.

In recent years, she has been a professional silversmith and also did studio jewelry training for silversmithing. She was also a licensed Oklahoma state Realtor but is now spending the bulk of her time writing.

Nancy feels that writing fiction for the sheer sake of entertainment is not good enough. She has always desired for her novels to touch her readers' lives and to even change them for the better in some small way. The many emails, texts, messages, and reviews she has received is a testament to that.

Also by Nancy Jackson

Novels

The Redemption Series

The Blood - Book 1

The Water - Book 2

The Fire - Book 3

The Redemption Series Box Set

The Box, a Carrie Border Novella

Carrie Border, The Prequel

Choices Like Rivers

Business Enrichment

How to Go From Hobby to Business

How to Write Publish and Market Your Book

Social Media Marketing Blitz Workbook and Planner

Please review this book and any others that you have read.

It will help me more than you know!